CAUGHT OFF-GUARD

"Something doesn't feel right," Summers said, staring down the slope after the old man.

"What do you mean?" asked Webb.

"I'm not sure. . . ." Summers looked back at the rest of the men riding toward them. He looked forward along the trail to where it disappeared into a turn. He looked up along the high rocky line above them, then down at the old man just in time to see him break into a run toward the cover of taller rocks, shooing the goats out of his way.

"Oh no," cried Summers, realization setting in and causing him to sit bolt upright in his saddle. "It's a trap."

WEBB'S POSSE

Ralph Cotton

A SIGNET BOOK

SIGNET
Published by New American Library, a division of
Penguin Group (USA) Inc., 375 Hudson Street,
New York, New York 10014, U.S.A.
Penguin Books Ltd, 80 Strand,
London WC2R 0RL, England
Penguin Books Australia Ltd, 250 Camberwell Road,
Camberwell, Victoria 3124, Australia
Penguin Books Canada Ltd, 10 Alcorn Avenue,
Toronto, Ontario, Canada M4V 3B2
Penguin Books (N.Z.) Ltd, Cnr Rosedale and Airborne Roads,
Albany, Auckland 1310, New Zealand

Penguin Books Ltd, Registered Offices:
80 Strand, London WC2R 0RL, England

First published by Signet, an imprint of New American Library,
a division of Penguin Group (USA) Inc.

First Printing, July 2003
10 9 8 7 6 5 4

For Mary Lynn . . . *of course*.

And for Curt and Malissa Beatty—
kinfolk, friends.

PART 1

Chapter 1

—————

"What the hell was that, Virgil?" Will Summers asked the bartender. Summers had started to take a sip of whiskey, but his shot glass stopped near his lips, suspended there as he recognized the sound of heavy gunfire coming from the far end of the street outside the Ace High Saloon.

Virgil Wilkes' face turned ashen. He shook his head slowly; his eyes widened in disbelief. "Lord God, I don't know, Will!" he whispered.

"Is that shotgun still beneath the bar?" Will Summers asked, already reaching a hand out across the polished bar top.

Virgil pulled up the sawed-off double-barrel and handed it over, swallowing a gulp of air. "What are you going to do, Will?"

"Beats me," Summers said, quickly tossing back his shot of whiskey. He broke the shotgun open, checked it, then snapped it shut. "But whatever it is, I feel better with one hand choked around a shotgun stock."

"What about me?" Virgil asked. "That's the only weapon in the place!"

"Are *you* going out there, Virgil?" Summers asked pointedly.

"No. . . . Are *you*?" Virgil countered.

"I intend to see what's going on out there," Summers said. He turned and headed for the batwing doors.

When the Peltry Gang had swooped up over the green hillside and onto the dirt street of Rileyville, launching a sudden and merciless attack, the townsmen had had no chance to react. Before anyone knew what had hit them, an old teamster named Roy Krill lay dead in the street. Then even the few townsmen wearing pistols made no attempt to draw their weapons. Like the rest of the citizenry, they bolted away from the oncoming barrage of rifle and sidearm fire and took shelter behind or beneath whatever cover they could find. The sound of pounding hooves and blazing gunfire lasted only a few short seconds.

In the wake of the attack, a woman screamed at the sight of the body in the street. From beneath a buckboard wagon, a baby cried. A large red hound appeared from an alley and barked fiercely at the armed horsemen as they circled and settled in their own cloud of dust.

"Shut that dog up!" yelled Goose Peltry, rearing his horse a bit with his big Lemat pistol cocked and raised for the benefit of the cowering townsfolk. A single rifle shot exploded; the barking stopped with an abrupt yelp. Silence loomed for a moment above the dirt street.

In the Ace High Saloon, the sound of the rifle shot caused Will Summers to stop in his tracks for a second. Then he stepped forward cautiously the rest of the way to the saloon doors and peeped out above them. Looking down the length of the street, Summers saw the horsemen spread out with their weapons aimed and ready. He jerked his head back inside the saloon. "Jesus," he whispered.

"What is it, Will?" Virgil asked, slipping around

from behind the bar with a billy bat raised in his right hand.

"It's a raid," Will Summers said, stepping to one side of the doors and slumping back against the wall. "It looks like Goose and Devil Moses Peltry."

"The Peltry Gang!" Virgil's billy bat drooped to his side. "What are we going to do now?"

"If you're smart, Virgil, you'll do like everybody else does. Keep your hands up and your mouth shut . . . hope they take whatever they want and ride out." Will Summers straightened up from the wall and started toward the rear door. "I'll bring your shotgun back directly."

"Wait, Will! Where you going?" asked Virgil, his voice shaky, the billy bat trembling in his hand. "You ain't going to try to fight them, are you?"

"Fight them?" Will Summers stopped at the back door long enough to look around at Virgil with a bemused expression. "No way in the world," he said. "But I brought in a string of new horses from Bently yesterday. Damned if I'm handing them over to that bunch."

On the street, Goose Peltry stepped his big bay stallion closer to the boardwalk. "All right, file out here, you bunch of flat-headed peckerwoods. . . . Anybody don't want to die, raise your hands." He cackled aloud at his little joke, shooting a glance around at his men for their approval. Goose Peltry ran a finger across his pencil-thin mustache, then along the strip of a thin goatee running down the center of his chin and coming to a two-inch point. The men chuckled respectfully, except for Moses Peltry. Moses spit a stream of tobacco juice and stared at his brother in disgust.

"Get on with it, damn it, Goose," said Moses, wiping the back of his gloved hand across his mouth. A long black-gray beard hung almost to Moses Peltry's belt line. His gloved hand squeezed around the middle of the long beard and rested there.

"All right, folks!" said Goose, sweeping his pistol barrel back and forth across the frightened faces venturing forward from cover, their hands high. "You heard him! Moses has spoken. Now hurry on out here and make a line. Since there's no bank in this dirt hole, we're here for your money, supplies, horses and what have you. Gather it all up and hand it over. . . . We'll get of here quick as we can." His eyes moved back and forth as the townsfolk formed an uneven line along the street in front of the boardwalk. "Have any of you men fit for the Union? Don't deny it if you have! Step up and admit it. . . . Take what's coming to you like the low, lousy dogs that you are!" His gaze turned more menacing. He scrutinized each townsman's face in turn. "None of you, huh?"

As Goose spoke to the townsmen, Moses motioned to the horsemen closest to him. "Gilbert, you and Frank go get a wagon; start cleaning these stores out. Smitson, get over to that livery barn and bring back any horses that look good enough to ride. Horses are getting worth their weight in gold."

As Moses issued orders to the men, Goose continued talking to the townsmen. "All right, none of you rode for the Union? That's to your favor. I hate Yankees worse than I hate snakes!" He looked back and forth again. "Anybody here who fit for the Stars and Bars?"

"I did, sir," said a shaky voice. "I fought for the Stars and Bars." A drummer named Odell Keithly stepped forward and offered a weak smile.

"Then get over here closer, sir," said Goose Peltry.

He jumped down from his horse and hurried forward, extending his hand in a gesture of friendship. The man looked relieved as he stepped forward himself. But as soon as Goose Peltry's hand closed down on his, Goose jerked him forward and swiped a hard blow from his pistol barrel across Keithly's face. Keithly crumbled to his knees; a bloody welt appeared across his cheek. "You cowardly bastard!" Goose Peltry shouted, striking the hapless man over and over. "You never fit hard enough though, did you?" Each blow from the pistol barrel sent blood splattering to the ground.

"Stop please!" a woman screamed. "You're killing him!"

"Oh, am I, sure enough?" Goose said, giving her a feigned look of concern. "I hadn't thought about it, but I believe you might be right!" He drew back and slammed a crushing blow straight down onto Keithly's head, the impact of the blow lifting Goose onto his tiptoes. When Goose let go of the man's hand, Keithly fell limp to the ground. A long moan issued from his lips.

"If he ain't dead now, he'll live to be a hundred," Goose shouted. "Come on everybody, dig real deep; come up with everything in your pockets. The Lord loves a cheerful giver, so pitch it out here. I catch anybody holding back . . . I'll cleave their hand off and nail it to a hitch rail!" The townsfolk gasped; men's wallets and women's purses hit the ground at Goose Peltry's feet. Goose stepped back as two of his men, Elmer Fitzhugh and Monk Dupre, scurried from their horses and began snatching up the booty.

In the livery barn, Will Summers had managed to slip back and forth from stall to stall until he had all six of his new horses strung to a lead rope and standing quietly in a line facing the rear door. When he heard the front door begin to creak open, he cursed under his breath and ducked down behind a stall door.

Bert Smitson stepped inside the livery barn with his pistol drawn and cocked, looking around in the semidarkness. "Well, well," he whispered aloud, seeing the horses strung and waiting. "What have we here?"

He moved silently alongside the string of horses, running a hand along their sides, keeping a close eye and his big army Colt on the darkened corners of the barn. "You can come on out now," Smitson said to the quiet barn. "I ain't gonna shoot yas. . . . Hell, I appreciate you getting these hosses ready for the trail." He stopped for a moment and waited for a reply. When none came, he moved back along the string of horses and chuckled under his breath. Letting down the hammer of his Colt, he blew out a tense breath, shook his head, and leaned back against the stall door.

"Sometimes, Bert," he said aloud to himself, "you just have to accept the good things in life when they're thrust upon you—"

His words cut short. Behind him, Will Summers rose up from the dark stall, gripping the shotgun by its short barrel, two-handed, and swinging it like a club. The whole string of horses flinched at the sound of the shotgun stock cracking across the side of Bert Smitson's head.

"Easy, boys. . . ." Will Summers settled the horses with a soothing whisper as he stepped from the stall and over Bert Smitson with the broken shotgun hanging in his hand. All that remained of the shattered walnut stock was a stub roughly the size and shape of a pistol butt. Summers hefted the shotgun, getting a feel for its newly modified design. Then he carried the gun pointed down as he walked to the rear door, leading the string of horses behind him.

On the street, Gilbert Metts and Frank Spragg came riding back to Moses Peltry in an open buckboard wagon. Between them sat Deputy Abner Webb, his hands cuffed behind his back, his dark hair disheveled, his shirt unbuttoned, his belt hanging loose around his waist. Sliding the buckboard to a halt, Frank Spragg threw Abner Webb to the ground. "Whooie, Goose!" he crowed. "Look what we brung ya! A real rootin'-tootin', honest-to-God lawman!"

Abner Webb landed with a grunt and struggled up to his knees, spitting dust.

"Where the hell's his boots?" Goose asked, looking Webb over, his cocked pistol turning from the townsfolk to loom above the lawman's head. Abner Webb's big bare feet looked pale and ridiculous in the glare of harsh sunlight. He tucked one foot over the other as if to hide them from sight.

"He weren't wearing any boots. He was barely dressed at all when we found him slipping along an alley," said Gilbert Metts. "He was hurrying to get his clothes on, trying to strap on his gunbelt." As he spoke, Metts pitched a holstered Colt .45 to the ground. "I reckon he heard the shooting and came running."

"I figure he was with a woman in this buckboard," Frank Spragg cut in, laughing. "Then we all came riding in and busted up his party. Found a pair of women's shoes and discarded unmentionables back there." As he spoke, Spragg reached around, picked up a pair of women's slippers and a pair of pantaloons and threw them to the ground. "She must've run off in hurry."

"Is that the truth, lawdog?" said Goose Peltry, giving Abner Webb a cruel grin. "Was you back there chasing the cat this time of day? In broad daylight?"

Abner Webb didn't answer. He kept his head bowed, avoiding the faces of the townsfolk.

"Answer me, Mr. Sheriff," Goose Peltry demanded, reaching down with his pistol and raising Webb's face with the tip of the barrel under his chin.

"I'm not the sheriff," said Abner Webb in a weak voice, still keeping his eyes lowered as much as possible. "I'm the deputy."

"Oh, I see," said Goose. "Hear that boys? He ain't the *sheriff*. He's just a *deputy*. . . . So it's all right, him taking time off for a little buckboard bouncing in the heat of the day!"

Goose Peltry reached with his pistol barrel, hooked the pair of pantaloons on it and raised them high in the air. With his free hand, he picked up one of the slippers from the dust and wagged it back and forth. "Any of you women missing these things, you best come on out here and claim 'em . . . else I'll keep them for a souvenir."

Among the townsfolk, Edmund Daniels' face swelled red as he recognized the pantaloons and lunged forward. "Webb, you dirty, rotten snake! I'll kill you!"

"Whoa, settle down!" shouted Goose. Two of his men grabbed Edmund Daniels and held him back. Goose and his men laughed aloud. Then he turned his attention back to Abner Webb. "I hope we ain't gone and spilled the beans on something here," he said.

Abner Webb hung his head and shook it back and forth, humiliated.

"Ain't you ashamed of yourself, Deputy?" Goose said, taunting Webb. "I bet this feller wouldn't say a word if I was to blow your head all over the street." He tightened his hand around the pistol butt.

"Cut it out, Goose!" Moses Peltry demanded, stepping forward and shoving his brother's pistol away from Abner Webb's head. "We ain't got time for this foolishness! Where's Smitson? What's taking him so long in that barn?" He cut a glance toward the livery barn, then said to Frank Spragg and Gilbert Metts, "Y'all get over there. . . . See what's the holdup. Has it occurred to any of yas that if this man is a *deputy* there might be a *sheriff* sneaking around here somewhere right now? You stupid bunch of cracker-neck peckerwoods!"

As Frank Spragg and Gilbert Metts hurried away on foot toward the livery barn, Goose Peltry reached back down and lifted Abner Webb's chin on his pistol barrel again. "Is that true, Deputy? Is there a sheriff sneaking up on us right now? Ready to heap fire and damnation upon my dear brother Moses here?"

"Don't you mock me, Goose. I'm warning you," Moses Peltry hissed.

"He's out of town today," Abner Webb said in a defeated tone of voice.

"There. You hear that, Moses?" Goose beamed. "The sheriff ain't here today. He's gone out of town!" He looked back down at Abner Webb. "Pray tell, where is the sheriff off to?" he asked in a taunting voice.

"He's gone . . . fishing," Abner said, dropping his voice to prevent the townsfolk from hearing him.

"Gone fishing!" Goose Peltry bellowed, laughing aloud and looking around at the sour expressions on the faces of the silent citizenry. "Lord God, folks, did you hear that? Here you people are on the very edge of death and destruction, and damned if your sheriff ain't gone off *fishing*!" He gestured down at Abner Webb with his pistol barrel. "One's off fishing. The other's laid up in a buckboard with another man's wife! What sort of terrible place have we stumbled into, brother Moses?"

"Get yourself under control or so help me I'll bust your head wide open!" Moses warned his brother, his voice lowered to carry just between the two of them.

"Hold on now, Moses," Goose Peltry responded, the humor leaving his voice quickly. "I don't take no more head bustings from you or nobody else." His hand tightened on his pistol butt.

Moses' nostrils flared. He took a step toward his brother as the helpless townsfolk looked on fearfully. But before Moses could say anything, Frank Spragg called out from the open door of the livery barn. "Moses! Goose! You better come quick! Somebody has knocked the holy hell out of Smitson!"

"Is he dead?" Moses called out.

"No, but his eyes might be crossed from now on," Spragg replied.

Beside Spragg, Gilbert Metts appeared with Smitson's arm looped over his shoulder. Smitson's head bobbed up and down as if attached by a loose spring.

"Damn it all," said Moses Peltry, looking back and forth along the dirt street. "This is what happens when we stand around here jawing and threatening people. We should be loaded and gone by now."

"Want us to go help them tote Smitson over here?" asked one of the men still atop his horse.

"Sit still, all of you," said Moses. The gunmen watched in silence as Metts and Spragg dragged Smitson along the street and lowered him to the ground. For a moment, Smitson managed to wobble back and forth on his knees. But then he crumbled to the ground, blood running down the swollen split along his jawline. Moses and Goose both winced at the sight of it.

Moses looked at Spragg and Metts. "Any horses in the barn?"

"None worth feeding," said Spragg.

"Every stall door is wide open," said Metts. "So's the rear door. Looks like somebody saw us coming and cleaned out every good horse in town."

"Well now, ain't you clever!" Goose shouted, keeping his voice loud enough to be heard anywhere along the dirt street. "Hear me good. . . . If you don't come leading them horses back here right now, we'll just start shooting people dead in the street!"

A gasp rose up from the townsfolk. They appeared ready to bolt away in every direction. "Nobody move!" shouted Moses Peltry, stepping around his brother and staring down at Abner Webb. "Who did it? Who took off with the horses?"

Abner Webb looked bewildered for a second. Then he remembered Will Summers' string of good riding stock from Bently. "Those were a trader's horses," said Webb. "Nobody took off with them. He must've just left town before you rode in. You can't blame the whole town for that."

"Oh?" Goose stepped in closer, Moses' arm holding him back from Abner Webb. "Then how the hell did Smitson's jaw get splattered all over his face?"

"I have no idea who hit him," said Webb, looking up at Moses Peltry as he answered Goose's question. "Don't kill any of these people; they had nothing to do with—"

"Shut up!" Moses shouted. "I'll say who we kill or don't kill here." He looked along the line of frightened faces. Then he said to Goose, "Get these men started cleaning out the stores. Any horse at the hitch

rails worth taking, get them gathered up." He looked
back down at Abner Webb. "Who's the trader?"

"I don't know," said Webb, stalling for a second
while he figured out whether or not there was any
harm in telling him.

"You better think real hard," Moses warned, cocking his pistol as he lifted it from the holster across
his stomach.

"All right, hold on," said Webb. "I believe his
name is Summers."

"Summers?" said Goose Peltry, jerking his attention back to Abner Webb. "You mean Will Summers?" Goose looked off across the grassy hillside
west of town as he spoke, as if searching for any sign
of Summers and the string of horses.

"Yes," said Webb, "I think that's his name." Abner
Webb studied the expression that swept over Goose
and Moses Peltry's faces.

"Well, I'll be double dog damned," said Goose,
still looking all around.

"One thing for sure," said Moses. "If they belong
to Will Summers, it's just as well we didn't take
them. We'd have to fool with him for the next
month . . . else blow his fool head off."

"So?" said Goose. "I don't mind blowing his fool
head off. Fact is, I'd kinda enjoy doing it."

"Sure you would," Moses said, sounding sarcastic.
He turned to the gunmen. "All right, men, let's get
busy. Strip these stores down . . . grub, guns, ammunition, anything you see worth taking."

"Don't forget—we like cash money too," said
Goose. He looked back at Moses. "What about shooting a few of these folks just for good measure? Leave
them lying dead in the street for Will Summers to
see in case he rides back this way."

"No," said Moses. "I got a better idea. Get everything we want loaded up."

"All right. Then what?" Goose asked expectantly.

"Then get some kerosene, lamp oil or whatever's on hand," said Moses.

"Yeah," said Goose Peltry with a wide, cruel grin, a dark gleam coming into his eyes. "I hear ya, brother Moses! Let's burn this place to a pile of cinders . . . every last store, house and privy jake!"

"Huh-uh," said Moses. "Not everything. We burn everything, these men have nothing left to lose. We'll burn just enough to keep everybody too busy to follow us."

"You're always thinking, Moses," Goose said with admiration. He turned to the gathered townsfolk. "After today, if anybody asks you who burnt this town, you tell them Will Summers done it. Whatever we do, you've got him to thank for it."

On his knee in the dirt, Abner Webb stared at the ground and shook his bowed head.

Chapter 2

In the small, rough-plank schoolhouse a half mile from the edge of town, schoolmaster Sherman Dahl hushed the two dozen excited students and continued to listen closely beyond the strip of shaded white oak surrounding the schoolyard. After a moment, when he'd heard no more gunfire, he turned to the children, who had assembled at the far end of the long single room near the door.

"Everybody pay attention," he said, raising his voice. "I have no idea what the shooting was about, but apparently it has ceased. Since we don't know what to expect, we are going to venture to the edge of town, single file, and see what we can find out. Each and every one of us is going to behave. Isn't that right, Eddie?" He raised a thin finger for emphasis, his gaze fixing on a red-haired ten-year-old boy who stood poking another child in the ribs, using his finger as a pistol barrel.

"Stop it, Eddie," the other child hissed.

"I *said*, isn't that right, Eddie Duvall?" Sherman Dahl's voice took on a louder, more impatient edge.

"Yes, Mr. Dahl," Eddie Duvall said grudgingly.

"Very good, children," Sherman Dahl said. "I want all of you to stay close together. Do not get out of line without my permission."

A thin hand shot up. "Yes, sir," said a thin lad

wearing thick spectacles, "but what if it's scalp-raising wild red Indians come to kill every one of us?"

"Take your hand down, Joel." Sherman Dahl offered a short, calming smile. "I assure you, if there's any wild Indians out there, I will give everybody permission to leave the line immediately."

"Don't worry. If it's wild red Indians, my pa probably already shot them down," Eddie Duvall boasted.

Joel Stevens nodded, seemingly reassured. The other children nodded in quiet agreement.

Drawing a key from his vest pocket, Sherman Dahl walked over to his battered oak desk. He bent down to a lower drawer and unlocked it. Concealing his actions from the children, he slid the bottle of rye whiskey to one side, reached farther back and picked up the loaded army Colt. He turned his back to the class, checked the pistol quickly and shoved it behind his belt, smoothing his vest down over its butt. He buttoned his suit coat, then closed the drawer and locked it, reminding himself how good a shot of the rye would taste. "All right, children: Form a line behind Constance Melton, and let's proceed in an orderly manner."

It would have been safer perhaps to keep the children in the schoolhouse, Sherman Dahl told himself. Yet now that the shooting seemed to have stopped, something compelled him to go investigate. With young Constance Melton leading the line of children a few yards behind him, Dahl kept a cautious gaze beyond the sparse stretch of white oaks between the schoolhouse and the edge of town.

"Whatever the shooting was about," said Eddie Duvall, "I bet my pa took care of it if he was there." A murmur of whispers rose up from the boys.

"Keep it down back there," said Sherman Dahl in

a hushed tone of voice. "Don't make me tell you again." Ahead Dahl saw the first rise of dark smoke lift up above the hillside. As he continued on, other rises of smoke joined upward on a sidelong drift of wind. "Oh my goodness," Dahl said under his breath. When he'd led the children a few yards farther along the path, he heard the sound of horses' hooves and the crack of a wagon whip. A man's voice gave a loud "Yee-hiii," and Sherman Dahl quickly shooed the children off the dirt path into the shelter of the trees as the first riders appeared above the roll of the hillside.

"Everybody duck down and remain quiet!" Dahl ordered. "Don't let them see you!" But it was too late. At the front of the riders, Goose Peltry and Frank Spragg caught a glimpse of Dahl's coattail as he tried to duck out of sight.

"Well now, what have we here?" Goose Peltry said, grinning, his voice in time to his horse's loping gait. Three small faces peeped out from behind an oak tree then jerked back out of sight. "Looks like we're about to be ambushed, brother Moses."

Nudging his horse up between Goose and Frank Spragg, Moses caught sight of the schoolhouse in the distant clearing. "I saw them, Goose. They're just kids . . . from that schoolhouse, I'd wager."

"Hell, brother Moses, of course I see they's just kids," said Goose. "I'm just having a little sport on such a lovely day. Come on, Frank," he said to Frank Spragg. "Let's scare the hell out of that little schoolmarm."

"That weren't no marm," said Frank Spragg. "It looked like a man to me."

"What's the difference?" Goose laughed. "If he ain't a woman, I bet he's always wanted to be." He spurred his horse's sides.

"Hold it, Goose!" said Moses Peltry, but his brother had already ridden forward, Frank Spragg right beside him.

On the path alongside the white oaks, Goose Peltry raised his pistol from his holster and cocked it. Beside him, Frank Spragg did the same. As the rest of the riders caught up to them, Goose called out to the hidden faces, "All of you in there, come out with your hands raised." He shot Spragg a wink and quick grin. "Any false move, and it'll be your last!"

"Please don't shoot," said Sherman Dahl, stepping out from behind an oak, his hands up. "There's only some schoolchildren in here. . . . They're no danger to you."

"Oh? Well, you don't look like a school kid to me," said Goose Peltry. "Get over here closer. . . . Keep them hands raised." Then he called out to the children as Sherman Dahl moved closer, "You heard your schoolmarm—get on out here. Else I'll take the top of his head off!"

"Schoolmarm?" Constance Melton whispered to the other children strung out alongside her on the ground behind a rising edge of rock and earth.

"We better get out there," said Joel Stevens, his voice quivering in fright.

"No. Sit tight," Eddie Duvall whispered harshly.

"But you heard him," said Joel Stevens. "He'll shoot Mr. Dahl!"

"Quit the yapping," said Goose Peltry, "and get out here before I commence peppering the woods with bullets!"

Moses and the other riders pulled their horses up to a halt around Goose and Frank Spragg. "What's going on here?" Moses asked impatiently.

"Nothing," said Goose. "Just some kids fixing to see this fool shot all to pieces"—he raised his voice

to the white oaks—"if they don't do like they're told
and get out here!"

"Children, listen carefully and do as I tell you,"
said Sherman Dahl, taking note of the dozen heavily
armed riders, some of them dressed in ragged Confederate issue. Many of them carried cavalry sabers
and field rifles strapped to their saddles. "Raise your
hands and step out far enough for these men to see
that we mean them no harm."

Behind the riders, Dahl saw a large freight wagon
loaded high with supplies and arms. A long string
of horses stood tied to the end of the wagon. His
eyes went from Goose to Moses Peltry, sensing
instinctively that this was the real leader. "I trust, sir,
that you won't harm innocent children." Out of the
corner of his eye, he saw the swelling dark cloud of
drifting smoke from town and heard the shouting of
townsmen as he pictured them trying to subdue the
licking flames.

"Bring them out," said Moses Peltry in a firm tone.
"No harm will come to them."

Goose Peltry didn't like being bypassed for his
brother, especially in front of all the men. He seethed
and pointed his cocked pistol at Sherman Dahl. "No
harm will come to them, but you're a different story
if you don't do like you've been told!"

There was a calmness to the schoolmaster that
Goose Peltry resented. Even as the man turned and
waved the children in around him, he didn't seem
frightened enough to satisfy Goose. "You. School-
marm . . . Get over here. I want to see you sweat!"

Moses Peltry stared, knowing he could stop his
brother at any time. Something about this young
schoolmaster seemed to say that Goose was in for a
disappointment. Sherman Dahl stepped closer as the
children drifted forward warily, their eyes wide with

fright and excitement. "That's close enough, school-marm," Goose instructed. Sherman Dahl stopped three feet from Goose's horse. Goose gave him a nasty grin. "Now, did anybody say you could talk to my brother instead of me?"

"No, sir," Sherman Dahl offered in a submissive voice.

"What's your name, schoolmarm?" Goose asked.

"Dahl, sir. . . . Sherman Dahl."

"Dahl, you cut a poor example for these younguns, speaking out of turn that way." He half turned in his saddle and said to two of the riders, "Thurman, Roscoe, you two take your can of coal oil, get over there and stick some fire into that schoolhouse. There's too damn many Yankees can read and write as it is." The two riders spurred their horses off toward the empty schoolhouse, both of them whooping aloud.

"Sir, please," said Sherman Dahl. "I beg you; don't burn down our school. It belongs to these children! Many of them even helped build it with their own han—"

"Shut up, schoolmarm!" Goose Peltry snapped, his hand tightening on his pistol butt. "You should have thought of that before you talked right past me." As they spoke, the two riders prodded their horses upward into the small plank building, both of them slinging small coal oil tins back and forth.

"Yes, sir. You're right," Dahl said, speaking fast, hoping against fate that there was still time for the leaders to call the two men back. "It was a rash and ill-considered thing for me to do. I—I apologize, sir."

"Oh, you do, huh?" As Goose spoke, he maneuvered his horse around sideways to the helpless schoolmaster. At the schoolhouse, the two riders reappeared, jumping their horses out the front door as

flames began to lick upward out of the open windows. "Well, I think an apology ain't going to get it
done. Your manners are in sore need of correcting!"

Seeing the schoolhouse aflame, Sherman Dahl felt
a sickness down deep in his stomach. Behind him he
heard the younger children sobbing, and he heard
Constance Melton trying to comfort them. There was
nothing Dahl could do now to keep this dangerous
situation from getting any worse but accept what had
happened and remain as calm as possible.

"I reckon that makes you fighting mad, don't it,
schoolmarm?" said Goose Peltry. "Bet you'd like to
take out on my head right here and now, eh?"

"No, sir," said Sherman Dahl. "I'm not a fighter.
Not me, sir. I only want to take these children away
from here."

"I bet you do," said Goose Peltry. The two riders
slid their horse back in among the others as the
schoolhouse became engulfed in high, swirling
flames.

"All right, Goose," said Moses Peltry. "You've had
your fun. Now let him go."

Fun . . . ? This was *fun* to them? Sherman Dahl
felt the bitter taste of dark anger rise at the back of
his throat. He swallowed hard and managed to keep
himself in check.

"Just one more thing, brother Moses," Goose said.

Dahl saw Goose's boot shift back an inch in the
stirrup. He saw what was coming and could only
prepare himself to take it. Even with the pistol
shoved down in his belt behind his suit coat, Dahl
knew he was powerless to take action, lest he cause
harm to the children.

"Maybe this will teach you!" shouted Goose Peltry,
his boot jerking back out of the stirrup and snapping
forward, kicking Sherman Dahl full in the face.

Dahl fell backward; the children gasped. But Moses saw that the schoolmaster hadn't taken as hard a blow as it looked. Moses had seen the way the young teacher had managed to roll back away from the kick, taking it at a glance instead of full impact. Pretty quick and savvy for a schoolmaster, Moses thought, seeing Sherman Dahl roll up from the ground onto one knee, his hands going up to cover his mouth. Yet looking closely, Moses saw no blood seep down behind his fingers. A kick that hard could have cost a man a couple of teeth, Moses thought.

Constance Melton hurried forward from the rest of the children and threw herself between Dahl and the mounted gunman, her long, gangly arms thrown out as if to prevent Goose Peltry from getting past her. "You leave him alone," she screamed. "He hasn't done anything to you. . . . Get away and mind your own business!"

The other children backed away as Goose Peltry stepped his horse closer, but Constance Melton appeared to have taken an unyielding stand. Moses Peltry chuckled under his breath, then called out to Goose. "Come on, brother Goose, before you get your eyeballs scratched out. We got lots of ground to cover before dark."

Goose scowled and started to say something to his brother. "But—"

Frank Spragg cut in with a shrill, mocking voice. *"Yeah, you leave him alone! He hasn't done anything to you. . . . Mind your own business!"*

The men laughed. Goose Peltry stopped his horse and turned to Frank Spragg, grinning. "Frank, that voice was a might too shrill to be a put-on. We're going to check you out one of these days, make sure you're all there." He jerked his horse away from Sherman Dahl and Constance Melton and shouted to the wagon driver. "Get that rig rolling! Who the hell said for you to stop anyway?"

On the ground, Sherman Dahl looked up at Goose Peltry, seeing the cocked pistol level down at him. Still he kept his hands to his mouth, taking only a split second to push Constance Melton away, making sure she was out of danger should a shot come blasting out of the pistol barrel.

"Bang!" Goose Peltry shouted. Then he cackled aloud, let the hammer down on his pistol and holstered it as he spun his horse and rode away with the others.

Sherman Dahl drew the children up close around him. They huddled in silence, watching until the riders fell from sight below the roll of the land. Then Dahl stood up, dusting himself off and looking anxiously toward the black smoke in the sky.

"My pa must not have been in town," said Eddie Duvall, giving Sherman Dahl a look of veiled contempt. "He wouldn't have let something like this happen."

"Be quiet, Eddie," said Dahl. He looked around at the other children and said, "Everybody listen to me." He gestured a hand toward the drifting, billowing smoke. "We have to go see what we can do to help the town . . . but we must be careful and not get ourselves injured. Stick close together." As he spoke, he adjusted his vest and brushed dust from it. Joel Stevens caught a glimpse of the pistol butt sticking up from Dahl's belt. His eyes grew large as he pointed at it. "Look! Mr. Dahl is carrying a gun!"

"Quiet, Joel," said the schoolmaster. But the children all stared in awe, seeing the imprint of the pistol clearly now that it had been pointed out to them.

"A lot of good it did," said Eddie Duvall. "You could have done something, but you didn't even try!

You just stood there and let them bully you, Mr. Dahl. You let them burn down our schoolhouse!"

"Children, that was a bad situation, and I did what I had to do. This is not the time to stop and explain it to you," Sherman Dahl responded. "The schoolhouse is gone." His eyes went to the twisting, spinning rise of flames and black smoke that only moments ago had been the Rileyville's first school, a structure that he, the townsmen and even the children themselves had built less than two years ago. As his eyes turned to it, he and the children saw the front wall collapse inward across rows of burning desks.

In the dirt twenty yards away, a shaggy brown housecat whose job it had been to keep down the rodent population sat staring as both her home and her livelihood disappeared before her eyes. "There's nothing we can do here," Sherman Dahl said gently to the children. "Let's hurry into town and help put out the other fires. At least we'll be doing *something*. . . ."

Chapter 3

In their haste, the Peltry Gang had not done their best work starting the fires. They had hurriedly set the fires at three random locations with no regard to the direction of the wind or to the structure of the buildings. Then the gang had left town quickly, without giving the fires adequate time to completely destroy the three large buildings. In spite of the overwhelming black cloud adrift above Rileyville, the fires were soon reduced to steam beneath the relentless efforts of the bucket brigade.

Abner Webb stood exhausted, his shirtsleeves rolled above his elbows, his face smeared with black soot. Beside him, Will Summers batted his wet hat against his wet trouser leg. Then he rolled the hat brim between both hands and put it on. "Looks like Rileyville has cheated the odds once again," he said. "This is a tough town to kill."

"Yeah, so it looks," Webb replied, looking all around. Wooden buckets littered the muddy street. Charred dry goods from the nearly destroyed mercantile store lay in a smoke-streaked pile. A long hose lay serpentine from the front of the smoldering barbershop to the hand pump attached to the edge of an empty water trough. "If I was you, Will, I'd make tracks out of here before these men have time to catch their breath. They'll start blaming you sure enough."

"Then I'm glad you ain't me, Webb," said Summers. "Leaving would be like admitting I was guilty of something. If I'd done anything wrong, I wouldn't have come riding back when I saw all the smoke."

"Suit yourself then," said Abner Webb. "I've got enough to worry about, explaining to the sheriff what I was doing when all this came about."

"You mean about you and the French woman, Renee Marie Daniels?" Will Summers asked in a lowered voice.

"How'd you know?" Abner Webb asked. "You weren't even here!"

"I just figured it," said Will Summers. "Different times I've seen the two of you together without you knowing it."

"You have?" Abner Webb looked crushed by the news.

"Sure have," said Will Summers. "The fact is, so have a lot of other people. There's few secrets in a town this size, Deputy; you ought to know that. I only pass through here a few times a year, but I hear everything that's gone on between. People love to gossip."

"Jesus," Abner Webb whispered, stung by the revelation, "you mean there's others who know about it?" He hooked a thumb in the empty pistol holster on his hip.

"Oh yes," said Will Summers. Taking note of Webb's empty holster, Summers took a Colt .45 from the shoulder harness under his left arm and handed it to him. "Here, take this. Ain't nothing looks more unnatural on a lawman than an empty pistol holster."

"Much obliged, Will," Webb said, taking the pistol, checking it and shoving it down into his holster. "It feels off balance too, going around with an empty holster—kept thinking I was walking in a circle."

"This thing with you and Renee Marie: It's been going on a while, ain't it?"

"Well, yes," said Webb, avoiding Summers' eyes with an embarrassed expression. "I thought we was pretty careful. But there's no denying it after today. We both might just as well have been caught in the act and raised up a flagpole. Goose Peltry made it worse, shooting his mouth off and waving Renee Marie's drawers back and forth."

"Right in front of Edmund, I reckon?" asked Summers.

"Oh, of course!" said Abner Webb. "The whole town saw them! Lucky for me Edmund wasn't armed at that moment. He was awfully upset about it."

"Lucky for you he didn't get his hands on you," said Will Summers. "Edmund is an awfully big man, Deputy. I ain't sure he'd need a gun. I heard he used to fight in the bare-knuckle ring in Chicago. Fought under the name 'Killer' Daniels, I heard." He offered a sympathetic wince. "Why *his* wife of all people?"

"There's just something about French women," said Abner Webb. "I never have been able to control myself around them."

"Maybe you better learn to," Will Summers suggested.

"Hell, it wasn't just her being French, I don't reckon," said Webb. "Look around you, Will. Rileyville ain't exactly blessed with pretty women. Besides, I didn't go looking to fall for Renee Marie Daniels," said Webb. "It just happened. It weren't neither one of our fault." Webb looked down in remorse and shook his head. "I wish I could go and talk to her, see if she's all right . . . see if I can do something for her."

"Sounds like you've done plenty. Best thing you can do now is keep your nose out of it . . . unless you and her are serious enough to take up together and run off."

"She knows I'm not looking for a wife any more than she's looking for a new husband. We just sparked a deep, passionate desire in one another, is the way she said it. We didn't mean it to ever go any further. Edmund would never have known, hadn't been for Goose Peltry."

"Yep, I can just picture ole Goose," said Will Summers, keeping himself from smiling, "waving them bloomers back and forth like a flag."

"Cut it out, Will. It's no joking matter," said Abner Webb.

"You're right. I'm sorry," said Summers. He looked back along the street to where his string of new horses stood tied at a hitch rail. "Miss Renee Marie is a fine, handsome woman. . . . I can't blame Edmund if he comes looking for satisfaction one way or the other, guns or knuckles."

"I know," said Webb. "Don't think I ain't already pictured that in my mind. I look for it most any time."

"At least you're not going to be caught unaware then," said Will Summers. "Be thankful for that."

"Believe me, I am. I won't be breathing easy until this gets settled between him and me some way or another. I just wish none of this ever happened."

"When's the sheriff coming back?" Summers asked.

"Any time now, I would think," said Abner Webb. "One man dead, another beat to hell, the town looted and burnt—I expect he'll want to put together a posse first thing. I sent Bobby Dewitt out to round up some horses and guns from the nearby ranches . . . if they've got any to spare."

"Good luck on that," said Summers. After a second's pause, he asked, "Who was it the Peltrys killed here?"

"That was old Roy Krill. He teamstered freight twixt here and Montydale. Poor old man never knew what hit him, I reckon."

"Never met him." Summers spit and ran a hand across his mouth.

"Nobody knew much about him," said Webb. "He was a quiet old fellow, kept to himself. Soon as our lines are back up, I'll wire Montydale and see if he had any kin there."

"I don't envy you riding posse," said Summers. "All those long hours in the saddle under a blazing sun. *Whew!*"

"Yeah, I know," Abner Webb sighed. "I'll be living in the saddle for quite some time, I reckon." But then he took a deep breath, finding some good in the prospect. "It might be the best thing for me though: get away from here a while, let things cool between Daniels and me."

"Good idea. The Peltrys will be headed straight down across the desert badlands then on into Mexico is my guess," said Summers. "Ever been there?"

"Nope, neither place, but I've always wanted to. I've heard plenty of talk," Webb replied.

"Always *wanted* to?" Summers shook his head, finding the notion absurd. Then he added, "You haven't missed anything, take my word for it."

"You've been through the desert and Mexico both?" Webb asked, looking Summers up and down.

"More times than I ever wanted to," Summers remarked.

"Then I reckon we can count on you riding posse with us for the good of the town?"

"Nope," Summers said flatly. "If there was going

to be a posse, you should have been on their tails before their dust settled. It could take weeks now—that's if you ever catch up to them at all. I'm too busy to turn loose right now, not for free anyway."

"Oh, you think you ought to get *paid* for doing something good for this town?" Webb asked.

"You get paid, don't you?" Summers responded.

"That's a whole different thing, Will."

"Okay, forget it." Summers shrugged. "Let's just say that Rileyville ain't really my kind of a town. Never was."

"Damn, Will, you don't want none of these men to hear you say something like that. Not after what happened here."

"Why? My conscience is clear." He smiled. "Unlike some I could mention."

"That's enough, Will. I mean it," said Webb. "Here they come now." He nodded toward the gathering of soot-streaked townsmen walking toward them, some of them dropping empty buckets to the ground as they neared. "Sure you don't want to cut out while you're able?"

"Yep, I'm sure of it," said Will Summers. "I've done nothing wrong."

"Just don't go losing your temper and start talking short to them," Webb cautioned, his voice dropping quieter as the townsmen neared.

"Don't worry, I won't let things go that far," Summers murmured, keeping an eye on the approaching townsmen.

"You've got some tall explaining to do, Will Summers!" said Ned Trent, leading the men with his fists balled stiffly at his sides, his right fist wrapped tightly around a shovel handle. His breath hissed in and out through his clenched teeth. A black smear

stretched down his cheek. Fifty yards behind him
and his followers, the Trent Mercantile Store lay in
a charred, smoldering heap.

"How so?" Will Summers asked calmly, his left
thumb hooked in his lapel, his right hand resting on
the pistol butt at his hip.

"*How so? By God, you *know* how so!*" Ned Trent
raved. The rest of the townsmen seethed in their
rage. Summers looked past Ned Trent, seeming to
ignore him. Among the angry faces, Summers spotted Virgil Wilkes, the bartender; the town blacksmith,
Big Miles Michaels; Carl Margood, the livery
owner—

"Look at me when I talk to you, Summers!" Ned
Trent bellowed. "I lost my store because of you! The-
odore Logsdon lost his barbershop! Ike Stevens lost
his drugstore!" As Ned Trent ranted, young Joel Stevens slipped in and stood close to his father's side.
Ike Stevens dropped a tired arm across his son's
thin shoulder.

"You're out of your mind, Trent," Summers remarked in an even tone. "I'm sorry you people lost
your stores. I'm sorry the town got looted. But, folks,
don't blame me."

"I *am* blaming you!" said Ned Trent, poking his
finger close to Will Summers' face. "If it hadn't been
for your damned horses, they would have just taken
what they came for and rode on!"

"You're a fool, Trent," said Summers. "And you
better back off a step before you get in deeper than
you want to." Still, Summers didn't raise his voice.
Abner Webb stood watching, not wanting to say any
more than he had to, knowing he too was on thin
ice with the townsfolk.

"You don't scare me, Summers," said Trent with

contempt. "You and your big gun and your big, tall hat!"

"My hat?" Summers looked bemused. "What the hell does my hat have to do—?"

"You know what I mean," shouted Trent, cutting him off. "Don't think we haven't all seen how you look down on the rest of us like you're some kind of big sporting man! Highfalutin horse trader!"

"That's enough out of you," Summers hissed, his hand slowly raising the pistol from its holster.

"Oh! I see," said Trent, throwing a hand to his waist in a gesture of superiority. "Are you threatening me, Summers? What are you going to do, shoot me? I reckon it's easy enough to do, knowing my guns have all been stolen!" He tossed a glance over his shoulder to the rest of the men. "There, you see? He gets brave now that there's no one here but honest, hardworking—" His words stopped short as he turned his eyes back to Will Summers just in time to catch the full impact of Summers' pistol barrel across the bridge of his nose.

"Aw, damn it, Will!" said Abner Webb, stepping toward Ned Trent and trying to catch him as he fell. Blood flew from Trent's nose as he collapsed to the ground.

The townsmen started to surge toward Summers. Summers cocked his pistol and leveled it at them. "I didn't shoot him, but that don't mean I won't shoot you!" His words were directed at everyone. The townsmen stopped short and shied back a step.

"You can't shoot the whole town, Summers," said Louis Collingsworth, a cattle buyer and land speculator.

"You might be right about the whole town, Collingsworth," Summers replied, sidestepping backward along the hitch rail as he spoke. He felt his way along his horse's side and jerked the broken sawed-off shotgun from beneath his bedroll. Holding it by the short stub of the stock, he cocked it. "But I can knock some fair-sized chunks of meat off with this."

"That's my shotgun, Will!" Virgil Wilkes said, outraged by the condition of the sawed-off.

"Sorry, Virgil," said Summers. "It couldn't be helped." His eyes went back to Louis Collingsworth. "You ready to be the first to drop? If you are, just say so. . . . I'll take it from there."

"Hold it, Will!" Abner Webb shouted, stuck between the townsmen and the menacing shotgun and pistol in Summers' hands. "Damn it, you said you wouldn't let things go this far!" He cast a quick glance through the crowd, searching for Edmund Daniels. Not seeing Daniels caused him to cast a quicker look over his shoulder as he spoke.

"I said I wouldn't fly off and lose my temper," Will Summers said, correcting him. "So far, I haven't. I'm just accommodating the crowd." He looked back at Louis Collingsworth. "What about it, Louis?"

From behind the townsmen, Sherman Dahl's voice rose above the tense silence. "Lower the guns, Mr. Summers. We all see that you mean business."

"Oh?" Will Summers stared in the direction of Dahl's voice as the schoolteacher stepped forward, parting the crowd. "And what are you bringing to this little gathering, Mr. Schoolmaster?"

Sherman Dahl's voice was as calm as Summers' as he slowly opened his coat and drew the right side back out of the way. The butt of the big army Colt stood leaning a bit toward his right hand. His right hand was thin and pale, but dead steady. "I'm bringing nothing, sir, unless I have to," said Dahl. "I'm just asking you to lower those weapons before somebody gets hurt. There's children here. . . . Let's show some civility."

"I couldn't agree more," Abner Webb said quickly. "Listen to the teacher, Will. He's talking good sense."

"Can't you see how bad this whole town is suffering, Mr. Summers?" Sherman Dahl continued, his voice calm and level. "Of course it wasn't your fault what happened here. Everybody will realize that once they've had time to think. Right, Mr. Collingsworth?" He turned his eyes evenly to Louis Collingsworth then back to Will Summers.

"All right," said Collingsworth. "Maybe I wasn't thinking straight." He wiped a hand across his forehead. "This is a terrible damn thing to have happen to a good bunch of people. I admit it might have us all a little stunned, not thinking clearly."

Seeing the townsmen ease back at the sound of Collingsworth's words, Summers lowered the shotgun barrel an inch. He looked back at the face of the young schoolmaster, not quite sure what he saw in the man's eyes. He started to ask Sherman Dahl what his intentions had been with the big army Colt. But before he got a chance to speak, a whip cracked from the far end of the dirt street. All eyes turned toward the sound of the southern stage from Greely as it rumbled forward in a rise of dust.

"He's in a powerful big hurry," said Abner Webb, relieved that Summers' and the townsmen's attention had been diverted away from one another.

"Yeah," said Will Summers. "Reckon he ran into the Peltrys out there?" As he watched the stagecoach driver pull back on the brake lever with all his weight and slide the big coach to a halt, Summers slid a glance at the schoolmaster, still wondering how far the young man would have gone with the big Colt.

"Let's see what Matthew's so excited about," said
Abner Webb, starting forward as the old stagecoach
driver dropped down from his seat and slung open
the stagecoach doors.

"Oh Lord!" said Carl Margood, seeing the stage
driver pull Sheriff Hastings from the coach and lower
him to the ground.

"Somebody get the doctor!" Matthew Bowden
shouted out to the townsmen. "Hastings is about
done for!"

"Damn, what a day," Will Summers said, moving
forward yet staying a few steps behind the rest of
the men. A few feet away from Will Summers, Sherman Dahl walked along at the same pace, staying
parallel, not allowing Summers to drop back behind
him. What was the story on this young schoolmaster?
Summers asked himself.

The door to Dr. Silas Blayton's office stood wide
open, the crowd of townsmen having filled the waiting room and spread out along the boardwalk and
into the street. Cigar smoke hung thick and low in a
blue-gray cloud. The doctor fanned a hand back and
forth as if parting a way for himself when he stepped
out of the door to his treatment room and closed it
behind him. Deputy Abner Webb moved forward,
holding his hat in his hand and nervously fidgeting
with the battered brim. "Well, is he going to make
it, Doc?" he asked in a hushed voice. Will Summers
stood three feet back, listening, still keeping a cautious eye on the crowd.

"It's too soon to tell," said Dr. Blayton, shaking his
bald head. "He's taken two bullets; one barely
missed his heart. He's lost a dangerous amount of
blood."

"Can I see him?" asked Webb, moving a step closer to the door as he asked.

Dr. Blayton raised a hand, stopping him. "Not now. He needs to rest some . . . get some blood back in his system."

"But I got to find out what happened to him, Doc!" Webb protested. "I need to hear what he wants to do about raising a posse!"

"I can tell you the whole story, Deputy," said Doc Blayton, maneuvering Webb back from the door. "Sheriff Hastings told me everything." He looked around at all the anxious faces, then back to Abner Webb. "The sheriff ran into the Peltrys on his way back from Little Dog Creek. Goose Peltry shot him. They took his horse and everything else he had . . . left him for dead." Doc Blayton looked back and forth at the eyes staring at him, then added, "Everybody go home now. If you want to do something for the sheriff, you might think about praying for him." He started to turn and go back inside the treatment room.

"Wait a minute, Doc!" said Abner Webb. "Did he give you any instructions for me? I need to know what to do here! Should I get on the Peltrys' trail or what?"

"Don't ask me," said the old doctor. "That's a matter for a lawman to decide."

"Yeah," said a voice full of contempt, "but where are we going to find a *real* lawman around here?"

Abner Webb snapped a harsh glare at the crowd. "All right, who said that?"

Before anyone could answer, Dr. Blayton gave Abner Webb a slight shove, getting him headed toward the front door. "I want this room cleared. Any discussing you need to do can be done on the boardwalk. I'll keep everybody posted on how the sheriff's doing."

As the men began filing out onto the boardwalk, Abner Webb looked back over his shoulder at the door to the treatment room, not knowing what to do next. As he hesitated, Will Summers coaxed him forward. "Come on, Deputy. The sheriff can't help you now."

Outside on the boardwalk, a skinny young cowboy slid down from his saddle holding a lead rope to a string of five dusty horses. Under one arm he carried three rifles wrapped in a wool blanket. A few townsmen stepped to one side as the cowboy tied the lead rope to the hitch rail and bounded up onto the boardwalk. Looking past him at the five-horse string, Abner Webb said, "Doggone it, Bobby, is that all? Just five horses?"

"That's all," Bobby Dewitt replied. "Five horses, three rifles, two boxes of cartridges." He handed the rifles over to Will Summers, who unwrapped them and tossed them out one at a time to the reaching hands of the townsmen. Two boxes of ammunition fell from the blanket, but eager hands snatched them up as soon as they hit the boardwalk. Bobby Dewitt slapped dust from his jacket with his gloved hand.

"McAllister sent everything he had," said Bobby Dewitt. "He's got his whole herd and crew off in the high grasslands. Said we're welcome to more horses, but it'd be three days getting to them. The Big R spread said pretty much the same: offered to send you every man he's got once they get back from their drive two weeks from now."

"Two weeks!" shouted a voice from the crowded street. "Hell, they'll be no need even looking for them in two weeks!"

"All right, men," said Abner Webb. "I know we

need more horses and guns." His eyes swept across the crowd and saw that many of the men were now wearing old pistols they had scraped up from their homes or barns. "But before you all go flying off the—"

"What we *need* is somebody who can *take charge*," Miles Michaels, the blacksmith, interrupted. "All we've seen Abner Webb do is *take advantage*!"

Deputy Abner Webb rubbed his temples as if suffering from a headache. Then he looked out from the boardwalk at the angry faces. "All right, we've only got five horses. Anybody got any idea how we're going to get by with *five* horses? Any of you want to join a *walking* posse?"

"That polecat has horses!" shouted Ned Trent with a nasal twang, his nose swollen to twice its normal size. "Make him give them up!"

"You don't learn easily, do you, Trent?" said Will Summers, stepping to the edge of the boardwalk as Abner Webb grabbed his arm and held him back.

Trent touched a wet rag to his broken nose as he shied back a step. "In an emergency situation, I say the town can confiscate a man's horses for its own use."

"Watch me break your nose again," Summers said. But Abner Webb held him back as he replied to the crowd.

"Men, we're not confiscating anybody's horses." He turned to Summers. "Will, how much will you take for those six horses?"

"It doesn't matter how much I'll take," said Summers. "None of you have any money. The Peltrys cleaned everybody out."

"Damn it! I plumb forgot." Abner Webb let out a breath of exasperation. "All right, Will. Can you hold the town's marker until we can round up enough money to pay you?"

"Nope." Will Summers shook his head. "I'm strictly cash only, all sales final."

Abner Webb stepped in close and said to Will Summers under his breath, "For God sakes, Will! These men are ready to tar and feather you. Can't you bend a little? I'm trying to save your hide!"

"By taking my horses and giving me a marker? No thanks," said Summers, keeping his own voice low between the two of them. "But don't worry, Deputy. I've got an idea that'll work out for both of us."

"What kind of idea?" Webb asked warily.

"Come on," said Summers. "Let's go to the sheriff's office, where we can talk in private." He turned to the townsmen and said, "Gentlemen, if you'll excuse us for just a few minutes, I believe we can work this out to everybody's benefit." He looked back and forth from one face to the next. "Meanwhile, decide among yourselves which ten of you are going to ride posse with us." The townsmen looked at one another, then began to nod and comment among themselves.

"There now, Deputy," Summers said to Abner Webb. "That'll keep them busy for a while." He offered a thin smile. "Long enough for us to work everything out."

Chapter 4

In the sheriff's office, under Will Summers' urging, Deputy Abner Webb went to a wooden file cabinet standing in a corner and took out a folder full of wanted posters. When he handed the folder to Summers, the two stood looking down as Summers took out the posters and spread them across the worn wooden desk. "There, first one out of the pile," said Summers, his finger pinning a rough, bearded face to the desk. Gilbert Metts, five hundred dollar reward . . . participation in bank robbery in the State of Texas."

Summers shuffled the posters back and forth, then fingered another face. "Here is another one: one thousand dollar reward, dead or alive. I'm telling you, Deputy, this gang is money on the hoof if we play our cards right." He started shuffling through the posters again.

"All right, I get the idea," said Abner Webb, feeling a little foolish that he hadn't already thought of this himself. "By the time you add it all up, the Peltry Gang could be worth, what, three or four thousand dollars?"

Will Summers just looked at him for a second, then said, "More like twelve or fourteen thousand, I'll bet. I haven't added it all up. But whatever it is, it'll be more than enough to rebuild what the Peltrys burnt down here."

"All right, Will. You don't have to sell me on the idea. We go after the Peltry Gang, and any of them we find, we turn in for the reward." He shrugged. "Sounds simple enough to me. You furnish the horses; we pay you for them when it's over."

Will Summers winced and raised a finger for emphasis. "See, right there is where I seem to lose you, Abner. I'm not providing horses unless there's cash on the barrelhead. But on the other hand, I will provide half the transportation for this posse if you agree to split any reward money fifty-fifty."

"Fifty-fifty? You've gone completely loco!" Abner Webb looked stunned by the proposition. "There's no way the town will stand for that!"

"I don't know why they won't," said Summers. "So far none of them have even thought about the rewards. . . . You neither, far as that goes."

"But they would have, Will, or else I would have." He shook his head. "It don't even matter. The fact is, fifty-fifty is too damn high!"

"Not if you think about what you're getting from me," Summers responded quickly. "I'm not only providing the horses. I know some men near here who can come up with all the guns we need."

"Gunrunners?" Abner Webb's eyes widened.

"Never mind what they are," Summers said, undaunted. "It's what they can do for us right now that counts." Without missing a beat, Summers continued. "I'll also be acting as guide across the desert— some of the most dangerous country in the world." He paused and studied the contemplative look on Abner Webb's face for a second. Then he said in a lowered, more serious voice, "And since it's just you and me here, let's be honest, Deputy. Have you ever killed a man? Ever shot one? Ever even shot *at* one, for that matter?"

He watched Abner Webb's expression as the deputy wrestled to come up with the answer. Webb started to lie but then thought better of it and let out a tense breath. "No, I haven't." He looked Will Summers up an down skeptically. "Have *you*?"

Summers looked all around the small office as if checking it before answering. Then he said, "Let's put it this way, Deputy. It's a whole lot different than shooting game: an elk, say, or a mule deer."

Webb gave him a stare. "That's no answer, Will."

"Of course it is, if you listen close to what I'm saying," Summers insisted. "It's not something I can come right out and admit to a lawman."

"Like hell," said Webb. "You asked me, and I gave you an honest answer. You're talking about leading a manhunt, so I'm asking you the same question. Yes or no. Have you ever killed a man?"

"We're getting off the subject here," said Summers. "The main thing is, I can—"

"I don't think we're getting off the subject at all," Webb said, cutting him off. "You brought it up. You must've thought it meant something. You're using it to bargain for half the reward money. So I've got a right to know. Have you ever killed anybody?" He folded his arms across his chest and waited for an answer.

"In Waco, three years ago," said Summers, "I faced a man in the street. It was just him and me, and when he reached for his gun, all I could do—"

"Twenty percent of the reward," Abner Webb said, cutting him off again.

"Twenty percent? *One-fifth!* Now *you're* talking loco," said Summers.

"I see you're not going to give me a straight-out yes-or-no answer," Webb said.

"I'm trying to answer you in a roundabout way," said Summers, "only you're too hardheaded to hear what I'm telling you."

"I don't listen to *roundabout* answers," said Webb. "All they do is confuse things. I figure you never killed a man either, else you would have said so by now."

"I don't know how this killing part got so all-fired important all of a sudden," said Summers. "But whether I have or not, I ain't going into the desert and risking six of my horses for twenty percent of what might turn out to be nothing but a lot of cold nights sleeping on hard ground. No, sir."

"Then let's forget it," said Webb. "I can't sell this town on the idea of fifty percent. I won't even try. They're mad enough at me already."

Summers cocked a shrewd eye. "Can you sell them on forty percent, providing ten percent goes to you? I'm talking about under the table from me, of course."

Webb seemed to consider it. "I just might be able to . . . but strictly to get back what this town has lost. That's my only reason for going along with it."

"I understand," said Summers. "Now get out there and pitch it to them, Deputy. We need to start making some time."

"Let me ask you something first, Will." Now Abner Webb cocked an eye. "Out there today, Moses Peltry said that if those horses belonged to you, it was just as well they didn't take them. Said if they did, they'd have to fool with you for the next month or else blow your head off. What did he mean by that?"

"I would try to tell you, Deputy," said Summers, "but I ain't about to offer another *roundabout* answer, knowing how picky you are."

"Just how well do you and the Peltrys know one another, Will?" Webb asked.

"I best take these along to keep score." Ignoring the question, Summers reached down, swept up the wanted posters, folded them and stuffed them inside his shirt. "While you convince the good townsfolk, I'll just slip out the back door, go on over to the livery barn and see if there's any grain to take with us for the horses."

Abner Webb didn't reveal Will Summers' proposition to the townsmen all at once. Instead, he told them a little at a time and checked on their reaction as he went. First he told them the part about the reward money, which Summers had assured him would be well over ten thousand dollars for the entire Peltry Gang. When he'd finished telling them, the townsmen spoke in a hushed whisper among themselves as Webb stood on the boardwalk and looked back and forth across their faces. After a moment of staring toward the pile of charred rubble that used to be his mercantile store, Ned Trent took a wet rag from his broken nose and said, "Never thought I'd be saying this about Will Summers . . . but God bless him after all!"

A murmur of agreement came up from the crowd. But then Sherman Dahl asked, "Are you saying that Summers is going to let us use his horses and provide us with firearms, then we deduct the cost of everything from the reward money once we collect it?"

Abner Webb cleared his throat. "Well, not exactly, although that was what I figured at first. But it turns out Will Summers knows his way across the desert. Lucky for us, he's agreed to guide us the whole way until we run these rascals down. I say we owe him

our gratitude for that. What do you say?" Abner
Webb began clapping, just enough to prime the rest
of the townsmen into doing it. Then he raised his
hands to quiet them. "Now, the thing is, we can't
expect Summers to work for free," said Webb. "So
he and I came up with an agreement that gives him
forty percent of what bounty we collect."

"Hunh?" The townsmen fell silent again.

"That moneygrubbing sonsabitch!" said Ned
Trent, his attitude changing quickly. "I should have
known better."

"Now hold on, everybody," Webb said. "I know
forty percent sounds steep, but let's take a look at
what we're getting for that amount. Summers is taking a chance on us getting his fine horses lamed or
killed. He's taking us through country we'd never
manage to get through ourselves without getting ambushed or having our throats cut in our sleep. . . ."

From inside the door of the livery barn, Will Summers smiled to himself, hearing Abner Webb pitch
the idea to the townsmen, working hard for his ten
percent. Twisting the top of a half-filled bag of grain
that the Peltrys had overlooked, Summers hefted it
over his shoulder then looked around at the few
dusty saddles lined up along a wall. He turned and
walked through the door and toward the sound of
Abner Webb's voice.

In the throng of townsmen, Sherman Dahl turned
to Virgil Wilkes and said in a quiet voice, "Are you
sure you want to miss all the drinking business while
you're off riding with the posse? Who will tend bar
for you?"

"A time like this," said Virgil, "I'll have to rely on
every man keeping tabs on what he drinks and leaving the money for it in the cigar box under the bar."

"I understand," said Dahl. "But as honest as these

men are, with money in short supply right now . . .
I'd say you're taking quite a chance. I'd be happy to
ride in your place."

"Oh?" said Virgil. "Why the change of mind? A
while ago you turned it down, said you had a school
to build here."

"I know," Dahl replied. "But the fact is, I won't
be building anything here without the funds to build
with. If I ride with this posse, I'll see to it we take
the cost of our new school out of the Peltrys' hides."

"That's powerful talk for a schoolmaster," said
Wilkes. He looked Sherman Dahl up and down. He
started to laugh, yet something about the look in
Dahl's eyes advised against it.

"They burnt down the children's school," said
Dahl. "In my book that makes them nothing but
vermin . . . cowards and low trash. Let me ride in
your place, Mr. Wilkes, sir. I implore you."

Virgil Wilkes looked around and scratched his
head, a bit embarrassed. "Well," he grinned, blush-
ing, "I never had anybody *implore* me before, unless
they did it while I weren't looking and I never found
out. If it means that much to you, schoolmaster, you
go right on ahead. I'll stay here and tend business. I
was just going to show my support."

"Thank you, sir," said Sherman Dahl, grasping
Wilkes' hand firmly and shaking it. While the two
had talked between themselves, Webb had continued
pitching Summers' plan to the townsmen. Summers
listened as he walked up behind the crowd from the
livery barn.

"How do we know he ain't lying about twelve or
fourteen thousand dollars?" Ned Trent asked, keeping the wet rag to his nose.

Before Webb could answer, Will Summers called
out "You *don't* know it" as he parted his way

through the crowd, the feed sack slung over his shoulder. Trent spun around at the sound of Summers' voice then backstepped as Summers came past him to the front of the crowd and stepped up onto the boardwalk. "And you'd be damned fools to take my word for it."

Abner Webb whispered close to Summers' ear, "It sure took you long enough getting back here."

Summers smiled, set the sack of feed down at his feet, took the wanted posters from inside his shirt and fanned them for the townsmen to see. "But right here is the proof . . . for anybody who wants to check it out. I went through these flyers. It's not twelve or fourteen thousand like I said earlier. Counting the five thousand apiece for Goose and Moses Peltry, the whole bunch is worth a total of *twenty-seven thousand, five hundred dollars*, on their feet or slung over their saddles."

Abner Webb stared at Summers, doubting he had gone through all those posters and added up the total.

"Can we see them?" a voice asked from among the men.

"Be my guest," said Summers. He waved the handful of papers back and forth. "Anybody wants to, feel free to figure it all up yourself." Without hesitation, he quickly stuffed the posters back inside his shirt, then said before anybody could step forward to look at them, "But I want to remind all of you: The longer we waste time here, the farther away these skunks are going to be."

Wild Joe Duvall stood at the front of the crowd, his thumbs hooked in his gunbelt. A wide handlebar mustache mantled his lip; a roll of beer fat drooped over his belt buckle. "This is all moving a mite too fast is what I think. Hadn't we oughta wait and see what the sheriff wants us to do? He might want us to contact the army . . . turn this over to them."

Will Summers saw a few heads nod in agreement. He spoke quickly, taking control. "Gentlemen, I can safely guarantee you this: Once Sheriff Hastings comes to, you don't want to face him and tell him you had a chance to catch up to the Peltry Gang but didn't do it!"

"But still, there's the army." Wild Joe Duvall shrugged. "Why not let them take the Peltrys on? We're scrounging around for horses and guns, but the army has plenty of both."

"Hear that, men?" said Will Summers. "Wild Joe Duvall wants to turn this thing over to the army. Well, yes, you can do that sure enough. But you be sure and tell the army to bring some hammers, some roofing tin and nails, so they can rebuild these places for you." He locked his gaze onto Wild Joe Duvall. "Is that what you really want? Do you want the army to wipe your noses for you? How will you face each other afterward?"

"Yeah, Joe," a voice called out. "What's wrong with you? You act about half scared!"

"That's a damn lie," Wild Joe Duvall raved, looking back and forth for the owner of the voice. "Anybody calling me a coward better be ready to step out on the street! You men all know me! There ain't a wilder, bolder fighting sonsabitch alive than me when I take a notion!"

"That's good enough for me," said Summers, starting to clap his hands. "Let's all hear it for Wild Joe Duvall—he's riding with us! Now, who else is going?"

"Wait a minute," Wild Joe said, looking worried.

"I got lots to do around my house. I can see sky through the holes in the roof!" But his words were drowned out by the crowd.

"That's my pa!" shouted Eddie Duvall. "Whoop the living hell out of them, Pa! Show everybody how it's done!"

Wild Joe's face reddened. At the sound of his son's cheering, he relented. Raising a hand to the crowd, Wild Joe offered a brave grin and shouted, "All right! What the hell are we waiting for? Let's get after 'em!"

"You heard him," said Summers above the crowd. "Everybody who's going, get one of these horses. Get over to the livery barn and grab yourselves a saddle while they last. We're pulling out of here in ten minutes flat, no ifs or buts about it!"

As the men scrambled, picking through the two strings of horses hitched at the rail, Abner Webb leaned close to Will Summers and said, "I can't believe I'm saying it, but damned if we ain't got ourselves a posse. Think there's any chance we might run down the Peltry Gang before they even get down in the territory?"

"It's possible," said Summers, "but I wouldn't count on it. To tell you the truth, it might be better if we don't."

"Why's that?" Webb asked.

"Look at this bunch of knotheads," said Summers. "Don't you think it'd be better to get a few miles behind them first? Let them have time to work all this out in their minds before they get to a point where they might have to drop the hammer on a man?"

"Yeah, come to think of it." Abner Webb's smile of confidence faded as he considered it, watching all the men except Sherman Dahl scurry away toward the livery barn. Sherman Dahl took his time, picked out a strong deep-chested bay and stooped down to inspect its forelegs. "I reckon it might be better to let them ride off some steam first at that."

"Yes, it would," said Summers. "Meanwhile, don't worry about catching up to the Peltrys. They're in no big hurry yet. They'll hit a few places twixt here and the territory. That's why they cut the telegraph lines. . . . They want to buy enough time to do some more raiding."

Webb gave Summers a look. "You sure seem to know an awful lot about how these kind of people think, Will."

"Do I?" said Summers. "I hadn't noticed."

Chapter 5

Will Summers stood waiting for Abner Webb on the boardwalk outside the sheriff's office. On the street, ten of the townsmen sat atop their horses, restless and tense, ready to get under way. At the head of the riders sat Sherman Dahl, calm and collected, his hands lying crossed on his saddle horn. Around his left shoulder he carried a leather possibles bag with a rolled-up blanket tied to the top of it. Next to Sherman Dahl sat Bobby Dewitt, restless but keeping himself in check, fidgeting with a four-foot length of lariat.

As Will Summers watched the group of mounted men, he saw a bottle of rye rise up in a long swig then go to a pair of reaching hands. He shook his head and murmured, "No respect, Deputy," as if Abner Webb were beside him. In fact, Abner Webb was still inside the sheriff's office.

When Webb finally stepped out of the office and closed and locked the door behind him, Summers looked him up and down. "Are we ever getting out of here?"

"Yeah, let's go," Webb growled. "I had to leave a letter for the sheriff, let him know what we're up to."

"I think it's a sure bet the doctor or somebody would've told him," said Summers.

"I know," Webb responded. "I just wanted to tell

him myself. Now I'm ready to ride." He looked around at the stoic faces of the townsfolk standing along both sides of the street. "I'll feel better getting out on the trail for a while . . . let these people get all their gossip out of their system."

They stepped down from the boardwalk and toward their horses at the hitch rail. Summers took up his reins, swung up onto his saddle, then caught a glimpse of Edmund Daniels leading a big gray horse down the middle of the street toward them. "I wouldn't go feeling a lot better just yet, Deputy," he said. "Look what's coming here."

"Aw for crying out loud," Webb said under his breath. "There's no way in the world I'm allowing him to ride along. I wouldn't see a minute's peace knowing he was riding behind me."

"Then you best straighten things out right now," Summers said, keeping his voice quiet. "Looks like he's got in his head he's going."

"You're right, Will. I can't keep putting it off." Abner Webb had already taken up the reins from the hitch rail. But now he respun them, then stepped away from his horse and out into the dirt street, facing Edmund Daniels. "All right, Daniels, that's close enough," he said. He kept his thumbs hooked in his belt rather than let his hand poise near his pistol. "You're not going on this posse."

"I've got as much right to go as the next man," Daniels replied. He looked at the mounted possemen for support. "Isn't that right, men?"

Ike Stevens looked at Wild Joe Duvall, who in turn looked at Carl Margood. Eyes exchanged glances back and forth until Louis Collingsworth spoke up. "He's got a horse and a gun. There's no need turning down an able-bodied man just because there's dirt between you, Deputy."

"That's right," one voice agreed, followed by others.

"There you are, Deputy," said Daniels. "The town agrees with me. I'm going."

"No, you're not," said Webb, loosening his gunbelt and letting it fall to the ground. "Not as long as I'm standing on two feet and able to say otherwise."

"Fair enough," said Daniels. "I plan on changing all that." He dropped the reins to the big gray and took a step forward.

"Where did you get a horse anyway?" Webb took the big knife in its sheath from behind his back and pitched it to one side.

"None of your business where I got it. I didn't sneak up and steal it away from somebody. . . . It ain't *another man's* horse, you can count on that." The accusation in his voice was too clear to be missed. He raised the pistol from his belt with two fingers, pitched it to the dirt, unbuttoned his shirtsleeves and began rolling them up.

"All right, Daniels," said Abner Webb, the two of them coming to a halt with less than four feet between them. "I reckon it's just as well we do this now and get it over with. Before we start, I want to tell you one thing. I never meant to cause you any—"

Edmund Daniels' big left fist snapped out into Abner Webb's jaw so quick even the spectators had no time to see it. Webb's head jerked back with a sound like raw meat slapped against an iron door. He staggered back a step. Daniels stepped forward. "All right," said Webb. "I figure I deserved that . . . so I'm letting you take the first lick. But now we're even. Now it's no-holds—"

Daniels' big left stabbed another hard punch to his jaw. "Lord God!" Will Summers whispered. "Stop talking, Webb," he said aloud to himself.

"That's it then, Daniels!" Abner Webb quickly wiped a hand across his already swelling jaw. "Now we're going to—"

Twice more Abner Webb tried to speak; each time, the big left fist stopped him.

"Lord!" said Will Summers aloud, still speaking to himself. "Why don't he shut up and fight?"

Abner Webb staggered in place, a trickle of blood running from a gash on his cheekbone. "Well, he's dead," Will Summers whispered, seeing Edmund Daniels take his time, letting his guard down, stepping in and grabbing the half-conscious deputy by the front of his shirt.

Edmund Daniels drew back his big right fist for what Summers decided would be a killing blow. But before swinging, Daniels stopped and held Webb out at arm's length. "Nobody has their way with my wife, Deputy . . . and lives to talk about it!" He let the big right fist fly. But Webb staggered to one side just in time to feel only the wind of the punch fly past his face. Daniels had put so much power behind the blow that when it missed its mark he flew forward, turning Webb loose and struggling to keep his balance.

To Will Summers' surprise, Webb saw a chance and took it. His consciousness seemed to revive some; he swung just as Edmund Daniels turned to him, still off balance. Webb's roundhouse right caught Daniels full on the chin and sent him a full flip backward. He hit the ground with a loud outburst of air. Webb staggered forward. As Daniels rose upward onto his palms, his head still lowered, Webb took a step back, cocked his boot and kicked Daniels full in the face, the force of it flipping Daniels up and backward again.

"That's more like it," Summers said under his

breath, showing a faint smile. "I was beginning to wonder what kind of man you are. Now finish him off and let's get going."

Abner Webb staggered toward Edmund Daniels as if having heard Summers' instructions. Edmund, in spite of being dazed by the hard kick to his face, shook his bloody head and rose up on shaky legs. He raised his guard and advanced on Webb, swinging one blow after the other as Webb walked backward to keep them from connecting. "Don't back away, Webb, you coward," Daniels said in a low growl. "I'm going to take you apart!"

"Damn it, Webb," Summers said to himself, watching. "You had him. Now you've let him up."

A solid punch caught Abner Webb in the face, snapping his head back. Before he regained his footing, another punch shot in and walked him backward to the boardwalk. He stopped when his back met a wooden support post. The post creaked with his weight against it. Webb slumped there and tried to clear his throbbing head.

"Stand up and fight!" Daniels shouted, not about to stop. He came forward, throwing a hard right. But Abner Webb rolled away from the post just in time. From his saddle, Will Summers heard the sickening thud as Daniels' powerful fist slammed into the wooden post so hard it dislodged the post from the boardwalk. Daniels shrieked in pain and grabbed his wounded hand. Webb saw what had happened and took advantage. As Daniels staggered in place, Webb lurched forward and caught him a hard clip on the jaw. Daniels stumbled onto the boardwalk and tried to steady himself on the loose post.

"Look out!" Summers shouted, seeing the pole come free, Daniels' big arm wrapped around it, ripping it from the wooden porch overhang.

Abner Webb barely jumped back in time. Then a thick pine beam fell free and landed with a hard thud on Edmund Daniels' head. Daniels fell from the boardwalk facedown into the dirt street, still hugging the post. Behind him, with no support to hold it in place, the rest of the boardwalk overhang crashed down in a cloud of dust and a spray of pine splinters.

"Good Lord," Summers said in a hushed whisper, staring at the high puff of dust where Abner Webb stood weaving back and forth, his fists still balled at his sides. Townsmen hurried forward as Will Summers slid down from his saddle and hurried over to Abner Webb. "All of you stay back!" Summers demanded. "He don't need your help."

"I . . . don't?" said Webb in a thick voice, falling to his knees. His face was bloody and battered, already swelling and turning the color of bruised fruit.

"That's right, you don't," said Summers, coming to a halt and spreading his arms to keep the rest of the men from assisting Webb to his feet. "Listen to me, Deputy," Summers whispered just between them. "You just won a lot of respect for yourself, knocking this big ape out."

"I . . . knocked him . . . out?" Webb asked, barely keeping from falling on his face.

"Well, it took half the porch ceiling falling on him, but he's out cold any way you look at it." Summers shot a quick glance at the townsmen closing in. "You'll make a wide gain for yourself if you get up off your knees on your own. The fact is, it's something we really could use if you're going to lead these men."

"All . . . right then," Webb groaned, pushing up from the ground. Summers stood back three feet, making no attempt to help him.

"That's the way, Deputy," Summers whispered. "You're doing fine." He watched Webb wobble back and forth, pressing a hand to a swollen cut on his jaw. "Now drag Daniels to his feet and throw him up on his saddle."

"Do . . . what?" Webb's breath heaved in his chest. He gave Summers an incredulous look through swollen, bloodshot eyes. "I just . . . fought to make him stay here."

"I know, but it's different now that you won. Now you've got to let him ride with us!"

Webb gave an exhausted shrug. "That makes . . . no sense at all."

"It will once you've thought it through," Summers whispered. "Do like I'm telling you."

Webb looked down at Daniels' broad back. "I can't . . . lift that big son of a—"

"You've got to, Deputy," Summers insisted, still in a whisper between them. "Think what it'll do for you in the town's eyes."

"Lord have . . . mercy, Will," Webb groaned. "I'm . . . beat all to hell!"

"You can do it, Deputy. I know you can," Summers insisted. "Now lift him up . . . throw him on that saddle." Summers stepped back out of the way. "These men will follow you anywhere."

The townsfolk along the street and the men mounted and ready to ride posse watched in hushed silence as a struggling Deputy Abner Webb pulled Edmund Daniels up and looped an arm across his shoulder. "Give him room!" Will Summers shouted. The townsfolk pulled back and watched Webb drag the knocked-out man to the big gray gelding standing in the middle of the street. With all his strength, Webb pushed upward against

Daniels until finally the limp figure flopped across the saddle like a corpse.

Summers saw the deputy was about to fall, so he hurried over to him and grabbed the reins to the gray. "There now, you saw Deputy Webb make things right with Edmund Daniels," Summers shouted to the mounted possemen. "Does anybody have any more to say on the matter?" He looked from man to man, making sure his eyes met theirs. When no one replied, he said, "All right then. Let's be off and gone!"

While the possemen filed by, Will Summers held the reins to Webb's horse. Webb struggled upward until he flopped over into his saddle. Summers handed him his reins, then handed him the reins to Daniels' big gray. "Here, Deputy, sit tall," Summers said. "You've earned the right to hold your head high."

"I . . . need to see . . . the doctor," Webb rasped. "I believe he's broke . . . something inside me."

"Don't whimper like a pup," Summers snapped at him. "You've just done a big thing for yourself. Be proud of it."

"At least . . . let me wash my face, Will," Webb moaned.

"Don't worry, Deputy." Summers pulled a wadded-up bandanna from inside his coat and shook it out. "Soon as the posse is farther down the street, you can clean your face up. Don't let these men see you're hurting though." Summers reached down with the bandanna and gestured young Eddie Duvall toward them. "You, kid, take this over, dip it in the horse trough and wring it out for us."

"The horse trough?" Webb moaned.

"Is he going to die?" Eddie Duvall asked, staring in awe at Abner Webb's battered face.

"Naw, kid, this man is tougher than a pine knot."
Summers chuckled, handing the boy the bandanna.
"When he catches up to the Peltrys, they won't know
what hit them."

Abner Webb just stared at Will Summers through
swollen eyes.

Seeing his son, Eddie, run to the water trough and
back with the wet bandanna, Wild Joe Duvall cut
away from the rest of the posse and circled back to
Summers and Webb. "Son, you finish up what you're
doing and get on back to the house," Wild Joe told
young Eddie. "You look after your ma and your sis-
ter like I told you to."

"Yes sir, Pa," Eddie said, wringing out the bandanna and passing it up to Will Summers' hand.
"Mr. Summers asked me to fetch this back to him,
so I did. Golly, Pa! Did you see the fight? I never
saw nothing like it!" Eddie exclaimed.

"Yeah," said Wild Joe grudgingly. "It was all right,
as fights go. I've been in worse and not come out
looking so bad." He gave Abner Webb the once-over,
then looked back down at his son. "You still here?"

"No sir, Pa. I'm gone," said Eddie. Turning and
bolting away, he called back over his shoulder.
"Don't forget—you said you'd bring me back one of
the Peltrys' shooting fingers!"

"Hope you brought yourself a sharp knife," Summers said to Wild Joe Duvall.

Wild Joe's face reddened as he saw the amused
look in Will Summers' eyes. "That son of mine thinks
I'm some kind of hero. I don't know why," Wild Joe
said, looking away and adjusting his wide-brimmed
hat. When Summers didn't answer, Wild Joe looked
at Abner Webb again. "Come to think of it, that was
one hell of a fight, Deputy. I couldn't have done
much better myself to be honest about it."

"The roof . . . fell on him," Webb said across thick blue lips, wiping the wet bandanna carefully across the welt on his jaw.

"Call it how you want to," said Wild Joe, passing a glance over Edmund Daniels lying draped across his saddle. "But I think you're just being modest. Daniels is a big piece of work, roof or no roof."

Abner Webb looked at Will Summers. Summers only shrugged. "Wild Joe's right, Deputy. You're in a saddle. Daniels is across one. That's how simple it plays in my book." He turned his horse and heeled it toward the rear of the posse as the horsemen made their way out of town.

"What do you think Goose and Moses Peltry is up to about now, Deputy?" asked Wild Joe Duvall, stepping his horse alongside Webb's. Abner Webb noted the nervousness in the man's voice as he continued. "Think there's a chance we might miss them altogether? Maybe they'll cut for the border and get away from us."

Leading Edmund Daniels' gray by its reins, Abner Webb heeled his horse forward, one hand holding the wet bandanna to his throbbing jaw. "If they want to keep their shooting fingers, I reckon they ought to," said Webb.

Lieutenant Freeman Goff stood up in his stirrups and gazed ahead at the lopsided wagon sitting sideways in the middle of the high pass trail. "Dagblast it!" the lieutenant said. "This just rips it for me. First the big gun jams. Now this!" He noted the wagon was heavily loaded and sitting up on an axle jack. A front wheel was off, leaning against the side of the wagon where the driver sat with an open tin of grease, slowly smearing the inside of the hub.

"Sergeant Teasdale!" Lieutenant Goff demanded.

"Take two men up there and see if you can help that fool get under way. He's blocking the whole confounded trail!"

"Indeed he is, sir," said the big rawboned sergeant as his eyes went warily along the ridgeline above them. "And if you don't mind my saying so, sir, we best keep a close lookout for some sort of—"

"Yes, I do mind you saying so, Sergeant!" Lieutenant Goff snapped impatiently, cutting Teasdale off. "For God sakes! Can't anyone simply follow an order so we can get this detail finished? It's hotter than a boiling pot out here. Do as I say."

"Yes, sir, Lieutenant," Sergeant Lawrence Teasdale said, his eyes still scanning the ridges, searching the black holes of shade among the jagged rocks. "Corporal Burnes . . . Trooper Frieze: up front on the double!"

"Speed this up, Sergeant," Lieutenant Goff said. "I'll be waiting in the shade back here behind the gun wagon." He turned his horse and moved it back a few feet along the trial as two sweaty bays fell out of the short single column and bolted forward.

"Yes, sir," said Teasdale.

As the two horses slid to a halt beside Sergeant Teasdale, he nodded toward the broken-down wagon thirty yards ahead. "Flank me, men, and be alert," Teasdale said. "The lieutenant wants us to assist this man." He nudged his horse forward, drawing his rifle from his saddle boot. The corporal and the trooper watched him check the rifle then cock it, keeping his thumb across the hammer. "Draw yours as well, men," Teasdale said quietly. "The lieutenant doesn't think this is anything to be concerned about."

"Uh-oh," said the corporal, tossing a quick glance along the ridgeline. Both he and Trooper Frieze immediately snatched up their rifles and cocked them.

"Any time the lieutenant ain't concerned, *I am*," Burnes commented. "Does this smell like the makings of an ambush to you, Sergeant?"

"Not only smells like one . . . I think it's going to taste like one any minute," Teasdale replied. "Stay sharp, Corporal. You too, Frieze." He nudged his horse closer to the man on the ground beside the wagon.

At twenty feet back, Sergeant Lawrence Teasdale stopped his horse between Burnes and Frieze, then stepped his horse a few feet ahead of them and sat staring down at the wagon driver. "What's the matter, Sergeant?" said the wagon driver, his fingertips blackened by axle grease. "I don't smell that bad, do I? Come on over here. I can use some muscle to shoulder this wheel on." He nodded past Teasdale toward the gun wagon and the eight mounted soldiers sitting alongside it. "Would that be a Gatling rifle I see under that tarpaulin? If it is, you have little cause to fear anything on foot or hoof out here."

"Indeed, it is a Gatling gun," said Teasdale, stepping his horse forward another slow step while looking all along the snaking trail before him. "And it would be a mistake to misinterpret my caution for fear of anything . . . on foot or hoof."

"No offense intended, Sergeant," said the wagoner. He raised his drooping hat, ran his shirtsleeve across his forehead, then lowered the hat back into place.

"None taken, sir," said Sergeant Teasdale. Yet as his eyes darted quickly to the high ridgeline then fell back upon the wagoner, Teasdale raise his cocked rifle and leveled it. "I saw that, you bloody bastard!" The cocked rifle bucked in Teasdale's hand. The wagoner flew backward as his grease-stained hand raised a pistol from his lap.

"He signaled somebody!" Corporal Burnes shouted back at the short column of men. "Take cover!"

His words were partly drowned out by the pounding of rifle fire from the rocks above them. Looking back, Trooper Frieze saw the lieutenant spring up into his saddle then melt down the horse's side as a bullet punched its way through his forehead. "Holy saints above!" Frieze bellowed. "We're in for it now!"

Chapter 6

"That hateful sonsabitch!" Goose Peltry yelled, standing up as his men opened fire on the troopers below. "He shot Otis Hirsh before Hirsh could bat an eye!" Goose jerked up his rifle from the rock beside him. "I will personally carve that Yankee bastard's heart out and eat it before it cools!" Rifle fire from the soldiers below zipped past Goose's head like mad hornets. He jacked round after round into his rifle chamber and fired until the gun barrel was too hot to touch.

"Get down there and kill every damned one of them!" Goose bellowed at the men along the firing line. The men looked at one another and rose up from the ground. But Moses Peltry stopped them with a raised hand as they headed back a few feet to their horses.

"Wait, Goose! Damn it to hell!" shouted Moses above the exploding rifle fire. Keeping his hand raised toward the men as if holding them in place, Moses turned to his brother. "Did you even see Hirsh's signal? Are you sure they were even carrying a Gatling machine rifle?"

The six riflemen stood staring, anxious to get under way. Moses Peltry wouldn't let them go until he heard something from Goose. Along the ridge, six other riflemen kept a steady barrage of gunfire on the trail below. Goose Peltry stared back and forth wild-eyed, outraged that his brother had contradicted his order. "Yes, damn it, I saw Hirsh's signal!" said Goose, his words broken up by the steady explosions. "He raised his hat and rubbed his forehead right before that Yankee put a hole in his belly! The Gatling gun's there! We just got to be bold enough to get it."

"You better be right about this!" Moses said in a threatening tone. "I ain't risking these men for an empty wagon! We're short of men as it is."

From below, one of the troopers had managed to get inside the gun wagon and swing the Gatling rifle upward along the ridgeline. Bullets ripped up a long line of dirt and rock twenty feet below the edge of the ridge. "Well there, brother Moses!" shouted Goose. "Does that tell you anything?"

"All right, men," Moses shouted. "Let's get down there and cut them to pieces!" The riflemen seemed to come unstuck. They bolted toward their horses. Goose growled under his breath, "Damn it to hell, I can't stand it when he does me that way!" Then he hurried to his horse along with Moses and the six other men. "Keep us covered!" he shouted to the riflemen firing down from the ridge.

On the narrow trail, a young trooper named Doyle Benson swung the Gatling gun back and forth, beating the rear of the mechanism with his fist. In the cover of the wagon blocking the trail, Sergeant Teasdale called out through the barrage of rifle fire raining down on them, "Damn it, man! What's wrong now?"

"Sergeant, it's jammed again!" shouted Benson. "I can't get it angled up to where they are, and now the damn thing's gone and jammed on me!" He stepped back and kicked the Gatling gun stand as bullets whistled past his head.

"Then get yourself down out of there and listen to Hargrove, you fool," shouted Sergeant Teasdale from his stooped position behind the broken-down freight wagon thirty yards away, "before they shoot your eyes out!"

The young trooper dropped from the wagon, but not before a bullet sliced through the sleeve of his blue wool shirt. "Who's up there, Hargrove?" he asked the older trooper huddled against the side of the gun wagon beside him. "Think it's Apaches come to steal that broken-down freight wagon?"

"No, you mallet-head!" Trooper Lyndell Hargrove replied, firing upward as he spoke. "They're white men! Ambushers! The freight wagon isn't broken down! It's a trap! Didn't you hear the sergeant say the wagon driver gave them a signal? You best start learning to pay attention if you plan on seeing your next birthday!"

"How am I suppose to see and hear everything going on at a time like this?" Doyle Benson asked. He jerked a pistol from beneath his holster flap and checked it as he glanced around at two dead troopers on the ground. Nearby, a big bay lay mortally wounded, raising its head in a pitiful whinny as blood flowed from its wounded flanks. "Can you believe this is the first action I've seen?" Benson said through the melee.

"I can believe it all right," said Hargrove. Hearing the thunder of hooves clamor down from a steep path leading up toward the ridge, the older trooper jacked a fresh round into his rifle and said, "Careful it's not your last."

Behind the cover of the freight wagon, Sergeant

Teasdale also heard the thunder of hooves. He looked at the dead, staring eyes of Corporal Burnes. Blood ran down from a bullet hole in Burnes' cheek. Then he turned to Trooper Frieze and asked, "How bad are you hit, Trooper?"

"It's in and out, Sergeant," Frieze replied. "I've got some fight left in me, if that's what you want to know. To hell with that border trash. They're not about to kill me."

"Good man," said the sergeant. "Benson and Hargrove are under the gun wagon. Everybody else is dead. They're coming down now to finish us off. We're making a run for it. Get ready!" Sergeant Teasdale looked around for any live horses but saw none. He shook his head.

"A run for it?" Frieze looked all around. "A run to where?"

"Over this edge and down into the rocks," said Teasdale. "It's steep and too rough for horses. If they want us, they'll have to dig us out of there. I'm betting we ain't that important to them once they get their hands on that machine rifle."

"I'm with you, Sergeant. Just say the word," Frieze replied, touching his fingertips to the wound in his right shoulder. "I hate the thought of dying without taking some of them with me."

"That's the way to think, Frieze," said Teasdale. "It'll keep you alive." He turned and called to Benson and Hargrove through the bullets raining in from over their heads. "They're coming down for us! Get ready to follow me!"

Benson looked confused, but Hargrove understood. "He wants us to follow him down the slope and into the rocks," Hargrove told Benson. "He thinks they won't take us on down there—it'll cost them too much."

"How do you know he thinks that?" asked the young trooper.

"Because that's how a good sergeant thinks. That's how I always thought when I was a sergeant." He gestured toward the darker blue area on his sleeve where three stripes used to be. They watched Sergeant Teasdale point his rifle barrel toward the steep rocky slope over the edge of the trail.

"Is it the right thing to do?" Benson asked.

"If the sergeant's game for it, so am I," said Hargrove, hearing the hooves draw closer. "As long as he leads us right, I've got no complaints. But the minute he makes a bad move, I'll take over then and there. Are you with me if I have to?"

"I'm all for staying alive," said Benson. "Whatever that takes, count me in." He looked around quickly, then added, "Think I should make a grab for the Gatling rifle?"

"Why?" said Hargrove. "The damn thing keeps jamming. It's not worth dying for." He saw Teasdale and Frieze make a run for it, bullets from the high ridge stitching a trail behind them until they dropped out of sight into the cover of jagged rocks. "Stay close to me, Benson," Hargrove said over his shoulder. As soon as he heard Teasdale's rifle and saw the puffs of smoke rise up from the rocks, Hargrove jumped from the cover of the gun wagon and ran zigzagging back and forth like a wild hare, bullets licking at his heels.

Trooper Doyle Benson ran right beside him but split away just as they cleared the edge of the trail and ducked down into the sheltering rocks. "Are you hit, Benson?" Hargrove called out.

"No, I'm all right. You?" Doyle Benson asked.

"I'll do," said Hargrove, a hand squeezing his side where a bullet had grazed him. He looked toward

Teasdale's rock a few feet away. "What about you and Frieze, Sergeant? Either one of you hit?"

"Frieze took one through the shoulder. I'm good." On the trail above them, the horses' hooves fell quiet, replaced by the sound of men's voices. "Let's work our way farther down this slope, Hargrove," said Teasdale, keeping his voice in check.

"Right away, Sergeant," said Hargrove, taking his yellow bandanna from around his neck and pressing it to his bleeding side. He glanced over toward Doyle Benson. The young trooper sat staring at him, awaiting instructions. Hargrove nodded farther down the slope, then watched to make sure Benson understood. When Benson began crawling down the slope, Hargrove followed.

On the trail, Goose Peltry reined his horse close to the edge and shouted down into the rocks, "Come back, you yellow-bellied bastards, and take what's coming to you! You've murdered a fine man in the prime of his life!" He drew his Confederate saber from its sheath and waved it in a circle above his head as he reared his horse high in the air. "Come taste the temper of my steel!"

"Goose! Get down!" Moses shouted, circling his horse a few feet behind his brother, near the gun wagon. "We've got what we came for!"

But Goose would have none of it. He kept his horse reared, his saber still flashing, and shouted, "If there's a real man among you cowards, you'll turn and fight!"

A shot from Sergeant Teasdale's rifle exploded up from among the rocks. Goose's hat spun upward. The shot left a long red gash across the top of his head. His reared horse staggered backward in fright then crumbled to the ground. In a desperate leap, Goose Peltry managed to keep his horse from falling

on him. "God almighty! They've kilt my poor horse!"
Goose raged.

Moses Peltry jumped from his saddle and ran to
his brother on the ground, looking him over. Goose's
horse rolled up and shook itself off, its saddle having
slid halfway down its side. "The horse is all right,
you idiot!" Moses yelled. "Your scalp's grazed!" He
dragged Goose a few feet farther back from the edge
as he spoke, then jerked him to his feet. "What kind
of lunatic would do something like that?" he asked.
He slapped Goose across the face with a rough hand.
Goose staggered backward. His hand went to his
pistol.

"That's it, you fool. Draw on me," said Moses.
"See if I don't take that gun and whip you senseless
with it!" Moses' eyes locked onto his brother's until
the force of his stare caused Goose to drop his hand
from his pistol and step sideways to where his hat
lay in the dirt. He picked his hat up, dusted it against
his leg and examined the fresh bullet hole, poking
his finger through it. Moses Peltry kept his stare on
his brother but spoke to the men. "Metts, ride out
and round up any loose horses. Catch up to us along
the high trail. The rest of you get that gun wagon
turned and headed up the trail. Throw that wheel
back on the freight wagon and get it ready to roll."

"What about poor Otis?" asked Goose, trying to
overlook the shame of his brother slapping him in
front of the men.

"Otis knew the risk of being a soldier," Moses said.
"Leave him where he lays. . . . He might have
wanted it this way."

"We've got no way of knowing if he might have
wanted it that way or not," said Goose. "We at least
owe him a few kind departing words."

"Then you go think of some kind words and get

them said," shouted Moses. "I'm just trying to run an army here!"

"What about them murdering bluebellies down there?" Goose asked, nodding at the edge of the trail. "Ain't we going after them?"

"Hell no," said Moses. "They got in those rocks knowing what an awful task it would be for us getting them out. Forget about them. They're on foot, probably shot all to pieces. I count this quite a victory for our side." Moses closed his hand around his long beard and squeezed it down.

Goose considered it and grinned. "I agree, brother Moses." He leaned forward and called out down the rocky slope. "Anybody asks who done this to you, tell them it was the Peltrys: *Devil* Moses and the *Goose* himself! Tell them we said, 'This war ain't over by a long shot!' "

Crawling farther down the hill, Sergeant Teasdale and Trooper Frieze met Doyle Benson and Hargrove behind a large boulder. Trooper Lyndell Hargrove shot a glance up toward the sound of Goose Peltry's voice. "The Peltrys, eh? That figures. They were never Confederate soldiers. I doubt either of them have ever been down South."

"If they're not soldiers," Benson asked, "then what are they?"

"Damn it, Benson," said Hargrove. "Don't make me sorry I saved your hide up there."

"I can't help it if I never heard of them," Benson said. "I'm the newest man in the company. If I don't ask questions, I'll never learn nothing."

"You might not anyway," Hargrove said.

"They're freebooters, Benson," Sergeant Teasdale cut in. "Low-down cutthroats that should have hung long ago."

"They're thieves wearing army uniforms, is all

they are," Hargrove added. "Before the war ended, even the Confederate states had a price on both their heads. They like to think of themselves as border guerrillas, but they wouldn't make a good scab on a Southern guerrilla's ass."

"That may be so," said Trooper Doyle Benson, "but we're the ones down here hiding in the rocks, and they're the ones with our Gatling gun."

Sergeant Teasdale gave the young man a hard stare. "That's all going to change just as soon as they clear out of here."

"Don't start talking crazy on us, Sergeant," said Hargrove, giving Teasdale a wary look. "There's only four of us. Frieze is bleeding like a stuck hog. We don't even have horses."

"I saw which way our horses ran. They haven't gone far. Now the shooting's stopped, they'll stop too. I heard one of the Peltrys send a man after them."

"Then I say we get on back to the fort and tell what's happened out here," said Hargrove.

"You don't *have* any say, Hargrove." Teasdale's voice was filled with determination. "The lieutenant's dead. That puts me in command. We're going after this bunch of vermin." He looked at Trooper Frieze and asked, "Are you in any shape to ride?"

"Just throw me into a saddle and watch me," said Frieze.

"Good man," said Teasdale. He looked at Hargrove, then Benson, saying to them as he slid away on his belly, "Stay put here until they ride away with the gun. Help Frieze clean that wound and cover it."

"Where the hell are you going, Sergeant?" Hargrove asked in a harsh whisper.

"I'm going to get our horses," said Teasdale, slowing long enough to cast a warning glance at Hargrove. "Make that the last question you ask me until you get some stripes back on your sleeves."

Gilbert Metts had no trouble locating the spooked army horses. Three of the big bays stood grazing less than a mile away. As soon as he spotted the horses in a stretch of wild grass alongside a thin stream running down from the hills, Metts swung wide of them and eased up slowly. When he saw the horses weren't going to bolt away at the sight of him, he sidled his horse up close, picked up the dangling reins to the first one, then made his rounds until all three were in tow. Before heading back to the rest of the men, he took a pint bottle of whiskey from inside his shirt, uncorked it and tipped it toward the big army bays.

"I'll say one thing . . . these damn Yankees are finding better-looking horses every day." He threw back a long drink, corked the bottle and put it away. Checking the front of his shirt to make sure the bottle didn't show, he heeled his horse forward, leading the army bays behind him. For the next few minutes he trotted his horse, hoping to catch up to his comrades before they left the narrow trail with their new machine rifle. But when he neared the trail, he saw a drifting rise of dust where the men had taken the gun wagon upward.

"Damn it," Metts cursed under his breath as he stopped beneath a cliff overhang less than four feet above his head. He pulled the three bays up beside him, wrapped their reins around his saddle horn, took out the whiskey bottle again and had a quick sip. Then he corked the bottle and put it away. "Now we'll have to ride like hell to catch up to them," he said to the horses and the empty land surrounding him. Heeling his horse forward, he'd begun to unwrap the reins to the bays when Sergeant Teasdale swept down behind him and clamped a thick forearm around his throat.

Gilbert Metts stiffened upward in his saddle as the blade of Teasdale's big knife sliced deep between his ribs and found his heart with expert aim. Metts let out a long groan, turning loose of his reins and clawing at Teasdale's forearm with both hands. But only for a second. Then Metts' hands feel limp to his sides. Teasdale removed the bloody knife blade and wiped it across Metts' chest. Quickly, he reached inside Metts' shirt and jerked out the bottle of whiskey. Then he gave Metts' body a shove as he slid forward into the saddle and grabbed the reins. "Whoa, boys," he said to the nervous bays. "You're back where you belong now."

Putting his knife back into his boot well, Teasdale downed a quick shot of the whiskey, corked it and shoved it down into his waistband. "Now back to work," he whispered to himself, studying the dust from the Peltry Gang as it drifted upward across the hilltops. "You've stepped on the wrong dog's tail today," he said to the rise of dust.

By the time Teasdale had arrived back on the slope where Hargrove, Benson and Frieze lay waiting behind the cover of a large boulder, the rise of the Peltry Gang's dust had all but settled. The sky above the ridgeline shone clear and blue with no regard for the dead men and horses strewn along the rocky trail below. At the sound of the horses' hooves moving up from the bottom of the long slope, Hargrove peeped around the side of the boulder long enough to recognize Teasdale. "Relax, men, it's the good sergeant," Hargrove said, slumping back against the boulder. "He brought us horses just like he said he would." Hargrove offered a slight, begrudging grin.

Frieze caught the cynical edge to Hargrove's words and said, "I know how much it galls you taking orders from a man who started out under your wing, Hargrove. But it ain't Teasdale's fault you lost your stripes."

"Did I ask you anything, Frieze?" Hargrove leaned toward him with a malevolent stare.

"No, you didn't," said Frieze, holding a wet bandanna pressed to his wound, "but it's my hide on the line here too. This is no place for you and Teasdale to go seeing who can outsoldier the other. You taught him everything he knows. . . . You better back him up, not go against him."

Hargrove stared at Frieze, knowing he was right but not able to turn the matter loose. "Shut your mouth, Frieze, before you become the first wounded man I ever had to rap in the teeth."

"Damn it, you two," said Doyle Benson. "This ain't no time to go fighting among ourselves!" He looked back and forth between Hargrove and Frieze.

"See," said Frieze to Hargrove. "Even a new man knows that much."

Hargrove spit on the ground then turned away and waved Sergeant Teasdale in. "Over here, Sergeant," he said in a lowered voice.

Teasdale hurried the horses the remaining few yards up the slope and into the cover of the large shading boulder. As the sergeant slipped down from the saddle, Hargrove took the reins to the army bays and looked the three horses over. "You sure took a big chance riding up here in the open that way, Teasdale," Hargrove said. "If we'd been dead and the Peltrys were waiting here . . ."

Teasdale overlooked Hargrove's insubordination, giving a slight grin. "I had faith in yas, Hargrove," he said, reaching down and taking the whiskey bottle from his waistband as he spoke. Teasdale pitched the bottle to Hargrove. "Hit it and pass it on. I figured you men could use a good snort of dust cutter about now."

"Well, all right now!" Hargrove smiled, catching the bottle and examining it. This time his smile looked real. "We've got horses and whiskey," he chuckled. "Things are starting to look better all the time." He took a drink from the bottle, then passed it to Frieze's reaching hand.

"Kill it quickly," said Teasdale. "I figure the Peltrys are headed for the settlement at Little Sand River. I wish to God we could flank them and get there before they do. But I know it's impossible."

"Why do you figure the Little Sand?" Hargrove asked, his disposition more agreeable now as he wiped a hand across his lips.

"Just a hunch," said Teasdale. "I figure it was a fluke, them spotting us down here and seeing we had a Gatling rifle. They'll have to backtrack to get to Little Sand, but I figure as bloodthirsty as they are, they'll be itching to try out their new weapon."

Hargrove considered his words for a minute, then said, "Well, we'll know where they're headed once we top the trail and see their hoofprints, won't we?"

"That's right, Hargrove," said Sergeant Teasdale. "They're not counting on us following them." He grinned. "They know there's only a few of us. They figure nobody would be that crazy."

"Then I guess you'll show them otherwise, eh?" Hargrove said, squinting into the afternoon sunlight as he looked up along the high ridgeline.

"Exactly," said Sergeant Teasdale, taking the bottle from Doyle Benson. "Take yourself a horse and prepare to ride. We've got daylight left and a long night ahead of us." He looked at Frieze. "Is that wound good and clean?"

"As well as we could do, Sergeant," said Frieze. "It's not hurting or nothing. See?" He raised his arm and stretched it.

Sergeant Teasdale looked at Hargrove and saw the dark look in his eyes. "I helped him clean it best we could, Sergeant," Hargrove said in a lowered voice, "but it's full of dirt and blue wool from his shirt. You know how bad that is about infection."

Teasdale turned from Hargrove as if not hearing him. "Good man, Frieze. Keep it wet and keep tending to it. Now, let's cover some ground."

Chapter 7

Evening shadows stretched long across the hills and grasslands as Will Summers and Abner Webb slowed their horses and looked back at the rest of the posse twenty yards behind them. "When we get down into that valley," said Summers, "it's important you keep this bunch back a ways until I let these gunrunners know it's me. Dick Vertrees has been known to shoot a man's head off for just looking at him suspicious."

"Dick Vertrees?" A worried look came to Abner Webb's battered face. "You didn't mention Vertrees, Will."

"Well, I would have if I thought it made this much difference," Will Summers said with a trace of sarcasm, looking Webb up and down. "What's wrong with you, Webb? You look like I threw a snake down your shirt!"

"Jesus, Will," said Abner Webb. "I had no idea you knew people like Vertrees."

"I know lots of people everywhere, Webb," said Summers in his own defense. "When a man buys and sells horses for a living, he meets a wide range of people."

Webb stared ahead into the shadowed valley as the rest of the men came to a halt a few feet back. "Then I suppose you know Jim Tunley and Arch Baumgartner?"

"I know everybody who runs with Dick Vertrees, Deputy," said Summers. "What of it?"

"They're all wanted by the law, Will . . . that's what of it," Webb protested. "I can't be dealing with the likes of Vertrees, Baumgartner and Tunley. They're no different than the ones we're hunting! What kind of lawman do you think I am?"

"A poorly armed one," Summers responded. "If we don't get down there and talk Vertrees into selling us some guns, you might just as well send these men home . . . or else you'll get them killed. Are you with me on this or not?"

Before Webb could answer, the other possemen sidled closer, Louis Collingsworth at the lead. "Is there a problem here, Deputy?" he asked Webb.

Abner Webb looked at the men, noting some of the old and outdated firearms sticking from their belts and saddle boots. Lagging back from the others, Edmund Daniels sat with a glazed look on his swollen face, a large, bloody knot shining atop his bare head. "Everybody listen to me," Webb said. "These men we're going to be buying guns from are not the most law-abiding men you'll ever meet. I want to make sure you all know what we're getting ready to do here."

"They're gunrunners, is that it?" said Carl Margood, the livery owner. "We already figured they weren't church deacons." A short, nervous laugh stirred across the men, then settled.

"I don't want nobody here thinking we're going to start making a habit of stepping outside the law," said Webb. "These men just happen to have guns, and we need—"

"That's right, they *are* gunrunners," Summers cut in, answering Margood. "That makes them a bit skittish by nature . . . and seeing us ride in is going to make them even worse. So if you don't want to get yourself shot, stay back with Webb and don't make any sudden moves while I talk to them. Don't say nothing these men could take the wrong way."

When Summers finished talking, Wild Joe Duvall looked at Abner Webb and said, "Deputy, nobody here cares who we get guns from, if that's what you're concerned about. Ain't that right, men?" He tossed the question over his shoulder and heard the rest of the men agree with him. "Don't worry about us. We'll be meek as mice if we need to be, so long as it gets us some guns." A grin crept onto Wild Joe's lips as he added, "Once we get ourselves better armed, that might be a different story."

"I just wanted to make sure everybody knows where we stand," said Abner Webb.

Will Summers turned his horse toward the narrow trail into the valley. "Looks like everybody knows," he said. He heeled his horse forward at a walk. Abner Webb and the rest of the riders fell in a few yards behind him.

They followed the downward winding trail until it stopped at the edge of a wide, shallow stream. On the other side of the stream stood a weathered plank shack with a curl of smoke reaching up from a tin stovepipe. Will Summers raised a hand and said to Abner Webb and the others, "Stay back on this side of the creek until I see that everything's all right." He gigged his horse forward and made it across the water. But then a voice called out from a grove of trees near the shack. "That's close enough, Summers. What the hell are you doing, bringing this bunch of flatheads into our hideout?"

"Easy, Dick," Summers replied to the grove of trees. "These men are riding with me. We're here on business."

"What about that piece of tin on that one's chest?" Dick Vertrees asked, stepping warily into sight from behind a tree trunk and pointing his rifle barrel loosely at Abner Webb. "It sure looks like a badge to me."

"You're right, Dick. It's a badge," said Will Summers. "This is the sheriff's deputy from Rileyville. The town got hit by the Peltry Gang. They took most of the guns with them. That's why we're here. We want to buy guns from you."

"Deputy, huh?" said Dick Vertrees. "Where was the sheriff?" He looked around as if expecting an ambush any minute.

"He was gone fishing," said Summers.

"Gone fishing!" Vertrees' grin widened. "That was mighty fortunate for Goose and Moses, weren't it? Do you reckon they knew the sheriff wasn't there, or do you call the whole thing a coincidence?"

"You know me, Dick," said Summers. "*Coincidence* is just one more card in the deck."

"I see. . . ." Dick Vertrees' eyes made a suspicious sweep across the posse then across Abner Webb as he considered what possibilities might be at work.

Seeing the question in the gunrunner's eyes, Summers headed off any further discussion. "The sheriff ran into the Peltrys along the trail. Now he's shot all to pieces," said Summers. "But that's neither here nor there to you. The point is, I brought you some customers. Do you want to do some business or not?"

Dick Vertrees considered it for a second, scratching his shaggy beard. "Me and the boys keep all the business we can handle. Twixt the Mexican *Federales* and whatever rebel forces happen to be at war, we stay busy on both ends. I don't know that we want any more business right now."

"I'd consider it a personal favor if you'd help these

men out, Dick," said Will Summers. "Goose and Moses left Rileyville in pretty bad shape."

"I've come to expect that from the Peltrys," said Dick Vertrees, looking past Will Summers and across the creek at the faces of the townsmen again. "I don't mind telling you there's little love lost between me and old Goose and Moses." As he looked the townsmen over, he called out to the grove of trees. "What do you say in there, Tunley? Baumgartner? Want to do some business with the good folks of Rileyville?"

"The good people of Rileyville don't mean squat to me," said a voice on one side of the grove. "Far as I'm concerned, we can drop them right where they stand."

Another voice called out from the other side of the grove. "Why not sell them what they want? Their money is as good as the next."

Dick Vertrees grinned at Will Summers. "See what a job it is being in charge? I now have what you call two conflicting opinions here." He lowered his rifle barrel an inch but kept his thumb across the cocked hammer. "What's your stake in this, Summers, if you don't mind me asking?"

"I just want to see the right thing done," Summers lied. "If I can help out by getting these men some firearms, then I feel like I've done my part."

"I see." Dick Vertrees nodded, not falling for his spiel. "So they're paying you, huh?"

A short silence passed. "Well . . . we do have sort of an arrangement," said Summers, "but nothing that would interest you. What about those guns, Dick? Daylight's getting away from us."

"We're talking about cash money, ain't we, Summers?" asked Vertrees.

"You know me, Dick. It's the only way I deal." Will Summers offered a thin smile.

"All right, boys, lower them shooters," Dick Vertrees called out to the trees. He uncocked his rifle
and let it hang over his forearm. "Summers, you and
your friends wait where you are. We'll bring out
what guns we've got and let you look them over."

"Sounds fine to me," Will Summers said, looking
around and giving Abner Webb a nod as he slipped
down from his saddle.

By dark, the posse had purchased six Winchester
repeating rifles, eight army Colts and enough ammunition to allow each man close to two hundred
rounds each. In addition to the arms and ammunition, Will Summers talked Vertrees into selling them
coffee, flour and a full quarter of smoked elk meat.
When the posse left the shack, Summers and Webb
led them upward alongside the stream until they
reached a high clearing in the light of a half-moon.
Bobby Dewitt built a low fire and fixed a pot of coffee while the men carved cold elk meat and ate it by
itself, all of them too tired to fix any biscuits to go
with it.

Will Summers sat with a blanket wrapped around
him, leaning against the trunk of a tall pine near the
horses. He watched the men settle in for the night,
their faces dropping out of the firelight one and two
at a time and forming a circle of blankets and saddles
around the flickering flames. They hugged their new
rifles and pistols to their chests. At length only Sherman Dahl remained awake. He sat staring into the
glowing embers. On the other side of the camp,
Abner Webb walked in from the cover of darkness
with his rifle cradled in his arm. Summers watched
him stop at the fire long enough to rub his hands
together above the low flames. Then Webb walked
toward the line of horses.

"Summers, where are you?" Abner Webb whispered into the blackness as he drew nearer beneath the tall pine canopy. When Summers didn't answer, Webb ventured closer and whispered again. When Summers still didn't answer, Webb came to a stop less than two feet from where he sat in invisible silence. "Will, answer me!" whispered Webb, his voice starting to sound concerned. "Are you all right out here?"

To quiet the deputy, Will Summers reached out with his rifle barrel, tapped it against Abner Webb's foot and whispered as soft as he could, "Down here, Webb."

Abner Webb let out a startled gasp, his boot instinctively jerking away from the touch of the rifle barrel. "Jesus!" he said, letting out a tense breath as he recognized Summers' low whisper.

Before Webb could speak again, Summers grabbed his boot and pulled down? "Keep your voice down, Deputy!" Summers said, slicing his words beneath his breath.

Abner Webb stooped down beside him in the dark and rubbed a hand across his face. "Damn it, Will," he rasped. "You 'bout gave me heart failure! I thought those gunrunners had already hit us and gone." He looked around in the darkness, relieved at the shadowy images of the horses along the rope line.

"If you're that fainthearted, you're riding the wrong trail, Deputy." Will Summers scooted to one side, giving Webb room to sit against the trunk of the big pine. "I told you I was going to settle in out here for the night . . . keep an eye on the horses."

"I know," Webb whispered. "You really think we've got something to worry about from Dick Vertrees' men?"

"If I didn't, I wouldn't have brought it up a while

ago, Deputy," Summers snapped in reply. "They steal guns and horses from the army and sell them to the *Federales*. They steal from the *Federales* and sell to the Mexican rebels. Do you figure they won't try to steal these guns and horses from us?"

"Then why didn't they just rob us in the first place," asked Webb, "before we got better armed?"

"Because we came upon them all of a sudden," said Summers. "They saw we had some guns. Dick Vertrees saw how I didn't bring everybody in close. He saw I left us a way out in case they tried anything. That's why I told you to keep the men back across the water." He paused for a second, then asked, "How'd they take what I said about watching out for an ambush tonight?"

"As well as you can expect," said Webb. "They're so dog-tired from being in the saddle all day, I reckon all they could do was get some shut-eye until something happens . . . *if* it happens." Webb let out a breath and added, "You might have told me before you told everybody else. They're pretty edgy over it. If we get hit in the dark, I hope they don't shoot each other."

"Tonight's as good a time as any to find out who we can count on and who we can't," said Summers. "You'll be surprised who sticks and who cuts and runs."

"All I know is Sheriff Hastings will throw a wild-cat fit over me consorting with that bunch of outlaws."

"No, he won't," said Summers. "He'll understand that the main thing is, we got what we came for."

"I hope so," Webb whispered. "Of course, now we got to worry about them stealing it all back from us. You figure there was more men there than Vertrees, Tunley and Baumgartner?"

"Not at that minute, no," said Summers. But I know for a fact that Cherokee Rhodes, Bufford Gant and his brother Davis have been holing up there all summer. There's others too. We happened to get there when they were all off somewhere, I reckon."

Abner Webb shook his head in the darkness. "Cherokee Rhodes, the Gant brothers . . . Lord! The list just gets worse as it goes. I swear, Will."

"We needed guns, Deputy," whispered Summers. "If you're that worried about the sheriff, tell him it was all my fault . . . tell him I twisted your arm, made you do it."

A silence passed as Summers trained his hearing to the surrounding darkness. In the distance, a coyote cried out long and mournful to the glittering night sky. "That ain't what you came over here to talk about though, is it?" Summers whispered. As he spoke to Webb, he watched Sherman Dahl sip slowly from a tin cup and stare into the glowing fire.

"No, it's not," Webb admitted. Another silence passed as the deputy weighed his words. Then he said, "When you and Vertrees were talking, and he asked about the sheriff being gone fishing when the Peltrys raided us . . . ?"

"Yep, what about it?" Summers asked, his voice barely audible.

"It sounded like Vertrees was saying somebody might have tipped off the Peltrys about Sheriff Hastings being out of town."

"You have to admit, Deputy, it sure came in handy to the Peltrys: swooping down like that, and nobody there to stop them."

"What about me, Will? Don't forget I was there," Webb whispered.

"You weren't exactly on the job, Deputy—no offense," said Summers. "Even if you had been, nobody handles things like a good sheriff. He's the one the town has their trust in, and he's the one can bring a town to make a stand in a second's notice. That whole thing might've gone bad for the Peltrys had Sheriff Hastings been there. We both know it."

"Then you're thinking somebody in Rileyville is in cahoots with the Peltrys?" Webb whispered in astonishment.

"Thinking it?" Summers whispered. "Hell, I thought it the minute I heard the first shots fired. I've thought it ever since. I'm just glad it finally come to you."

Webb whispered grudgingly, "I can't say the thought hadn't crossed my mind. I never brought it up because, to tell the truth, I didn't want to start a bunch of suspicions among the men."

"That was wise of you, Deputy," said Summers, sounding a little skeptical as to whether or not Webb was being honest about it. "I never mentioned it because for all I know it might be you in cahoots with the Peltrys."

"That's a hell of a thing to say to me!" Webb rasped, barely keeping control.

"Shhh, keep it down, Deputy. You're the one brought it up. I'm just airing it out for us. The fact is, it could be anybody in Rileyville . . . could be one of these men riding with us." He nodded at Sherman Dahl. "It could even be your schoolmaster for all we know."

"Or it could even be you," Webb added.

"Yep . . . and if it was, I damn sure wouldn't admit to it, not until we got into a pinch. Then it might just be too late for all of you." Summers smiled to himself in the darkness. "Now, there's an idea that'll really give you cause for some serious thought."

"Dang it!" Webb hissed. "I hate having to deal

with this kind of stuff . . . especially with everything else going on."

"Then put it out of your mind, Deputy. When the time comes, we'll find out who it is . . . if it's anybody at all. Don't forget what I told Vertrees: Coincidence is just one more card in the deck."

"Yeah," said Webb. "Trouble is, it just might be a *wild* card. I don't need any surprises out here, Will."

"I know it. We've got plenty more to think about," said Summers. Again, the lonesome call of a coyote resounded from within the distant ridges.

Noting the strangeness in the sound of the coyote's voice, Abner Webb said in a hushed tone, "That ain't no real coyote out there, is it?"

"Nope," Will Summers whispered. "That's Cherokee Rhodes. He's one coyote I'd recognize anywhere." Summers slipped his blanket off and raised up into a crouch, cocking his rifle softly across his knee. "You best get over on the other side of these horses. Careful you don't shoot me when this all comes to a head."

"Don't worry about my aim; mind your own," said Webb. He nodded at Sherman Dahl in the glow of firelight. "Think I better slip over there first, tell him and the others what's going on out there?"

"Nope, he's already on his toes," said Summers. "He's telling the others." He studied Sherman Dahl for a second, then said, "I noticed there ain't much that gets past that schoolmaster." They both watched as Dahl stood up slowly and slung the last drops of coffee from his cup. The young schoolmaster drifted quietly among the sleeping men, nudging each of them with the toe of his boot until he was sure they were awake and understood his message. Then he drifted out of sight into the surrounding darkness as quiet as a ghost.

"What do you know about him?" Summers asked in a whisper.

"Not much," said Webb. "He responded to an advertisement the town placed in the Denver newspaper last year for a schoolmaster. The kids are learning what he teaches; that's been good enough for everybody."

"He's skilled at soldier-craft," said Summers. "He didn't learn it at no teacher's college."

"No, I reckon he didn't," said Webb, seeming to have a hard time tearing himself away from Will Summers' side.

Finally Summers looked at him in the darkness and whispered, "Are you going or not, Deputy?"

Webb cursed under his breath without answering, then turned and moved away in a low crouch. In moments he had taken a position on the other end of the string of horses.

Forming a protective guard around the camp, Abner Webb, Will Summers and Sherman Dahl lay in tense silence, listening for the sound of approaching footsteps across the rough terrain. The awakened men had abandoned their blankets around the low campfire and crawled off to take cover in the outer circle of darkness. When Will Summers caught the faint rustle of a trouser leg against the surrounding brush, he honed onto it and followed it as it crept around his position and stopped somewhere back behind the string of horses. Summers lowered himself silently onto his belly. He turned on the ground and adjusted himself and his rifle barrel, preparing for the coming battle.

Chapter 8

Abner Webb did not see the men sneaking in through the line of horses, but he visualized them as he heard the nervous animals begin to nicker under their breath and thrash back and forth against their ropes. Not wanting to hit one of the horses, and not sure how to keep from it, Webb waited, his hand trembling a bit on his rifle stock, a trickle of cold sweat running down slowly beneath his shirt collar.

In the brush and scrub trees fifty yards beyond the far side of the camp, Dick Vertrees turned to the poncho-clad man beside him and said in a lowered voice, "Get going, Cherokee. Make sure the Gants and Tunley and Baumgartner don't leave any live witnesses. And see to it Creek and Odell do their part. They're both new; it's time we see what they're made of. I'll get back there and keep an eye on our horses."

"Why don't you go in there and check things for yourself?" said Cherokee Rhodes, looking Vertrees up and down. "I can go back and watch about our riding stock." He checked the rifle in his hands as he spoke quietly in the darkness. "Better still, why don't we both go in there and help out with the killing? It would give our boys better odds."

"Ha," said Dick Vertrees. "If they need our help

against that cowardly bunch of house cats, they don't deserve to call themselves outlaws."

"I don't recall Will Summers ever being known as cowardly," said Cherokee Rhodes.

"He's not," said Dick Vertrees. "But Summers is just along for what he can get out of them. Shooting starts, he'll lay low or else cut and run. He ain't putting himself in danger for that bunch. Summers only does something if it's worth serious money to him. That's something I can garun-damn-tee you. Now get in there and wrap this thing up. I already know where we can sell them horses for top dollar."

"I hope you're right about Summers," Rhodes said quietly.

"Don't worry. I'm never wrong about men like us. Summers is a straight-up outlaw, no different than you and me. He just keeps it well-hidden most times."

"Since you're so sure of yourself, I don't see why you don't go on and—" Cherokee Rhodes' words cut short as a shot exploded from the direction of the glowing campfire.

"Damn it, half-breed!" Dick Vertrees hissed, giving Rhodes a shove toward the campsite. "All hell's breaking loose! Get in there and kill somebody!"

Gunshots blossomed in the darkness surrounding the campsite as Cherokee Rhodes ran toward the melee. He slid to the ground when he saw Bufford and Davis Gant come charging from among the line of horses and into the campfire light, firing down at the empty blankets. "They're not here!" Davis bellowed. "Where are they?" He threw a quick glance around the abandoned campsite.

"Damn it to hell, Davis!" screamed Bufford Gant. "We've been tricked!" Shots caught him from all directions at once, jerking him back and forth like a rag doll as the bullets sliced through his body. Davis Gant managed to dive to the ground, grab two of the saddles lying near the campfire and pile them together for cover. Cat Creek and Lester Odell had also just charged into the campsite. But seeing Buford die on his feet, Lester Odell dove over beside Davis Gant and began firing from behind the saddles. "Get back, Cat!" he shouted. "Take some cover!"

"I ain't leaving you, Lester!" Cat Creek vowed. But he quickly dropped back into the darkness, fired two hasty shots, then disappeared when four possemen's rifles concentrated their fire upon him.

Cherokee Rhodes fired shot after shot at the muzzle flashes until the rifles turned from the campsite and sent bullets whistling past his head. With a long yell, Rhodes jumped up and ran wildly zigzagging back toward the horses. Catching a glimpse of the outlaw and hearing his yell, Sherman Dahl said to Carl Margood and Louis Collingsworth, who lay firing beside him, "Pour it on the camp! I'm going after that one! If we let any of them get away, they'll be dogging us this whole trip!"

Seeing Sherman Dahl spring up in the midst of rifle fire and take off behind the fleeing outlaw, Louis Collingsworth asked above the explosions, "What the hell's got into that schoolmaster all of a sudden?"

"Beats me!" shouted Margood, firing and levering his rifle without missing a beat.

Near the horses, Will Summers lay firing at the two outlaws still trapped in the center of the campsite with only the two bullet-riddled saddles for cover. In the racket of gunfire and the commotion of men locked in battle, the line of horses reared frantically against their ropes. At the other end of the line of horses lay Abner Webb, also firing at the two outlaws. But as he stopped to reload, Lester Odell and

Davis Gant took advantage of the lessening of bullets kicking up dirt around them. They rose up as one into a crouch amid the continuing fire from the other possemen. Snatching up the saddles as shields, they bolted out into the greater darkness, a sawed-off shotgun swung on a strip of rawhide down Davis Gant's back.

"Stay after them, men!" Will Summers bellowed, still firing at the fleeing figures as he came to his feet. "Don't let them get away!" He ran over to Abner Webb and pulled him to his feet as the rest of the men gave chase to the outlaws. "You okay, Deputy?" Summers asked.

"I'm all right. What about you?" Abner Webb gave himself a once-over, brushing dust from his shirt front and feeling for any wounds he might have missed in the heat of battle. "We better get with them, Will!" He levered a fresh round into his hot rifle chamber and turned to take off behind the other men. But Summers grabbed his arm, stopping him.

"Take it easy, Deputy. Let these men feel like they're earning their keep."

"But they'll get themselves killed," Webb protested.

"No, they won't. Not unless they run off a cliff. Vertrees' men are hightailing now. They won't stop till they figure they gave us the slip." He let out a breath and looked all around. But before he could relax, they both heard the sound of someone dragging something through the brush. "Who goes there?" shouted Summers, aiming his rifle.

"It's me, Dahl. Don't shoot," said the young schoolmaster. "I'm bringing one in. . . . I think it's Vertrees himself."

"Vertrees?" said Summers, giving Abner Webb a surprised look in the flicker of low firelight. "This teacher's starting to impress me," he added under his breath.

"Bring him on over here, Dahl," said Abner Webb. "Let's take a look at him." In the brush fifty yards off to their right, they heard the possemen yelling and firing as the two outlaws fled on foot. A blast of Davis Gant's sawed-off shotgun resounded loudly through the brush.

"Yep," Will Summers said, stooping down over the body when Dahl brought it and laid it on the ground. He took a close look at the dead face with a long veil of blood stretching halfway down the chest from beneath the stubbled chin. "That's Dick Vertrees all right," said Summers. The surprised look on his face matched his surprised voice. "You—you cut him like this, schoolteacher?" he asked, sounding even more stunned.

"I had to," said Sherman Dahl. "It turned into a risky situation.

"I bet it did," said Summers, looking him up and down.

Dahl continued. "I chased another man into the brush toward the horses. He slipped away in the dark, but this one was hiding nearby. I didn't know how many more might be around. So to keep quiet, I chose the knife. That was all I could do," he added with finality.

Will Summers looked at the deep, perfect gash across Dick Vertrees' throat. "This wasn't your first time using a blade though, was it?" he asked in a somber tone.

"No," said the young schoolteacher. "I'm a veteran of the Civil War: fought in the Wilderness Campaign. Saw a lot of action as a forward scout."

"Forward scout would have been my guess," said Summers, turning his eyes away from Dick Vertrees' slit throat and up to Dahl's solemn, cold blue eyes. "Who'd you fight for, the North or the South?"

"That's right," said Sherman Dahl bluntly. He stared at Will Summers until at length it became apparent to Summers that further information would not be forthcoming.

"Either one, you do good work, teacher," Summers offered. They turned at the sound of winded voices and brush scraping against trouser legs. The possemen came trotting in one and two at a time from the darkness like hounds fresh off a scent.

"Collingsworth and Edmund Daniels caught one of them bushwhacking rats, Deputy!" said Carl Margood, out of breath, his rifle dangling in his hand. "They're dragging him in right now!" As he spoke, he caught sight of Dick Vertrees' pale face, the vacant, wide-open eyes seeming to stare up at him. "Lord God! Quick, boys, come look at this!" Carl Margood exclaimed, his breath heaving in his chest. "Somebody's nearly cleaved this one's danged head off!"

The men gathered, looking down at the grisly sight on the ground at their feet. "Oh no!" said Wild Joe Duvall, throwing a hand over his mouth and looking away.

"Joe? Are you all right?" Abner Webb asked.

"Huh-uh," Joe grunted, shaking his head, not looking at the deputy. "I'm . . . not feeling so good."

"Then get off into the brush," Will Summers insisted. "We're going to be sleeping here tonight."

Wild Joe hurried away, his right hand planted firmly against his puffed out cheeks.

Hearing the angry, winded voices coming out of the brush, Abner Webb and Will Summers turned and saw Louis Collingsworth and Edmund Daniels throw Davis Gant into the dimly lit campsite.

"You're making one damn bad mistake, you bunch of square-headed sonsabitches!" Gant cursed. "I was just passing through the tree line and heard the ruckus going on! That's the truth, so help me God!"

"Oh yeah?" said Collingsworth. He raised his panting voice to the rest of the men. "Somebody get a rope! He started out just passing through the tree line. . . . We'll put him right back where we found him. Only this time, he'll be hanging from a limb!"

"Easy, Collingsworth," said Webb. "Don't get carried away. He's a prisoner now; he's under my custody. There'll be no hanging while I'm in charge."

"Like hell," said Collingsworth. "He's killed Ike Stevens. Go look for yourself. Are you the one who's going to face Ike's woman and boy and tell them this skunk is still alive while poor Ike's lying with dirt on his face?"

"Ike Stevens is dead?" Abner Webb looked all around.

"Here he is, Deputy," said Miles Michaels, the blacksmith. "He ain't far from it."

The men stepped to one side so Webb could get through them to where two men had just laid Ike Stevens on the ground near the low fire. "It's true, Deputy," Ike Stevens said in a failing voice, both hands clasped to the gaping hole in his stomach where he'd caught the full blast from a load of buckshot. "I'm all numb down both . . . legs. I'm missing . . . some stuff down here." He nodded grimly at the surging stomach wound, then lay back, trying to clasp it shut with both hands.

"Oh good Lord, Ike," said Deputy Webb, looking away from the terrible wound. "What can I do? Tell me what to do for you!"

"Get me home . . . and buried, first thing," Ike Stevens murmured, his breath becoming more shallow and weak. "Tell Martha . . . tell my boy . . . tell them—" He struggled for a second, seeking one last gasp of air. But when it didn't come to him, he relaxed with a long sigh and settled limply on the dirt.

"I ain't the one who gut-shot him. I swear to God I ain't!" Davis Gant pleaded.

"You rotten, murdering son of a—!" Louis Collingsworth hurled himself at Gant, his spread fingers plunging toward the outlaw's eyes like an eagle's talons.

"No!" Abner Webb caught Collingsworth and held him back. "He's a prisoner!"

"Let me go, Deputy!" Collingsworth screamed.

"String that bastard up!" one of the men cried out.

All of the men advanced on Davis Gant at once, forcing Abner Webb to turn Collingsworth loose and take a stand between them and Gant.

"Men, you can't lynch him! I won't have it!" Abner Webb shouted. He tossed a worried glance at Will Summers for support. "Will, come on! Do something here! Help me out!" The men pressed closer.

Ted Logsdon, the barber, had hurried over to his horse and now came back waving a coiled-up rope. "Let's see how he likes wearing this straight to hell!"

"Lay the rope down, barber," said Summers. "You won't be using it tonight."

"You've got no authority to stop me," said Logsdon, gripping the rope tighter and staring into Summers' eyes.

"I know that," Summers said calmly. "I'm just appealing to your good sense."

Davis Gant let out a dark chuckle, seeing Will Summers draw his pistol and cock it. "There you go, Summers," Gant said. "You can't let these square-headed poltroons hang me, can you?"

Summers turned to Davis Gant, his gun cocked and held at arm's length. "So long, Gant," he said.

"Hunh?" Gant looked confused. Ted Logsdon jumped away.

The bullet hit the outlaw in the center of his forehead and flipped him backward, a long ribbon of blood spouting from the back of his head and turning into a wide spray.

"God almighty!" Abner Webb shouted, startled. Davis Gant's warm blood splattered his face. In the chilled night air, steam swirled from the hole in Gant's head.

"Sorry, Deputy," said Will Summers. "You was standing too close."

In the tense silence, the possemen stood stunned, their eyes wide, their mouths agape. Will Summers lowered the pistol back into his holster. He looked from one to the other of the men. "What're you looking at? You were going to hang him, weren't you? He had to pay up for Ike Stevens, didn't he? Now it's done."

"It's done, Will, but my God," said Webb, wiping blood from his face.

"What?" Will Summers looked back and forth between Webb and the other possemen. "Now none of you can stand the sight of blood?" He stared at each man in turn. "You better take a good look at this man lying here. . . . Then you better look at yourself as well. This ain't no child's game we're playing out here. Men bleed and die here!" He gestured a hand toward Ike Stevens. "There's what death looks like up close. It's bloody and terrible, and it stinks to high hell. Turn Ike over, five to one says he's shit himself!"

The men looked at one another and milled uneasily in place.

"You don't like hearing about that, do you?" Will Summers continued. "But you'll all do the same thing out here if somebody puts a bullet in you. You better remember that before you go any further with this."

"Damn it, Will, what are you doing?" Webb asked, trying to get him to shut up. "These men just fought one hell of a fight. Don't take that away from them."

"I'm not taking nothing from them," said Summers. "You men fought and won. But then winning wasn't enough for you. Then you needed to see somebody hang!" He pointed again to the body of the outlaw on the ground. "Well, there he is. He's not been hanged, but he's as dead as I can make him for you. Is everybody satisfied?"

"That was nothing but stone-cold murder, Summers," said Ned Trent, his broken nose still affecting his voice.

"Oh, was it, Trent? But you saw something right in hanging him?" Summers stepped forward, grabbed Trent by his coat and jerked him forward, forcing him to stoop down over Davis Gant's body. "There now, tell us what you see!"

"Turn me loose, Summers!" Trent protested.

"I said tell us, Trent!" Summers insisted. Holding Trent firmly, Summers reached down with his boot toe and kicked Davis Gant's closed hand. A small derringer pistol fell into the dirt and glinted in the flickering firelight.

"Oh, Jesus," said Ned Trent, his voice sounding shaky all of a sudden. "He was holding a hideout gun. . . . One of us was fixing to die before this was over."

"Thank you, Trent!" said Will Summers, turning him loose with a shove. "That's right, men," he added, looking back and forth among them again.

"One of us *was* going to die before this was over."
He let the hard cast of his eyes convey the gravity
of his words to each of the townsmen. "These are
dangerous men we're hunting. Do you think they
give up, call it quits, just because you've managed to
catch them?" He shook his head. "No . . . that's not
the way it works. They die bloody, fighting and clawing like a wildcat. They're a danger to you as long
as there's a single breath left in them. When you
wound one, you better wound him bad, then keep
both eyes on him."

"We made a simple mistake, Summers," said Edmund Daniels, both of his eyes still swollen and dark
from his fistfight with Abner Webb. "Quit making it
seem like—"

"A simple mistake?" Summers cut him off. "You
were all so broken up over Ike Stevens and so full
of yourselves over catching the man who shot him
that you didn't even search him down good before
you brought him back here. You stupid bunch of
peckerwoods!"

"Take it easy, Will," said Abner Webb. "We all
get your point now. These men aren't experienced
lawmen. They never pretended to be. They're just
hardworking, everyday citizens. They done the best
they could."

Will Summers ignored him and spoke to the men.
"While you good, hardworking, everyday *citizens*
were busy deciding whether or not to hang Davis
Gant, he'd already decided clear as day what he was
going to do. He'd made up his mind that he was
going to take one more of us with him."

"All right, Summers," said Edmund Daniels, still
trying to finish what he'd started to say. "We all
made a mistake here not searching this outlaw. But
it's over now, and we all learned from it."

"I sure as hell hope so, Daniels," said Will Summers, sounding disgusted as he turned and walked away. At the edge of the campsite, he said over his shoulder to Sherman Dahl, "Schoolteacher, you and Bobby Dewitt come with me. Let's see if we can bring in their horses."

As Sherman Dahl and Bobby Dewitt hurried to join him, Will Summers said to the rest of the men, "I smelled whiskey on at least four of you. Come morning, any whiskey left over is going into the fire. Drink it while you got it, right, Webb?"

"Who the hell does Summers think he is?" a muffled voice asked among the men. The men turned their attention to Abner Webb to hear his take on things.

"Summers is right about the whiskey, men," said Deputy Webb. "This is neither the time nor the place to be drinking hard liquor. You all see what's at stake here." He nodded at Ike Stevens' body. "We've already lost one good man. Let's do whatever we've got to do to keep from losing any more."

PART 2

PART 2

Chapter 9

Deputy Abner Webb awakened before dawn to the quiet sounds of men readying their horses for the trail. Standing up from his blanket, he looked across the campfire at Will Summers and Sherman Dahl, who sat drinking coffee with solemn expressions. Behind Summers and Dahl, on the other side of the campsite, the townsmen were raising Ike Stevens' blanket-wrapped body across a saddle. "What's going on here?" Webb asked Summers and Dahl, rubbing sleep from his eyes with both hands. "I said we'd break camp at first light."

"Yep, that's what you said all right." Will Summers tossed a disgusted glance over his shoulder at the townsmen, then looked back at Webb. "They're all leaving. I reckon they were hoping to get out of here without having to face you."

"Damn it!" Webb jerked his hat up from the ground and jammed it down on his head. "And you was just going to sit there? Why didn't you wake me up?"

"Don't get yourself all worked up," said Summers. "We wouldn't have let them leave without you knowing it." He shrugged. "We just figured to let you sleep until they were ready to travel."

"Well, that's damn considerate of you," said Webb, raising his gunbelt from beneath his saddle and quickly throwing it around his hips. As he fastened his belt buckle, he looked at Sherman Dahl and asked, "What about you, schoolteacher? Are you cutting out too?"

"No," said Dahl. "Mr. Summers and I have discussed it. I'm continuing on with you."

"So am I," said Edmund Daniels, his voice coming from the outer circle of firelight. Webb turned to face him. Daniels sat cleaning a rifle, his swollen eyes looking strange and demonlike in the thin, flickering firelight. "I plan on being with you every step of the way," Daniels said with resolve, the end of the sentence punctuated by his hand levering a cartridge into his rifle chamber. Abner Webb just stared at him for a tense second.

"The cowboy is staying with us too," said Summers. "He's just helping the men get Stevens' body ready for the trail."

Webb looked over at the townsmen and saw Bobby Dewitt tying the blanketed corpse down to the saddle. The townsmen avoided Webb's stare and busied themselves with their horses. "Forget them, Deputy," said Summers. "All they would do is get themselves killed out here. We're better off without them."

"The Peltrys have a dozen or more men," said Webb. "What chance will the five of us have against them?"

While Summers and Webb talked, the townsmen finished preparing for their ride back to Rileyville. They spoke to one another in a huddle for a moment, then led their horses over closer to the campfire. Keeping his eyes lowered, Ted Logsdon spoke on the townsmen's behalf. "Deputy, we don't want you thinking this is any reflection on you. We just figured since we need to take Ike Stevens' body back to Rileyville anyway, this is a good place to call a halt to hunting the Peltrys. We're all tired, and we need to get back to our homes and families."

"Jesus, Logsdon," said Webb. "We've only been gone two days! As far as hunting the Peltrys, we haven't even gotten started. One little run-in with some gunrunners, and you men give up? I can't believe what I'm hearing!"

"We're not making excuses, Deputy," Logsdon continued. "I can't afford to be away any longer. I've got a business that needs to be run."

Webb shook his head. "Ted, you're a barber."

"That's true," said Ted Logsdon. "And in the barbering business, two days can make a big difference in the whole appearance of a town."

Webb just stared at him. "Logsdon, your barbershop burnt to the ground. Don't you want to track down the men who did that and make them pay?"

"Hell, no," said Logsdon. "Not if it means more of this." He nodded at the dead outlaws lying on the ground to one side of the campfire. "This is the worst thing I ever took part in. I can't stand no more of it. Besides," he continued, "I do the undertaking too. My services will be required for poor Ike there." He thumbed toward the blanket-wrapped corpse across the saddle.

Webb looked past Ted Logsdon at the others. "What about the rest of you? Is this how you want to be looked at by the town? Where's your self-respect?"

Logsdon started to speak, but Louis Collingsworth stepped forward first. "Let me answer that, Ted," Collingsworth said. He stood with his hands on his hips. "Deputy, we thought this was a good idea at first. We'd catch the Peltrys ourselves and collect the rewards on them. Use the money to rebuild what they destroyed. But damn, this is a gruesome busi-

ness. We've got no business out here. Summers
showed us that last night. We're lucky Davis Gant
didn't kill one of us."

"But what about learning from your mistake?"
asked Webb.

"Well . . . last night we might have said some things
that ain't really the way we feel. Shooting and getting
shot at makes a man say and do strange things. But
that's neither here nor there. We're going back to Rileyville, and nobody's going to talk us out of it."

"What about the reward?" asked Webb.

"Well . . . if you five collect it, it's up to you five
to decide how to share it. Fair's fair. We don't want
something we didn't earn."

"What about my guns and horses?" Will Summers
cut in. "I put up the guns and horses for you men
to use. Who's paying me the money I put out for
this expedition?"

"There's no cause to be insulting, Summers," said
Collingsworth. "I have reserve capital in a bank in
Denver. You have my word before all these gentlemen that I'll pay for everything. These men have
agreed to pay me back over time, right, men?"

The men nodded in unison. "Whatever it takes to
get out of this thing in one piece," said Logsdon,
"we're willing to do it."

Louis Collingsworth saw the relenting look come
to Abner Webb's face. "Look, Deputy," he said. "We
all realize this whole thing was a big mistake. We
were angry, in shock and not thinking straight. Now
we've tasted blood, and it's made us sick. There's
nothing says you can't ride back with us and put this
thing out of your mind. We need you to look after
Rileyville until the sheriff is back on his feet. He'll
thank you for it, and we'll none of us ever forget
how you tried to go after these criminals."

Webb looked back and forth across the faces of the men. Ned Trent nodded in agreement with Collingsworth. "Louis is right, Deputy. Come on home with us." He looked past Webb at Sherman Dahl and added, "You too, schoolmaster. We'll find a way to rebuild that schoolhouse."

Sherman Dahl saw the indecision in Abner Webb's face. He stood up from the fire with his rifle cradled in his arm and looked down at Will Summers. "If Deputy Webb goes back to town, are you still going after the Peltrys?" Dahl asked in a mild manner.

"Oh yes," said Summers. "I'm in it for the money. That hasn't changed."

"And you?" Dahl asked Bobby Dewitt. "Are you still going with him?"

"I am," said Bobby, stepping away from the townsmen and closer to where Will Summers sat on the ground. Summers leaned back against his saddle. He watched and listened.

From the other side of the campfire, Edmund Daniels stood up quietly and walked around closer to Will Summers. He sat down and laid his rifle across his knees. "Count me in," said Daniels. "I want a piece of the Peltrys' hide."

"And me also," said Sherman Dahl. "I can't abide the thought of those common thugs denying the children of Rileyville their education." He stepped over beside Bobby Dewitt.

Seeing Daniels, the schoolteacher and the young cowboy make their stand, Abner Webb put any thought of turning back out of his mind and said to the townsmen, "There you have it, men. The four of us are sticking on the trail with Summers. We'll be back when we've bagged the Peltrys, not before."

"I think you're making a bad mistake, Deputy," said Collingsworth, "but if that's your decision, we'll

respect it. I'll tell the sheriff you're still on the job."
He and the others turned to mount their horses.

"Hellfire," said Wild Joe Duvall, pulling his horse
forward instead of stepping up into the saddle. "I
can't go back to Rileyville just yet. I promised my
boy I'd bring him the Peltrys' trigger fingers. He'd
never let me live it down."

Collingsworth started to say something to Wild
Joe, but before he could, Joe went on. "Louis, will
you be sure to tell little Eddie I'm out here about to
mix it up with these bad *hombres*? But tell him not
to worry though. Tell him there ain't none of that
bunch too tough for his ole pa to handle. Will you
tell him that for me?"

"I'll tell him first thing, Wild Joe." Collingsworth
nodded. He turned his horse with the rest of the
townsmen, and in moments they had faded into the
gray morning mist.

For the next few silent minutes, the six men sat
close to the low campfire, their hands wrapped
around hot cups of coffee. "Looks like they'll have
something to talk about the rest of their lives," said
Webb. "How they once went out in a posse looking
for a gang of outlaws."

"Yep," said Bobby Dewitt, "and you can bet the
story will get better and better in the telling of it."
The men nodded as one.

Another silence passed. Then Will Summers said,
"Well, Deputy, what do you think the sheriff is going
to say now? Think he'll throw a fit over you staying
out here?"

"I couldn't give a damn less," said Abner Webb.
He looked from one pair of eyes to the next, his
resolved stare making its way around the glowing
fire. "From here on, I answer only to myself." He

absently raised a hand, loosened his deputy's badge from his shirt and dropped it into his vest pocket.

Will Summers stood up and tamped out the last remnants of the campfire, then poured the coffee grounds onto the ashes. "Time to saddle up and get on the trail," he said. The rest of the men stood up and walked to their waiting horses. In moments they had mounted and left the campsite behind them on their way up toward the high trail.

Abner Webb and Will Summers rode abreast a few yards ahead of Sherman Dahl. Behind Dahl rode Bobby Dewitt and Wild Joe Duvall, followed by Edmund Daniels. Daniels wore a sour expression on his swollen face. Coming onto a stretch of flat trail, Summers and Webb both reined their horses up quickly at the sight of Cherokee Rhodes sitting on a large rock with the reins to a horse in his hands.

As Summers' and Webb's pistols came up from their holsters, the half-breed raised his hands and said calmly, "Don't shoot. I'm not here to cause you any trouble."

Behind Summers and Webb the other men rode forward, their rifles coming up from across their laps. Summers heeled his horse ahead of Webb's and turned it sideways to Cherokee Rhodes, keeping his pistol pointed down at Rhodes' face. "You never travel alone, Rhodes! Tell your pals to come out with their hands high."

"I'm alone this time, Summers," said Cherokee Rhodes, watching Webb and the rest of the posse spread out along the trail, facing him with their weapons cocked and ready. "You boys took care of most of my pals last night."

"We left them lying back there in the rocks," said

Summers. "If they're your friends, you best go bury them before the critters get into their bellies."

Rhodes shrugged, keeping his hands up. "Critters can have them, far as I'm concerned. Serves them right for not listening to me. I told them to leave you boys alone. Told them Will Summers ain't nobody to be trying to rob in the night. But you know how that goes: Nobody listens till it's too late. Can I lower my hands now?"

"Yeah, go ahead," said Summers. "While you're at it, raise that pistol from your holster real easylike and pitch it aside."

Cherokee Rhodes looked at the ground. "I hate getting it all dirty."

"I'd do it anyway if I was you," said Summers.

Rhodes nodded, stone-faced, then raised his pistol with two fingers and pitched it halfheartedly aside. Summers stepped down from his saddle, picked up the pistol and stepped forward. He spoke as he reached his free hand out, opening Cherokee Rhodes' vest one lapel at a time and looking for any hidden pistol. "So, you're telling me you wasn't a part of all the commotion last night?"

"Think I'd be sitting here waiting for you if I was?" asked Rhodes.

Will Summers didn't answer. Instead, he offered a tight smile, stepped back, shoved Cherokee Rhodes' pistol down behind his belt and said, "Why *are* you sitting here waiting for us?"

"Dick Vertrees told me you're looking for Moses and Goose Peltry," said Rhodes. "As soon as I heard it, I knew you and me would be riding the same trail."

"You're looking for the Peltrys too?" Summers asked.

"Yep," said Cherokee Rhodes. "I've been wanting

to run into them ever since last year, when me and
some of the boys delivered a wagonload of ammunition to them over in Mexico. You might say there's
bad blood twixt Goose and me."

"You don't say." Summers looked him up and
down, uncocking his pistol and lowering it. "Are you
sure you're not just saying that because Dick Vertrees
mentioned that I'm hunting them for money?"

"To be honest, that did have a lot to do with it."
Cherokee Rhodes looked embarrassed. "But what's
the difference why I'm looking for the Peltrys? The
fact is, I know their stamping grounds across the border, and I'm betting you don't." He looked pleased
with himself. "I always wanted to be a guide; I suppose it runs in my Indian blood."

"If I agreed to let you ride along with us, what
kind of money are we talking about?" asked Summers without revealing whether or not he knew his
way to the Peltrys' hideout in Mexico.

"Hold on, Summers!" said Abner Webb. "You're
not really thinking about letting this cutthroat gunrunner ride with us? I won't stand for it."

"It never hurts to hear a man out, Deputy," Summers replied. "If he can save us some long days in
the saddle by leading us to the Peltrys, I say it's
worth giving some thought." He turned his attention
back to Cherokee Rhodes. "Okay, Rhodes, what kind
of cut are you looking for?"

"Let me do some figuring. . . ." Seeing Summers'
interest, Cherokee Rhodes cocked his head to the side
as if considering it for a moment. "I see where it
could be worth as much as a third of the bounties to
you, seeing as how it's going to save you all those
long, hard days in the saddle you just mentioned."
His smile widened. "How does that sound to you?"

"A third? You've got to be joshing me." Summers

shook his head, chuckling under his breath as he raised his pistol and cocked it toward Cherokee Rhodes. "It's better to kill you right here and take our chances finding the Peltrys on our own." He drew a bead down his pistol barrel. "So long, Cherokee." The half-breed watched Summers' knuckles grow white as he braced the pistol for the coming shot.

"Wait, Summers! Damn it, man!" said Cherokee Rhodes. "That was just a starting figure I tossed out!" His face had turned pasty white. "Everything can be adjusted up or down either one—we both know that!"

"Then tell me your price," Summers said, keeping his pistol pointed but letting his grip ease up. "This time tell me like you really mean it."

Cherokee Rhodes swallowed hard. "All right, Summers. How about ten percent? That sounds fair, don't it?"

"Ten percent of what we collect," said Summers. "If we get nothing, you get nothing. If you get us into a bad spot and try to cut out on us, I'll put a bullet in your back and leave you lying in the dirt. Sound fair enough to you?"

"I wouldn't have it any other way, Summers," Cherokee Rhodes said quickly.

Will Summers turned to Abner Webb and the men. "What do you say, Deputy? I put up five percent of my money, and the town puts up the other five. If he ain't lying, it could save us a lot of time and trouble."

Abner Webb let out a breath of exasperation. "I must be losing my mind." He looked Rhodes up and down, then looked back at Summers. "Do you really think we can trust this man to lead us to the Peltrys?"

"If he wants to make any money, he *better* lead us to them," said Summers.

"That's not what I mean," said Webb. "I'm worried about him trying something while we ain't looking. For all we know, he could be working for the Peltrys. He could be leading us smack into a trap!"

"Then say the word, Deputy," said Will Summers, his pistol coming up, leveled again at Cherokee Rhodes. "We both know I don't mind putting a bullet in him."

"No," said Webb. "You don't have to kill him. Unload his gun and throw it over in the rocks. We'll be long gone by the time he finds it. He won't cause us any trouble."

"If you believe that, what you said is right, Deputy," Summers replied. "You really are losing your mind." He looked Cherokee Rhodes up and down, then said to Abner Webb. "Either he goes with us, or we've got to do something with him. I'm not leaving him on the trail behind me."

Having sat quietly until now, Sherman Dahl said in a lowered voice to Abner Webb, "He's right, Deputy. Either we've got to kill him or take him in. He knew this when he stopped here and waited for us, didn't you, outlaw?" His eyes fixed on Cherokee Rhodes as he spoke.

Dahl's cold stare made Cherokee Rhodes shift uncomfortably back and forth. "All I can tell you is that I know where the Peltrys lay up across the border. If there's some money to be made, I want to make it. Can you fault a man for that?" He looked from Dahl to Webb, then to Will Summers, a look of desperation coming to his dark eyes.

"All right then, damn it!" said Abner Webb, jerking his horse's reins and putting the animal back onto the trail. "But one false move, Rhodes, and it'll be your last."

Cherokee Rhodes turned to Will Summers as Webb and the others fell into loose single file, casting a glance at him as they passed by. "I'll need my gun, Summers," said Rhodes when he and Summers were the only two left alongside the trail.

"Don't push your luck, Cherokee," Summers said, stepping up into his saddle. He gestured toward Rhodes' horse. "You said you always wanted to be a guide. . . . Get on out in front of us and start guiding. But make damn sure you keep in sight. Every time I look up, all I want to see is your back."

The half-breed nodded. He stepped up into his saddle and heeled his horse forward, feeling the eyes of the men upon him as he rode past them and ten yards ahead. When Will Summers rode forward and cut his horse in beside Abner Webb, the deputy said, "I sure hope to hell you know what you're doing."

"So do I, Deputy," Summers replied.

Chapter 10

The four soldiers had pushed hard throughout the night, only slowing for a while atop a high ridge where they listened to the sound of distant gunfire. As the posse battled Dick Vertrees' gunrunners five miles behind them, Sergeant Teasdale and his small, haggard band sipped tepid water from a canteen and offered opinions about the unseen combat. "I'm thinking it's some of the Peltrys' men," said Hargrove, sloshing the water around in the nearly empty canteen. "They must've split up along here for some reason. Part of them went back along the high trail."

"Since you know all that, Hargrove, go ahead and tell us just who they're fighting back there," Teasdale remarked.

"A posse, maybe?" Hargrove rubbed his beard-stubbled chin, wishing he could come up with at least one more possibility. When none came to him, he finally said with a halfhearted shrug, "Hell, I don't know; it was just a hunch is all. Who do you think is back there, Sergeant?"

"I have no idea," said Teasdale. He turned his horse back along the trail in the darkness and heeled it forward.

"Well, squat," Hargrove grumbled under his breath. "His opinion was no better than mine." In moments, they had passed on into the velvet darkness beneath a dome full of starlight.

At daybreak the sound of gunfire erupted again, this time in the nearer distance ahead of them. Teasdale stopped the other three soldiers with his raised hand. "Listen to that now," he said to Hargrove as the big man rode up and stopped his horse beside him. "I can tell you most certainly where that's coming from and who's doing it," he said.

"That's coming from the settlement at Little Sand," Hargrove said, his eyes staring ahead through the silver mist of morning.

"Notice anything missing?" asked Teasdale.

"Missing?" Hargrove looked puzzled. "No. Why would I notice anything missing?"

"It's the Gatling gun." Teasdale allowed a faint, tight smile as he stared ahead. "They've had no better luck then we did getting it to fire. That helps our odds considerably."

"By the saints, Sergeant!" Hargrove shook his head in exasperation. "We're still outnumbered beyond any sane measure."

Teasdale ignored him, then turned to Trooper Frieze as he and Doyle Benson rode up on his other side. "How's the wound, Trooper?" he asked.

Frieze shivered in a cold sweat. "I'm fine, Sergeant. I might have me a touch of infection . . . but it'll soon pass. I'm hoping so anyway."

"Good man," said Teasdale. "Just hold on a couple of hours longer. We'll find a doctor for you in Little Sand."

"He's looking worse by the minute," said Doyle Benson, giving Frieze a quick once-over in the grainy dawn light. "God almighty, look at his face! Frieze, your eyes are all blue underneath like some kind of dead man's!"

"That's enough out of you, Benson!" Sergeant

Teasdale commanded. "Get yourself back there twenty yards and guard our rear."

"Our rear?" Benson looked confused. "Sergeant, everything from me back *is* our rear. I can guard it from where I sat—"

"Shut up, Benson!" Hargrove bellowed. "Come with me!" He grabbed the young soldier's horse by its bridle and jerked it along beside him. In the gray morning, Teasdale and Frieze heard him chastise the young man as they rode farther back. "The hell's wrong with you, Benson?" Hargrove growled at him. "You never say something like that to a badly wounded man!"

"I thought it wasn't that bad," said Benson. "He said himself it's just an in-and-out wound."

"Never mind. . . . Just shut your stupid face!" said Hargrove.

As Hargrove's and Benson's voices faded, Trooper Frieze tried to sound as if nothing was wrong. "Soldiers always have to bicker and bellyache, don't they, Sergeant?"

"How bad is it getting, Trooper Frieze?" Teasdale asked instead of answering him.

"Aw, heck, Sergeant. Like I said, it ain't nothing," Frieze offered bravely.

"On the square, Trooper," said Teasdale. "I need to know so I can figure it into our plans."

"On the square then," said Frieze. "It's the strangest feeling I ever had. It wasn't bad at all till the past couple hours. . . . Then, Lord have mercy, this fever hit me all at once. I swear I never felt nothing like it before in my life."

"All right then," said Teasdale. "You just hang on. We'll get the doctor in Little Sand to treat you. We'll leave you with him a few days, just until you're past the fever stage."

A silence set in. Then Frieze said, "What if this fever hangs on and gets worse? I've heard how it is to die of blood poison."

"Blood poison? Who said anything about blood poison?" said Teasdale. "You might come out of this sicker than a dog for a few days, but that's a long way from—"

"Begging your pardon, Sergeant Teasdale," said Frieze, cutting him off. "I thought we was still talking on the square here."

Teasdale stopped himself and let out a breath. "Sorry, Trooper. You're right. This is still on the square. As fast as that infection came on you, we haven't a moment to waste getting you some medical attention. But we will be in Little Sand by midmorning at the latest. Hang on till then, all right?"

"I'll sure try. You count on that," said Frieze. "I can't say that I feel like I'm dying. . . . But I swear, this is the damndest thing ever." His voice nearly gave in to the deep shiver in his chest, but he managed to hold it off. "I hate the thought of living through a bullet wound only to die from the sickness of it. It don't seem fair somehow."

"Quit thinking about dying. Put the *fair* part out of your mind too, Trooper," said Teasdale. "A few days from now, you might be laughing about this."

"Suits me, Sergeant," said Frieze. "Dying ain't exactly something I ever planned on doing."

"That's more like it," said Teasdale. "I need you to stick in here real tough for me. Will you do that?"

"You know it, Sergeant," said Frieze, making an effort to sit taller in his saddle.

"Good man." Teasdale heeled his horse forward, this time speeding it up a bit.

By the time they reached the outer edge of the valley where the settlement of the Little Sand River stood, the sun was high and boiling. Entering through broken-down timber gates on a narrow path that ran between rows of shacks and crumbling adobes from a time long past, Teasdale raised his hand and once again stopped the other three soldiers in their tracks. From a tall pole just inside the broken gates, the body of a man clad in buckskin swayed back and forth on the hot, still air. Thirty feet farther along the thin path, another body hung from a similar pole, this one with a feed sack down over its head.

"Those dirty murdering bastards," Sergeant Teasdale whispered. He turned to Hargrove and Benson. "Get up there and cut them down. Frieze and I will go raise the townsfolk from hiding."

"Stay where you are," said a voice from behind the burnt remains of a hide wagon. "Nobody does nothing till we say so!"

"Easy, sir," said Teasdale, raising his hands chest-high in a show of peace. "We're soldiers."

"So was that last bunch came through here," said the voice. "Look what they done."

As Teasdale and the other three soldiers watched cautiously, a half dozen men and women stepped out from behind the smoking pile of charred wood and bent metal bracing. In front of them stood a portly older man dressed in greasy buckskins. He carried a big fifty-caliber buffalo rifle in the open crook of his left arm. His dirty thumb lay across the cocked hammer. At his moccasined feet stood a skinny spotted hound with its hackles raised. The dog held a low, steady growl in its throat.

"I differ with you, sir," said Teasdale. "The men who did this were not soldiers. They're a murdering band of thieves called the Peltrys."

"I know all about them," said the old man, lowering the rifle an inch now that he had a better look at the men and their dusty uniforms. "It's Moses and Goose. I knew them back when they were snot-nosed babies. Pity somebody didn't mash their heads back then, save the world all this grief." He gestured a hand toward the body hanging from the first pole. "That's Rance Stofeild. He cut new trails with Bridger back before this land had ever seen a white man's footprint on it. Sonsabitches have no respect for nothing anymore."

"We'll help you cut him down," said Teasdale. Behind him, Hargrove and Benson stepped down from their saddles and helped Frieze to the ground. Three men and a woman rushed forward and assisted Frieze. "Is there a doctor here?" Teasdale asked.

"No," said the woman, "but I'll see to him." They hurried Frieze away toward a whitewashed shack.

"Thank you kindly," said Teasdale, tipping his dusty cavalry hat. "I'll be right along, Trooper," he said to Frieze.

"They like to call themselves Southern guerrillas," said the old man, continuing on about the Peltrys, "but Rance lost two grandsons who fought for the Stars and Bars, and he wasn't about to hear the Peltrys pretend they were decent Southern boys. He called the Peltrys what they really are, and it got him hung. I oughta have done something. . . . But I didn't." He looked ashamed and remorseful.

"Now, you stop that kind of talk, Campbell Hayes. There was nothing you could do," said a matronly woman standing close behind him. She looked at Sergeant Teasdale as he stepped down from his horse. "He stood up to them when they first got here, and one of them knocked him cold and tied him to a hitch rail."

"It was the first time in my life I felt just plain powerless," said Campbell Hayes, his glance going up to Rance's body hanging in the air. "What a hell of a time to go flat in my old age." He looked back at Teasdale. "But by God, sir! If you're hunting them polecats, I'm going with you."

"Ordinarily, sir, I would be glad to have you join us," said Teasdale. "But as you can see, we're hard-pressed and ill-outfitted for this task. I won't jeopardize your safety."

"My safety be damned, Sergeant," said Campbell Hayes, looking up to where Benson, who had shinnied up the rough wooden pole, had taken a pocket-knife from his trouser pocket and begun to cut through the taut rope holding the dead man suspended above the ground. "I just want to kill the Peltrys and watch Stofield's hound, Junior, piss in their dead faces." On the ground, the dog recognized his name and deepened his steady growl. "What put you on their trail anyway?"

"We're part of a guard detail," said Teasdale, "accompanying a gun wagon to the camp up in the hills. We had a Gatling rifle that was supposed to keep the area safe from Mescaleros this winter. The Peltrys hit us yesterday. These men and myself are all that's left of the detail."

"I saw that Gatling gun," said Campbell Hayes. "Good thing the Peltrys weren't smart enough to get it working. They tried spraying this whole settlement with it. Seems like the army would better protect a weapon that fierce."

"Yes, I agree," said Teasdale, leading his horse along in the direction the townsfolk had taken Frieze. "By the same token, you'd think a weapon that fierce would be capable of protecting itself. And it would have, if it hadn't kept jamming on us. But that's all water under the bridge now. I have to get that gun back and take down the Peltrys in the process."

"Then you best be prepared to ride into Old Mex," said Campbell Hayes, walking along beside him, keeping his eyes turned away from the sight of his dead partner's body hitting the ground like a sack of feed. "They hole up in the north. . . . The *Federales* in the provinces turn a blind eye to their thieving, cutthroat ways so long as they keep their noses clean over there. Everything for the right price, of course."

"Of course," said Teasdale. He seemed to consider things for a second, then he said, "If I have to cross the border, I will. Can you tell me where we might get fitted with some civilian clothes around here?"

"All depends," said Hayes. "Am I going with you or not?"

"What about your business?" asked Teasdale. "The buffalo won't wait for you to get back here."

"The buffs are about played out anyway," said Hayes. "Besides, I'm short a hide wagon now . . . and skinning ain't a one-man job. Hadn't been for Stofield, I'd have drug up from it two seasons back. I know the northern hill country over there, if the fight goes that far . . . which I know it will."

Thinking about it as they walked along, Teasdale looked down at the dog staying close to Hayes' heels. "What about your partner's dog? Is there anybody here you can leave him with?"

"Anybody here in Little Sand would be honored to keep Junior," said Hayes, "but I wouldn't think of leaving him here. He'll be worth his weight in gold to us in the Mexican wilds. After what they done to his master, Junior will sniff us out a Peltry from a mile upwind."

"Just keep him out of my way," said Teasdale,

passing a glance down to the skinny canine. "Gather what supplies you can find for us," he said. "Whatever these folks can spare." He stopped dead in his tracks as if just reminded of what the Peltrys had done. "Are these folks going to be all right?"

"Why, hell yes," said Hayes. "They was ready to shoot your eyes out if you and your lads weren't what you should be. Fighting people are *whole* people, I always say." He grinned behind his long silver beard.

"All right then. Be ready to ride as soon as I see how the trooper is doing."

"He ain't going with us, the shape he's in, is he?" Campbell Hayes asked, looking astonished by the prospect.

"You saw him," said Teasdale. "You tell me where you think he's going."

"Ummph." Hayes winced and grunted under his breath. "It's a damn shame, a young feller like that. Does he know how serious it is?"

"He knew it before I did," said Teasdale, shaking his head. "I never seen a wound go bad that fast. We cleaned it with water the best we could. Still, it didn't help. One of my troopers said it was full of blue wool from his shirt."

"Nothing makes any difference when a man's time is at hand, Sergeant," said Hayes. "The Lord calls it the way it falls. I'll get to gathering up those supplies."

Teasdale stopped a few feet from the whitewashed shack and spun his reins around the hitch rail. As he stepped up onto a rickety boardwalk, the woman who had taken charge of Trooper Frieze met him at the open doorway and motioned him inside. "Wait right here, Sergeant. We'll have him cleaned up in no time." She turned and left the room.

Teasdale paced back and forth across the plank floor until the woman appeared again a few minutes later. "He's asking for you, Sergeant," she said in a low whisper. "You best come on in here quickly. This poor boy is in a terrible way."

Inside the small room, Teasdale took off his hat and stooped down beside the cot where Frieze lay, shirtless now. His pale chest glistened with sweat, and the color of the skin surrounding the bullet hole had turned puffy and bluish green. The young soldier looked into Teasdale's eyes, trying hard to keep from shivering. "Don't know what the fuss is all about, Sergeant," he said. "I can ride once I get a shirt on and get some water in my belly."

"I want you to lay still here, Trooper," said Teasdale. "These folks will take good care of you."

"Stay here?" Frieze offered a weak chuckle as if the sergeant were joking. "I can't stay here. What about the Peltrys and our Gatling gun?"

"We'll take care of it, Trooper," said Teasdale. "You need to rest and get rid of this infection. Do you understand me?"

Trooper Frieze saw the resolved look in Teasdale's eyes and felt cold terror move through him. "No! I'm not dying, Sergeant! Don't even think it! It's bad luck thinking it!" As he spoke and tried to raise himself up, firm hands seemed to appear out of nowhere and pressed him back down onto the cot. He looked into the faces of the townfolk gathered around. In his fevered state, he pictured them as grim angels of death. "Mother of God, no!" he screamed. "Don't leave me here! Don't let me die! I can't stand it!"

"Don't fight the hand of the Lord, young man," said the lady's voice, soothing and frightening at the same time. Frieze looked at her face as Sergeant Teasdale backed away from the cot. Behind Teasdale,

Hargrove and Benson came into the shack, Benson closing the blade of his pocketknife. "Hargrove!" Frieze pleaded. "Don't let him leave me! Tell them I'm not dying! Please tell them!" Sweat glistened on his pale, trembling face.

"Come on, now; get a hold of yourself, Frieze," said Hargrove. "That bullet has killed you—you know it as well as we do. Let these good people comfort you, soldier. It's all that's left for you to do."

Frieze sobbed for a second, then stopped himself and looked from Hargrove to Trooper Benson. "Tell them I'm all right, Benson! Please tell them I'm going to live."

Doyle Benson looked away, his eyes filled with tears. "I'm sorry, Frieze," he said. "There's nothing I can do."

"We've got to go, Frieze," Sergeant Teasdale said softly. "I give you my word the Peltrys will pay for this."

The three soldiers backed to the door and slipped outside. Lyndell Hargrove closed the door behind them and leaned back against it. "Those rotten, good-for-nothing murderers! I won't rest until they're all dead."

"Me neither," said Doyle Benson, running his sleeve across his eyes.

"I'm glad you both feel that way," said Teasdale. "Let's see if you mean it."

"What are you talking about, Sergeant?" asked Hargrove.

"You'll see." From the far end of the narrow path, Campbell Hayes led a big paint horse toward them, Junior the hound trotting alongside. Over his shoulder he carried a feed sack filled with dried beef, beans, coffee and flour. Sergeant Teasdale nodded toward him, seeing the pile of civilians' clothes draped over the paint horse's saddle. "He's riding with us, men," said Teasdale.

"That old relic?" said Hargrove. "What on earth for, Sergeant?"

"His name is Campbell Hayes," said Teasdale, "and he knows the Mexican hill country. That's good enough for me."

"The hill country?" said Hargrove. "You don't think for one minute that we're—"

"That's right," said Teasdale, cutting him off. "I had him find us some clothes to wear once we cross the border. We can't go over there in army uniforms."

Hargrove sounded stunned. "We can't cross the border, *period*, Sergeant!" said Hargrove. "We'll wind up facing a firing squad! If not theirs, then one of our own!"

"I'm crossing," said Teasdale. "If you don't want to come along, that's up to you."

"Damn it all," said Hargrove. "I don't know who's the craziest: you for doing this or me for following you." He turned to Doyle Benson. "Get our horses, Trooper. We're about to make some strange history for ourselves."

Chapter 11

———

It was noon when Abner Webb and Will Summers led their posse onto the narrow path through the broken timber gates at Little Sand. They kept Cherokee Rhodes riding between them. Sergeant Teasdale, Hargrove and Benson looked up from busily preparing their horses for the trail and saw the six horsemen come to a halt, staring at them from twenty yards away. Having changed into civilian clothes, Teasdale suddenly realized there was nothing to identify him and his men as soldiers. "Don't touch that pistol, Hargrove," Teasdale warned, seeing the horsemen spread out abreast across the path.

"Whatever you say, Sergeant," Hargrove said quietly. His hand inched away from the holster on his hip. "But that's Cherokee Rhodes with them. He's one gunrunning, back-shooting, low-down sonsabitch."

"Duly noted," said Teasdale. "Now stay calm." He took a slow step sideways, away from the horses.

Will Summers glanced up at the short stubs of rope hanging from the poles where earlier Doyle Benson had cut the bodies free. He looked around at the smoldering ashes of the hide wagon and the debris the Peltrys had left in their wake. "Does this look familiar, Deputy?" Summers asked Webb without taking his eyes off the men standing before them.

"Yep," said Webb, "but that's not the Peltrys."

"I know it," said Summers. "Stay back here while I find out who it is." He heeled his horse forward, raising his hands slightly.

Sergeant Teasdale kept his hand away from his pistol and stood facing Summers in the middle of the narrow street. "Who goes there?" Teasdale asked.

Summers stopped his horse fifteen feet away and turned it sideways to Teasdale. "We're a posse out of Rileyville," said Will Summers. "I've got a feeling you already know who it is we're trailing." He sat still, watching for a reaction. "I'm Will Summers. Now, who are you?"

Teasdale cocked his head slightly. "Will Summers, the horse trader?"

"Yep, that's me. Do we know one another?" Summers asked.

"No," said Teasdale. "I've heard of you though. You sold some horses to us up at Fort Bent a couple of years back."

"Were they good horses?" Summers asked.

"As I recall, yes, they were," said Teasdale.

Summers nodded, looking relieved. "That was me, sir. Now, who are you?"

"I'm Sergeant Lawrence Teasdale, United States Army," said Teasdale.

"You could have fooled me," said Will Summers, looking Teasdale up and down. As he spoke, Deputy Webb and the others inched their horses forward until Webb stopped close beside Will Summers.

"We're out of uniform at present," said Teasdale. "We're also tracking the Peltrys." He nodded along the pillaged plank shacks. "This is some of their handiwork. They left two men hanging from poles."

"Yes, sir," Campbell Hayes cut in, taking a step forward from the horses, his big buffalo rifle in hand.

"And one of them was my best friend, Rance Stofield." His eyes narrowed coldly on Cherokee Rhodes. "Is that man your prisoner?"

"No, he's not," said Will Summers. "But we ain't exactly friends either."

"He's agreed to show us where the Peltrys' hideout is down in Mexico," Abner Webb cut in.

"Call him our scout," Summers offered.

"I see," said Teasdale. "We heard gunfire late last night. Was that coming from you people?"

"Yes, it was," said Summers. "If you'll invite us down from our saddles, we'll tell you all about it."

"Step down then," said Sergeant Teasdale. "It may be that we can do one another some good."

"I wouldn't be at all surprised," said Summers, easing down from his saddle, the men behind him doing the same.

"You can't trust anybody riding beside Cherokee Rhodes," Hayes said to Teasdale in a lowered voice.

Teasdale looked down at Junior the hound standing near Hayes' feet as the riders stepped down from their horses. "Why didn't that mutt warn us that somebody was coming?"

"I don't know," said Hayes. "Maybe he didn't think they was the enemy."

"And neither do I," said Teasdale. He looked around at Hargrove and Benson. "Finish up with the horses and supplies. Let's see what these men have to offer."

Summers, Webb and the other possemen formed a half circle in front of the hitch rail. With their reins in their hands, the men squatted down on their haunches or rested with one knee to the dirt and listened as Summers, Webb and Teasdale exchanged stories. A gallon jug of whiskey made its way into the circle and moved from man to man. When it had come into Wild Joe Duvall's hands and he'd lowered it from his lips and wiped a hand across his wet mustache, he passed it to Sherman Dahl beside him and said between the two of them, "Is my boy Eddie doing like he's supposed to in school?"

"He's headstrong," said Dahl without diverting his attention from Sergeant Teasdale as he told Summers and Webb about the stolen Gatling gun, "but he learns quick. He can be a bit of a bully sometimes, but I try not to let that happen." Dahl raised the jug, drank from it, then passed it on to Bobby Dewitt. "He could use some help at home on his arithmetic."

"Headstrong, eh?" Wild Joe beamed with secret pride, passing over the arithmetic part. "I expect I know where he gets that *headstrong* from." Then his expression turned more serious as he caught himself and said, "But I'll get on him about the bullying part. I always hated bullies when I was a kid. If I saw somebody bullying others, I usually whopped the living hell out of them. Made them beg for mercy."

"I'm sure you did," said Dahl, trying to listen to Teasdale.

"What does that mean?" asked Wild Joe.

"Nothing, sir," said Dahl. "Nothing at all."

"Oh . . ." Wild Joe fell silent for a moment, then said, "Well, I'm glad we got this chance to talk some. I think it pays to know the man you're fighting next to, don't you?"

"I couldn't agree more," said Dahl.

"I'll tell you what," said Wild Joe. "You're not a very big feller. If we get into a hard scrape with the Peltrys, you just holler out. . . . I won't let them hurt you. That's my personal promise."

"Thank you," said Dahl. "I feel much better."

On the other side of Sherman Dahl, Bobby Dewitt leaned forward and looked around at Wild Joe Duvall. "Hey, Wild Joe, didn't you see what the school-master did to that outlaw, Vertrees? He cut him from asshole to appetite."

"I know it," said Wild Joe. "I'm just offering is all."

"Both of you shut up and listen," Edmund Daniels hissed.

"Sure thing, Edmund," said Bobby Dewitt, stifling a whiskey belch. Having taken a long swig, he passed the jug into Edmund Daniels' eager hands. "By the way, how's the head?"

Edmund Daniels just stared at him, not sure whether or not the young cowboy was making fun of him. Finally he said as he raised the jug to his lips, "Don't worry about my head; worry about your own."

Hearing the stir of conversation among Daniels and Dewitt, Deputy Webb cast a firm gaze in their direction. But before he could say anything, Edmund Daniels said, "Don't worry, Deputy. We're not missing a thing. Our eyes and ears are wide open."

Bobby Dewitt snickered under his breath at Daniels' words, but then he shut up quickly when Daniels turned his eyes to him. Sherman Dahl and Wild Joe Duvall stared ahead and listened as Sergeant Teasdale explained how the Gatling rifle had kept jamming on them. "But God help us if they ever get it working properly," he said, looking from one face to the next, one hand reaching out for the jug as it came into sight.

Inside the whitewashed shack, Trooper Frieze heard the sound of voices out front through a fevered haze. In a thick voice, he asked the woman standing over him, "What are they doing out there?"

"Shhh. Lie still now, young man," she whispered, pressing him back down as he tried to rise up onto his elbows. "The fighting's all over for you. It's best you lie still here what time you've got left. Make peace with your creator."

Her words sent a new shiver up his spine. "I'm not dying, damn it to hell!" Frieze shouted in his hoarse, trembling voice. "Do you hear me, God?" He raged at the plank ceiling. "It's me, Chester Frieze! Tell this old bag that I'm not going to die! God! Somebody! Anybody! *Please!*"

Outside, the men gathered around the hitch rail looked toward the sound coming from the side window of the shack. As the woman stepped over and closed the window, cutting Frieze's voice in half, Teasdale said to the men, "He's one of my troopers. His wound infected overnight. He's starting to talk out of his head. I regret to say he's not going to make it." The sergeant stopped for a second as if to let his words sink in.

From the room beyond the window, Frieze screamed, "Take your hands off me!"

Teasdale raised his voice and said, "He's just one more reason I want to see the Peltry Gang dead! The longer these killers go free, the more decent people are going to suffer!"

The soldiers and possemen nodded in agreement. "I can see where it's to all of our advantage to ride together, Sergeant," said Will Summers. "But I better tell you right now that I have a deal with the town of Rileyville and these men here. We're sharing the bounty money on the Peltry Gang."

"That's strictly between you gentlemen," said Teasdale. "I'm military through and through. I'm going after them for the murdering animals they are. Whatever you people make, you're welcome to it."

Crouched in the dirt beside Hargrove, Doyle Benson said to him in a whisper, "How much money do you think they're talking about?"

"Makes no difference," said Hargrove. "You heard the sergeant. We'll not see a dollar of it." He grinned mockingly. "We're military through and through."

At the hitch rail, Sergeant Teasdale asked Will Summers and Abner Webb, "Which one of you is in charge?"

"I suppose you might say we both are equally, Sergeant," said Will Summers. "The deputy here is officially in charge on behalf of Rileyville, but I'm more familiar with the country twixt here and the border."

"I don't want to sound like my being a soldier gives me any longer spurs than either of you," said Teasdale, "but I also know the desert, and I have Campbell Hayes here to show us around in Mexico."

"So you think you should be in charge?" Webb asked bluntly.

Teasdale looked a bit embarrassed. "Not if the three of us can work together. But I'd like to think my word carries at least as much authority as either of yours," he said.

"And so it will," said Summers. "Only fools turn down good advice. Speak your piece at any time, Sergeant Teasdale. We're all after the same thing: bringing down the Peltrys."

In the desert settlement of Diablo Espinazo, only a day's ride from the Mexican border, a small band of Mexican and American goatherders kept their distance from the Peltrys and offered no resistance as the gang helped itself to their meager food and precious wellwater. In the scorching heat of the day, one of the outlaws stood shirtless and glistening with sweat as he turned a slaughtered goat above a licking mesquite fire. The goatherders stared at the gun wagon through caged eyes as Goose Peltry cursed and raged at his men.

"Then what good is this rotten, no-shooting son-sabitch?" Goose shrieked, out of control, standing in the gun wagon with Thurman Anderson and Roscoe Moore. He kicked the Gatling gun stand. Then he kicked the ammunition crates stacked beside it. Then he kicked the wagon's sideboard. He spun around toward Thurman and Roscoe. They jumped back with fear in their eyes. "Make the damn thing work! I'm sick of owning a machine rifle, hauling it all over hell and not being able to get it to fire a shot?!" He kicked wildly at the big cylinder of rifle barrels, missed it and fell backward onto the wagon bed in a puff of dust.

Standing on the ground watching, both hands clutched around his long beard, Moses Peltry shook his head in disgust at his brother's insane antics. "Get down here, Goose!" he shouted. "Before you break your idiot neck."

Goose stumbled to his feet, slapping at Thurman and Roscoe, who had reached out to help him stand. "I want this gun fixed and firing! I don't want no more excuses!" He narrowed a hard stare at Thurman Anderson. "You had it working earlier. . . . How did you do it?"

"It only fired a few shots. Then the blasted thing jammed again," said Thurman in a nervous voice. "I held this switch here up while Roscoe turned the crank. Soon as I turned the switch loose, it got stuck again. I've worked on every kind of weapon there is. But this piece of junk has got me and Roscoe both stumped." He looked at Roscoe Moore for support.

"It's the truth, Goose," said Roscoe. "Seems like

this gun's got a mind all its own. We've tried." He shrugged.

"Then try again, damn it to hell!" Goose lunged forward, shouting in his face. Roscoe and Thurman stepped backward out of the blast of Goose's rage.

"Goose, get down here," Moses demanded again, his poise the same but his hands clutching tighter around his long beard. "If we can't get it to work right, we'll have to abandon it. A gun that won't shoot is no better than a woman who won't cook. Let Thurman and Roscoe work on that blasted thing. You've never been worth a tinker's damn with machinery."

But Goose ignored his brother and shoved Thurman and Roscoe out of his way. "Let me get my hands on this damn thing!" He reached down, wrapped his arms around the big gun and jerked it into the air, tripod and all. Staggering in place under the heavy weight, Goose yelled, "Roscoe, hold the switch up. Thurman, start turning the crank! We'll get her barking!"

"Goose! Put it down!" shouted Moses Peltry. "This is getting out of hand." He turned loose of his beard and hurried forward toward the gun wagon.

"Oh shit," said Monk Dupre, who'd been standing beside Moses along with three other men. All four of them ducked away, each seeking cover for himself. Dupre raced for shelter behind the stone wall of the well in the center of the clearing. A small herd of bleating goats scurried in every direction as he charged through them.

"Thurman, for God sakes, don't turn that crank!" Moses pleaded. But he was too late; Thurman had already started. The sound of rapid gunfire drowned out Moses' words. The hard, steady recoil of the big gun caused Goose, Thurman and Roscoe to bounce around in a circle, the sweep of bullets kicking up dirt across the clearing. Goose clung to the gun with all his might. The line of fire crawled up the side of an ancient adobe building, leaving fist-sized bullet holes in the hard earthen wall, shattering clay pots and water gourds that stood along a shelf beneath an overhanging canopy.

"Turn it loose, Thurman!" Moses Peltry bellowed, ready to duck beneath the gun wagon as the three men and their deadly gunfire came circling toward him. On the far side of the clearing, skinny chickens rose up, batting their wings and screaming shrilly. A cat had jumped atop a crumbling adobe ledge only to disappear in an explosion of fur. "You're killing every damn thing in sight!"

Thurman would not or could not stop turning the crank; but in all the jerking and bouncing back and forth, Roscoe's hand came off the switch he'd been holding up, and the gun stopped firing with a loud metallic clunk. Goose and Thurman fell in the wagon; Roscoe flipped over the side and landed in the dirt at Moses Peltry's feet. "God almighty!" Moses shouted.

"Get it off me!" Goose screamed from inside the wagon bed, the hot rifle barrels burning his chest.

"I ought to let you lie there and bake under it," said Moses. He dragged Roscoe to his feet and shoved him away. Climbing up into the wagon, he looked down at Goose and Thurman as the two wallowed beneath the gun and its tripod. "Nobody touches this gun again unless I say so!" Moses shouted, pulling the gun from atop them. Moses yanked his brother to his feet. Goose tore open his shirt and rubbed the long red burns across his chest.

Moses Peltry and the rest of the men were so consumed with watching Goose fire the Gatling gun that none of them had noticed the seven scalp hunters who'd slipped up alongside the clearing and now sat atop their horses twenty yards away, watching with stonelike expressions on their weathered faces. Their saddles were adorned with long black strands of hair, bits of human bones and other unsavory mementos of their profession. "What do you make of that, Doc?" asked a skinny little killer named Pip Magger.

The leader, Elvin "Doc" Murdock, wore a long riding duster, a wide-brimmed hat and high Spanish boots that came up to his knees. A long, sharply waxed mustache mantled his upper lip. He stared at Goose Peltry as he said quietly to Pip and the rest of the riders gathered around him, "I've always said the Peltrys' folks were too close kin to sleep in the same room."

A slight chuckle rippled across the serious faces of the scalp hunters. Doc Murdock continued. "Moses can make you think he's not a complete lunatic if you're not paying attention. But that poor Goose . . ." He shook his head. "There's a mercy killing in the making. Somebody shoulda felled him the first time they found a possum under his pillow."

More dry, muffled laughter rose and fell among Murdock's men. From the gun wagon, Moses Peltry caught a glimpse of the scalp hunters and growled under his breath at Goose, "Damn it, here's Murdock. See if you can act like you've got some sense— bad enough he had to ride in and witness something like this."

"If he don't like it, he knows where he can go," Goose grumbled in reply.

"That's real smart of you, Goose," said Moses. "Bad as we need men to put this outfit ahead, you better show Doc Murdock some respect." Stepping down from the gun wagon, Moses raised an acknowledging hand toward Murdock and his men.

"Howdy, Doc. Howdy, boys. Come on in. Step down and make yourselves to home."

"Howdy, Devil. Sure we're not interrupting anything?" Doc Murdock asked coolly, nudging his horse forward, his men gathered close behind him. He looked all around at the shot-up adobe and the broken pottery as he stepped his horse over to the gun wagon. His eyes settled on the Gatling gun lying on its side. "I never like to interfere in a family discussion."

"Never mind about us," said Moses. "We've just been having a hard time with this blasted Gatling rifle."

"No kidding?" Murdock sounded bored. He said over his shoulder to one of his men, "Spears, see what's wrong with this gun."

"Sure thing, Doc," said Mort Spears, jumping his horse forward and stepping down beside the gun wagon. He climbed up onto the wagon and stood to one side as Goose Peltry stepped past him and down, grumbling under his breath.

"Hope you haven't been waiting long for us, Devil," said Doc Murdock to Moses Peltry.

"Nobody calls him *Devil* anymore," Goose said grudgingly, "unless it's me or some close, longtime friend of ours."

Ignoring Goose, Moses said to Murdock, "We ain't been here long, Doc. Have you given any more thought to throwing in with us? We've just had ourselves a hell of a run . . . all the way down from the Milk River. The only ones big enough to stop us is the Yankee army. They've pretty much got their hands full with the Lakota up along the Bozeman Trail. "We've got ourselves an open door from Mexico plumb up to the high Montana line, providing we keep striking while the iron's hot. From now on, everything's going our way."

"Then why do you need me and my boys?" Murdock grinned slyly. "Just need somebody to keep your Gatling gun repaired?"

Goose cut in. "Don't get cocky, Murdock. My brother just made you the best offer you ever had in your life. If you're too good to ride with us, we understand. The fact is, I never thought you was anything but—"

"Goose!" Moses barked, cutting him off. "Why don't you see if you can help Spears fix that damn Gatling gun?"

"He's wasting his time," said Goose. "The only way to fix that gun is with some gunsmithing tools."

"There—all done," said Mort Spears, standing up from beside the Gatling gun and wiping his hands on a wadded-up bandanna.

"Like hell," said Goose with a sneer, seeing Roscoe and Thurman raise the gun on its tripod and aim it out across the wide desert floor. "I wouldn't be afraid to stand right smack in front of it."

A string of blasts resounded from the barrels as Spears leaned down behind the gun and turned the crank three full turns. Fifty yards away, a tall cactus toppled over on its side.

Doc Murdock spread a thin smile and nodded at Goose as he said to Moses Peltry, "Shame we didn't have time to take him up on his offer."

"Get out of the way!" shouted Goose, his face swollen and red with rage. He jumped up onto the gun wagon, shoved Spears aside and grabbed the Gatling gun's crank. He tried turning it briskly, but the crank seized up and wouldn't budge. "Damn it to bloody hell!" he shrieked. "Why won't this sonsabitch work?"

"Spears, show him *again* how it's done," said Murdock. "I'm afraid he must've missed it the first time." He turned to Moses Peltry and said, just between the two of them, "If you ever decide to have that fool put to sleep, I'd be glad to do it for you free of charge."

Moses stared at him with a mixed expression. "That's my brother you're talking about, Doc."

"I know," Murdock said flatly, his eyes searching Moses.

Moses dismissed the idea. "Are you throwing in with us or not, Murdock?"

"Sure." Murdock shrugged, taking a quick glance around at the men, then turning his eyes back to Moses Peltry. "I wouldn't miss it for the world."

Chapter 12

When every horse was fed and watered, and every canteen and water keg had been filled, the men gorged themselves on hot goat meat, beans and tortillas. Moses Peltry and Doc Murdock sat in the shade of a blanket-draped lean-to and watched the evening sunlight simmer and spread across the western horizon. "Listen up, men," said Moses Peltry to the circle of faces on one side of the fire. They turned their stares from Murdock's scalp hunters on the other side of the fire and looked at Moses.

"Looks like we're going to be riding together from now on," Moses continued. "While we're all together on the same spot here, it's time I introduced you to Elvin Murdock and his boys." Moses wiped his greasy fingers on his shirt and said to Doc Murdock as he pointed a finger at the far end of the row. "That one with his head swollen like a Georgia melon is Bert Smitson." His finger bounced from one man to the next. "Next to him is Thurman Anderson and Roscoe Moore, who you seen earlier working on the gun. Next is Monk Dupre, Frank Spragg and the Catt brothers, Big Catt and Little Catt. Then there's Cap Whitlow, Jake Barnstall, Elmer Fitzhugh, Dog Belly Kelso—I believe you already know Dog Belly?"

"Yep," said Murdock. "Howdy, Dog."

Dog Belly stopped chewing long enough to nod at Murdock.

Moses went on. "Next is Flat Face Chinn . . . and of course you know brother Goose."

The men all acknowledged Murdock respectfully except for Goose, who continued to stare at the faces of Murdock's men across the fire. "Now maybe you'll tell us these men's names, if they have any," Goose grumbled.

"Sure thing," said Doc Murdock, nodding at his men. "On the end there is Pip Magger, then Mort Spears. Next to him is Handy Phelps, Brayton 'Comanche Killer' Cane and Andy Merkel." He looked around, then added, "Duckbill Grear is over keeping watch on the trail." Murdock rose to his feet and looked all around. "I'm Doc Murdock, boys, and just so's you all understand something about my men right off, they are the meanest, roughest, bloodiest bunch of devils ever thrown out of hell. They can lift a scalp and be gone with it while some poor sonsabitch raises his hat to say howdy."

A dark chuckle rose and fell around the fire. Then Doc Murdock sat down slowly.

"After spending half the war riding with most of this bunch, I can safely say the same for my men," Moses Peltry intoned, standing up and dusting his seat, "except for the scalping part." He hooked both thumbs in his gunbelt, his long beard hanging down between them, past the belt buckle. "These men are straight-up Southern guerrillas . . . tempered by the flames of war and forged and honed to the finest cutting edge of killing. They hate a Yankee worse than they hate a—"

"Wait a minute," said Brayton Cane. "Excuse me for interrupting, but I happen to have fought for the Union back in '63—even took some rebel metal in my back." He patted a thick hand to the small of his back as he stared at Moses Peltry. "We ain't going to have no problems over our personal opinions, are we?" His fiery eyes swept from man to man.

"No problem at all, Brayton 'Comanche Killer' Cane," said Goose Peltry, cutting in before Moses could respond. "I've heard of you. My brother likes to preach for the Southern cause, but believe me, so long as you're out to get your hands on as much money as we can steal or kill for, we're all of the same accord here."

Moses Peltry started to chastise his brother, but hearing the cheer go up along both sides of the fire, he decided to keep quiet about it. As the men joked and hooted back and forth, Moses Peltry and Doc Murdock sat back down and picked up their cups of coffee. "For some reason, Moses," said Murdock, "I thought you had more men than this."

"I did," Moses replied. "But I've lost a few over the past few months. It's gotten hard to stay alive out here. I sent a man to gather stray horses when we took the Gatling gun from that army patrol. . . . Damn fool never made it back."

"Did you leave any soldiers living?" Murdock asked, a concerned look coming to his face.

"A couple or so maybe." Moses shrugged. "But they were afoot and retreating down a steep rock bank last we saw of them. They would never have been able to get the drop on Gilbert Metts. He's one of them kind of men who has eyes in the back of his head."

"Then what happened to him?" Murdock asked.

"I don't know," said Moses. "Maybe he deserted on me." He grinned. "Maybe he sold them horses somewhere and hightailed it out of here."

Murdock stood up and looked off along the trail

in the failing evening light. "I hope so . . . else you could have soldiers on your tail right now."

"Relax," Moses chuckled. "This ain't the first army patrol I ever bushwhacked. If they did get their horses back from Metts and start trailing us, let them come." He nodded at the men gathered around the fire. "This bunch might look ragged, but don't ever think they can't fight. There ain't a day goes by that I ain't prepared for somebody attacking us from some direction or another. Me and these men live for the smell of battle, Murdock. I wouldn't have it any other way."

"You and your men have been at it a long time, Moses," said Murdock. "I didn't mean to cast any doubt on your judgment."

"I know you didn't," said Moses. "You just want to know more about the kind of man you're riding with. I don't blame you." He gave Murdock a serious look as he sipped his coffee. "You'll see soon enough for yourself, I reckon. I've got a sneaking hunch we've had a posse fanning our trail ever since we left Rileyville. I think it's time we sent them packing, don't you?"

Doc Murdock grinned and said, "Damn right, Moses. Why not?"

Cherokee Rhodes and Campbell Hayes rode abreast forty yards ahead of the others on the trail to Diablo Espinazo. Junior the hound loped along near Hayes' horse. The riders had pushed hard throughout the night. At the first glimpse of sunlight, Hayes drew his tired horse to a halt and slumped a bit in his saddle, his lack of trust in Cherokee Rhodes causing him to keep his right hand ever close to his holstered Walker Colt. Junior circled once and sat down in the dirt, his tongue hanging out of his mouth.

"We stop here, Rhodes," Hayes said to the half-breed. "Let the rest of them catch up to us and rest their horses."

"We've already stopped too much overnight," said Cherokee Rhodes, drawing his horse down and circling it in closer to Hayes. "If we're ever going to catch up to the Peltrys, we best keep moving."

Campbell Hayes kept his horse turned sideways to the half-breed as he spoke. "If we run these horses into the ground, we'll never catch up to them either." He eyed Cherokee Rhodes closely and added, "Or is that what you're hoping for?"

"Maybe you wasn't listening, Hayes. I showed up on my own. Nobody is forcing me to do this." He thumbed himself on the chest. "I've got my own reasons for wanting to catch up to the Peltrys. If you don't like it, you can go to hell!" He pointed at Junior, who had stood up and stepped forward with a low growl. "Keep that stinking dog away from me, or I'll hammer its head in with a pistol butt!"

"Make no mistake, half-breed," said Hayes, his big, rough hand closing around the bone handle of the Walker Colt. "Lay a hand on that dog, and I will kill you graveyard dead. Put us in a jackpot, and I'll go to hell all right . . . dragging you with me by the hair on your greasy head."

"Damn it! They're ready to kill each other," said Will Summers from thirty yards back. Seeing Hayes' hand on the big pistol and seeing Cherokee Rhodes back his horse a step and point a warning finger at Hayes, Summers kicked his horse's pace up a notch. Abner Webb and Sergeant Teasdale did the same and followed Summers to where the two men faced off in the middle of the trail. "Hayes! Rhodes! Both of you settle yourselves down! Take your hands off your guns right now!" Summers shouted, sliding his horse to a halt almost between the two. His hand snapped up from his holster with his Colt .45 cocked and ready. "Rhodes, don't make me sorry I gave that pistol back to you."

Hayes and Cherokee Rhodes both cut their gaze to the gun in Summers' hand, then to Abner Webb and Sergeant Teasdale as the two came sliding in beside Summers, both of them with their pistols drawn as well. "Him first," said Rhodes, keeping his hand clenched around his pistol butt.

"Both of you!" shouted Summers. "We're too close to the Peltrys to tip our hands this way! What the hell's wrong with you two anyway? One shot, and we've lost any element of surprise!"

"I can't abide this thieving, back-shooting trash riding near me," said Campbell Hayes, "let alone riding front scout right beside me!"

"All right then," said Summers, seeing that neither man was willing to back down first, "let's get it going then . . . all three of us. You hardheaded son-sabitches want to go out this way, I'll go right out with you. When I count three, you better both make a move, 'cause I'm just going to start shooting!"

"This ain't got nothing to do with you, Summers," said Hayes, still glaring at Cherokee Rhodes. "Stay out of it."

"No. I'm in it," said Summers. "One . . ." He raised his cocked pistol slightly and fanned it back and forth from one to the other.

"Stay out for just a couple more minutes, Summers," said Cherokee Rhodes. "I'll shoot this stiff-necked peckerwood, and we'll go on after the Peltrys. The way he's going, we'll never catch up to them anyway."

"No," said Will Summers. "I'm in on this. You boys better get ready. Webb, Teasdale, you better step your horses away." He kept the pistol moving back and forth slowly between them, a resolved look on his face. "Two . . ."

Beside Summers, Abner Webb and Sergeant Teasdale widened the space between their horses and his. Teasdale said in a low, warning voice, "Hayes, I brought you along so you could avenge your friend, not so you could fly off the handle and jeopardize this whole party. I swear to you right now, if Rhodes or Summers doesn't kill you, I will."

"Same here, Rhodes," said Deputy Webb, pointing his pistol in Rhodes' direction.

"Three . . ." said Summers. His hand tightened on his pistol butt.

"*Hold it*," said Campbell Hayes quickly, knowing that Will Summers wasn't bluffing. His hand moved upward away from his big Walker Colt. "There. It's settled. The sergeant's right. I came along to avenge my friend's death . . . not shoot it out with the likes of this saddle tramp."

Cherokee Rhodes bristled at Hayes' words, but he held himself in check and lifted his hand away from his gun butt. "It's been a long night. I might be a little bit testy. Mighta said things I shouldn't have."

"That's more like it," said Will Summers, keeping his cocked pistol moving back and forth just in case. "Both of you back your horses away from one another. Keep some distance until you both start acting like you've got some sense." He sat watching until both men had backed their horses and pulled away from one another. Hayes moved his horse back beside Sherman Dahl and crossed his wrists on his saddle horn—a gesture of peace after the tense encounter. Cherokee Rhodes swung wide of the others and sat looking back at Summers.

"Damn it," said Abner Webb. "We can't put up with any more of that kind of stuff."

"We're not going to," said Summers, just between Webb and Sergeant Teasdale. "Any more trouble between those two . . . shoot them both." He nudged his tired horse forward, saying over his shoulder, "Keep an eye on Rhodes. I'll ride on and scout the trail a while."

No sooner had Summers ridden out of sight around a turning in the trail than Bobby Dewitt came leading his horse up behind the rest of the men. Looking at Sherman Dahl, he asked, "What's going on, schoolmaster?"

"Just a little trouble between the buffalo hunter, Hayes, and Cherokee Rhodes," said Dahl.

He nodded forward along the trail. "Looks like we'll be in Diablo Espinazo before long. Maybe we can rest our animals there . . . for a couple of hours anyway."

"Yeah, maybe so," said Bobby Dewitt, staring at the trail ahead, where thin slices of morning sunlight spilled sidelong through towering rock.

For the next twenty minutes, Will Summers rode ahead of the others toward the small clearing where Diablo Espinazo stood on a terraced level of rough rocky ground high on a mountain trail. At a spot where fifty feet of trail lay engulfed by rock wall on either side, Summers hurried his horse along until the trail opened back up beneath him. Where a thin elk trail snaked down from above and crossed the main trail, Summers stopped at the sound of a goat's bell clanging, coming down from the rocks. An old man followed four goats out onto the main trail, not seeing Will Summers until Summers touched his hand to his hat brim and said *"Buenos días"* to him.

The old goatherder stopped abruptly with a look of fear in his eyes. *"Sante Madre!"* he whispered. The goats scurried across the trail and disappeared down the rocky slope on the other side.

Will Summers knew why the old man looked so frightened. He added quickly, "Don't worry, old fellow, I'm not one of the Peltry Gang. Are they still there?" He nodded in the direction of the small town.

"No, they go in the night . . . thanks be to the blessed Virgin Mother," said the old man, sweeping his broad straw sombrero from his head and making the sign of the cross. "They are terrible animals, these Peltry *hombres*! They come to our little town, and they force us to do their will! Every time they come to these mountains, someone dies before they are through."

"Which way did they go?" Summers asked.

"Southwest," the old man said without hesitation. "They go to cross the border. Always they spend the cold months in México, as if that poor country of my birth can tolerate their kind." He shook his head and walked on, turning his back on Summers, following his goats off the trail down into the rocks. Summers relaxed in his saddle and waited until Webb and Teasdale came riding up to him ahead of the others.

"What did he have to say?" asked Webb, nodding toward the old man as he descended down the slope behind the goats.

"He said the Peltrys pulled out in the night," Will Summers replied. "Sounds like they're headed for the border."

Teasdale and Webb both looked disappointed. "Well . . . then we stay on their trail," said Teasdale. "At least, as far as I'm concerned."

"Me too," said Abner Webb. They both looked at Summers.

"Something doesn't feel right," Summers said, staring down the slope after the old man.

"What do you mean?" asked Webb, exchanging a glance with Teasdale.

"I'm not sure. . . ." Summers looked back at the rest of the men riding toward them. He looked forward along the trail to where it disappeared into a turn. He looked up along the high rocky line above them, then down at the old man just in time to see him break into a run toward the cover of taller rocks, shooing the goats out of his way.

"Oh no!" cried Summers, realization setting in and causing him to sit bolt upright in his saddle. "It's a trap!" He swung his horse out into the middle of the trail and yelled at the rest of the men as he jerked his hat from his head and waved it at them. "Get back! Stop! Take cover!" But the men did not stop all at once. Instead, they slowed behind Hargrove and Sherman Dahl as the two men raised their hands and checked their horses down.

"What's got into him?" Hargrove asked Dahl.

Sherman Dahl hadn't the slightest idea. Yet no sooner had he seen Summers waving his hat than he caught a glimpse of morning sunlight glinting off the end of a rifle barrel atop the rocky ledge above Will Summers. "It's an ambush! Don't ride in!" Dahl shouted, his reflexes sharp and already responding. His rifle came up from his lap as he spoke.

In the middle of the trail, Will Summers had done all he could. He'd warned the others. Now, seeing Dahl's rifle belch a streak of fire upward along the rocky ledge, Summers ducked low in his saddle as rifle fire began to explode above him. Just as he jerked his horse around and spurred it to where Teasdale and Webb had jumped down and taken cover in a rock crevice, a body thudded to the ground at his horse's hooves. Dahl's shot had nailed the gunman before he could get his shot off at Summers. Even as Summers' horse reared and spun away, Summers caught a glimpse of Dahl's smoking rifle as the young schoolmaster levered a new round into the chamber.

"Get into the rocks! Protect your horses!" Hargrove bellowed at the men. They had broken into a run in every direction, diving for any cover they could find. Some of their horses had already bolted away. They ran back along the trail, whinnying loudly, escaping bullets that whistled past them.

Summers gigged his horse toward the safety of the crevice where Teasdale and Webb stood firing up at the ledge. "You're wasting your bullets!" Summers shouted, sliding down from his horse's back and jerking his rifle from his saddle boot. "We've got to get on the other side of the trail—get a better angle of fire!"

"I'll cover you both," said Teasdale. "Make a run for it. Get over there, then cover me."

"Ready when you are," said Will Summers, shoving his horse farther back into the crevice and spinning his reins around a jut of rock.

"I'm ready right now," said Webb, his gun barrel smoking from the shots he'd just fired upward at the riflemen.

"Go!" said Teasdale.

Summers and Webb darted zigzagging across the trail, their rifles in hand. Bullets kicked up dirt and rock at their feet. On the other side of the trail, the two lunged over the edge and rolled among dirt and rock until they stopped themselves and crawled quickly behind a low-standing rock terrace. "Here he comes—cover him!" shouted Will Summers, aiming and firing upward along the rock ledge where long drifts of rifle smoke wafted on the air.

The rifles concentrated their fire on Sergeant Teasdale as he made his run for the rocky slope. When he came sliding in beside Will Summers, a shot sent his hat spinning from his head. "Are you hit, Sergeant?" asked Abner Webb.

"No, I'm fine," said Teasdale without even checking himself. He began firing upward at the riflemen. "They've got our men pinned down over there— we've got to help them!"

"Damn it!" said Summers, stopping long enough to hurriedly reload his rifle. "If only I'd seen through this thing sooner. The old goatherder fooled me."

"We're lucky you saw though it at all," said Teasdale through the sound of rifle fire. "Another few feet and our men would have been stuck on the open trail with nowhere to hide."

"Was that old man one of the Peltry Gang?" asked Abner Webb, firing as he talked.

"No," offered Teasdale. "That old goatherder wasn't one of the Peltrys; they just made him come down here and stop us on the trail, hoping to bunch us up as much as possible. They're probably holding his family to make sure he did what he was told."

"Either way," said Summers, raising his loaded rifle and taking aim along the rock ledge, "they've caught us with our britches down around our ankles."

"Then we better pull them up and get out of here quick," said Teasdale, "before they cut our men to pieces."

On the other side of the fifty feet of walled trail, Sherman Dahl and Trooper Hargrove had pushed and goaded Wild Joe Duvall, Trooper Doyle Benson, Edmund Daniels and Bobby Dewitt farther down the side of the steep rocky slope. But then, seeing where the men were headed, Sherman Dahl yelled, "No! Stop! Don't go out there!"

Not far from Dahl and Hargrove, behind a short rock barely large enough to protect them both, Campbell Hayes, Cherokee Rhodes and Junior the hound lay piled upon one another, watching "The damned mindless fools," Hayes cursed as the other four men stepped out onto the footpath.

To get out of the rifle fire, Wild Joe, Trooper Benson, Daniels and Bobby Dewitt began to work their way down the narrow footpath, clinging to the rocks hand and foot. Wild Joe Duvall felt his rifle slip from his hand, but he dared not try to grab it or look down as it clattered away against the side of the rock wall. Rifle fire pelted down above them. Beneath them lay nothing but thin air for a distance of two hundred feet. Wild Joe grasped his stomach, then looked at his hand and saw that it was covered with his blood. "Oh Lord . . ." He swooned slightly. Behind him, Edmund Daniels helped to steady him. "I swear, I do believe I've been shot in the belly." He let out a crazy, halfhearted laugh. "Ain't this the damndest thing?" He sank almost to his knees before he caught himself and stepped backward against Edmund Daniels.

"Hang on, Joe—damn your hide!" said Daniels. "You're going to cause us both to fall!"

Still on the slope, hunkered down behind a large, half-buried boulder, Sherman Dahl and Hargrove fired upward as shots pounded all around them. Dahl cut a glance to the line of men inching their way along the narrow footpath where Wild Joe had stopped and caused the others to come to a halt behind him. "They'll die out there if we can't stop them!" Dahl shouted above the gunfire.

"What have you got in mind?" asked Hargrove.

"I'm going up there," said Dahl, nodding upward toward the line of steady rifle fire. "There's another ledge thirty feet above them. If I get in there, I can do us some good."

"You're crazy, young man," said Hargrove. "You won't make it across the trail, let alone up the rock wall. They'll kill you!"

"I can make it," said Dahl. "I've got to try . . . else we're all dead!" He ventured a look toward Summers, Webb and Teasdale sixty yards away. "If they can see what I'm doing, and all of you give me some support fire, I can get a good start up there. Once I'm tucked in above them, the Peltrys will have a devil of a time getting to me. It'll cost them some men, that's for sure."

Hargrove considered it as he bit his lip and ventured a gaze along the higher ledge. Shots concentrated in his direction, forcing him and Dahl to flatten behind the rock. When the fire slackened, he turned to Dahl. "All right, schoolmaster. I'll cover you."

Chapter 13

"What the hell is he doing?" shouted Abner Webb, seeing Dahl leap forward and make a run across the trail.

"I don't know, but give him some help," said Teasdale.

"Looks like our schoolmaster has more guts than he does good sense," Will Summers said as he fired.

The three men fired as one, hard and steadily, sending a heavy barrage of fire in the direction of the riflemen above Sherman Dahl. Along the rocky ledge, Goose Peltry, Moses Peltry and Doc Murdock ducked back as bullets whistled past them from the trail below. "Whooieee!" Goose laughed aloud. "I love seeing Yankees trapped like bugs in a bucket!"

"Yankees?" Doc Murdock shook his head. "I'm starting to think that to you two a *Yankee* is any poor sonsabitch you happen to be mad at."

"What's the difference?" said Goose. "Just be thankful you ain't one of them." He ventured a peep down over the edge. When he stood back, he looked at Moses and said, "Most of them has taken cover along that footpath that winds around the mountain. If you want to really have some fun today, brother Moses, send a couple of men down below the trail and watch them pick 'em off like ducks in a shooting gallery." Goose spread a flat, evil grin at Doc Murdock and Moses Peltry.

"I believe that's a sterling idea, brother Goose," said Moses with a bit of haughtiness to his voice, a bit of swagger in his stance. "Murdock," he added with a smug tilt of his head, "you're getting an eyeful of how my men work. Pay attention: You might learn something."

As the Peltrys and Murdock had been talking back and forth above the fray, Sherman Dahl had climbed hand over hand up the side of the rock wall with bullets slicing past him. The rifle fire from Summers, Webb, Teasdale and Hargrove partially protected him as he struggled upward. Soon he had flanked the gunmen and climbed up past them along a taller stand of rock wall fifty yards to their right.

"By damn, sir!" said Hargrove aloud to himself. "He's done it! He's climbed up above them!" He poured rifle fire up at the gunmen with renewed effort, seeing Sherman Dahl settle in on a short perch of rock from which he could easily fire down into the Peltrys without them being able to draw a bead on him. "Now let's give them hell, schoolmaster," Hargrove whispered.

Goose, Moses and Doc Murdock stood talking, still safely back a few feet from the cliff's edge, when Sherman Dahl opened fire on the line of gunmen. The first man to take a bullet was one of the Catt brothers, Little Catt, who stood up laughing at the trapped man only to feel an impact like the blow of a sledgehammer atop his head. He twisted down to the ground like a corkscrew, a crazed look of surprise frozen on his dead face.

"Little brother! Little brother, wake up!" demanded Big Catt, grabbing Little Catt and slapping his limp face.

But Goose, Moses and Doc Murdock already saw that the man was dead. "What hit him?" shouted Moses. They looked all around quickly, not noticing in the heat of battle that the killing shot had been fired down from above them.

On the firing line, lying next to Flat Face Chinn, Frank Spragg let out a grunt and relaxed down onto his face as a fountain of blood rose up from between his shoulder blades. "What the hell is this?" Chinn said, looking baffled for a second. But then, realizing what had happened, he scooted back from the firing line just as a bullet thumped into the ground where he had been. "They're above us!" he shrieked, turning and firing blindly at the high wall of rock where Sherman Dahl sat well protected in his nest of solid stone.

"You're right about me learning something, Moses," said Doc Murdock as he and the Peltrys ducked into a crouch and ran for cover. "I'm learning that one man with a rifle can send your whole gang packing."

"What?" Moses asked, not hearing Murdock in the melee.

"Nothing," said Murdock, dismissing it, grabbing his horse and pulling it away from the line of horses as another shot exploded down and nailed another gunman to the dirt.

"Damn it, pull back, men!" shouted Moses Peltry. "They've gotten the drop on us . . . the bush-whacking bastards!"

"There's only one man up there," said Doc Murdock. "Send a couple of my scalp hunters up there—they'll tan him for you!"

"No . . . not now," said Moses. "We've spent too long here as it is. We taught them a lesson . . . got them off our trail. It's time we cut out."

"What about sending a couple of men down below the trail like you said you were going to do?" asked Murdock, already knowing the answer but asking it just to put the Peltrys on the spot.

"This ain't the time or place, damn it, Doc," shouted Moses, grabbing his horse as another shot thumped into the ground near the animal's hooves.

Duckbill Grear and Andy Merkel ran in beside Doc Murdock, hearing Moses Peltry's words. "Doc, say the word," said Duckbill. "Me and Andy will slip down there and kill every one of them sumbitches."

Doc Murdock considered it quickly, watching Moses and Goose Peltry mount their horses and ride off toward a stretch of tree line along a flat terrace. "All right, men. Go do it . . . but keep these knot-heads from seeing you. Meet up with us down the trail. I'm starting to think I could scrape a better bunch of fighting men off a shithouse floor."

"We're gone, Doc," said Andy Merkel. Murdock watched the two men make their way around the high wall of rock and disappear onto a downward footpath.

Behind their rock on the lower side of the trail, Will Summers said to Abner Webb and Sergeant Teasdale, "Listen . . . they've stopped firing. I believe that schoolmaster has turned this fight around for us." The three looked upward, seeing only the tip of Sherman Dahl's rifle barrel reach out from behind a rock and fire down into the line of fleeing gunmen.

But as they spoke, Abner Webb caught sight of the two riflemen, Andy Merkel and Duckbill Grear, working their way down the slope on the other side of Hargrove and the men still clinging to the side of the mountain on the narrow footpath. "Look there!" he said.

"Blast it," said Teasdale. "Hargrove should have

seen them coming!" Behind his rock sixty yards away, Hargrove lay scanning the ledge above the trail. "The men on the path will never know what hit them," Teasdale said. "I better slip around behind the gunmen before they get into firing position."

"No, you stay here," said Summers. "I'll take care of them. If there's any bounty on them, I want to be the first one to know it." He slipped down onto his belly and crawled away into the rock and sparse brush along the steep slope.

Teasdale looked at Abner Webb as Summers moved unseen across the sloping mountainside. "What kind of man is he that bounty money is all that matters to him?"

"I can't say what kind of man he is anymore, Sergeant," said Webb. "I thought I knew until the other night. But now I can't say." In his mind, Webb pictured Will Summers pulling the trigger on the shot that killed Davis Gant. As he saw the scene play itself out, he recalled every second of it, every move, every flicker of an eye. . . . Yet, as he saw the outlaw fall dead on the ground, he realized that he could not recall the look on Summers' face as he let the gun hammer fall. "I can say this," he said, looking back at Teasdale and shaking the scene from his mind. "I trust him with my life."

Through the brittle brush, Will Summers belly-crawled until he'd circled down behind the two gunmen, coming to a spot behind a deadfall of sun-bleached pine. He raised his rifle up over the pine trunk just as a shot exploded from one of the men's rifles. On the exposed footpath, Summers watched Doyle Benson sink down on his knees, barely hanging on with Bobby Dewitt's help. Blood ran down the center of the young soldier's back. Bobby looked back and forth helplessly, realizing there was no place to hide. "Damn you to hell!" he shouted. "You could give us a fighting chance, you damn, yellow cowards!"

Summers raised up and took aim at Duckbill Grear as Duckbill prepared for a shot at Bobby Dewitt. Both rifles exploded at once. Bobby Dewitt slid down on his knees beside Doyle Benson, the two wounded men weaving back and forth, supporting one another.

"Two damn good shots, Duckbill!" said Andy Merkel, rising to his feet beside Duckbill. When Duckbill didn't answer, Andy turned to him and saw the dark blood running down from under Duckbill's hatband. "Duck! Are you okay?" Andy asked, seeing the strange distant look in Duckbill's eyes as the blood ran down into them. A strange sound came from Duckbill's chest. He toppled forward and landed flat on his face, the force of the fall sending his hat out onto the ground and exposing the large, steaming hole in the back of his head.

"Whoa now!" Andy Merkel sidestepped away, looking all around, his rifle chest-high, his thumb across the trigger. He'd only backed up three steps when Will Summers' shot hit him in his thigh, slamming him to the ground and sending his rifle sliding downward in loose gravel and dirt. He lay still on the ground for a second, listening to the footsteps move toward him through the brush and then stop.

"Throw your pistol out," said Summers, crouched and ready for whatever move the wounded man might try to make. "I know you're wounded; you best give up now. The rest of the gang has gone off and left you."

"They'll be back for me," said Andy Merkel, lifting a big Hoard pistol from his holster and cocking it quietly, listening, judging how close the footsteps were to him. "If you know what's good for you, you'll cut out now while you're still able."

"Drop the gun," said Will Summers, stepping suddenly into view, his pistol out at arm's length, cocked and ready.

But Andy Merkel would have none of it. He swung the big Hoard up. Will Summers shot him in the forearm. The pistol flew from Merkel's hand. He writhed in pain, clamping his left hand around his right forearm. Blood flowed down the sleeve of his filthy buckskin shirt. "Son of a bitch!" he bellowed. "What the hell is this? You shoot a man in the arm?" His enraged eyes glared at Will Summers. "You think that's all it takes for me? Then you're dead wrong!" He snatched at his boot well for his knife, but Will Summers kicked him backward, then stepped forward and clamped a boot down on his good hand, pinning it to the ground.

"Settle down, outlaw," said Summers. He looked at the body of Duckbill Grear, the dirty buckskins, the ragged headband and bits of bone and hair souvenirs pinned to the dead man's shirt. Then he looked back at Andy Merkel and said, "You two don't look like any of the Peltrys to me. Maybe we ought to talk about it some."

"Slap a loaded gun in my hand, mister—that's all we've got to talk about. We'll see which one leaves here with a hole punched in his gut."

"I just *might* slap a gun in your hand if you play your cards right, outlaw. Tell me what I want to know about the Peltry Gang. I'd sure hate dragging you and your stinking friend's carcasses up this mountainside."

"I never rode with the Peltrys before now, and neither did he. And I don't have a diddling-damn thing more to say to you, mister," said Andy Merkel.

"You might not think you do right now," said Summers, grinding his boot down on Merkel's hand, "but I bet you will before it's over."

Teasdale and Abner Webb gathered the men together in a defensive circle behind a large rock near the edge of the trail. The men had rounded up the horses and tied them a few yards away in the narrow shelter of a crevice between two tall upthrusts of rock. A few minutes had passed since a single pistol shot resounded from the direction Will Summers had taken in order to stop the two riflemen. Teasdale, Webb and the remaining survivors kneeled beside Bobby Dewitt and Wild Joe Duvall, both of whom were wounded. The pale, limp body of Doyle Benson lay beside them, his hands crossed on his chest.

"That poor . . . soldier boy," Wild Joe said, his voice strained by the bullet wound in his big stomach. "Is he? Is he . . . ?"

"Yeah, Joe," said Abner Webb, holding a canteen down close to Joe's bloody lips. "He's dead. Here, sip you some water." As Joe managed a short sip, Abner Webb cut a glance to Sergeant Teasdale and shook his head slowly.

"You . . . don't have to hide nothing . . . from me," said Wild Joe. "I know I'm done for."

"Sorry, Joe," Webb said softly. "I wouldn't have had this happen for nothing in the world."

"Hell . . . I know it, Deputy," Wild Joe responded, his voice sounding weaker as he spoke. He turned his head sideways toward Bobby Dewitt. "Looks like me and you . . . are going to take the long ride together, huh, Bobby?"

"It looks it, Joe," Bobby Dewitt said, his eyes glistening with tears. "I ain't feeling nothing down my legs." He struggled to hold back a sob. Then he asked, "Where's Will Summers? I've got to tell him something before I go."

"He'll be here directly, Bobby. Just try to hang on a while," said Webb.

"I ain't got long," said Bobby Dewitt, trying to rise up on his elbows and look around for Summers.

"Lie still now, Bobby," said Webb, pressing him gently back down on the dirt. "Is it anything you can tell me instead?"

Bobby Dewitt grimaced and seemed to consider it for a second. "Naw . . . I best try to hang on till Summers gets here." He looked at Sherman Dahl, who had come down from his rocky perch and crouched on one knee, his rifle butt propped on the ground beside him. "Schoolmaster, I hope you won't hate me once you hear it."

"I won't hate you, Bobby, whatever it is," said Dahl.

"Sure you can't tell me?" asked Abner Webb.

Bobby Dewitt searched Webb's eyes for a second, then let out a breath of resignation. "All right. . . . I'll tell you, Deputy. It was me who let the Peltrys know that the sheriff was out of town that day." He looked down, ashamed to see the faces of the men around him. "I—I knew you'd be busy with the Daniels' woman. I told them that too."

"Aw, Bobby, no," said Webb with regret. "I wish you hadn't told me that." Junior the hound stepped forward and poked his wet muzzle into Bobby Dewitt's face. Webb pulled Junior back as the dog tried to lick the wounded cowboy's face.

"I feel awful about it," said Dewitt. "I figured I better square it up before I meet my maker."

Edmund Daniels stood back quietly from the others and stared off into the distance as if he hadn't heard Bobby's words. Sergeant Teasdale cut a glance to Daniels, but only for a second, starting to get the picture of what had gone on between Webb and Daniels' wife. "Man oh man," he whispered under his breath. The bruises on both Webb's and Daniels' faces began to make sense to him.

"What's done is done; it can't be changed now," said Deputy Webb. "But I'm glad you told us, Bobby, just to get it off your chest."

A painful moan came from Wild Joe Duvall, causing the men to turn away from Bobby Dewitt. "Lord God! This is . . . starting to hurt something fierce," said Joe.

"Hold onto my hand, Wild Joe," said Deputy Webb. "It'll help some."

Wild Joe's bloodsoaked gloves closed around Webb's right hand and squeezed. "Deputy . . . if it ain't no trouble . . . will you bury me some place pretty, not where it's just dirt and rock?"

"We'll try, Joe—you've got my word," said Webb. "I'll mark your spot real clear, so's if your wife and boy want to have you moved back home, you won't be hard to find."

"That's good, real good, Deputy." Wild Joe fell silent for a second, squeezing his eyes shut. A trace of a tear came to the corner of his eye. "I don't know how my boy'll take this. He thinks I'm a hero. I promised him . . . a shooting finger from one of the Peltrys."

"I'll talk to him, Joe," said Webb. "I'll tell him you done the best you could."

"I never really was . . . a tough fellow, Deputy. I just played it that way . . . for my boy, you know? Wanted my son to grow up a good man."

"I understand, Joe," said Webb. "We all understand."

Wild Joe looked around at the faces of the men. "I

had no business out here. Wish I could change it some way. Just stay home with my boy, my woman. All the rest never meant nothing, Deputy. I wish I'd known it then . . ."

Wild Joe Duvall's eyes glazed over as his breath ceased in his chest. His head went limp and relaxed on the ground.

"Damn the Peltrys for causing all this," Abner Webb said, his voice soft and cracking a bit as he spoke. "And damn us for coming out here. This was madness." He stood up from beside Wild Joe's body and rubbed his tired eyes. "I can't keep watching good men die like this. This is like being stuck in some kind of nightmare with no way to wake up."

"Take it easy, Deputy," said Sergeant Teasdale, seeing Abner Webb starting to come unraveled. "We're all upset right now. But we'll feel better after we get these men buried and get on our way."

"Yeah, we'll get on our way all right, Sergeant," said Webb, trying to steady his voice. "I'm taking these men home—what's left of them. This killing is going to stop right here and now. Dahl, you and Daniels get your horses ready. We're heading back for Rileyville."

"The hell you say!" Sergeant Teasdale gave him a look of disbelief. "Take a look there, Deputy." He pointed down at Doyle Benson's pale, dead face. "That young soldier is dead because he followed me and you. He gave his life for this manhunt. Now, because some blood's been shed, you want to strike up and cut out with your tail between your legs? Not unless you walk through me first, Deputy." Teasdale took a firm stand, his feet shoulder-width apart. "I owe this trooper that much."

"Don't face off with me, Teasdale. I'm warning you!" Webb growled. "I'm not going any farther, and

I'm not going to fight you or anybody else over it."
He looked back at Sherman Dahl and Edmund Daniels. "Let's go, men. We don't have to stick with this."

"Speak for yourself, Webb," said Edmund Daniels. "I said I'm staying, and I meant it. You want to show the world the color of your stool, suit yourself. I pegged you as a low, sneaking rat to begin with."

"I reckon I deserve that from you, Daniels." Webb bristled but kept himself in check, knowing Daniels' opinion of him. "I'm not going to argue with you either. Far as I'm concerned, you and I had our fight, and it's over."

"There ain't a damn thing over between you and me, Webb. It won't be over until one of us is under the sod."

"Have it your way, Daniels." Webb turned his attention to Sherman Dahl. "What do you say, schoolmaster? Are you ready to ride back to Rileyville and put all this behind you?"

"If it's all the same to you, Deputy," said Dahl in a soft-spoken tone, "I want to see this through."

"So does he," said Will Summers, cutting in as he stepped in among the others, a dusty feed sack hanging heavy in his right hand. "He's just blowing off some steam. Pay no attention to him."

"No," said Webb, turning toward him. "I mean it. I had no right getting these men to follow us out here—"

"They came because they wanted to come, Webb," said Summers. "Now turn it loose. We're just getting started." He hefted the feed sack up slightly, enough to draw Webb's and the men's attention to the weight of it.

Abner Webb stared blankly at the sack for a sec-

ond, unsure what Summers meant. But then he saw
the long drop of dark blood drip from the bottom of
the sack, and he recoiled at the sight of it. His eyes
went to the bloody knife handle sticking up from
Will Summers' belt. "My God in heaven, no," Webb
gasped. His voice sounded shaky and ill as he took
a step back. "Don't tell me you've done something
like that."

"It's done, all right," said Summers. "I brought
along that feed sack for this very reason. I'm not
about to haul their stinking carcasses all over the
desert when all we need is enough to get identifica-
tion for the bounty money." He dropped the sack on
the ground with a thud. "These two rode with Doc
Murdock. One said his name was Andy Merkel. He
claimed he wasn't worth anything, but I brought him
along anyway, in case he's lying. I recognized the
other one. He's Duckbill Grear. He's worth a thousand dollars, dead or alive." Summers looked
around, studying the faces of the men.

Abner Webb also studied their faces, seeing the
cold-edged resolve in the tired, wary eyes. Campbell
Hayes stood up and stepped over near the feed bag.
He reached out with his foot and rolled one of the
heads back and forth slightly. "I don't know about
the rest of yas, but this makes me feel a little better.
I'll feel better yet when it's Moses' and Goose's heads
in that bag. I know we missed some back there, but
it can't be helped. I reckon the buzzards and coyotes
get their bounty."

Cherokee Rhodes made a dark chuckling sound as
he looked down at the outline of the two heads. "I
knew both those boys. There ain't a better ending for
either one of them, far as I'm concerned." He looked
at Will Summers. "But if Doc Murdock and his hair

lifters have thrown in with the Peltrys, it's going to
make this job a little tougher. If anybody truly wants
to go home, this is the best time to do it."

Abner Webb avoided the eyes of the men and
looked off into the distance. "I got a little carried
away there, but I'm all right now." He turned to
Summers and nodded down at Bobby Dewitt on the
ground. Dewitt had been watching through fading
eyes, his hands grasping the bloody exit wound in
his stomach. "Bobby here just told us he's the one
tipped off the Peltrys."

Will Summers looked surprised, but only for a second. "That's too bad, Bobby," he said, stooping
down beside the wounded cowboy as he spoke. He
lifted the range pistol from Bobby's holster and
looked it over. "I thought a lot of you."

"I'm sorry I let you down," Bobby said in a
trembling voice.

"So am I," Summers whispered. He opened the
range pistol, dropped the cartridges out into his
palm, stuck one back in the cylinder and snapped it
shut. "In light of that, you wouldn't expect us to wait
here while you die, would you?" He laid the pistol
on Bobby Dewitt's chest.

"Wait a minute," said Abner Webb. "That's Bobby
lying there, not some stranger. Surely we can give
him a few minutes—"

"It could take hours," said Summers, cutting Webb
off. "When he tipped off the Peltrys, he became re-
sponsible for everything that's happened since." He
looked back down at Bobby Dewitt. "Does leaving
you a gun with one bullet seem fair enough to you?"

"I ain't complaining," Bobby said, his voice
weaker now.

"The Peltrys know we're on their tails, Deputy,"
Summers said to Webb. "We've got to press them

hard now." He turned to the others. "I hope nobody here is too shocked or outraged by all of this killing. It's exactly what we came here to do."

"Damn it," said Abner Webb. He swung around and grabbed a canteen from Hargrove's hands and pitched it down by Bobby Dewitt's side. "At least leave a dying man some water." He turned and stomped away toward the horses.

"I'll go talk to him," said Sherman Dahl, rising up slowly and cradling his rifle in his arms.

"Let him be, Dahl," said Summers. "He knows what I said is right. That's why he's upset by it. Killing is never what a man imagines it will be like." His eyes went across the men's faces, then he added in a lowered tone, "Thank God for that."

Chapter 14

Moses and Goose Peltry led the riders back into the Diablo Espinazo clearing at a hard gallop, the horses' pounding hooves raising a cloud of dust and sending the goats and their owners in every direction. The goatherders could tell by the look on the Peltrys' faces that things had not gone as expected. Goose Peltry slid down from his horse before it came to a complete stop. Moses circled his horse near the well in the center of the clearing. His men grouped up around him. A few feet away, Doc Murdock reined in and slid down from his saddle, his band of scalp hunters bunching up by his side. Murdock gazed back along the dusty trail, searching for any sign of Duckbill Grear or Andy Merkel.

"You're wasting your time looking for them two boys, Murdock," said Moses Peltry, giving Murdock a cold stare. "If they were still alive, they'd already been here by now. Looks like you mighta got them both killed."

Murdock gave him a curious look.

"That's right; I don't miss a thing goes on around me. I knew you sent them back the minute you did it," said Moses. "You just had to show me that your men could pull it off, didn't ya? Well, they're both dead now. Maybe next time you'll listen a little closer to what I've got to say." He wrapped both hands around his long beard and stared at Murdock.

"It was the right thing to do at the time," said Doc Murdock defiantly. "If those two men only took out a few of the posse, it was worth doing it. It'll make the rest of that bunch think twice before coming after us. If you hadn't left anybody alive the other day, they wouldn't be trailing us to begin with. Now that we had the posse dead in our sights, we should've stayed and finished them off."

"Hell, I just wanted to see how we worked together, Murdock," said Moses. "As far as getting the posse off our trail, we're old hands at that, Goose and me." He gestured with a toss of his head toward Goose Peltry. "Brother Goose is getting ready to show you a dandy way of doing that without wasting any ammunition on them." He nodded toward his brother, who came riding his horse over to them. Goose had a short rope in his hand. At the other end of it, an old goatherder wobbled along barefoot in the dirt. The old man's face had already turned blue from the rope circling his neck. His hands were tied behind his back. "You watch close now, Doc," Moses chuckled. "This works most every time."

"Dupre's bringing one more just like this one." Goose chuckled, swinging the old man forward toward the center of the clearing at Moses' feet. "If two ain't enough, we'll grab some more. It's like snatching chickens for a Sunday dinner."

A few yards behind Goose came Monk Dupre on his horse, leading an old woman on a rope in the same manner. "This one offered me her goat money to leave him alone," said Dupre. "Can you imagine her thinking I could be bought off like some common thug?" He slung the old woman forward. "Get over there, you old hag. You ought to be ashamed of yourself, trying to bribe an honest, upright man like me!" Dupre shouted. The woman landed in a puff of dust, sobbing and praying.

"What are you getting ready to do, Moses?" Murdock asked.

"Like I told you, Doc, I'm going to get that posse off our tails before we move down into Old Mex. These two are going to deliver a little message for us. Aren't you, old woman?"

"Por favor, tiene misericordia! No nos mate!" the old woman pleaded.

"Ain't that pitiful?" said Moses to Doc Murdock. "She's begging me not to kill her and the old man." Moses laughed, reaching out with his boot toe and raising her chin up to face him. "Kill you? Now, what ever gave you a notion like that?"

"This ain't going to make that posse think twice about staying on our trail," said Doc Murdock. "If anything, this will make them more determined."

"Either way, this'll tell what kind of men they are. Then we'll know how best to handle them," said Moses Peltry. He looked down at the woman's terrified face and gave her a flat grin. "Ain't that right, old woman?"

"Por favor, por favor!" Her frightened eyes flashed to Doc Murdock then back to Moses Peltry. "Do not let him scalp us!" she begged.

Moses laughed louder and shoved her away with the toe of his boot. "Did you hear that, Murdock?" he said. "She's begging me not to let you scalp her and her husband. Sounds like your reputation has preceded you."

"Yeah, I heard her," said Murdock, frowning down at the old couple in the dirt. "Can't say I

thought much of it either. That's what I get for trying
to be kind, I reckon."

"I always say it never pays," Moses Peltry said,
still staring down at the old woman.

Doc Murdock went on. "I admit there might have
been a couple scalps made it across the counting
table that weren't exactly Apache." He turned a flat
grin to Moses Peltry. "But hell, I never claimed me
and the boys were perfect." He reached down, entwined his fingers in the old woman's hair and lifted
her bowed head. She gasped. "But don't you fret,
old crone. You ain't worth a thin *peso* to me—unless
I just want to do it for practice." He turned her hair
loose and let her head fall to her chest.

"Don't beg these lousy pigs for nothing, Soledad,"
said the old man, rising up to his knees beside her.
He reached his tied hands to one side behind his
back and clasped her weathered hand in his. "If
they're going to kill us, begging won't stop them.
Don't give them the satisfaction."

Moses Peltry looked down at the old man. "Well
now, there's some spirit. Do I hear a little Alabama
accent there? You're American, ain't you, old
goatherder?"

"That's right, I'm an American . . . southern Alabama born and raised. And we won't beg you for
our lives! I've shit a better wad than you on an empty
stomach, you rotten bunch of saddle trash!"

On the trail less than two miles from Diablo Espinazo, Webb, Summers and Teasdale reined up for
a second at the head of the riders as the distant
sound of a pistol barked six times in rapid succession. "I've got a hunch that wasn't target practice,"
said Teasdale, heeling his horse forward again. They

rode on in silence until in the distance behind them they heard a single pistol shot, this one coming from where they had left Bobby Dewitt with his range pistol across his lap.

Webb shook his head. "It still doesn't seem right, us leaving Bobby Dewitt to die alone that way, no matter what he did."

"You heard him call it, Deputy," said Summers. "Your problem is, you think too much. Sometimes it's best to put things out of your mind. All things considered, we could have done a whole lot worse by him."

"Seems to me I'm putting too much out of my mind lately," said Webb. They rode farther in silence. Then he said, "The other day, when I asked if you'd done any killing, and you kept beating around the bush . . . I thought at the time it was because you were bluffing, not wanting me to know that you'd never really killed anybody." He looked Summers up and down as he spoke. "But that wasn't it at all, was it?"

"Nope," said Will Summers without facing him. Sergeant Teasdale remained quiet, listening to the two men as he rode along beside them.

"It's just something you don't like talking about or admitting to, isn't it?" Webb asked.

"That's right, Deputy," said Summers, staring straight ahead along the trail into Diablo Espinazo. "Killing ain't something I like confessing to. Talking about it just brings it up all over again."

"I understand that now," said Abner Webb.

"I bet you do," said Summers. They rode in silence until they came to another halt, this time less than two hundred yards from the small clearing of a town. When they reined up, Will Summers slipped his rifle from his saddle boot, checked it and laid it across his lap. "What do you think, Sergeant?" he asked.

"I think we need to split up into twos and threes and come in from different directions in case there's a trap waiting for us in there."

"That sounds good to me. What about you, Deputy?" Summers and Teasdale both looked at Abner Webb for approval.

"Sounds good to me too," said Webb, drawing his rifle. "I just want to get this thing done as fast as we can and get back to Rileyville."

Summers and Teasdale gave one another a look. Then Summers sidled his horse closer to Webb. "The deputy and me will swing up onto the slope and ride down," he said. "Schoolmaster, you, Rhodes and Daniels sit still until you see us coming down, then ride in from here. Sergeant, you and your trooper take Hayes with you and swing around and come in from the other end of town." He looked around. "Anybody got anything to add?"

"Yeah," said Teasdale. "Everybody be real careful we don't get one another caught in a cross fire." He looked at the others and added, "The fact is, the Peltrys are probably already gone . . . but we're taking no chances. Anybody in there makes a wrong move, don't think twice about shooting them. Just make sure it's not one of us."

Webb and Summers pulled away from the others, cut up onto the sloping mountainside off the trail and circled up above Diablo Espinazo. They sat atop their horses, watching as Teasdale, Hayes and Hargrove circled down off the trail and came back toward the small town from the far side of the clearing. "All right, let's go," said Summers, seeing the others begin to make their move. Riding down the slope, Summers and Webb arrived in the dusty clearing only seconds before the other four men. But in those few seconds, they saw the grisly scene awaiting them, and they slid their horses to a halt.

"Lord God, what is this?" Webb whispered in revulsion. In the center of a wide clearing beside the stone wall of the community well, the bodies of the old man and his wife swung slowly back and forth from the limb of an ancient white oak.

"I'd say this was what those six shots we heard was all about," said Summers, nodding at the bullet holes in the old man's chest. "Easy, boy," he whispered to his horse, feeling the animal grow nervous beneath him. Then he said to Webb, "Stay right here. Keep an eye on the adobe. There's almost always somebody here." He coaxed his horse forward, drawing his knife from his boot to cut the bodies from the oak limb. But as Summers neared the tree and stood up in his saddle to reach the ropes above the bodies, a young man came running from the adobe swinging a machete, sobbing and cursing in Spanish.

"Summers, look out!" shouted Abner Webb. As soon as the young man heard Abner Webb's voice, he spun in Webb's direction and charged toward him from twenty feet away, the machete swinging back and forth, making a slicing sound through the air.

"Murderers! *Asesinar a perros!*" the young man screamed in blind rage.

"No!" Webb shouted. But his instincts took over as the long blade came slicing closer to him. His horse shied back, whinnying loudly, and tried to rear up with him. Just as the horse's front hooves lifted, Webb's rifle came up from his lap, cocked and fired. The young man's feet continued to run, but the ground no longer lay beneath them. He flew backward with the impact of the bullet hammering his chest. Then he hit the ground dead, a circle of blood spreading across his shirt. The machete clattered for a second on the hard-packed dirt, then fell silent.

Coming into the clearing from one end of town,

Sherman Dahl, Cherokee Rhodes and Edmund Daniels spread out, their rifles raised and ready. From the other end of the clearing, Teasdale, Hayes and Hargrove did the same. From the adobe came a long wail as an old woman ran out and flung herself onto the body of the young man lying in the dirt. "My God, I killed him," Webb said, staring down at the body, his rifle still smoking in his hand. His horse settled beneath him and scraped a hoof in the dirt.

Will Summers trotted his horse up to him, having cut the ropes and let the old couple's bodies fall to the ground. "I saw the whole thing, Deputy. He gave you no choice. It was you or him."

"No choice?" Abner Webb stared at Summers, stunned. "I—I killed him, Will. He thought I was one of them . . . and I killed him. Do you understand what I'm saying?"

"Yeah," said Summers. "More than you think."

From inside the adobe, more goatherders ventured out, the men with their straw sombreros in their hands, the women with shawls drawn across their heads. "Mother of God," an old goatherder whispered.

"Schoolmaster," said Summers as Sherman Dahl and Edmund Daniels came closer, "ride him out of here. He don't need to be here, and these people don't need to see him." Cherokee Rhodes stayed back, keeping his rifle up and ready, his eyes searching back and forth along the edge of the trail.

"Come on, Deputy," said Dahl, reaching a hand out to Webb's horse's bridle. "There's nothing you can do here. Let these people take care of the boy."

"The boy?" Webb looked crushed, realizing for the first time that the young man in the dirt was not much older than the schoolchildren he watched play every afternoon on the streets back in Rileyville.

"I didn't mean *boy*," said Sherman Dahl, seeing the effect his words had had on Webb. "Come on, let's go." He took Webb's horse by its bridle and began leading it toward the other side of the clearing.

"Turn loose of my horse!" said Webb, jerking his reins and seeming to snap out of a dark, trancelike state. Dahl dropped back, and he and Daniels followed Webb until the deputy stopped his horse and turned it around. Then Dahl and Daniels flanked him. The three of them sat watching the old goatherders pick up the young man and carry him to the adobe. One old woman looked over at Abner Webb, spit on the back of her hand and slung it toward the ground, cursing him.

"I should have warned him first," said Abner Webb. "I should have fired a warning shot over his head or something . . . anything at all instead of this."

"There was no time, Deputy Webb," said Sherman Dahl. "It happened too fast. I saw what you did. We all saw it. I expect all these people here saw it too. If you had waited another second, it would be you out there, and us picking you up. It was all a terrible mistake. . . . But which end of that terrible mistake would you rather be on?"

"Right now, I honestly don't know," said Webb, avoiding Dahl's eyes as he replied. "All I know is it's going to be a long time before I ever sleep nights. You're right about it happening too fast though. I swear it happened so fast it seems like nothing could've stopped it."

Edmund Daniels had been sitting in silence watching the people carry the body away. Quietly he said, "This don't change nothing between us, Deputy, but the schoolmaster's right. One of you was going to die out there. It might just as well have been him as you. There didn't seem to be anything going to stop it. Now there ain't nothing going to change it."

Without answering, Abner Webb stared straight ahead, watching some of the people go to the bodies of the old couple on the ground and tote them away toward the adobe. The old man's chest was riddled with bullet holes. A large portion of the old woman's scalp was missing. Summers, Teasdale and Hargrove trotted their horses over, joining them in a huddle. Campbell Hayes and Cherokee Rhodes stayed out in the center of the clearing, watching the trail in each direction.

"Damn, Deputy, are you all right?" Summers asked, keeping an eye on the goatherders as he spoke.

"Yeah, I'll do," said Webb. "Don't bother telling me it couldn't be helped. I've already been told."

"All right, I won't," said Summers. He nodded at the old couple's bodies as the goatherders carried them away. "This was the Peltrys' way of getting our attention . . . telling us to get off their trail. Only we're not going to listen to it, are we?" He looked at the men. They nodded silently.

"We're in too deep to turn back now," said Sherman Dahl, nodding toward the adobe where the sound of the old woman's grief could be heard as if seeping out of the ancient blocks of sun-hardened clay.

"Then what are we waiting for?" asked Sergeant Teasdale. "Fill your canteens, and let's get riding."

"I feel like I need to go say something to those folks . . . apologize or something," said Abner Webb. His face was ashen in torment; his lips looked pale and dry.

"Apologize? Damn little good that'll do them. They know you didn't come here to kill him," said

Will Summers. "There's nothing more can be said about it. All they know is that the two of you come upon this same spot of ground at the same time. Now one of you is dead and one is living. These people don't need life and death explained to them, especially not by the likes of us. It's best you leave them alone. They've seen a damn sight more of this sort of thing than any of us have."

"He's right, Deputy," said Sherman Dahl. "We need to ride. We may never get this close to the Peltrys again before they hit the border. All talking to these people will do is make you feel better, but it won't help them one bit."

"Then to hell with all of you. Let's ride!" said Abner Webb, jerking his horse around away from the others and gigging it off along the trail.

"You men hurry and take on water for yourselves," said Will Summers, lifting his canteen strap from around his saddle horn and pitching the canteen to Sherman Dahl. "Fill mine too. I'll catch up to Webb and keep an eye on him. Looks like he ain't thinking straight right now."

The men watched in silence until Will Summers' horse disappeared around a turn in the trail. "Whatever's bothering the deputy, I hope he gets over it pretty quick," said Campbell Hayes. He reached a hand down and idly patted Junior's head as the dog came up and sniffed at his leg. "A man needs to be at his best on this kind of manhunt." He looked over at Sherman Dahl and Edmund Daniels. "You men are both from Rileyville. What kind of man is the deputy?"

Instead of answering Hayes, Sherman Dahl looked at Edmund Daniels, deliberately turning the question over to him. "You know him better than I do, Daniels. What do you say?"

Edmund Daniels' jaw tightened, but then he swallowed hard, as if ridding himself of a bad taste in his mouth, and said, "When it comes to law work, I reckon I've seen worse." The men looked at him, waiting for more, but Daniels had no more to offer.

"If you're all through socializing," said Teasdale, "get watered and move out. We've got a long way to go."

Chapter 15

The German captain, Hans Oberiske, had dropped back from the head of the dusty column of Mexican *Federales* to rest his horse for a moment in the dark shade of a cliff overhang. To Captain Oberiske, riding patrol along the border this time of year was as close to being trapped in a hot, raging hell as he could imagine. From beneath the overhang, he stared out across the valley below and watched the heat swirl and dance as it rose ever upward. The flatlands were a white-hot living demon, he had come to believe, and whatever assignment brought him here he accomplished as quickly as possible, then hurried back into the cooler climate of the high mountain valleys.

"*Salud,*" he murmured to himself, practicing his Spanish. He raised his canteen as if drinking a silent toast to such wisdom. When he lowered the canteen, he resisted the urge to pour the rest of the tepid water over his burning neck. But it was dusk now, and soon the crisp night air would blow in and soothe his torment. He could wait another hour . . . surely he could. Since his arrival here with the German training forces over a year ago, this terrible land had taught him patience if nothing else. As he capped his canteen, he saw Sergeant Hector Hervisu riding back toward him along the line of tired horses and men.

"Capitán," said Hervisu, jerking his horse to a stop and spinning the animal in place. "Riders . . . many of them. They are coming down from the border. I believe it is the *loco americano* brothers and their men. They are heavily armed."

"Oh?" Captain Oberiske looked at him. "How heavily armed?"

"They are pulling a gun wagon with a big Gatling rifle on it, and they are also pulling a supply wagon filled up past its sideboards."

"A machine rifle, eh?" Captain Hans Oberiske perked up instantly. "Come, let's take a look at them. Perhaps it is time we confronted those two and explained to them exactly who is the real authority here."

"Sí, Capitán," said Hervisu. "But there are many of them: over a dozen, I think. And they are some bold *hombres*, these Peltrys."

As Captain Oberiske tapped his spurs to his horse's sides, he said over his shoulder to Sergeant Hervisu, "We have twenty-eight of your Mexican light cavalry here, Sergeant. Are you suggesting we cannot handle this band of American rabble?"

"No, *Capitán*, I would not dare suggest such a thing to you," said Sergeant Hervisu, gigging his horse forward and catching up to Captain Oberiske. "But as long as they have such powerful weapons, perhaps it is wise that we do not provoke them."

"Provoke them . . . ha! What do I care if we provoke them? We are the law in Mexico. We are the ones who established peace and put down the revolution here. We are the ones who should have such weapons, not them! You must learn to think and act with deliberation, Sergeant, if you and your nation are ever to amount to anything in this world."

"Sí, Capitán, you are right of course," said the ser-

geant. He followed quietly until the captain came to
the front of the column and raised a hand, halting
the tired men and horses.

Captain Oberiske raised a pair of binoculars that
he wore tied to a cord around his neck. Looking out
into the valley below in the failing light, he saw the
procession of riders and the two wagons filing across
the flatlands, both men and beasts pushing hard
toward a trail reaching in between two tall standing
rocks. "Ah, they go to the river valley." He lowered
the binoculars, wiped the lens on his shirtsleeve, then
raised them again.

"That is wise of them," said Sergeant Hervisu.
"They can travel many miles through the rocklands
with graze and water for their horses without ever
being seen."

"No, Sergeant, they are not wise," said Captain
Oberiske, looking out through the binoculars. "They
are stupid American bandits, nothing more."

Sergeant Hervisu gave a guarded look at some of
the men and shrugged, saying submissively, "*Sí, Capitán*, that is what I really meant. They are nothing
but stupid bandits, these *gringos*, but at least they
have managed to go in the right direction . . . perhaps
by mistake." He stifled a sly smile and shrugged at
the men again.

"I will have that machine rifle, Sergeant Hervisu,
rest assured of that," said Captain Oberiske, lowering
his binoculars again, this time rubbing his eyes from
the strain of focusing in the near darkness. "What
right have they to bring such a weapon into this
country? It will be a token of Germany's willingness
to guard the Mexican borders . . . and quite a useful
tool to help us do so, eh?" He chuckled.

"*Sí, Capitán*," said Sergeant Hervisu. The men nodded and chuckled in agreement.

"Shall I prepare the men to charge these stupid *gringos*?" asked Hervisu.

"From here? In this light? On this terrain? Of course not! Are you insane, Sergeant?" Captain Oberiske barked. He ran a forearm across his sweaty forehead and seemed to settle down. "No, we will hurry ahead of them and cut down into the river valley. We will be waiting for them when they arrive."

On the valley floor, at the head of the hard-riding men, Moses Peltry lowered his dusty field telescope from his eye, collapsed it in his gloved hands and put it inside his shirt. "*Federales*, just like we thought," he called out to Goose and Doc Murdock, who rode beside him. "They're turning and leaving now."

"Want to guess where they're going?" said Murdock.

"Guessing's not my job," said Moses. "My job is *knowing*." He gestured toward the river valley ahead. "They'll be waiting there for us. . . . You can count on that. If we can't shake them off our tails, we'll have to keep swatting them all the way to Punta Del Sol."

"Is that where we're headed?" asked Doc Murdock.

"Yep," said Moses, "but keep it between us three for now. We've still got to get into that river valley first, without getting shot all to hell."

Murdock looked back at the tired men and horses. "We can't beat them to the river valley. Our wagon horses are about dead right now."

"Naw, we can't beat them there," said Moses. "And if we did, think how bad that would hurt their feelings." He grinned and poked a gloved thumb back over his shoulder. "We'll step aside up here at the last minute and let our posse run smack into them. That ought to keep everybody busy for the rest

of the night while we circle around and go on about
our business."

"Good thinking," said Murdock, appearing
impressed.

"Yeah, scalp hunter," said Goose with a sarcastic
snap, nodding at the old woman's scalp tied to Murdock's saddle horn. "We know our business, same
as you know yours."

"That's real good to know, Goose," said Doc Murdock. "I'm beginning to realize that maybe you're
not nearly as stupid as you look."

Goose bristled, but Moses looked around just in
time to see his expression darken. He dropped his
horse a step back between the two of them. "Take it
easy, Goose. Doc meant that as a compliment, I'm
sure. Didn't you, Doc?"

"Hell, yes. If we can throw those *Federales* onto that
posse dogging our trail, you better believe I meant it
as a compliment." He grinned, booting his horse
forward.

Inside the entrance to the river valley where the
trail narrowed between the two towering chimneys
of upreaching stone, Captain Oberiske had positioned his men. They crouched low along both sides
of the trail in the black shadows of rock, listening,
waiting, their horses within arm's length. Beside the
captain, Sergeant Hervisu whispered, "*Capitán*, it is
not my place to say, but this is very dangerous in
the dark. Most of our men are young and inexperi-
enced. They have never been in this kind of a fight."

"You are right, Sergeant," said Captain Oberiske,
letting out an impatient breath. "It is not your place
to say anything! It is your place to observe and learn,
if that is at all possible! It is my place to teach you
how to lead troops and develop this savage, godfor-

saken wilderness!" The sound of horses' hooves thundering closer into the valley caused him to stop and turn his attention from Sergeant Hervisu to the darkness stretched before them. "Here they come! Prepare your men to rise up and charge, Sergeant!"

Fifty yards inside the towering rocks, the Peltrys' men knew what to do. The supply wagon and half the men had already broken away in the darkness and taken another trail, one leading wide of the river valley and around the line of foothills toward the Peltry hideout in Dead Horse Pass. The rest of the men still riding ahead of the gun wagon cut away swiftly and doubled back at the last second, their only purpose being to let the *Federales* hear the sound of their horses' hooves in the darkness. As they doubled back and beat a hasty retreat out of the valley, the gun wagon swung around fast and began pelting rapid gunfire across the soldiers' positions.

"Holy Mother of God!" shouted a young soldier, one of the first to gather quickly on the river valley trail to meet the oncoming riders. But now there were no oncoming riders, only an endless spray of hot lead as bullets sliced through the black air and through the flesh and bone of man and horse alike.

"It's a trick!" shouted Sergeant Hervisu. "Retreat, men! Run quickly!"

"No, you fools!" Captain Oberiske screamed above the exploding gunfire. "Get off the trail! Back into the rocks!"

But the men were not retreating. Nor were they taking to the rocks. Instead, they were bunched up mid-trail, seemingly stuck there, melting into a dying, tangled pile of flailing limbs and horseflesh beneath the insistent pounding of the machine rifle.

Then the firing stopped as abruptly as it had started. A voice from the gun wagon let out a long

rebel yell in the darkness as a wagon whip cracked
and the team of horses whinnied loudly and thun-
dered away.

"They're running! Charge them!" screamed Captain Oberiske, crawling over a dead horse and its
rider in the middle of the trail. His hand caught onto
the stirrup of a spooked horse, and he managed to
pull himself upward and grab the horse, settling it
enough to throw himself across the saddle. "Do not
let them get away! We must have that machine rifle!"

"Like hell you will!" came a taunting reply in the
darkness. And the chase was on.

On the speeding gun wagon stood Mort Spears
with both hands holding firmly onto the machine
rifle. He stayed crouched low, bracing himself against
the bucking wagon floor as he rounded two full turns
on the gun's crank, leaving a stream of fire in the
darkness behind him. "Yiii-hiiii!" he yelled. Beside
Spears stood Monk Dupre, one hand holding onto
the gun stand for dear life, his other hand planted
down atop his hat to keep it from blowing off. Driv-
ing the wagon was Elmer Fitzhugh.

"Let me know when to hightail it out of here!"
Fitzhugh shouted over his shoulder. He rode leaning
forward from his bouncing driver's seat, the long
reins slapping steadily in his left hand. In his right
hand he wielded a long whip above the backs of the
team of horses. On either side of the racing wagon,
the riders had begun to cut away. They raced off into
the night to join the Peltry brothers and Doc Murdock on the other trail around the foothills.

"Stay on the trail for now!" Spears shouted. "I'll
let you know when to cut out of here."

A half mile away on the other trail, Moses Peltry,
Goose and Doc Murdock stopped their horses. Having heard the last blast of gunfire, followed by the

sound of hooves drawing closer to them in the night, Moses smiled in the thin moonlight. "That should give them all something to do the rest of the night," he said.

"Think the posse will fall for it?" asked Murdock.

"What is there to fall for?" Moses chuckled, stroking his long beard. "When someone rides at you in the dark, shooting at you head-on, your choices are pretty simple. You either shoot back or die." He laughed quietly. Goose and Doc Murdock joined in, hearing the sound of horses' hooves slow down and draw closer until finally the approaching horses stopped, and a voice called out.

"Moses? Goose? Is that you?" asked Bert Smitson.

"Yeah, Smitson, it's us," Goose replied. "Get on over here so's we'll know who's who as you men ride in. Who's that with you anyway?"

"It's me, Flat Face," said Chinn.

"And me, Comanche Killer," said Brayton Cane.

"Handy Phelps back here," said another voice. "And there's more not far behind me."

"Yeah, I'm back here," said Pip Magger. "Man oh man, you ought to heard them soldiers screaming! That machine rifle ate them up and spit them out like soft goat meat! I got to get me one of them guns someday just to chase jackrabbits with, if nothing else."

A chuckle rose above the gathering men. More scattered hoofbeats came in along the dark trail. In the distance, another rapid volley erupted from the Gatling gun. "Damn, I hope your man Spears don't melt the barrel," said Goose. The blast of gunfire died down. Then sporadic rifle and pistol fire resounded from the soldiers chasing the wagon along the black trail.

"It won't be much longer, men," said Moses Peltry,

listening closely for any change in the firing. The men fell silent for a moment until they heard return rifle and pistol fire coming from farther down the trail. "There comes our posse now," Moses grinned. But his grin would have faded fast had he been able to see what had just happened to the gun wagon.

As soon as the Gatling gun had done its job and drawn fire from the *Federales,* Elmer Fitzhugh had turned the wagon sharply off the trail and sped it across the rocky dirt toward the other trail where the Peltrys and Murdock's men were waiting for them. Behind Fitzhugh, Monk Dupre and Mort Spears held on tight to the side rails of the gun wagon. "Slow down a little, Fitz!" Monk Dupre shouted. "Before you break a whee—"

His words had cut short as the spokes of the right front wheel splintered inside the steel band. "Oh no!" shouted Dupre as the front edge of the wagon began breaking apart. In the darkness, Dupre caught sight of Elmer Fitzhugh sailing off the driver's seat with the reins still in his hands. Then Dupre saw nothing but a swirl of darkness and dirt as he and Spears went tumbling through the air.

"Look out, Spears!" Dupre bellowed, sailing high from the crashing wagon.

The two men rolled and bounced across the flatlands, the Gatling rifle and its stand ripping loose from the wagon bed and keeping right up with them. Six shots exploded as the gun's crank hit the ground and turned. Then the gun collapsed in the dirt with its barrels smoking. In the silence that followed, Monk Dupre let out a groan and said "Fitz, you crazy . . . sumbitch. Moses is going to kill you." But Fitzhugh didn't answer. His right wrist and left leg had become tangled in the long reins. His broken body bounced along in a wake of dust behind the fleeing team of horses.

Farther back along the trail, at the first sound of oncoming gunfire, Sergeant Teasdale had sensed something was wrong. But without hesitating, the possemen began returning fire at the sound of the Gatling rifle exploding on the trail coming toward them. "Hold your fire," shouted Teasdale as soon as he realized there were no bullets streaking past them in the darkness. "They're not firing at us!" But by the time the men heard him and stopped shooting, the gun wagon had already cut off the trail and gone on to its fate, leaving the two groups of riders facing one another in an onward rush.

Rather than face the Gatling gun bunched up in a long single column, the *Federales* had spread out abreast on the flatlands and charged forward relentlessly, knowing that they had to strike hard and fast while the deadly machine rifle was still silent. From where the possemen stood, the land before them came alive with blossoms of gunfire, bullets whistling past them like angry hornets.

"They damn sure *are* firing at us!" shouted Edmund Daniels, a shot grazing his forearm as he ducked low in his saddle. Another bullet grazed his horse's ear. The animal nickered wildly and bolted away. As the air filled with streaking lead, the other horses attempted to do the same.

"Do not return fire!" Teasdale demanded.

"Sergeant, they'll cut us to pieces," shouted Abner Webb through the sound of gunfire and pounding horses' hooves.

"Not if they can't see us," said Will Summers. "Do like he says."

At first it appeared that Sergeant Teasdale had done the smartest thing by getting them to cease fire in the darkness. In doing so, the possemen were no longer making targets of themselves through their muzzle flashes. For a moment, the gunfire began to slacken. But the hoofbeats never let up. Teasdale shouted for the men to turn their horses and clear the trail, knowing what was about to happen next. But it was too late. The men couldn't act quickly enough to prevent it. The oncoming light Mexican cavalry patrol closed ranks as it charged and slammed into the mounted possemen head-on in the darkness.

In the melee, both sides sought one another out blindly with pistol and knife. But Will Summers managed to move away from the throng at the core of the skirmish and fight his way toward the flat stretch of land on his right, the direction where he'd last heard the short burst of shots from the machine rifle. "Summers, down here!" shouted Sherman Dahl from the ground. Looking down quickly, Summers saw the dead horse lying at Dahl's feet. He threw out his hand to Dahl, felt the young schoolmaster grasp it firmly and swing himself up behind him.

"Go!" said Dahl, his pistol coming up and firing as the horse bolted forward. Warm blood splattered on his and Summers' faces. A *Federale* trooper fell away from his horse with a bullet hole in his forehead. Dahl snatched the horse's reins and pulled it along behind them. A young Mexican came charging alongside them swinging a saber, but Dahl raised a boot and kicked him from his saddle as the sharp edge of the blade sliced dangerously close to his head. "Circle and come back!" Dahl shouted. "We've got to help the others."

"No! Follow me," Summers demanded as they cleared the edge of the fighting and Dahl leaped onto the other horse. "I think I heard the gun wagon crash! We can do more good if we can get our hands on that machine rifle!"

"I'm right behind you," shouted Dahl, firing two shots into the Mexican uniforms gathered around the possemen. He caught a glimpse of Abner Webb and Edmund Daniels fighting from their saddles, their horses pressed together against overwhelming odds. But he forced himself to look away and follow Will Summers. They rode hard and fast across the stretch of flatlands, following the blanket of dust looming above the wagon's tracks. In a moment, while the battle raged behind them, Dahl cut away from beneath the drift of dust and called out, "Summers! Over here! Quick!"

As Will Summers reined his horse over to Sherman Dahl, he saw the first scraps of broken planks from the wagon bed. He saw an empty boot. Then, a few feet farther, he saw the big Gatling gun lying in the dirt without its stand. Dahl had just leaped down from his saddle, grabbed the gun and hefted it up into his arms. "Hold it still, schoolmaster," said Summers, leaping down from his saddle and running up to Dahl. "I'll turn the crank."

"Be careful not to aim it at our men," Dahl cautioned as Summers straightened the bent crank in his gloved hands.

"I'm not going to shoot it at anybody," said Summers. "I just want to get their attention." He helped Dahl swing the barrels out along the dark trail as he turned the crank hurriedly and sent a string of bullets streaking out into the night. The recoil jarred Dahl to his bones, but he held tight, the smell of burnt powder rising into his eyes. Summers turned the crank another two full turns, then said, "Come on— that's enough for now. Let's load it up and get out of here. The Peltrys just had a little fun at our expense. Let's see if we can turn it around on them."

Chapter 16

At the first burst of fire from the Gatling gun when the wagon crashed and tumbled across the flatland, Moses and Goose Peltry had looked at one another, stunned. "What's keeping that wagon so long?" asked Goose. No one responded. But moments later, as they formed the men into two short columns and waited, listening to the sound of the battle raging less than a mile away, Moses looked back and forth between Goose and Doc Murdock.

"That gun wagon should have been here by now," said Moses. "Something ain't right out there."

Goose and Murdock nodded, looking concerned. Still, they waited until the sound of the Gatling gun exploded again. Not realizing that the gun was now in the hands of Dahl and Summers, Goose Peltry said, "Do you suppose Spears and Dupre got into trouble out there? I always said Fitzhugh can't drive a wagon worth a damn."

"I don't know what's going on," said Moses, "but we better get out there and find out." He circled his horse quickly, drawing his saber, and said to the men, "Follow me! Everybody spread out as soon as we hit the flatlands."

The riders pushed hard and fast across the dark flatlands, hearing the rifle and pistol fire of the *Feder-*

ales lessen in the distance and seeing less and less of the blossoming streaks of fire.

"Here they come," said Will Summers, looking through the darkness to his right toward the sound of the Peltry Gang's horses' hooves. To their left, where the battle had all but stopped, the sound of hoofbeats also pounded toward them in the darkness. "Let's give them one more volley just to keep them interested."

A half mile away and closing fast, Captain Oberiske and Sergeant Hervisu rode side by side at the center of the *Federales*. When the burst of fire erupted from the machine rifle ahead of them, Oberiske called out to his men, "Spread out and concentrate on that position! Fire at will; kill them all. They are nothing but lawless American criminals!"

Hervisu shook his head but said nothing, knowing that whatever advice he offered Captain Oberiske would go unheeded. As the Mexican soldiers began firing in the darkness, revealing themselves by the rifle and pistol flashes, Sergeant Hervisu kept his pistol silent and veered farther away from the captain, saying to several of the men as he passed them in the dark, "Quickly, get over near *Capitán* Oberiske. Give him some covering fire!" Hervisu rode away, leaving Captain Oberiske in a storm of gunfire.

But Oberiske soon saw he'd made a mistake. As the *Federales* around him began to fall, their positions betrayed by their own muzzle flashes, Oberiske shrieked, "Cease fire! *For the love of God, cease fire!*" Bullets whistled and hummed. He spurred his horse to his left, in the direction that Sergeant Hervisu had taken, and shouted over his shoulder to his men, "Follow me!"

Three hundred yards away, the Peltry Gang

slowed their horses and began holding their fire as the darkness seemed to close back upon itself. "Who were they? Where the hell did they go?" Goose shouted to Moses, who rode beside him.

"I don't know!" Moses replied. "But whoever it was, if they had their hands on that machine rifle, they would have used it!" He pulled his horse back and forth, looking all around in the darkness. "I think we're being tricked! Fall back to the valley trail."

Across the flatlands, Captain Oberiske and Sergeant Hervisu listened to the sound of the hooves turn and ride away. "All right, *Herr* Sergeant," said Oberiske, fingering a bullet hole through his shirtsleeve, "you know this country better than I. What do you propose we should do?"

As the frightened young soldiers drew their horses up around the two leaders, Sergeant Hervisu said, "Leave a small patrol here to round up any survivors, *Capitán*. If we want the machine rifle, we must be where these men do not expect us to be. To do this, we must hurry."

"What about our dead lying back there?" Oberiske asked.

"For now, the dead must bury the dead. The patrol will find them in the light of morning."

"Where exactly are you talking about going, Sergeant?" Oberiske demanded.

Sergeant Hervisu did not answer. Instead, he kicked his horse forward. The men fell in behind Hervisu in a loose column of twos and rode past Captain Oberiske in the darkness. Oberiske cursed under his breath and hurried to catch up.

On the flatlands, a thousand yards behind the *Federales*, Abner Webb lay against the body of a dead

horse with his pistol in his right hand and a long
boot knife in his left. He listened in silence to the
moaning of a dying *Federale* and the low, painful
nicker of a wounded horse. He dared not make a
move or a sound until he knew for certain that all
the Mexican soldiers were gone. But as he lay there,
hearing the sound of gunfire in the distance and the
horses' hooves pounding away across the flatlands,
he heard a cautious voice whisper, "Is anybody alive
here but me?"

"Daniels?" Webb whispered in reply. "Is that
you?"

"Yeah, it's me," said Edmund Daniels. "Is that
you, Webb?"

"Yes, it's me," said Abner Webb. "We must be the
only ones left." As he spoke, he belly-crawled around
the dead horse toward the sound of Daniels' voice.

"That figures," Daniels said in a flat, disgusted
tone. "It had to be me and you left out here."

"At least we're alive," said Webb. "Are you hit?"

"Hell, yes, I'm hit. My leg's shot all to hell. How
would a man get through a scrape like that and not
get wounded some?" In an afterthought, he asked,
"Aren't *you* hit?"

"No, not a scratch, far as I can tell," sad Webb,
sounding almost apologetic about it.

"Well I'll be double dog damned," said Edmund
Daniels, letting out an exasperated breath at the un-
fairness of it. "I suppose that figures too."

Webb started to crawl all the way up beside the
dark figure he saw in the pale moonlight. But then,
hearing Daniels' tone of voice, he thought better of
it and stopped and shoved the big knife down in his
belt. He checked his pistol; there were only two
rounds left. "I suppose we better fix that leg wound
up. . . . Then we need to move around here, see if

all the others are dead." He kept an eye on Daniels' dark outline as he took bullets from his pistol belt and reloaded.

"They're not all dead," said Daniels. "Best I could see in the dark, it looked like your pal Will Summers got out of here while the getting was good."

"Good for him if he did, as far as I'm concerned," said Webb. "I wish to hell we all could've cut out." He looked at the body of a young *Federale* lying three feet from him. "What do you suppose made them attack us that way? Think they must have figured we were the Peltrys?"

"Who knows?" said Daniels. "Who really gives a rat's ass? They beat the living hell out of us. That's enough for me. It's time to pack it in, head for home. Rileyville can't say we didn't give it our best try."

With his pistol reloaded, Abner Webb crawled in beside him and felt the wet, sticky ground near Daniels' leg. "My God, Daniels, you're bleeding something awful."

"I don't need you to tell me that, Webb," said Daniels, the resentment still in his voice. "The bullet cut through the big artery in my thigh. I'm trying to hold back the bleeding with this tourniquet I made with a bandanna and my pistol barrel. I don't think it's helping much though. I can feel myself getting light-headed and weak."

"Here," said Webb. "Let me look at it. Maybe I can get it to—"

"Keep your hands off me, Webb," said Daniels, jerking his wounded leg away. "I know where we stand." He raised a rifle that he'd kept hidden down the length of his other leg. Even in the darkness, Webb could see the hammer was fully cocked. "I only came along to see you die . . . either by my hand or the Peltrys'. I never counted on it coming about this way. Looks like we're gonna leave this world together."

Abner Webb acted quickly, grabbing the barrel and shoving it away from his chest just as Daniels pulled the trigger. The explosion kicked up a chunk of hard dirt that broke apart and stung both men. "Damn it, Edmund! This ain't the time or place," said Webb, wrenching the rifle from his blood-slick hand and pitching it aside. "I hope that shot ain't going to bring them back down on us."

"What's it matter?" said Daniels. "You're going to kill me. I don't have a doubt about that."

"You're wrong," said Webb. "I don't want to kill you. I wish to God what happened between us never happened . . . but I don't want to kill you. I won't raise a hand against you unless it's in self-defense." He pushed Daniels' bloody hands away and looked down closely at the bloodsoaked tourniquet. "Let's call a truce between us, at least until we get out of this fix we're in. What do you say?"

Instead of answering, Edmund Daniels said, "Let me ask you one thing, Webb, since there's only the two of us here." Daniels looked down at the wound as Abner Webb untwisted the tourniquet to take it off and get a tighter grip on it. "When you and her, you know . . . did it. Would she ever say or do—"

"Hush, Edmund," said Webb, cutting him off. "I'm not going to talk about it with you. It ain't right. Besides, you've lost a lot of blood. You're not thinking clear right now."

"Who brought it on, Webb," Daniels asked. "You or her? Did you go looking, waiting for your chance . . . or did she come offering?"

"Stop it, Daniels," said Webb, feeling the heavy surge of blood as he completely let the pressure off the bandanna. He hurriedly retied the bandanna tighter. He stuck the bloody pistol barrel beneath it and twisted it, cutting off the blood flow, seeing the fountain of thick arterial blood ebb down to a steady trickle then stop almost completely. "There," he said. "Lay your hand right here on the gun handle and hold it in place. Can you do that while I see if any of our men are lying around here?"

"Yeah, I can hold the gun in place," said Daniels, his voice starting to sound a bit slurred. "Didn't you check this pistol while you had it loose? Make sure it's not loaded?"

Now that Daniels mentioned it, Webb wished he had. But it hadn't crossed his mind at the time. "No, I didn't. But we've got a truce, remember?"

Daniels shook his head slowly. "I never said we had a truce, Webb. It's just something you brought up."

Webb had already placed Daniels' hand down on the pistol and taken his own hand away. "If it's loaded, I'll just have to trust you not to shoot me," he said. "If you undo that tourniquet just to shoot me, you'd have to be a damned fool. I doubt if you could get it back on before you bleed to death. You'd be killing yourself."

"It might be worth it to me, Webb," Daniels said in his slurred voice.

"Then you decide for yourself," said Webb. "I'm going to take a look around."

Three hundred yards away on the flatlands, Campbell Hayes and Cherokee Rhodes had heard the single rifle shot. The sound of it had only made them spur their horses to get farther away. They strove hard to stay side by side as they fled the scene of the battle, neither man trusting the other enough to turn his back on him. After another hundred yards had passed beneath their horses' hooves, Campbell Hayes reined to a halt and said to Rhodes as the half-breed slid his horse down beside him, "This is crazy, Rhodes! We can't do ourselves no good if we have to watch each other like hawks. All we'll do is wear our horses to death."

"You can trust me," said Cherokee Rhodes. "You've got my word I ain't going to shoot you in the back while you ain't looking."

"Your word don't cut no ice in my river," said Hayes. "Ain't a half-breed alive ever gave his word and kept it."

Cherokee Rhodes seethed but kept control. "Then what idea have you got?" Rhodes asked.

"We need to split up," said Hayes. "We both know our way in the wilds. We don't need each other. I can cover my own back; so can you."

"All right, let's split up then," said Rhodes. "Which way are you going?"

"Why do you want to know?" Hayes gave him a suspicious look.

"Because, damn it," Cherokee Rhodes spit, "I need to know so's I can go the other way."

"Oh," said Hayes. He weighed his words and looked Rhodes up and down in the darkness. "I'm going to head for Mexico City soon as I can shake away from them *Federales*. I'm still going to get me a piece of the Peltrys' hide for killing my partner. But I'll have to bide my time till the soldiers are through out here."

"Well, then we've sure enough got ourselves a problem," said Cherokee Rhodes. "I'm headed for Mexico City myself. Looks like you're going to have to trust me after all."

"Huh-uh." Hayes shook his head firmly. "Only way I'll trust you is to kill you first."

Rhodes made a sucking sound in his teeth, then said, as if having given it quick consideration, "I'm not good at changing my direction to suit anybody." His hand rested on the pistol at his waist. "Are you sure we can't work it out no other way?"

"None that I can see," said Hayes.

"How you want to do it?" said Rhodes, swinging a leg over his saddle and stepping down without taking his eyes off Campbell Hayes.

"Take ten, turn and fire suits me," said Hayes. "If you're game for it."

"Seems a shame you can't just take me at my word," said Rhodes. "But I'm as game as a rooster for taking ten with you." He adjusted his pistol butt at his waist. "We best hobble these horses first so's we don't spook them away."

"Mine won't run off," said Campbell Hayes. "Hobble yours if you need to."

"Mine's good," said Rhodes. "Where you want to start from?"

"Right here," said Hayes. "Let's hurry up before more *Federales* show up."

"I'm with you," said Rhodes, turning his back to Hayes and standing rigid, his hand on his pistol butt. "Back up here and start counting."

Hayes turned around and stood back to back against him, his hand also poised on his pistol butt. "Ready?" he asked over his shoulder.

"As ever," Rhodes replied.

"One," said Campbell Hayes, taking a step away.

Cherokee Rhodes turned and shot him in the back three times, taking a step closer each time a bullet knocked Hayes farther away.

Campbell Hayes lay gasping on the ground, blood spreading across the back of his buckskin shirt. Rhodes stepped in, placed a boot down on the old plainsman's neck and lowered the tip of his pistol barrel a few inches from his head. "That's what you get for not trusting me, you pig-headed old turd you." He pulled the trigger. Hayes' head bounced from the impact, then settled into the dirt.

As Rhodes stepped back and punched the spent cartridges from his pistol, Junior the hound came running in, having followed the two horses away from the battle site. With his tongue hanging out, the dog circled over to Hayes' body, licked Hayes on the neck, then made a whimpering sound and slinked over beside Cherokee Rhodes with his tail tucked under his belly. Sticking new cartridges into the pistol, Rhodes snapped the cylinder shut, cocked it and pointed it down at Junior's head. "So long, dog."

Junior looked up at him blankly. Rhodes cocked his head slightly, looked at the gun in his hand and at how close Junior was standing to his trouser leg. "I'll be a month scraping your brains off my britches, won't I?" He lowered the hammer on the pistol, shoved it back into his belt, reached down and rubbed the dog's head. "Good boy," he said. Junior stopped panting and licked Rhodes' hand. "I won't tell if you won't," Cherokee Rhodes chuckled under his breath.

Hargrove lay flat on his back in the dirt, staring up at the wide, starlit sky. The bleeding from his chest had slowed to a trickle with Sergeant Teasdale's hand pressing down on the bandage Teasdale had quickly made from a dirty shirt he'd found in Hargrove's saddlebags. "That was pistol shots, wasn't it?" Lyndell Hargrove said in a labored voice, looking up at Teasdale's face in the darkness. "Maybe you best get on out of here, Sergeant. Leave me be."

"There's not a chance in the world of me leaving

you alone out here, Hargrove," Teasdale said. He offered a tight smile. "I'm not going to have you spreading the word that I'm the kind of sergeant who'd desert a wounded trooper."

"I've got to admit, you've surprised even me. I must've trained you well back then, didn't I, Teasdale?" Hargrove swallowed a knot in his throat as he spoke. "There's no doubt in my mind you can soldier with the best of them."

"That means more coming from you then it would from any general in the army," said Teasdale. "I was afraid you'd give me trouble once I sewed these stripes on my sleeves. I'm glad you didn't. . . . Not much anyway." He shrugged and offered a gentle smile. "Otherwise I'd have been the one to have to shoot you."

"Yeah, sure you would have," said Hargrove. He squeezed Teasdale's hand. "But no joking, Sergeant. Get out of here now, while you can. Save yourself. I'll surrender to the *Federales* when they come back," Hargrove insisted. "It's the smart thing to do, for both of us. I can heal up in an army hospital in Mexico City."

"Hush that kind of talk, Trooper," said Teasdale. "I don't know for certain that they'll come back, Hargrove, and neither do you. I can't leave here thinking a coyote is going to be chewing on your leg, now, can I?'

"The *Federales* will be back around," said Hargrove, ignoring the sergeant's attempt at humor. "That pistol fire was them going around among the wounded, looking for our possemen and finishing them off one by one, I figure." He caught himself and added quickly, "But they won't finish me off. I'll have my hands up soon as they get here. Plus, I can speak their language. I'll be all right." He coughed and spit a stream of blood. "I could use the rest. Might meet a nice *señorita* or two."

"Lie still, Trooper," said Teasdale, pressing the bandage more firmly. "Pistol shots could mean a lot of things out here. Might be one of our men trying to signal us."

"Oh?" Hargrove coughed, then went on in a strained voice. "Why don't you answer him then, if that's what it is?"

"I said that it might be . . . not that it *is*," Sergeant Teasdale replied.

"Yeah? Well, I believe you're wrong, Sergeant. I've seen more of these night skirmishes than you've got fingers and toes—" Hargrove's words cut short, turning into a broken rasp as he struggled for breath.

"Try not to talk. It's got you bleeding in your lungs," said Teasdale. "Give yourself a little while here; I believe we can get you through this."

"Save that talk for greenhorns and shavetails, Sergeant. I already know the outcome to this," said Hargrove.

"Am I going to have to stick a sock in your mouth to shut you up, Trooper?" Teasdale let up on the bandage just enough to see if the bleeding had slowed any. It had. He started to speak again, but the sound of horses' hooves moving toward them at a steady clip caused him to turn away from Hargrove and draw his army Colt from his flap-top holster. "Who goes there?" Sergeant Teasdale said to the looming darkness. "Halt! Come forward slowly and be recognized."

"Yiii!" said a voice. The horses' hooves sped up as they came closer, but there was no answer to Teasdale's question. "Halt!" he demanded again, stronger this time. Before he could start his next sentence, he heard the horses speed up toward him, and he leveled his Colt and fired four shots one after the other.

Two riderless horses raced past him, one on either side. Teasdale ducked down into a crouch, knowing there was little chance he could have blindly shot two men off their horses. He scanned his pistol back and forth in the darkness until he heard a rustle of footsteps coming up behind him. He swung around, ready to fire.

"Easy, Sergeant," said Sherman Dahl. "It's Will Summers and me." Dahl had stooped down beside Hargrove, taking a look at his chest wound.

"That's a hell of a way to ride in on a man," said Teasdale, holstering his Colt.

"Don't blame me, Sergeant. It was the schoolmaster's idea," said Summers, walking in from the outer darkness leading his and Dahl's horses. The feed sack with the two outlaws' heads in it still hung from Summers' saddle horn. "We wanted to know who it was here before we came in and got shot at." He jerked his head at Dahl. "Sherman says he learned that move in the war."

"Someday I'd like you to tell me exactly who it was you fought for, schoolmaster," said Teasdale.

"Make sure you really want to know first," said Sherman Dahl with a solemn expression. "It might not be who you'd like it to be."

"I bet," said Teasdale. Then he looked back at Will Summers as if letting it go.

"There's plenty of spare horses running loose out there tonight," said Summers, changing the subject. "We snatched these two strays up on our way across the flatlands. I'm glad you didn't shoot them."

"Me too," Teasdale said flatly. "I could use one of them for Hargrove. We had to share one getting away from the *Federales* a while ago. Glad to see you two made it."

"Don't worry about Hargrove," said Sherman Dahl quietly. "He won't be needing a horse."

Teasdale stepped over and looked down at Hargrove's wide-open eyes staring up at the wide, open sky. Starlight glittered on the dead man's pupils. "I'm sorry, Lyndell," said Teasdale. "I never should have gotten us into this."

A short silence passed, then Will Summers said, "No disrespect toward your trooper, but we're *still* in it, Sergeant Teasdale. We better get moving." He nodded toward his horse, at the Gatling gun strapped behind his saddle. "We've got what the *Federales* wanted all along."

"Jesus!" said Teasdale, giving them both a stunned look. "How did you two get your hands on it?"

"We found it lying on the ground," said Summers. "I thought I'd heard the gun wagon crash. We played a hunch, went looking and there it was . . . just lying on the ground."

Sergeant Teasdale shook his head. "Hearing it must've been enough to draw the *Federales* away from us and send them after it. No sooner had we heard a burst of fire than they all pulled away and took off toward it."

"That's what we hoped it would do," said Summers. He nodded down at Hargrove. "If you want to say some words over your dead trooper, get them said. We'll cut out, hide somewhere till morning, then see if anybody else is left alive."

Sergeant Teasdale stooped down, closed Lyndell Hargrove's eyes, then stood back up with a sigh. "He was a good man, a hard fighter and a brave soldier. Bold men respected where he stood. What else needs saying over a man?"

"Amen," said Will Summers. The three turned as one and reached for their horses' reins.

Chapter 17

In spite of the danger a small fire might bring upon them, Abner Webb had built one anyway, for Edmund Daniels' sake. He'd banked a saddle up on one side to help conceal the firelight from the long stretch of flatlands. He'd positioned himself and Edmund Daniels up close on the other side to draw whatever warmth they could get from it. Abner Webb listened to the silence of the flatlands beneath the low whir of wind through the darkness. Webb nodded and listened to Edmund Daniels' weakened voice above the sound of wind-whipped flames.

"When I saw her undergarments on that rifle barrel and heard Goose Peltry blurt it out in public like that," said Edmund Daniels, "my first thought was to go pick up a shotgun, come back and splatter your brains all over the street. I must've cooled off a little on my way to the house."

"I'm glad you did," Abner Webb responded quietly, placating a wounded man.

"Me too." Daniels shivered and continued with much effort, his head resting in Abner Webb's lap. "Because if I had of killed you, I would of had to kill her right along beside you. God knows I couldn't have done that." Wind blew across the fire, pressing the flames sidelong across the ground. Sparks tumbled and bounced and raced away across the dirt.

Daniels shivered more violently. Webb held him more firmly in the crook of his arm. "Sure, I whacked her a good one upside of her head—what man wouldn't under the circumstances?" Daniels said. "But Lord knows I could never do her no *real* harm." He paused, then added, "Or you neither, not after seeing what we've seen out here. If I ever raise my hand to another man, it'll have to be for something worse than him sleeping with my woman, I can tell you that. I fear for my immortal soul just thinking what all we've done out here. And this is all within the law."

"I think I understand what you mean," said Webb. "I'll never look at killing the same way. I'll never talk about it the same way either, law or no law."

Daniels closed his eyes and whispered, "God, I love that woman so much . . . that's really why I came along on this posse. I thought it was just so I could find a chance to kill you. But that wasn't it, Deputy. It was because I was so wild and tormented I didn't know what else to do."

Abner Webb listened with regret. "Dang it, Edmund, I wish I'd known you felt this way about her before anything happened between us. Maybe it would have made a difference." He rubbed his forehead with his free hand. His voice began to crack a bit as he spoke. "I'd never done anything like that before . . . not with another man's wife. I don't know what got into me."

"Really?" Edmund Daniels opened his eyes and looked up into Webb's. "Funny, I convinced myself that you had been telling all your friends, bragging about it. Having yourself a good old time at my expense."

"No," Abner Webb said firmly. "I'd never have done something like that." Then he admitted, "Well,

I did talk to Will Summers about it . . . but that was only after it was in the open."

"I expect Will Summers told you you'd better kill me before I killed you. That's what a devil like him would whisper in a man's ear, I reckon."

"I don't remember," said Webb, feeling more and more ashamed of what he'd done. "Why don't you take it easy, Edmund. Maybe you shouldn't be talking right now."

"I beg to differ with you, Deputy," Edmund Daniels replied, the cold of night causing his voice to tremble despite the nearness of the fire. "Right now is all I've got . . . talking or otherwise."

"You need hearing it, do you?" Webb asked softly. He took a deep breath and let it out slowly.

"Yeah, I believe I do," said Daniels.

A short silence passed, then Webb said, "I fell in love with her, Edmund. That's the whole of it. I never meant for it to happen. But it was in play before I even saw it coming. If it helps you any, I believe that's the way it was for her too. She didn't do it to hurt you, I'm sure of that much. She told me she couldn't help how she felt any more than I could. Said she'd sooner die than have you ever find out about it." He hesitated for a moment, then added in a lowered tone, "Said she loved us both . . . said she hoped she'd never have to choose between us."

"You mean she said all that to you . . . ?" Daniels let his words trail. "We never talked that much to one another since we was first married."

"That's too bad," said Webb. "But I believe what she said, that she never stopped caring about you. . . . Not that we talked that much about it, I mean," he added quickly. "The fact is, she never left you for me. She could have. To be honest, I even asked her to." He looked ashamed. "But she never did. That ought to tell you something."

"Yeah, I suppose it does," said Daniels. He sighed, reflecting on everything. Then he said, "It nearly killed me at first when I found out about it. The pain made me sick. It got down deep in my belly like something with sharp claws and hung on. It tore me up. I couldn't stand the picture of you being there, then of me being there afterward, never suspecting that she'd done the same things with you she'd done with me."

"Let's not talk anymore about—"

"No, let's do talk about it, Deputy," said Daniels, cutting him off. "Because right now I want to be with her so bad I can't stand it. For some reason, being here with you is like having her with me. Like you and me have become kin through her in some crazy kind of way. . . ." Daniels' voice drifted for a second. It appeared as if he'd dozed off.

"Edmund?" Webb shook him slightly, afraid he'd died.

But Daniels came back around, opening his eyes and taking a deep breath. "I want you to promise me something, Deputy."

"What's that?" Webb asked.

"Promise me you'll take good care of her," said Daniels.

"Don't—don't say that, Edmund." Webb winced. "I can't make you a promise like that. Besides, you ain't going nowhere. You've just lost lots of blood. You'll do better now that you're not bleeding."

"I got this feeling that I'm not going back, Deputy. Maybe that I'm going to die out here . . . or maybe not. Maybe that I'm just going to drift off on my own to someplace nobody knows me. Either way, take care of her. She's a good woman, no matter about this thing that happened."

"Hush, Edmund. I can't make a promise like that," said Webb.

"Why can't you? You told me how you feel about her. I'm not going to be around. I've no more hard feelings about it. . . . Well, that is, I'm not bent on doing anybody any harm."

"I just can't, Edmund," said Webb. But his voice lacked conviction as he realized how easily he could. "It's not right, this way."

Daniels heard his voice relent a bit, and he said, "Listen to me. We both know how we feel about her. Go back to Rileyville and the two of you be happy. There's seven thousand dollars in my name in the bank up in Cheyenne. She doesn't know about it. Go there, the two of you. Take it and enjoy it. Promise me you will! Damn it, I mean it! Promise me!" As he spoke, his voice became more and more insistent. He grasped Webb's forearm and began pulling himself up.

"All right. Settle down. I promise I will," said Webb, pressing him back down. "Keep quiet. It's risky enough having this fire going."

Daniels relaxed. "I'm all right now. Just see that you keep your word."

Webb didn't answer. Instead, he turned his eyes toward the sound of something moving in closer from the outer darkness of the flatlands. Daniels felt Webb tense up, and he whispered, "What is it, Deputy?"

"Shhh. Somebody's coming. Lie still," said Webb. "Maybe all they've seen is the firelight so far."

"Get ready," said Daniels, "and get out of here when I kill the fire."

"What? You're crazy. Lie still," said Webb. "Let's make sure it's not one of our own—"

His words cut short as Edmund Daniels cocked a pistol and rolled off his lap. "What the hell?" said Webb, his hand slapping the holster on his hip and realizing it was empty. While they'd been talking, Daniels had somehow snuck his Colt from his holster. *Why?* A cold realization came to him, but the thought barely had time to register before the sound of voices split the night, speaking in broken English.

"Hey you, *gringo!*" said a voice from a distance of thirty yards or more. "Stand up and raise your hands! We have you in our sights."

"They haven't seen us both yet," Daniels whispered. "Get out of here."

"I can't leave you," Webb whispered.

"Yes, you can," Daniels replied. "Here I go."

For a split second their eyes met in the low flicker of firelight. But it was long enough for Webb to see what Daniels meant to do. He started to say something, to try to stop Daniels somehow. But Daniels moved quickly—too quickly, thought Webb, for a man who'd lost a lot of blood. Before Webb could stop him, Edmund Daniels lunged forward across the small fire, aiming the Colt into the darkness with both hands. As the fire died beneath his belly, flames flared up around his sides and licked at his shirt, then went out with a terrible sizzling hiss. "Go!" he screamed as the pistol slammed round after round into the darkness.

The *Federale*'s rifles responded instantly. Bullets sliced past Abner Webb's head as he rolled away from the smell of burning cloth and flesh, hearing Daniels' sustained tortured scream through the cacophony of gunfire. Then Daniel's scream stopped

abruptly. Webb heard the hard thump of bullets
pounding into flesh and bone and dirt as he rolled
away instinctively and scrambled across the ground
on his belly. Black smoke rose high in his wake. He
caught a glimpse of his horse turning and bolting
away as he crawled toward it.

Only when he'd scrambled over a low rise of earth
did Abner Webb stumble to his feet and run blindly
across rocky ground and through scrub brush as the
rifle fire continued to explode behind him. "Jesus!"
he sobbed under his breath, looking back at the
deadly blossoms of rifle shots dancing and spinning
on the black belly of night. "What in the name of
God am I doing here?" He ran harder, knowing that
any minute the *Federales* would swoop down upon
him on horseback. He could almost feel the cut of
cold, sharp saber steel across his back.

In his panic and desperation, Abner Webb did not
realize the ground had run out beneath his feet until
he had taken three steps on thin air and begun to
fall. His scream lingered long and loud above him
as he sailed out and downward into what he could
only imagine to be a bottomless pit.

Near the sizzling body of Edmund Daniels, the six
Federales stopped in their tracks at the sound of
Abner Webb's scream. A corporal named Luna, who
wore a thick mustache, turned to the two young men
nearest him and said in Spanish, "Hector, Felipe, get
out there. Bring him back if he hasn't broken his
stupid neck."

"*Sí*, Corporal Luna!" said one of the men, fanning
his hand before his face to diminish the smell of
burning flesh. The two men hurried away.

"The rest of you drag this fool from the fire. The
smell is making me sick." He looked all around, then
added, "Everybody spread out . . . search for the

Gatling gun. That German pig Oberiske will not rest until he has his hands on it."

In the silver light of morning, Will Summers looked out and down on the wide valley from a perch where he, Sherman Dahl and Sergeant Teasdale had assembled the Gatling gun on its stand and taken turns keeping watch on the flatlands throughout the night. Sporadic gunfire had come and gone, but it had ceased over the past couple of hours. Will Summers had made a quick count of the bullets in his rifle chamber and pistol belt, contemplating what he and his two companions should do once the sun came up. Soon the silver-gray mist would vanish from above the low-lying brush and dry creek beds below. The heat of day would return with a vengeance.

For now, the sleeping land lay still as death. Yet as Summers raised the single field lens to his eye and scanned the breadth of the rugged terrain, he caught a glimpse of the *Federales* as they came into sight, two prisoners walking ahead of them. The prisoners staggered forward like drunkards, their hands tied in front of them.

"My goodness, Deputy Webb," Will Summers whispered aloud to himself, "look what you've gotten yourself into now." Through the lens, Summers could see the bruises and cuts on Abner Webb's face and chest. "No sooner does your face get back to its normal size than you go get yourself beaten half to hell again." He reached a hand down to Teasdale's shoulder and shook him lightly. "Wake up, Sergeant. You've got to see this."

Teasdale came awake and eased up beside him, rubbing his tired, bloodshot eyes. "What is it, Summers?" he asked.

Summers handed him the field lens. "It's the deputy," said Summers. "He's gotten himself captured. Looks like six soldiers in all. You can bet they'll be meeting up with the rest of their company before long."

As Teasdale looked down at the procession on the flatlands and Will Summers stared through his naked eye, Sherman Dahl awakened and rose up beside them. Having heard their hushed conversation, he said, "It's good to know one of our men is still alive."

"Yep." Teasdale watched through the lens and said, "The other one must be one of the Peltry Gang."

"We're all the same to the *Federales*," said Summers. "As long as we've got something they want, we better manage to keep one step ahead of their game."

"We'll have to take all six of them," said Dahl. "How're you two fixed for ammunition?"

"I'm low," said Will Summers. "But I've got enough to see me through the day . . . providing we take whatever the *Federales* are carrying on them. What about you, schoolmaster?"

"I'm down to less than twenty rounds between my pistol and this rifle," said Dahl. They both looked up at Teasdale as he scanned the flatlands. "What about you, Sergeant?" Dahl asked. "Have you got enough to last the day?"

"Not if we're going to start taking on the Mexican army before breakfast," said Teasdale without taking the lens down from his eye. "I'm holding about fifty rounds."

"How about the machine rifle?" Dahl asked Summers.

"Over a couple of hundred rounds left," said Summers. "But that big gun eats bullets real quick. We'll have to keep a close watch on how we shoot it."

"I understand," said Dahl, a ring of confident efficiency to his voice. "Think there's any chance of getting the deputy loose without any gunplay?"

"You saw how it all went last night, schoolmaster," said Summers. "What do you think?"

"I'd like to try reasoning with them first," said Dahl. "If nothing else, it'll give the deputy a chance to see it's us before the shooting starts."

"That might be a good idea," said Will Summers. "Got any tricks we might use this time?"

"Not this time," said Dahl, lifting his pistol from his holster, checking it and spinning the cylinder down his shirtsleeve. "I'm all out of tricks."

Watching how slickly and effortlessly Sherman Dahl handled the big pistol, Summers offered a thin smile and said, "I can't help wondering about you, schoolmaster. You sure have seemed right at home through all this."

"I learned a long time ago to take this life as it comes to me, Summers," said Dahl. "There's nothing special about it. I just refuse to let things rattle me." He returned Summers' smile. "I think it amuses you to watch a man get rattled. You're an observer of human nature, whether you realize it or not."

"Oh? Then thanks for telling me," Summers replied. "Suppose that's something that'll help me out once we get down there and tangle horns with the *Federales*?"

"I don't know, but it certainly can't hurt," said Dahl, spinning his pistol expertly back into his holster.

As Summers and Dahl talked, Teasdale swung the field lens across the flatlands to a rising drift of dust on the horizon. He saw the riders come into sight, their horses looking tired and dirt-streaked, moving slow. "Here come the Peltrys now." He lowered the lens from his eye and handed it to Will Summers. "I've got a feeling this could turn into a real busy day before we know it."

"I've got that same feeling," said Sherman Dahl. He stood up and began disassembling the Gatling gun from its stand.

Chapter 18

In a dry creek bed that snaked three miles across the flatlands, Monk Dupre and Abner Webb staggered along in front of the six mounted *Federales*. After an hour of rough walking, the creek bed narrowed to a rocky halt where thorny brush and cactus grew too thick to penetrate. Struggling up the side of the sandy bank to the trail, Abner Webb stopped and wobbled in place at the sight of Sherman Dahl sitting atop his horse and staring at him from less than thirty feet away. "Uh-oh," said Webb, his voice carrying a warning even to himself. Coming up the bank behind Webb, Monk Dupre bumped into him and stumbled to the side.

"Watch out, damn it!" Dupre cursed. But then he too saw the mounted figure sitting sideways across their trail. "Friend of yours?" he whispered sidelong to Abner Webb without taking his eyes off Sherman Dahl. "Because if he is, don't forget: I know every water stop, whorehouse and cantina twixt here and—"

"*Silencio!*" Corporal Luna shouted down at Dupre. Gigging his horse to one side to allow the rest of his men up the dry creek bank, Corporal Luna stared at the lone rider and waited until his last man had stepped his horse up over the edge of the bank and sidled it over near the others. "Steady, men," Luna purred in Spanish, watching his men spread out alongside him. Hands poised attentively on pistol butts. Rifles rested across laps in tense hands. Thumbs tightened across rifle hammers.

Sherman Dahl had also been waiting for all the *Federales* to appear up out of the creek bed. As soon as the last one rode up into sight, he called out to the corporal, "*Saludos, viajeros del compañeros.*" Then he smiled calmly, his hand resting on his rifle stock, the rifle lying across his lap and pointing straight at Corporal Luna's chest.

"Listen to this *loco gringo*," Luna whispered in Spanish to the man nearest him. "He tries to say, '*Greetings, fellow travelers*' to us? As if this is some mindless game we play here?" He appeared astonished by Dahl's insolence. He looked around quickly, trying to understand why a lone rider would act this way. Then he settled a bit and took on a devil-may-care attitude himself, looking back at Sherman Dahl. "*Saludos* to you as well. What can I do for you this fine, clear morning, *por favor*?"

"I came to offer you a trade," Dahl said, keeping his horse perfectly still beneath him. He nodded toward Abner Webb. "My friend there for something you value most highly."

Corporal Luna perked up. "Oh? You have the machine rifle? You are willing to trade it for your *amigo*?" He cocked his head, looking Webb up and down. Then he grinned, enjoying the game, and said, "I have to tell you, he don't look so good, your *amigo*. I think I would be taking advantage of you." The line of *Federales* stifled nervous laughter.

"Huh-uh." Sherman Dahl shook his head slowly, "The machine rifle's not what I had in mind."

"Oh, it's not?" Corporal Luna's expression turned cold and serious. "Then what is this thing of value that you will trade me for your *amigo*?" He shrugged for his men's sake. "Go on, we are all listening."

A ripple of laughter rose and fell among the *Federales*. But then they settled into tense silence, awaiting Dahl's words.

"Your lives," Dahl said flatly. His thumb cocked the hammer back on his rifle as if for emphasis.

From within a cover of brush, Will Summers tightened his grip on the Gatling gun and said under his breath, "You have to admit, the schoolmaster doesn't beat around the bush."

The corporal's face turned ashen at Dahl's words. But then he tried to keep calm, not let his men see the consternation running through his mind. He forced a stiff smile and waved his hand slowly at his men, signaling them to spread out. "You damn crazy *Americano*! Why do you play around like this? You know we spent the night looking for that big gun! Who do you people think you are, that you come here, keep my men up all night, then tell me you trade this man to me for *my life*!" He gave his men a quick glance, making sure they were ready as he cocked his hand slightly and prepared to make a grab for his holstered pistol. "You make me laugh! Ha ha! See how I laugh, *gringo*?"

"Yep, I see," Sherman Dahl said grimly, seeing the corporal's hand make the slightest twitch toward his pistol. Dahl's rifle bucked across his lap. The shot lifted Corporal Luna from his saddle and slammed him sidelong into the man sitting next to him. Before the men could grasp what had just happened to the corporal, Dahl's pistol streaked upward in his right hand, firing as his left hand slung his rifle forward, levering up a fresh round.

"Get down, Webb!" Dahl shouted. His rifle fired a second behind his pistol. Two *Federales* flew from their saddles. Abner Webb caught a glint of morning sunlight on the Gatling gun barrels sticking out of a dry stand of brush. He flattened against the ground as the big gun began its deadly song.

Monk Dupre was too stunned to even dive for cover. He stood frozen in place, his hands bound in front of him, his shoulders scrunched up as if to make him a smaller target. He stood wild-eyed on one foot, his other foot raised knee-high like some strange, frightened waterfowl. Shots screamed past him from both directions at once. His face formed a tortured scream, but the sound of it went unheard amid the solid pounding of gunfire.

As the last of the *Federales* fell and their spooked horses scattered, Abner Webb managed to leap up and catch a set of loose reins with his tied hands and run along, checking the horse down. By the time the horse stopped struggling, the Gatling gun had fallen silent. Will Summers turned loose of the smoking gun and leaped out from behind the brush in time to slow down a fleeing horse and divert it right into Sergeant Teasdale's hands. "Good Lord!" said Abner Webb, keeping the spooked horse under control as he looked around at men lying dead on the ground.

"Get armed and ready to ride," said Sherman Dahl, punching spent shells from his Colt and replacing them. "Everybody between here and the hill country must be looking for the machine rifle." He stepped down from his saddle and lifted a knife from his boot well. Abner Webb held his hands out. Dahl sliced through the rawhide strips binding the deputy's wrists together.

As Webb stepped away, rubbing his raw wrists, Monk Dupre held his hands out to Dahl, saying quickly, "Thank God you showed up when you did.

They would have slit our throats before the day was over."

"Get out of here," said Dahl, shoving Dupre away.

"Are you three all that's left?" asked Abner Webb, stepping over to the bodies on the ground. He picked up a loose pistol and checked it over, then tossed it aside and picked up another.

"So far," said Sherman Dahl. "Hargrove died in the night. We haven't seen Cherokee Rhodes or Hayes or Daniels." Dahl stooped down and picked up a bandoleer of ammunition, looked at it and dropped it to the ground.

"Edmund Daniels is dead," Abner Webb said, wincing at the memory of it. "He died last night when this bunch come upon us. He was wounded bad . . . took a stand against them and gave his life to save mine."

"Saved *your* life?" Sherman Dahl gave him a surprised look, then looked him up and down, noting the dried black blood down Webb's side, his lap and his left leg.

"That's right," said Webb. "I couldn't believe it myself at first. But me and him did some talking before he died." Webb hesitated for a second, then added, "I'm glad we got to."

"I bet you are," said Will Summers, stepping up beside him, leading the horse he'd just caught. "If I was you, I'd be careful how I told that story to people. It's going to be hard to believe you didn't kill him."

Abner Webb bristled. "Don't say that even joking, Will! Daniels and I made peace. That's the truth, so help me!"

"All right then. Settle down, Deputy," said Summers. "Speaking of killing—" He nodded at the knife still in Dahl's hand. "While you've got your knife out, go ahead and stick this one before we leave." He turned a cold stare at Monk Dupre.

"Whoa now, hang on!" said Dupre, taking a shaky step backward. "There's no need in that. Where will all this violence end? It sickens me, all the killing I've seen lately. Men who have no more regard for life than to—"

"Shut up, Dupre," said Abner Webb, cutting him off. "The fact is, he rides with the Peltrys . . . says he knows where they hide out in the high country."

"Dupre?" said Summers. "Monk Dupre? There's some money on your head . . . a few hundred dollars, as I recall."

"No, you've mistaken me for another Monk Dupre," said the worried outlaw. "I admit I've done some things I shouldn't have done, riding with the Peltrys, but no, *huh-uh*." He shook his scraggly head. "There's no money on me. Believe me, I'd know it if there was."

"I still think your head would look better in that bag with those two scalp hunters, Duckbill Grear and Andy Merkel," said Will Summers, nodding toward the feed sack hanging from his saddle horn as Teasdale led their horses forward.

"Oh Jesus, no," said Monk Dupre, looking at the outlines of the heads in the bag. "Is *that* them? Grear and Merkel?" His voice trembled.

"Yep," said Summers. "They're a lot shorter than the last time you saw them."

"I'm getting sick." Dupre looked away from the bag, his face taking on a sour expression. "I—I can't hardly breathe here." He turned his bound hands to his side. "Please cut me loose. Send me on my way. I swear you'll never see me again! I won't tell a soul I saw you out here."

"He might be some use to us," said Abner Webb. "It wouldn't hurt to keep him alive a while. If he crosses us, you can always bag him any time you feel like it."

"That's right," said Monk Dupre, talking fast. "Only that won't happen. So help me God, I won't cross yas. I'll lead you straight to the Peltry hideout. I'll ambush them with you. . . . Hell, I'll kill them both myself! Just say the word!"

"Can you keep him quiet?" Will Summers asked Abner Webb.

"I'll try," said Webb.

"Then he's with us, schoolmaster," Summers said to Sherman Dahl, "but keep his hands tied for a while." He took his horse's reins from Teasdale and walked away with Abner Webb.

"You men won't be sorry," said Monk Dupre.

Summers and Webb stepped in among the bodies of the *Federales,* searching for any canteens of water, weapons or ammunition they could use. "So you and Daniels got things straight between you before he died, huh?" asked Summers.

"Yeah, we did, Will. It was strange. He—he made me promise something before he died. I still don't know what to make of it."

Summers stood up, lifting a belt full of .45 caliber pistol cartridges from around a dead man's shoulder and slinging it over his own. "Men say strange things before they die. . . . I never felt bound by anything a dead man asked of me," said Summers.

"I do," said Webb. He stopped and looked at Will Summers and said, "In case something happens to me, I want you to tell Ren—I mean *her* . . . his wife, that is—that there's a bank account in Cheyenne that belongs to her."

"What's wrong, Deputy? Can't you say the woman's name?" Summers asked. "As close as the two of you's been? You can't say her name? That must have really been some talk you and Edmund Daniels had. . . ."

"Cut it out, Summers," Webb demanded. "I can say her name. It's Renee Marie, so there." He looked embarrassed. "Anyway, there's a sizable amount of money I'm supposed to tell her about. So in case I don't make it back, I want you to tell her."

"But you are going to make it back, Deputy, so don't even start talking about dying. I won't have it," said Will Summers.

"But if it happens, you tell her, all right?"

"All right," said Summers, "but it won't happen." He mused over the conversation for a second, then said, "And that's it? That's the promise you made him?"

"No, there was something else," said Webb. "I promised him that no matter what, I'd never see her again or have anything more to do with her."

He started to walk away, but Will Summers grabbed his arm. "Hold it. You promised him something like that?"

"That's right, I did," Webb lied, seeing Edmund Daniels' eyes in the flicker of firelight from the night before, feeling the man's lifeblood warm on his chest.

"But you don't have to keep that promise," said Summers. "I thought you was crazy about her!"

"I *was*. . . . I mean, I still am, Will," said Webb, avoiding Summers' eyes. "But a promise is a promise. I've got to keep my word." He raised his face to Will Summers, and Summers saw something deep at work, some remnant of the past night and what it had left in its wake.

"I understand," said Summers as if reading some revelation in the deputy's caged eyes.

"Good," said Webb. "I don't ever want to talk about it again."

"Then we won't," said Summers.

They both looked over to where Sherman Dahl had reached down and pulled a rolled-up blanket from around the shoulder of a dead *Federale*. Dahl unrolled the blanket, shook it out and stuck his knife blade in its center, making a ten-inch slit. "I mean it, Will," said Abner Webb. "It's not something I ever want to be reminded of."

"I said I understand," Summers responded quietly, "and I meant it."

Sherman Dahl pulled the faded wool blanket down over his head, adjusted it over his gun holster, then put his hat on his head and looked around at the others. "Let's get moving before every gunman in this hellhole shows up wanting to kill us."

"Right you are, schoolmaster," said Will Summers, taking a step forward and leading his horse from amid the dead.

At the sound of the Gatling gun in the distance, Goose Peltry had spun his horse toward it and let out a long string of profanities. Moses, Doc Murdock and the rest of the men also turned their horses and looked back, but they remained calm. "Looks like somebody came out ahead of us on the machine rifle," said Doc Murdock. "I reckon we can't win every time."

"Says you," Goose sneered. "Give me three men, Moses! Just three men! I'll go back and get that gun and drop it on the ground at your feet. I swear an oath to it!" He raised his weathered right hand to the sky. "Turn me loose on them!"

"Turn you loose on who?" said Moses. "We don't even know for sure who has the gun. We've got Mexican *Federales* and a law posse back there on the desert floor. That's a bad mix, brother, and you know it. Doc's right; we lost this time. It's time we took this as a loss and went on about our business."

"I can't stand knowing somebody has something that belongs to me, even if we did steal it in the first place." Goose clenched his fists in rage. "Just imagining some sonsabitch's hands on that machine rifle sends fire through me!"

Doc Murdock gave him a bemused look. "Damn, Goose," he chuckled aloud, "you better start sleeping with your head up off the cold ground."

"What the hell is that suppose to mean, Murdock?" Goose Peltry hissed.

"It means you're starting to sound too strange to be trusted around firearms and livestock, you crazy-acting bastard," Doc Murdock growled in return. He turned his horse and started to heel it away.

But Goose Peltry had sidled his horse closer to Doc Murdock as they spoke. Now, having heard all the insults he could stand, Goose let out an insane yell and hurled himself from his saddle onto Doc Murdock's back. The two hit the ground rolling, punching and gouging, raising dust. Horses and riders jockeyed back and forth, the animals stepping high-hoofed, trying to keep from stepping on the pair. Moses Peltry shouted at the other men, scalp hunters and guerilla fighters alike. "Get down there, some of you! Break these damn fools up before they kill one another!"

The men jumped down from their saddles and pulled Murdock and Goose Peltry apart. Moses Peltry stepped his horse over close to Goose, grabbed him by his hair and kicked him soundly in the back of his head. Then he turned his brother loose, and Goose sank to his knees with a dazed groan. Doc

Murdock struggled against the men holding him. "Turn me loose! I'll eat that rotten sonsabitch's heart!" He managed to free his gun hand and slapped his palm around his pistol butt.

But then Murdock froze at the sound of Moses Peltry's big Walker Colt cocking. Looking up, Murdock saw the big open pistol bore staring down at his face from three feet away. "You ain't really drawing that pistol on my brother, are you?" Moses asked in a low, steady voice.

Doc Murdock thought better of it and drew his hand away from the pistol butt. He shook himself free of the men holding him and said to Moses, "The man's a complete lunatic! You saw what he just did! Only my respect for you keeps me from killing him like the mad dog he is! You shoulda taken up my offer to put him to sleep the other day! He's nothing but trouble!"

"Hush up, Murdock, before you and me go to shooting chunks off one another," Moses warned. His left hand gripped his beard at chest level. His right hand extended the cocked Walker Colt out at arm's length.

Murdock saw Moses' knuckles turn white and bloodless on the trigger. He took a step back. "Easy, Moses. There's no trouble between you and me."

Moses relaxed his gun hand a little, letting the Walker barrel slump. "We're all tired and getting edgy," said Moses. "We need to get over to Punta Del Sol and rest some before we start splattering one another."

"You're right, Moses." Doc Murdock eased back and took a deep breath. He ran a hand across his upper lip, wiping away a trickle of blood. "No harm done. I reckon I mighta brought some of that on myself."

Moses uncocked his Walker Colt and backed his horse a step. As Doc Murdock turned and took his horse's reins from one of the men, Moses backed his horse over, holstered his pistol and bent down in his saddle. Goose had struggled halfway to his feet. Moses grabbed his shoulder and helped him up the rest of the way. "What was he talking about, Moses," Goose asked in a dazed voice, "saying you shoulda took him up on his offer to put me to sleep?"

"Nothing, Goose. It was just loose talk. Forget you even heard it," said Moses.

"Nothing? He's talking about putting me to sleep like I'm a sick dog or something. You say forget it?"

"Yeah, Goose, that's exactly what I'm saying," Moses spit in exasperation. "You're my brother. Nobody is going to do you harm so long as I can help it. Don't you have enough sense to know that? Now shut up and put it out of your mind. We've got more pressing things to concern us."

"All right then. It's forgotten." Goose rubbed the back of his head and watched his brother turn his horse and ride away a few feet.

"The fight's over, men," said Moses. "Get mounted and get moving. To hell with the Gatling gun and the *Federales*. It's time we ride on to Punta Del Sol, take a few days of drinking and whoring."

"It's a three-day ride from here to Punta Del Sol," said a voice among the men.

"So what? It's a three-day ride from here to *anywhere*," Moses laughed. "We can hole up under a hot rock out here if everybody prefers." He looked around at the sunburnt, haggard faces. "But if it's drinking and whoring you want, speak now or forever hold your peace."

The men hooted and cheered. As they turned away from Doc Murdock and Goose Peltry, Brayton "Comanche Killer" Cane picked up Murdock's hat from the ground, slapped it against his leg and handed it to him. "Don't worry, Doc," he said between the two of them. "When you get ready to kill that wild-eyed rat's ass, I've got you covered."

"Keep it in mind, Comanche Killer," said Murdock. "It's coming most any time. Nobody jumps me from behind that way. First chance I get, I'll kill him quicker than a fly can lick its snout."

"That sounds good to me, Doc." Cane looked over at Goose Peltry with a strange smile and tipped his ragged hat as he continued speaking to Murdock. "You kill him, and I'll lift his scalp for you before his dead ass hits the ground."

PART 3

PART 3

Chapter 19

Before riding into Punta Del Sol, Moses Peltry had sent two men upward into the high rocky cliffs lining either side of the trail. When the men waved their rifles back and forth slowly, Moses Peltry looked at Doc Murdock and said, "Now that we've made it through that little stretch of adventure, how do you feel about our partnership so far?"

Doc Murdock returned Moses' flat smile. "All's well that ends well, I suppose. But to tell the truth, I can't see where me or my men made a dime traipsing across those flats and badlands."

"Don't worry about the money, Doc," said Moses. "We'll soon be making it hand over fist. I've got plans that will cross your eyes once you hear them."

"I'm all ears," said Murdock.

"In good time, Doc," said Moses, heeling his horse forward.

"I'd kind of like to know now," Doc said, raising his voice a bit as Goose and Moses Peltry rode forward side by side, leaving him sitting.

"You'll know when we're damn good and ready to tell you," Goose said, turning slightly in his saddle and giving Murdock a hard stare.

Beside Doc Murdock, Brayton "Comanche Killer" Cane said under his breath, "God almighty, I want to kill him so bad it's making my teeth ache."

"Settle down, Comanche Killer," Doc Murdock whispered, heeling his horse forward. "Let's try to enjoy ourselves while we're here. If you see any scalps that could pass for Apache, don't forget we've still got a good market for them."

"Let them say what they will about scalp hunting becoming a dying profession," said Comanche Killer Cane. "I miss it something fierce every day of my life."

"We all miss it, Comanche Killer," said Murdock.

They rode on, coming to a point where a large, crumbling sandstone wall crossed the trail. Two wide wooden gates stood open before them, revealing a community of ancient adobe structures, sun-bleached chozas and skeletal lean-tos wrapped in weathered canvas and skins of animals both domestic and wild. "Everybody watch each other's backs," said Moses Peltry, stepping his horse through the open gates. The men looked all around cautiously, their hands poised on rifles and pistols across their laps.

Once inside the gates, the riders watched two women shy away from the large well where they had stood drawing water in the early-morning light. A thin old man came limping forward with a cane as the two women hurried their steps, their water crocks resting atop their bare shoulders. Beyond the well lay the empty, criss-crossing dirt streets of Punta Del Sol. Somewhere a rooster crowed as if raising the town from its slumber.

"You gals needn't rush off on our account," one of the riders called out to the women. But the two women ignored them in their haste, one offering a trace of a playful giggle as they scurried away. From his saddle, Moses Peltry gazed down at many fresh hoofprints in the dust. But he only looked down for a second before raising his eyes as if not having noticed the prints.

The old man stopped in front of Moses and Goose Peltry and leaned sideways on his cane. *"Buenos días, señores,"* he said, offering a stiff, uncertain smile. He swept a narrow-brimmed soft felt hat from atop his head and held it to his thin chest.

"Habla inglés?" Moses Peltry asked bluntly.

"Sí," said the old man. "I speak English ever since I was a small child. I am Hector Roderio. What can I do for you?"

"If you speak English, keep speaking it then, damn it!" said Goose, cutting in. "I hate the way you people always try to talk to us in a foreign language."

Moses gave his brother a look, silencing him, then turned back to the old man. "Hector," he said with an air of familiarity, raising one of his big Walker Colts and cocking it, "I'm going to ask you something that I already know the answer to, and if you lie to me, I won't ever ask you another thing. Are we clear on that?"

"Sí." Hector shrugged nervously. "Always I pride myself on being an honest man."

"That's commendable, Hector," said Moses, taking aim at the old man's frail-looking chest. "Have any *Federales* been through here in the past few hours, heading in either direction?"

"Sí! Yes!" said Hector. "The soldiers came through here three days ago, headed south. Then they came back through last evening, headed north. They go back to the garrison at—"

"That's all I wanted to know, Hector," said Moses, interrupting him. "Were they carrying a big machine rifle when they came through last evening?"

Hector seemed to consider it for a second, then

shook his head. "No, not that I can recall. I know the kind of gun you are talking about, and I did not see one with the *Federales*."

Moses nodded, apparently satisfied as he looked past the old man and along the dirt streets of the hill community. "We're a Southern military force in exile, Hector. I hope the good folks of Punta Del Sol are prepared to go out of their way to make us feel welcome here. I always said the future of a town like this relies on its hospitality toward armed strangers. Don't you agree?"

"*Sí*, of course I agree with you, *señor*," said Hector. "We are a town of commerce. For a price, you will find whatever you want here. Owing to my religious beliefs, I cannot condone the drinking of alcohol or consorting with loose women. But I can tell you where such items and activities can be found."

"We can't ask for more than that." Moses grinned. "Now here's the deal, Hector." Moses clasped his free hand around his long beard and let it rest there as he gestured with his big Walker Colt toward the waking town. "Instead of us paying for everything now and then robbing the town and taking our money back before we leave, why don't you just give us everything for free to begin with and save everybody the labor?"

Behind Moses Peltry, the men laughed and hooted.

"Hell, Moses," said Doc Murdock, "with ideas like that, you could have been a politician!"

Hector Roderio shrugged in resignation and stepped to one side as the riders moved slowly by. "Our town is your town, *señores*," he said meekly.

"That's exactly the kind of talk we like to hear," Goose Peltry chuckled, heeling his horse up into a trot ahead of the others. He stopped the tired horse in the middle of the dirt street out front of an adobe cantina. Letting out a loud yell, he raised his pistol and fired three shots upward into the closed double doors of a balcony atop the cantina. "Ladies, wake up in there! Get on out here, *pronto!*" he yelled. "Don't even bother about dressing. You can come as you are . . . it's just us ole rebel boys!"

At first the women approached the balcony doors fearfully, peeping out around the corner of the jamb. Then, as they heard the whistles and catcalls of the men, they became emboldened. Gold coins hit the balcony floor, and they became more emboldened yet. They ventured out, some with blankets clutched around them, some wearing soft cotton robes. "Lord God, don't let it all be a dream!" a man shouted hoarsely.

Quickly the women's blankets loosened in the morning sunlight, revealing smooth brown shoulders. Robes became undone, revealing breasts and thighs. Pistols fired wildly in the dirt street. Men flung themselves from their horses, smoking pistols in hand, and crashed through the thick wooden door of the closed cantina. Trampling across the cantina door where it fell, the men left a trail of discarded boots and shirts behind them on their way to the narrow stairway leading to the floor above. "Get the hell out of my way!" one of the scalp hunters shouted, giving the man in front of him a hard shove.

Halfway up the stairs, the man fell and caused a logjam of bodies between the wall and a thin banister that soon broke free of the stairs and swung back and forth as men fell to the floor below.

"*Por favor!* Please! Please!" shouted the proprietor, running out from his room adjoining the cantina. As he shoved his shirttail into his trousers and hiked his galluses over his shoulders, he pleaded, "Don't destroy the stairs! There are plenty of women to go around!"

"Not for me there ain't!" shouted a scalp hunter climbing up the backs of downed men on the congested stairs.

Outside, Moses, Goose and Doc Murdock watched and listened as the adobe cantina shuddered and trembled beneath the stampede of boots and hooves—a few men having elected to remain in their saddles and ride their horses inside. "I like to see my men enjoy themselves," Moses said to no one in particular. He looked down at Hector Roderio and asked, "Now then, Hector, who lives in the best *hacienda* around here? I mean somewhere close by but still offering a man some solitude from the back and forth of street traffic?"

"*Señor*, that would be Juan Richards' house," said Hector, pointing with his cane to a large adobe-and-log structure seated atop a steep trail up on the hillside. "His family were *Americanos*, but they have lived here for many generations, even before the war with Texas and California."

"That ought to do," said Moses, gazing up the trail at the big hillside *hacienda*. "Hector, you go tell Juan Richards to get himself down here. Tell him that I'll be needing his house for a couple of days while I do some military planning."

"But he cannot come down here, *señor*," said Hector. "I am sorry."

"What?" Moses looked taken aback. "Why can't he come down here, Hector, pray tell?" he asked mockingly.

Because he cannot walk, *señor*. Juan Richards sits in one of those what-you-call-it, chair with the wheels on it?"

"A wheelchair?" said Moses.

"*Sí*, a wheelchair." Hector nodded.

"He's in a wheelchair, living on a hillside like that?" Moses asked, a dark chuckle starting to creep into his voice. "What kind of man is this Juan Richards anyway?" He looked at Goose and Doc Murdock as if for an answer.

"An *adventurous* man, I'd say." Goose grinned.

"On second thought, Hector," said Moses, "maybe you better wait here with me. Brother Goose, ride up there. Roll *Señor* Richards down here to me."

As Goose Peltry galloped off up the steep trail, Moses looked down at the spotted hound that seemed to have appeared out of nowhere and stood at Hector's side. Hector reached his free hand down and scratched the dog's head.

Moses Peltry cocked his head to one side, giving the dog a curious once-over. "Hector, where'd you get that dog? I've seen him before."

Hector jerked his hand away from the dog as if the animal were diseased. "He is not my dog, *señor*! No! He just wandered into town last night."

"Is that so?" asked Moses, starting to remember the dog. "As I recall, I saw that dog a while back in a town the other side of the border." He recocked the Walker Colt, staring hard at Hector Roderio. "Best I recall, I had a run-in with the man who owned him." He started to raise the pistol toward Hector, but a voice in the street stopped him.

"A run-in? Your memory's nearly as long as your beard, Moses," said Cherokee Rhodes, stepping out from around the corner of the cantina. "What happened was, you shot that poor bastard deader than a pine knot."

"Cherokee Rhodes," said Moses, easing his grip on the Walker Colt but keeping it cocked. "The only half-breed I know who can eat a rattlesnake while it's still trying to crawl away." He looked Rhodes up and down. "Didn't I hear some Texas Rangers hanged you a while back?"

"They tried. It didn't take," said Rhodes, stopping a few feet back and resting his hand on his pistol butt.

"Tell me, Rhodes," said Moses. "How come you to know so much about that dog and its owner?"

"Because I met the owner's partner. We rode together with that posse that was fanning your trail. He vowed to kill you soon as he caught up to you." Cherokee Rhodes offered Moses and Murdock a guarded smile. "Come to think of it, I vowed the same thing."

Doc Murdock stepped his horse a couple of feet away from Moses, his hand going to the pistol on his hip.

"Easy, Doc," said Moses. "If Cherokee was getting ready to throw down on us, he wouldn't have announced it first. Right, Rhodes? I mean, not if you had a choice between that or a good, clear shot in the back?"

"You know me better than my closest kin," Cherokee Rhodes chuckled. "Fact is, that's exactly what happened to the partner of that dog's owner. He turned his back on me . . . wanted to have a duel of all things."

"I bet that was quick and sweet," said Moses.

"Quick, yes. But *sweet*? I doubt it." Rhodes looked up the steep trail at the commotion as Goose Peltry came pushing Juan Richards into sight. "Is Goose going to shove that poor sumbitch down here, steep as this trail is?"

"I'm wondering that myself," said Moses, watching Richards curse and plead, flailing his arms back and forth wildly. "I bet he does, if I know Goose."

Cherokee Rhodes shrugged. "Anyway, I threw in with the posse trailing you boys . . . told them I had personal reasons to want to see you dead. This is where I landed after that row the other night with the *Federales* over the Gatling gun."

"You was in on that, eh?" Moses asked, still gazing up the trail at Goose and the hapless Juan Richards.

"Yep, up to my elbows in it, Moses," said Cherokee Rhodes. "And I'll tell you truly, that bunch out of Rileyville is not the kind of posse I'd want on my trail. You took their horses and guns, and damned if Will Summers didn't bankroll them to new ones."

"Will Summers. . . . I might have known," said Moses. "That's who figured out how I sicced the *Federales* on them, then turned it all around on us. That sonsabitch." Moses gritted his teeth. "I bet he's the one got our machine rifle too."

"Can't say on that," Rhodes replied. "But he's riding up front with that posse, you can believe that. He's doing it all for the reward on everybody's heads."

"So they're really nothing but straight-up bounty hunters is what you're telling me." Moses shook his head in disgust, thinking about it. "That's pure evil, Rhodes. It ought to be against the law."

A long scream of terror resounded from atop the steep trail. Looking up, Cherokee Rhodes, Moses Peltry and Doc Murdock saw the high-backed wooden wheelchair zigzagging crazily as it raced downward toward them, leaving a bellowing wake of dust. "Yep, brother Goose gave him a shove all right," Moses said, stepping his horse to one side and giving the speeding wheelchair room to streak past him. Juan Richards continued screaming, wide-eyed, his hair swept back by the onrush of air.

"Look at him go!" said Rhodes, turning his head quickly, keeping up with the wheelchair as it shot past them and careened across the dirt street. All three men winced when the wheelchair struck the boardwalk and came to an abrupt halt. "Whooiee," Moses whispered, seeing Juan Richards hurled from the chair and through the broken door of the cantina. A crash of splintered wood and shattered glass erupted.

"You have to admit," said Cherokee Rhodes, "the man held on pretty damn good."

"Yes, he did," said Moses. Then, dismissing the whole matter, he asked Rhodes, "So, you're wanting to throw in with us? You're giving up the gunrunning business?"

"I've got to go where the money is," said Rhodes. "That posse busted the hell out of the gunrunning. If you've got a place for me, I'll jump right in." As he spoke, Junior the hound sidled up to him and sniffed his trouser leg. Rhodes dropped a hand to the dog's head and scratched it, looking up at Moses for an answer.

"Yeah, you're in," said Moses. He grinned. "Just make sure you don't shoot none of us in the back. I know it's a hard habit to break."

"I'll do my best," said Cherokee Rhodes.

"Good," Moses replied. He nodded at the cantina, where three men had carried Juan Richards out onto the boardwalk and pitched him into the street. "Now go stick that man in his wheelchair and roll him away from here. Tell him as long as we're still using his house, he better stay out of my sight, or I'll kill him."

                    *   *   *

By noon, the cantina at Punta Del Sol was packed
with men, horses and whores. Pistol shots roared
above wild laughter and harsh curses. Bottles crashed
against walls. A young woman was hurled naked
through a front window in a spray of shattered glass.
She sprang to her feet like a cat, screaming, cursing
and slinging broken glass from her hair. A fire broke
out in a corner of the cantina but was soon extin-
guished, leaving a black streak of soot up the wall
and across the ceiling.

At the bar, Cherokee Rhodes produced a leather
bag full of dried peyote cactus buttons and passed it
along. The men chewed the powerful hallucinogens
and washed them down with mescal, tequila and
wine. Fistfights soon broke out. Knives were drawn.
One of the scalp hunters who'd eaten a handful of
the powerful cactus buttons soon stabbed himself in
the thigh by accident, thinking he'd stabbed the man
standing beside him. The stairway leading up to the
brothel had been torn away from the wall and
thrown through the broken front window. Drunken
patrons had stacked chairs and tables against the
wall and begun climbing hand over hand to the waiting arms of the whores who stood half naked on the
balcony, taunting and encouraging them upward.

"Maybe it was a bad idea giving them the peyote
buttons," Cherokee Rhodes said to Moses Peltry. He
scratched his jaw, watching the surrounding debacle
spin further and further out of control. Goose Peltry
threw his head back in a loud shriek of drunken
delight as he swung back and forth on a large
wagonwheel chandelier. A thick crosstimber in the
ceiling sagged a bit and let a stream of dried earth
trickle down onto the drinkers at the bar.

"They can handle their festivities," said Moses, shrugging the matter aside. He picked up two cactus buttons and popped them into his mouth.

"Careful Moses," Cherokee Rhodes cautioned him. "Somebody's got to stay sane here . . . to keep an eye on the rest of this bunch."

"Oh? You've been here long enough you're going to start telling me how to run my gang?" asked Moses.

"Don't mind me, Moses. Sometimes I just talk to make sure my jaws are working good." Cherokee Rhodes backed off, raising his hands chest-high.

Moses Peltry's eyes followed the trickle of dried earth falling from the ceiling. "If you want to worry about something, worry about this place falling in around us." He threw back a mouthful of tequila from a large wooden cup. "Where'd Doc Murdock go?"

"He grabbed that whore with the long black hair and carried her out of here over his shoulder," said Rhodes. "Last I seen, he was headed to the cripple's house with her."

"Good for him," said Moses. "If you're smart, you'll drag something away from here yourself. Once we hit the trail, it'll be a long, dry spell before we find another place like this."

Chapter 20

In the late afternoon, Sherman Dahl rode back along the trail to the cliff overhang where he'd left the others waiting while he scouted the ridgeline above Punta Del Sol. Webb, Summers and Teasdale stepped forward as Dahl rode into sight. Monk Dupre sat against the wall of the overhang with his tied hands folded on his lap. "The Peltrys are down there all right," said Dahl, reining in. "From the sound of things, the town will be lucky if it's still standing when they leave."

Summers, Webb and Teasdale looked at one another as if all three were asking themselves the same question. Then Summers turned to Monk Dupre and asked, "How far are we from their hideout?"

"It's thirty miles, give or take," said Dupre flatly. "It's easier to show how to get there than it is to try and give directions."

"Don't worry, Dupre. We're keeping with you the whole trip," said Summers. "Just make sure what you tell us comes up right." He turned back to Teasdale and Webb with a determined expression as Dahl slipped down from his saddle and joined them. "I hate passing up the opportunity to chop them down in the street," said Summers.

"It can't be helped," said Webb. "We're about out of ammunition for the Gatling gun. Without it, the four of us don't stand a chance."

"I know," said Summers. "We might just as well put it out of our minds for now. We need to get ahead of them and be waiting at their hideout. We're outnumbered. But a good four-rifle ambush can cut them to pieces before they know what hit them, especially if we catch them by surprise coming into their own front yard."

"Then we need to push on," said Teasdale.

"I can't go any farther right now," said Dahl. "That horse I'm riding is ready to drop in his tracks. I've got to either rest him or kill him."

"All our horses are in the same shape, schoolmaster," said Summers. "The best thing we can do is make a dark camp here, rest these horses and ourselves and head out tonight around midnight. The Peltrys aren't going to break up their party any time soon." He looked from one man to the next for their agreement. Webb, Teasdale and Dahl nodded.

"I'll take the first two-hour watch," said Dahl. He led his horse over beside the horse carrying the Gatling gun and tied its reins around an upthrust of rock.

By the time the last glow of light sank down below the horizon, the men sat eating cold jerky that Abner Webb had taken from his saddlebags and passed around. They ate the dry, stiff meat in silence, washing it down with tepid water from their canteens. With his hands still tied, Monk Dupre looked from one grim, shadowed face to the next as he pried a sliver of jerky from between his thumbnail and spit it away. "I know it's not my place to mention this," he said in a lowered voice. "Has it crossed any of your minds that maybe it's time to break off here and head back to Rileyville? I mean, nobody can say you men didn't give it your all. But the odds against you taking down the Peltry Gang was slim to begin with, and it's only gotten slimmer since then."

Silence loomed until Monk Dupre felt himself grow uneasy. "Not that I can't agree you've got every right to stay here and fight it out after all that's—"

"Keep your mouth shut, Dupre," Summers hissed. He stood up, dusted the seat of his trousers and turned to Sherman Dahl. "Wake me up in two hours, schoolmaster. I'll take the next watch."

But in the darkness of night, when the two hours had passed, it was not Sherman Dahl who awakened Will Summers. Instead, it was the cold edge of steel pressed against the side of his throat that caused Summers to open his eyes as his hand reached instinctively for the pistol lying beneath his saddle.

"No, no, *señor*," said Sergeant Hervisu's gravely voice. His rough boot clamped down on Will Summers' wrist and pinned it to the ground. A lantern glowed in Hervisu's hand, revealing the shadowy forms of numerous *Federales* standing over Abner Webb, Lawrence Teasdale and Monk Dupre with their rifles pointed down in their faces. Beside Sergeant Hervisu stood a young soldier with his rifle cocked and pointed at Will Summers.

"It is over for all of you now," Hervisu said to Will Summers. "For the sake of your friends there, do not attempt something foolish."

"I won't," said Will Summers, easing down a bit, looking around in the flickering light of the lantern. "We've had our play. Looks like you've won."

"You are wise to see it that way," said Hervisu. With his boot still on Summers' wrist, he gestured for the *Federale* beside him to reach down and get the pistol from beneath Will Summers' saddle. When the young man stood up and handed Sergeant Hervisu the holstered pistol, Hervisu looked at it and draped the gunbelt over his shoulder. Then he took a step back from Summers and looked all around in the darkness.

"We're not outlaws," said Will Summers, "If that's what you're thinking."

Sergeant Hervisu tipped his chin up and patted his hand on the gunbelt on his shoulder. "I am thinking that you are not gunfighters either." A trickle of laughter spilled from his men, and he added, "We have taken all of you without firing a shot."

Summers ignored the insult. "We're a legally sworn posse trailing the Peltry Gang. We didn't come here to break any laws of Mexico."

Sergeant Hervisu offered a knowing smile and wagged a thick finger back and forth. "But you break the law simply by coming here in the first place. You *Americanos* always think it is *your* border. Why do you never stop and realize that it is *our* border too?"

"You can bet I'll remember that in the future," said Will Summers. He tried raising himself up, but the boot held his wrist to the ground.

"It is best you speak no more unless you are first spoken to, *señor*." Sergeant Hervisu looked around again, then said to Summers and the others, "Now then, *señores* . . . where is the machine rifle? My *capitán* says I must bring it to him right away. He does not like to be kept waiting."

In the flickering light, Webb's, Teasdale's and Summers' eyes met, each man taken aback by the realization that both the Gatling gun and Sherman Dahl were missing. Thinking quickly, Will Summers said, "We don't have it. We thought you did."

Sergeant Hervisu quickly turned the tip of his

saber toward Monk Dupre. "You . . . you are a prisoner here, *sí*?"

"Yes, I am," said Dupre. "But I don't know why.
I haven't done anything to—"

Hervisu cut him off. "Where is the gun? If you lie
to me, I will open your belly here and now." The tip
of his saber came to rest at the center of Dupre's rib
cage. Dupre looked down at it, his eyes bulging in
fear. Yet he sensed that his best chance at staying
alive was to stick with the possemen's story, knowing that somewhere in the shadows surrounding
them, the Gatling gun could be poised, ready to fire
at any second.

"I—I haven't seen any Gatling gun," Dupre said,
"and that's a fact, so help me God! I was an innocent
hostage of the Peltry Gang before these men captured
me. They had a Gatling gun when the fight started
the other night in the river valley, but that's the last
I saw of it."

Sergeant Hervisu stared at him coldly for a moment as if having difficulty making up his mind.
Then he said, "If I find you have lied to me, I will
quarter you limb from limb like a roasting animal."
He spun to the *Federale* who had his rifle aimed at
Will Summers. "Get them to their feet and chain
them together. By morning we will be in Punta Del
Sol. We'll see what *Capitán* Oberiske wants to do
with them."

In the wispy gray predawn air, Punta Del Sol slept
in its own sour smell like a diseased animal. The
cantina was the sore at the center of its disease.
Within the ragged walls behind the broken windows
and doors, the light of one thin candle glowed amid
the low drunken babble of the last two men standing

at the battered bar. One of the whores lay sprawled facedown on the bar top between Flat Face Chinn and Handy Phelps. Flat Face stood naked from the waist down save for his gunbelt and a long knife shoved down behind it. He picked the whore's head up by her hair and said drunkenly, "Wake up . . . this dance ain't ended yet."

"Turn her loose, Chinn," Handy Phelps demanded. "Can't you see she's bleeding all over hell?"

Chinn saw blood on the bar from where she'd passed out earlier with a shot glass raised to her lips. "Damn, what a mess," said Chinn. He turned loose of her hair. Her head bounced on the bar. She let out a short groan, then lay still. "I don't know about you," Chinn said in a slurred voice, looking down and kicking a broken guitar out of his way with his bare foot, "but I could eat something hot and greasy . . . get my guts working again."

"We et up everything in town last night," said Phelps. The two weaved back and forth in place, looking across the floor at the half-naked whores and outlaws whose bodies lay entwined in twisted blankets, broken furniture, torn clothing and empty bottles.

"What happened to that spotted hound that kept licking and sniffing around here last night?" asked Chinn.

"I don't know," said Phelps, "but I don't eat dog except in a pinch."

"Me neither, I reckon," Chinn resolved, reaching for a half-full bottle of tequila someone had left standing on the bar. He took a long, gurgling drink and passed the remains on to Handy Phelps. As Phelps turned up a long drink, three young *Federales* slipped inside the cantina and stepped silently over the sleeping bodies on the floor. They spread out, listening to the drunken conversation between the two outlaws.

"*Sante Madre*," whispered one of the *Federales* under his breath, looking all around. The body of the cantina owner hung upside down at the end of a rope someone had thrown over a ceiling timber. Looking at the dead, blank eyes, the young Mexican soldier made the sign of the cross, then raised his rifle to his shoulder.

"Every one of you, wake up and raise your hands!" the young soldier shouted. "We have this place surrounded!" Behind him, four more *Federales* stepped through the open door and spread out among the sleeping men on the littered floor. On the floor, a few men moaned and cursed in their sleep, but none awakened.

"Now, what the hell is this?" Chinn demanded in his drunken voice.

"It's a swarm of bugs," said Handy Phelps. "Mexican hopping bugs!" He lowered the bottle from his lips and let tequila run down his scraggly beard. "Lord God, I'm never eating no cactus buttons ever again. I swear it!"

"You two, raise your hands quickly!" said the young Mexican, he and the others swinging their rifles toward the strange-looking pair. Beside the naked Flat Face Chinn, Handy Phelps stood missing a boot and his hat. Sometime in the night, a whore had pulled one of her garters down around his forehead.

"Why?" Phelps asked the young soldier bluntly, a look of defiance in his bloodshot eyes. "You bunch of kids ain't going to shoot nobody."

"That's right," said Chinn, thrusting his nakedness forward. "You boys want to see something, come take a look at this."

The young *Federale* looked away, stunned for a second. His face reddened in embarrassment. He nodded at the pair of dirty denim trousers hanging from the bar. "Put on your bitches, *señor*, right now!"

"Ha!" said Flat Face Chinn. "I ain't got a damn thing I'm ashamed of!"

"Careful, Flat Face, these bugs ain't kidding," Handy Phelps laughed.

"Hell, neither am I," Flat Face Chinn bellowed, a weird, crazed look coming to his eyes. He reached down and shook himself at the shocked young Mexicans. "I said get over here and take a look at this!" he raged, his free hand grabbing the butt of his pistol.

Across the street, atop the steep trail in Juan Richards' *hacienda*, the volley of rifle fire from the cantina caused Moses Peltry to awaken from a mescal-and-peyote-induced stupor. He batted his blurry eyes and tried to focus on something long enough to stop the room from spinning. "Hey, Moses, wake up," said Cherokee Rhodes with a dark chuckle, poking a pistol barrel into Moses' chest. "If you sleep late today, you're going to miss an awful lot."

"Get that damn pistol out of my face," Moses demanded, swatting the pistol barrel away as if it were a fly. On his right, a young whore lay naked against him, her arm thrown across his chest, his beard wrapped around her forearm like a furry white snake. Moses unwrapped his beard, shoved the woman away and sat up. He wiped his face with both hands and kept his head bowed as he asked, "What the hell was that rifle fire about?"

Cherokee Rhodes looked around at Captain Oberiske with a flat smile. The German officer stood rigidly with his gloved hands on his hips, a riding quirt hanging down his thigh. "I told you that peyote would knock their heads off," Rhodes said. Then he looked back at Moses Peltry. "What you heard was Mexican soldiers shooting the hell out of your men, Moses. You best wake up and pay attention here before life decides to pass you by."

Moses sat slumped for a moment longer, his long beard piled in a random coil in his lap, his forehead in his hands. He struggled, trying to make sense of what Rhodes had said. Finally he raised his face slowly and stared once again into the barrel of Cherokee Rhodes' pistol. "If you shove my pistol away this time," said Rhodes, "I'll have to shoot you just to keep from looking weak in front of my friend here."

"Rhodes, you rotten sonsabitch," Moses hissed. "You've sold us out. You came to me looking for work, and all the time you was setting us up for the law!"

"There you are," said Rhodes. "I couldn't have said it any plainer myself."

"So you was out to try and kill me after all," Moses growled.

"No." Rhodes wagged his pistol barrel back and forth. "But when Will Summers and his posse came to buy guns, and I later heard he was hunting your gang for bounty, damn if it didn't sound like a good idea!" He tapped the pistol barrel to his head, then leveled it back at Moses Peltry. "It was only after him and his posse killed all the gunrunners that I decided I would help hunt you down. Then I ran into the captain here and explained my intentions, and, well, you know how one thing always leads to another, eh?" He chuckled under his breath. "We've got all your men disarmed and in custody. Captain Oberiske here wants you to hand him over that Gatling gun. I told him you'd more than likely be glad to. Don't disappoint me now."

Moses Peltry shook his head, wincing against the

sharp hangover pain in his temples. "I've got to disappoint you, Rhodes," he said, lowering his head again. "I ain't got it. We lost it the other night near the river valley."

Captain Oberiske stepped forward impatiently, reached out with the tip of the riding quirt and raised Moses' eyes to his. "Do not waste my time, outlaw! I want the truth, nothing less! We gathered many boxes of ammunition from the spot where your wagon crashed. Now, I must have the gun."

Moses batted his blurry eyes, glancing past the German captain and seeing the armed soldiers gathered inside the door. He saw Juan Richards in his wheelchair behind the captain. Richards' face bore a strange, grim expression. Dark circles lined his sunken, hate-filled eyes. "Let me question him for you, Captain Oberiske," Richards whispered, his voice deadly calm. "I'll make this pig tell the truth. I owe him and his brother both for what they've done to me, to my home, to this town."

"Why don't you crawl off somewhere and die, you crippled, legless old poltroon!" Moses snarled. He looked back at Captain Oberiske and asked, "Where the hell is my brother?"

"He's chained up and under heavy guard in the old Spanish mission at the edge of town," said Oberiske. "Both he and the leader of the scalp hunters. You will be going there yourself. As soon as I find out who has the machine rifle, I will accompany the lot of you to the border and set you free. You can make it hard on yourself or easy. Either way, my only interest is the gun." He turned, slapping the quirt impatiently against his thigh, and summoned the *Federales* who stood at the door with their rifles pointed at Moses. "Quickly, take him out of my sight."

"What about me?" asked Juan Richards. "Can't I cut some meat off him . . . make up some for what they've done to me?"

"Perhaps later," said Captain Oberiske, appearing to have dismissed the matter. "Right now I am waiting for all parties to stand on the same spot and tell me about the Gatling gun."

"I already told you. I don't know where it's at," said Moses Peltry as the *Federales* lifted him to his feet and dragged him toward the door.

"Of course you did," said Oberiske. "But now I am curious to see what you will say when I stand your men one at a time in front of a firing squad."

"Whoa! A firing squad!" said Cherokee Rhodes, beaming with a wide smile. "Hear that, Moses? They're going to kill you and your idiot brother just like you were *real* soldiers! You ought to be proud as a painted peacock." He turned, laughing, and grabbed Juan Richards' wheelchair with both hands. "Come on, crip. You're not going to want to miss any of this."

Rhodes rolled Juan Richards out behind the *Federales*, hurrying to keep up with them. Moses Peltry spit over his shoulder at him, saying, "You better hope to God I never get loose long enough to get my hands around your throat, you jackpotting sonsabitch!"

Cherokee Rhodes laughed, taunting Moses. "I don't know what's wrong with all these fools, crip," he said to Juan Richards. "They all know what a low, back-shooting weasel I am, yet they still keep inviting me along." Juan Richards only stared grimly ahead in silence, his eyes livid in his rage and riveted to Moses Peltry's naked back.

On their way along the dirt street toward the old Spanish mission, Cherokee Rhodes spotted Sergeant

Hervisu and his patrol riding in from the east ahead
of a long, glowing shaft of morning sunlight. "Well
I'll be double dog damned," said Rhodes. "Looks
like the Summers-Webb posse is still alive and
kicking . . . just not nearly as high as it was before."
He veered Juan Richards' rickety wheelchair toward
the oncoming patrol. "Stick with me, Juan. You're
going to meet all kinds of new faces today."

Trudging along on foot in front of the Hervisu patrol, Will Summers said to Abner Webb and Lawrence Teasdale in a lowered voice, "Of all people,
look who made it through alive." With four feet of
chain connecting the three men by their wrists, Summers lagged long enough to let Webb and Teasdale
close ranks at his back.

"I'd love to hear how he's managed to stay alive,"
Webb whispered near Summers' ear.

"Can't blame Cherokee Rhodes for going with
what's no more than his nature," said Summers.

"Yeah, at least we should have expected it from
him," said Abner Webb. "What should we have expected from Sherman Dahl, sneaking out on us the
way he did?"

Will Summers' eyes scanned the ridgeline above
the western edge of Punta Del Sol, where the sunlight had not reached the long black holes of shadow
across the breast of the hillside. "Don't discount the
schoolmaster," he said. "Something must have gone
wrong for him back there—who knows what it was.
Maybe he saw he couldn't warn us before they got
to us. If that's the case, he might've saved our lives
letting us get caught in our sleep. Whatever it was,
I'll wager my life he'll be back in this game before
it's over. Schoolmaster's the kind of man who has to
make things right. Nothing else will do for him. He's

a true hero, that schoolmaster. Count on him to always do what a hero does."

"I sure hope you're right about him, Summers," said Lawrence Teasdale, trudging along without missing a step. He spit dryly through parched lips and did not bother rubbing a hand across his mouth.

Along the boardwalk out front of the cantina, Summers, Webb and Teasdale saw an old man leaning to one side on his cane. Hector Roderio shook his head, looking back and forth, first at Sergeant Hervisu's patrol with its three ragtag prisoners, then at the half-naked outlaws who spilled blindly through the doors of the cantina and were jostled into a loose line to be herded off to the old Spanish mission.

Chapter 21

In the home of Juan Richards, Captain Oberiske stood with the empty feed bag hanging from his right hand, his left hand clasped firmly over his nose and mouth. On the floor, the two outlaws' heads lay amid chips of dried mud that had flaked and broken off when Oberiske shook them from the sack. "What kind of men are these?" he whispered in awe. "How do they live? How do they think? What in God's name makes them do something like this?"

Sergeant Hector Hervisu and old Hector Roderio looked at one another, then stared back down at the heads. Hector Roderio tapped his cane on the wooden floor. "I think you would be wise to kill these men and be done with them, *Señor Capitán*. No good is served by these men remaining alive."

Captain Oberiske ignored Roderio and looked to Sergeant Hector Hervisu for an answer. But Hervisu only shrugged. "I have seen this means of bounty hunting many times, *Capitán*. Is it any different than a man who takes the pelt of a mountain cat or a wolf for the reward?"

"Oh yes, indeed. I dare say there *is* a difference!" Captain Oberiske replied strongly. "It is not the taking of these outlaws' heads for *reward* that I find profane. It is the very act of chopping off heads, for any reason! Perhaps you must come from an older, more civilized race in order to recognize the inhumanity of such a deed."

"Sí, that must be it," Hervisu said, relenting to his superior officer. "My people still have much to learn. Lucky for us we have people like you to teach us."

Hearing Sergeant Hervisu, Cherokee Rhodes stifled a short laugh and cleared his throat. He had wheeled Juan Richards to the Spanish mission, then returned to the *hacienda* with Sergeant Hervisu, carrying the feed sack with its gruesome contents. "Yep, I think you're both right," he said quickly, making sure Captain Oberiske heard the gravity in his voice.

Oberiske turned to a guard by the front door and said, "Remove these—these hideous things!" He brushed his hand through the air as if sweeping the heads out the door. "Have them burnt and disposed of in some—"

"Whoa!" said Cherokee Rhodes, cutting in. "Begging your pardon, Captain . . . but I put a stick to the dirt on this thing and did myself some serious figuring. There's a few hundred dollars on these heads alone. It turns into several thousand if I can put some more of the Peltry Gang with them, especially Goose and Moses themselves. I don't know how much that sounds like to you in Germany money, but in good ole American it's a *whole bunch*, let me tell you!"

Captain Oberiske just stared at Cherokee Rhodes blankly for a moment. Then he batted his eyes as if to clear his head and make sure he'd heard correctly. "What did you say? Did you say *several thousand*?"

"That's right, Captain," said Rhodes. "It took me a minute or two for it to sink in when I first heard it, but there it is. There's big money in dead outlaws! Will Summers saw a good thing and jumped right on it. Soon as I saw it, I did the same." He nodded at the two grisly, mud-packed heads on the floor and said, "I know that machine rifle is mighty important to you, but surely we can work something out between us on all this bounty money, can't we?"

Captain Oberiske didn't answer. Instead, he slapped the riding quirt against the side of his leg and said, "We will soon close the subject on the machine rifle for good. Either these men will give it up, or we will begin killing them one at a time, every hour on the hour until they do." He turned haughtily and walked out the door.

In a large stone-walled wine cellar beneath the old Spanish mission, Will Summers, Abner Webb and Sergeant Lawrence Teasdale huddled together in a dark corner as the armed *Federales* shoved more and more of the Peltry Gang down the wide wooden stairs. Most of the outlaws were still in a drugged stupor, barely able to stand on their own, the powerful combination of peyote and alcohol still singing frantically inside their ragged heads. They only cast passing glances at the three possemen as they took in their new surroundings. Then they crawled off to their own spots along the stone walls as one of the guards walked down the stairs with several sets of ankle chains draped over his shoulder.

"What the hell is that for?" Dog Belly Kelso growled drunkenly at the young soldier who bent down and dropped a pair of ankle chains at his feet. From his spot in the dark corner, Will Summers took note of the key the young soldier took from his waist belt to unlock the cuffs on the end of the two-foot chain. Gigging Abner Webb with his elbow, Summers whispered to him and Teasdale, "Keep an eye on the one with the key—he'll be our way out of here."

Webb and Teasdale nodded, already honed in on the young soldier.

"This is to keep you from getting shot should you try to break free and run away, *amigo*," the young soldier said to Dog Belly. He shoved the key back down into his belt, grabbed Dog Belly's bare feet and cuffed them quickly, before Kelso had a chance to think about it and offer resistance. Atop the wide stairs, three armed *Federales* watched over the young soldier with their rifles at port arms, their thumbs poised over the rifle hammers.

Will Summers' eye moved from face to face along the row of handcuffed outlaws lined along the stone wall. He said their names silently to himself, sorting out the ones he'd seen on the wanted posters. "There sits our bounty money, Deputy," he whispered to Abner Webb.

Webb nodded, his eyes still fixed on the young soldier and the key to their freedom. "To tell the truth, I've forgotten all about the bounty money, Summers. I just don't want to end up dead down here."

"Neither do I," whispered Sergeant Teasdale. "To hell with the reward, and the Gatling gun too. All I can think about is staying alive." He shot a quick glance around Webb to Summers. "Think we'll really get any help from that schoolmaster? Or is he high-tailing it back to the border about now?"

"He'll be back for us," Summers whispered confidently. "It's the only thing he'll allow himself to do."

Against the wall next to Dog Belly sat Brayton "Comanche Killer" Cane, Big Catt, Pip Magger and Cap Whitlow, the four dressed only in their trousers, having lost their boots, hats and shooting gear. Across the narrow hall, facing them in the same condition, sat Thurman Anderson, Roscoe Moore and

Bert Smitson. As the young soldier moved from Kelso to Pip Magger, the big outlaw drew his feet up away from the set of ankle chains. "I've never let another living human being touch my bare feet, and I never will," Pip Magger hissed, his eyes aswirl on peyote and mescal. He clenched his already cuffed hands into fists and snarled at the young soldier.

"I understand," said the young soldier, jerking his hands back from Magger's dirty ankles. He shrugged, pulled a pistol from beneath the safety flap on his holster and shot Magger squarely in the forehead.

"Lord have mercy!" Comanche Killer Cane bellowed, sitting next to Pip Magger, Magger's blood stinging his drunken face. The bullet had gone through Pip Magger's head and thumped flat against the stone wall. A great rosette of blood, brain and bone matter spun out, showering the rest of the men. "You didn't have to splatter that fool all over me, did you, *Peewee*!"

"Pee-wee, *señor*?" The young soldier turned the smoking pistol to Comanche Killer's face.

"It's just a figure of speech, boy," said Cane, raising his cuffed hands chest-high in a show of submission. "Nothing to get in an uproar about." Blood and brain matter ran down and dripped from Cane's face.

The young soldier's face and voice took on a sharp edge as he fanned the pistol slowly from face to face along the wall. "Does anybody else object to me touching his bare feet?" The pistol made its rounds from man to man, then aimed back at Comanche Killer Cane as if expecting an answer for the group.

"Well, hell no, we don't mind you touching our feet," said Cane, giving a low, drunken laugh. "The truth is, neither did that ole boy." He nodded at the slumped head of Pip Magger next to him. "He was just drunk and confused . . . mistook his bare feet for another part of himself, I reckon."

"Make no mistake, any of you," the soldier said, raising his voice for everyone's benefit. "I will put a bullet in any man who hampers my job." He slowly lowered the pistol and holstered it, then went back to his task with the ankle chains.

"So there's that," said Comanche Killer Cane, still laughing under his breath. The soldier looked at him and shook his head in disgust, realizing the outlaw was still under the influence of the peyote.

Down along the wall, Goose Peltry had been passed out ever since the soldiers had peeled him up off the floor of the cantina. But now the gunshot caused him to raise his face from the cool dirt floor and rub his blurry eyes. "What the hell's going on?" he asked, looking across the dirt floor at the dark corner where Will Summers, Abner Webb and Lawrence Teasdale sat staring at him.

"You're a prisoner of the Mexican government, Goose," Will Summers said flatly. "We all are."

Goose looked all around, rubbing his face, having a hard time understanding. Then he tried harder to focus and said, "Will Summers? Is that you?"

"Yeah, it's me. Howdy, Goose," Summers responded.

Goose squinted, then opened his eyes as he recalled the events of the past week. "You're the ones been trailing us all the way from Rileyville, ain't yas?"

"Yep" said Summers. He nodded toward Abner Webb. "This is the deputy you and your men shamed in front of the whole town."

Webb seethed, then said, "Remember me, you rotten sonsabitch?" He leaned slightly forward, but Summers blocked him back with his forearm.

"This is Sergeant Teasdale," said Summers, nodding toward the other side of Webb. "He's the one you stole the Gatling gun from."

"Really now?" Goose gave Webb and Teasdale a hard stare, feeling the peyote and mescal loosen its grip on his brain a little. "I suppose the two of you can't wait to settle up with me?"

"That's right," said Teasdale. "The only thing keeping you alive is circumstance, Goose. The minute that changes, you're dead."

"Says who?" came the gruff voice of Comanche Killer Cane from the other end of the wall. "Just cause we're prisoners, don't go thinking we won't kill you."

"You heard him," said Goose Peltry to Teasdale. "You're just as outnumbered here as you was out there."

"That won't be for long, Goose," said Summers. "The way I figure, you either got to tell these boys where the machine rifle is, or they start trimming down your numbers for you."

"Me?" Goose looked confused. "I don't know where it's at. Last I knew, either you or the *Federales* had it."

"You better hope you can sell them on that story, Goose," said Summers. "Otherwise you're cooked."

"Real funny, Summers," Goose sneered. He looked back and forth along the wall where he lay, seeing the faces of his men and Doc Murdock's scalp hunters. "Where's my brother and Murdock?" he asked.

"We saw Moses being led out of the big *hacienda* on our way over here," said Comanche Killer Cane. "I ain't seen Doc Murdock since late last night when he left the cantina with that Mexican woman. I hope they haven't bushwhacked him. You know they killed poor Flat Face Chinn and Handy Phelps . . .

shot them down in the cantina a while ago, these dirty, rotten poltroons."

"It's been a rough night on all of us. They'll be missed," Goose said. Then, keeping his voice lowered, casting a glance toward the young soldier as he worked his way along the wall from one man to the next, Goose said to Will Summers, "You know it weren't nothing personal against you, Summers, what happened back in Rileyville. We just needed horses awfully bad . . . and damned if you didn't take off with the best ones in town."

"So you tried burning the whole town down because of it," said Summers. "Shame on you, Goose. Imagine how that made me feel. Hadn't been for that, I wouldn't have come looking for you, bounty money or no bounty money. I've got better things to do than to chase a bunch of misfits who don't have enough sense to know the war's over."

Goose started to say something more, but the door at the top of the stairs opened and three soldiers walked down to the cellar, escorting a naked Moses Peltry between them. At the bottom of the stairs, Moses stopped and stood as the young soldier hurried over and threw a pair of dirty striped trousers against his chest. "Here, put these on," the soldier commanded.

Moses stepped into the trousers, pulled them up and gathered them at his waist. Then the young guard bent down and clamped a set of ankle chains on him. When the soldier stood up and backed away, Moses looked along the faces of his half-naked men and said, "If any of us make it out of this alive, remember this. Cherokee Rhodes is the man who set us up and sold us out. He told me so himself."

"Against the wall with you, outlaw," said one of the guards, giving Moses Peltry a shove from behind.

The guards turned as one and walked back up the stairs, except for the one still clamping chains on the prisoners' ankles.

"Come down here with me, Moses," said Goose, waving his brother toward him.

Moses Peltry looked down at the body of Pip Magger without changing his cold expression, then walked barefoot to where Goose had pushed himself up and stood against the wall. The men murmured greetings to Moses as he passed by. When he joined his brother, he stopped at the sight of Will Summers standing against the opposite wall and staring at him.

"Will Summers. . . ." Moses looked him up and down. "Rhodes told me it was you back there dogging us. You never should have trusted that half-breed any more than I should."

"Who said we trusted him?" Summers replied. "He said he knew your stomping ground."

"Yeah," said Moses. "He said you was after the bounty on everybody's head. I never knew you to go out for that kind of money, Summers."

"You burnt Rileyville in my name, Moses." Will Summers returned Moses Peltry's harsh stare. "Whatever made you think I'd stand still for that?"

"Call it the heat of the moment," said Moses. A tense silence passed, then he said quietly, "Any reason we can't call a truce for a while . . . just to see what it's going to take to get us out of this mess?"

"Why not?" Will Summers shrugged. "But it won't change anything once we're out of here."

"That sounds fair enough to me," said Moses. "I never wanted any trouble with you anyway." He looked at Abner Webb. "You're that deputy from Rileyville, ain't you?"

"Yep," Webb said, tight-lipped.

"And you?" said Moses, looking at Sergeant Teasdale. "How do you play into all this?"

"I was with the army patrol you and your men bushwhacked," said Teasdale. "As far as I'm concerned, you and I can go at it tooth and nail right now." He nodded toward Will Summers. "But if he calls a truce, I'll honor it as long as the next man does."

"Wait a minute, brother Moses!" said Goose, also gesturing toward Will Summers. "You can't trust this damn horse trader! He's part of the reason we're trapped here . . . dogging our trail the way he has."

"What do you want to do, brother Goose?" Moses demanded, squeezing both hands around his long beard. "You want to start fighting here and now like this Yankee soldier said?"

"It beats belly-crawling," said Goose.

"Belly-crawling?" Moses Peltry shook his head and said to Will Summers, "See what I have to deal with?" Then, turning back to Goose, he said, "You never know when to keep your mouth shut, do you? When you've lost everything you've got, all the way down to your bare ass, it's time to stop and look at every possibility!"

"Never thought I'd see the day we'd have a truce with a Yankee, a lawman and a horse trader," Goose mumbled. He hung his head and looked down at the floor.

Will Summers said to Goose, "All we're talking about is trying to stay alive until we get out of here."

"So shut up and pay attention," Moses cut in. "What do you have in mind, Summers?"

Will Summers looked along the hall to where the soldier was still busy clamping ankle cuffs on the rest of the men. Keeping his voice lowered, Summers said, "It's plain enough what these soldiers want. They want the machine rifle. The sergeant said they were going to start killing us if you don't give it to them."

"We don't have it," said Moses. "I figured you've got it."

"It doesn't matter which of us has it. We've got to keep them from knowing. Once they get their hands on that gun, there's no reason to keep us alive. We've got to keep them guessing which of us has it for a while."

"For a while?" Moses gave him a questioning look. "Are you expecting some company, Summers?"

"Maybe," said Summers. "But I'm not saying when or how many, so don't even ask. But when the right time comes, I'll need you and your men ready to make a move with us. We all bust out of here together."

Goose looked suspicious. "Why are you being so good to us, Summers?"

"Because there's only three of *us* in here, Goose," said Will Summers. Wasting no further explanation on Goose, he said to Moses, "As soon as we get free of this place, the truce is off. We'll settle everything between us. Deal?"

"Deal," said Moses.

"A deal, huh?" Goose spread a wide, sarcastic grin, looking the three possemen up and down. "Like you said, there's only three of you. What makes you think the three of you stand a chance out there any more than you do in here?"

"I never said we didn't stand a chance in here, Goose," said Will Summers. "Your brother Moses is the one who asked for the truce. We're just being obliging."

Dead silence followed, until finally a slight smile

came to Moses' face. Then a low chuckle, then a laugh, as Summers, Webb and Teasdale joined in. Finally, after looking confused by it for a second, even Goose joined in.

"You always was one bold, crazy sonsabitch, Summers," said Moses Peltry. "I almost hate thinking I've got to kill you before this is over."

"Don't worry about killing me, Moses," said Will Summers, still smiling. "You don't stand a chance in hell."

Chapter 22

———

Sherman Dahl had spent most of the night hiding in the darkness of the crevices and gullies along the trail toward Punta Del Sol. After he'd escaped with the heavy Gatling gun and its folded stand tied across his horse's back behind his saddle, he'd stayed as close to the *Federale* patrol as he dared, just to make sure no harm came to Teasdale, Webb or Summers along the way. Dahl hated having to abandon his companions the way he did, but he'd really had no other choice. The Mexican army patrol had come upon them swiftly and silently in the night. By the time Sherman Dahl could have fired a warning shot, the soldiers were already within a few slim yards of the sleeping men. There was no doubt in Dahl's mind that Summers, Webb and Teasdale would have made a fight of it. And that fight would have been their last, Dahl thought.

At daylight, when the patrol entered the town, Sherman Dahl stepped his horse quietly up into the surrounding hillside and lay in watch like a mountain cat. In the thin morning light, he saw the naked, drunken outlaws being herded from the cantina to the old Spanish mission at the edge of town. He saw Summers, Webb and Teasdale also taken there. Then he watched Cherokee Rhodes appear alongside the tall officer in the German uniform on the porch of the large *hacienda* atop the steep trail. "Good thing I saw you first, Cherokee," he whispered to himself.

As the gray mist of morning lifted, burnt away by the hot sun, Dahl saw the supply wagon sitting inside a livery corral, where the Peltry Gang must have left it. Now there were three soldiers standing guard around it. Through the canvas tarpaulin draped over the rear of the wagon, Dahl saw the outline of the ammunition crates. His eyes instinctively followed an imaginary line away from the wagon to the closest point of steep, rocky hillside where he could find cover for himself. Then he unloaded the Gatling gun, affixed it to its stand a few steps back out of sight and checked it over thoroughly.

Sherman Dahl waited and watched and rested. He sipped tepid water from his canteen as he kept an eye on the comings and goings of Punta Del Sol. In the early afternoon, Cherokee Rhodes and Junior the dog walked out to the corral. Rhodes carried a goatskin of water that he passed around to the three guards. In a moment, Rhodes and two of the guards left, probably going for their noon meal, Dahl thought, grateful that now there was only one guard to take care of. But then he saw that Junior had found himself a slice of black shade beneath the wagon and dropped down in it.

"Please get out of there, Junior," Dahl whispered. "Don't make me kill you." He drew the long knife from his boot well and tested its edge with the flat of his thumb. He hoped the dog wasn't going to be a problem. With the sun reaching the hottest point of the day and heat wavering upward from the dirt streets of the town, Sherman Dahl crawled down from his lofty position and headed for the supply wagon.

Dahl carried his repeating rifle with him as he

snaked downward but stashed it behind a rock when he reached the bottom of the hillside, where his cover ended. He couldn't take the rifle any farther with him, but he wanted it close by in case he needed it on his way back. He lay behind a brush thicket and watched as three guards dragged one of the scalp hunters from the old Spanish mission to the wide clearing in the center of town.

"This ain't fair, damn it to hell!" Comanche Killer Cane shouted. One guard shoved him over near the stone well, where he staggered back and forth, trying to get his footing, his cuffed hands reaching out uselessly in front of him. "You could give a man a fighting chance, you jake-legged bunch of rotten—!"

His words cut short as the one guard stepped away and the other two raised their rifles and fired unceremoniously. Both shots hit Cane in the chest and drove him backward to the ground. But as the other guard stepped forward again, Cane managed to turn himself over and struggle upward onto his hands and knees, blood flowing freely from his shattered chest. "All right now," he said in a groggy voice. "Let's just hold on. You've done what you . . . set out to do." His voice began failing as his life spilled out into the hot dirt. He tried to say more, but the young soldier drew a short sword from a sheath on his side, grabbed a handful of Cane's hair and jerked his head up.

From his position in the brush thicket, Sherman Dahl winced at the sight of the blade passing sleekly across Cane's exposed throat, leaving a ribbon of spinning blood behind it. The soldier turned loose of Cane's hair and let him drop facedown in the dirt. He wiped his sword blade across Cane's naked back and stepped away. Joining the other two soldiers, he slid the sword back into its sheath. Dahl watched the three march single file back to the old Spanish mission. On the supply wagon, the guard had also watched the execution intently. He rubbed a hand on his sweaty throat and whispered the name of the Blessed Virgin under his breath.

As soon as the three soldiers stepped inside the doors to the old Spanish mission, Sherman Dahl drew his knife from his boot and prepared to make his move. But the sound of a pistol cocking and the feel of the steel barrel tip against his head caused him to freeze. "Make one sound," Doc Murdock whispered, "and I'll open your head up all over the ground."

Sherman Dahl spread his hands before him, letting the big knife fall from his fist. He lay silent, awaiting the next move in what he knew to be a most deadly game. "Good boy," whispered Doc Murdock. "Now back up behind this brush. I don't want to be seen no more than you do."

When Sherman Dahl had crawled backward a few feet, Doc Murdock stopped him with a nudge of his pistol barrel. Still whispering, Murdock asked, "Now, who the hell are you? What's your angle in all this?"

"I'm one of the four possemen left," said Dahl, seeing no point in hiding the fact. "The other three are in there." He nodded toward the Spanish mission.

"I'll be damned." Doc Murdock grinned, shaking his bare head slowly. "I'll say one thing for you bunch of fools, you don't give up easy."

"You're Doc Murdock, I presume?" Dahl asked, turning his face around enough to look him in the eyes.

"Yeah, you *presume* right," said Murdock. "But me and my men threw in with the Peltrys *after* they hit your pig-shit town. So you've got no call to have a mad-on at me." He offered a tired grin. "Anyhow, it looks like both your side and mine are in the same bad spot over there." He gestured his pistol barrel away from Sherman Dahl and toward the Spanish mission. "Don't tell me you risked your neck coming down here to save your possemen."

"That's right," said Dahl. "I'm here to do whatever it takes. What about you? Are you here to free your men?"

"Me?" Murdock chuckled under his breath. "Hell, no. I got caught off-guard, wild-eyed on peyote and pinned to a young whore's belly. We was damn near stuck together like dogs. We both dived out the same window. But she landed on the bottom and couldn't take the fall, I reckon." He spit. "Anyway, I hope to hell you came here on horseback. I need to get out of here fast!"

"What about your men?" Dahl asked.

"What about them?" Murdock retorted. "They're all old enough to die. They knew what to expect when they started riding with me. Now let's get going. Show me where that horse is."

"Huh-uh," said Dahl, glancing down at Murdock's bare feet then back to his sweaty face. "I'm not showing you anything. I came here to get my men, and that's what I'm going to do." His hand dropped to the ground and closed around the knife handle. "You want a horse? Sure, I've got one hidden up there. . . . In fact, I've got a half dozen horses up there," he lied. "But nobody rides until this job is finished."

Murdock's hand tightened around his gun butt. "Maybe you're a little thick, young man," he said in a harsh whisper, "so let me remind you: I'm the one holding the cocked pistol. You might get a swing started with that knife, but it ain't going to do anything for you. You'll still be dead when this hammer falls."

"Yep, and you'll still be here, barefoot and without a horse, *Federales* making round holes in your belly. Now, either pull that trigger or get ready to help me make a move. I'm not going to lay here in this heat all evening."

Doc Murdock considered the situation. He glanced around the edge of their brush cover at the guard sitting on the tailgate of the supply wagon and looking in the opposite direction. "You've got guts, young man, I'll give you that." He let out a breath, uncocked the pistol and lowered it. "What is it you're getting ready to do anyway?"

"I'm getting ready to take out that guard, grab some ammunition for the Gatling gun, then get out of here before they see what I've done."

Murdock's eyes lit up. "You've got the Gatling gun?" He laughed low and quietly and shook his head. "Lord, man, why didn't you say so to begin with? That gun is just what we need to get us the hell off the spot here."

"Then you're with me?" Dahl asked.

"With you? If you've got that machine rifle, we're just like cousins, you and me," said Murdock. "Tell me what you need me to do." Even as he spoke to Sherman Dahl, Doc Murdock was busily sizing him up, weighing his chances at dropping this young man along the trail, taking whatever horses and supplies he had and hightailing it out of there. The Gatling gun would be worth taking too, he thought.

"Just cover my back until I take care of him," said Dahl. "Then come grab as much ammunition as you can carry. Once we get the Gatling gun loaded, we'll see what we need to do to get our men out of there."

"That's it? That's your whole plan?" said Murdock.

"That's where it starts," said Dahl. "We'll see

where it goes from there." He turned his gaze toward
the guard. "Get ready," he whispered over his
shoulder.

Murdock just stared at him for a moment, wondering if he was serious. "Have you done much of this
kind of fighting?" he asked.

"I've done my share," said Dahl. Without another
word, he crawled away on his belly like a lizard,
circling wide of the wagon, keeping himself on the
guard's blind side until he got within a few feet from
the wagon's tailgate. Beneath the wagon, Junior stood
up and looked at Dahl, causing him to freeze to the
ground for a second and close his hand around his
pistol butt. But then Junior stepped out from beneath
the wagon without a sound, shook himself off and
dropped back down in the dirt, facing the guard.
This time the dog sat staring at the guard as if inten-
tionally drawing his attention.

For a moment, Doc Murdock lost sight of Sherman
Dahl. But then, as quick as a streak of lightning, Dahl
sprang into sight. He came up over the edge of the
tailgate, swung an arm around the guard's neck and
jerked him backward onto the hard, sharp point of
steel.

Murdock watched, mesmerized, seeing Dahl rock
the blade up and down brutally between the guard's
ribs, making sure it pierced his heart. Junior the dog
stared with detached fascination. When Dahl slid the
guard forward and pulled the blade from his back,
Murdock saw the calmness, the cold deliberation, of
Dahl's movements as he sat the guard back into place
on the tailgate and adjusted his hat on his head. Dahl
crouched down out of sight beside the wagon and
motioned for Murdock to join him. "Damn, boy,"
Murdock whispered to himself. "You do know your
business, don't you?"

As Murdock hurried forward, Dahl had already raised one corner of the canvas tarpaulin. He began grabbing the ammunition crates by their rope handles and dragging them down to the ground. "Get two of them and go," Dahl whispered. "I'll get two more!"

"That's not enough!" said Murdock, grabbing the two crates by their handles.

"It'll have to do," said Dahl, shooting a quick glance toward the old Spanish mission. "They'll be coming back soon. We need to cover some ground before they catch on to us."

"Anything you say, posseman," said Murdock. He turned, half carrying, half dragging the two crates toward the brush. Junior stood up from the dirt and trotted off behind him as if following an old friend.

They slipped into the cover of brush and rock and moved along in a crouch until they came to the base of the hillside where Sherman Dahl had stashed his rifle. Doc Murdock had stopped a few feet in front of Dahl. When he looked back and saw the rifle in the young man's hands, he silently commended himself for not having tried to make a move on Dahl just yet. He was learning more about this man every step they traveled. He would bide his time. "You're full of surprises, ain't you, posseman?"

"Stop calling me posseman," said Dahl. He checked the rifle with a serious expression and cradled it in his arm. "My name's Sherman Dahl."

"All right then, Sherman Dahl." Murdock agreed with a nod, catching his breath, taking advantage of their stopping if only for a moment. "You don't strike me as a full-time lawman. What are you, a deputy? A town councilman?"

"Neither," said Dahl. "I'm Rileyville's schoolmaster."

"You're kidding?" Doc Murdock stifled a surprised chuckle. "A nice young schoolmaster out here on a manhunt? How the hell did that come about?"

"I came along because your pals the Peltrys burnt down the schoolhouse. Whatever bounty reward we get, my cut of it goes to rebuild the school." He nodded at the uphill path before them. "Let's get going. We've got a hard climb."

"Right," said Murdock, yet he made no move toward grabbing the rope handles of the ammunition crate. Instead, his right hand rested on his pistol butt as he wiped a shirtsleeve across his sweaty face. "Only, I was just thinking. What's keeping me from shooting you right here, leaving these heavy crates where they lie, working my way on up this trail, finding those horses for myself and getting out of here?" He spread a crafty grin.

"What about helping your men escape?" Dahl asked.

Murdock shrugged. "I already told you how I feel about them. They knew the risks." His stare turned sharper, bolder.

"Then I suppose there's nothing keeping you from it," said Dahl, straightening up, letting his right hand poise near his pistol butt, "provided you're a good gambler."

"Good gambler?" Murdock's brow raised slightly. He still bore the crafty grin.

"That's right," said Dahl calmly. "You'll be betting on my having told you the truth about there being horses there. You'll be betting that even if there are, you can kill me so quick I won't have time to put a bullet or two in you . . . slowing you down while the *Federales* come running." Dahl returned the crafty grin. "It's a whole lot to be betting on, you have to admit." His hand inched a fraction closer to his pistol butt.

Doc Murdock chuckled aloud now, his hand coming up away from his pistol. "It would be at that." He reached down with both hands, grabbed the rope handles and started off up the path. Junior trotted along close at his heels. "Anyway," he said over his shoulder, "I don't want to run out. I've got some unfinished business with Goose Peltry that needs settling."

"Oh?" That was all Sherman Dahl said, but it was enough to keep Murdock talking.

"Yep. The fact is, I'm going to kill that sucker," said Doc Murdock.

"But he's one of the leaders," said Dahl. "How do you expect to pull that off? What about his brother?"

"Ha! I'm not worried about his brother. If Moses wants to jump in, that's all right too." Murdock glanced back as he moved ahead. "I suppose hearing something like that surprises the hell out of a man like you, but that's the cold, hard way things work in this world me and the Peltrys live in."

"Yep," said Dahl, hurrying along behind him. "It does surprise me. But I'm getting more used to it every day I'm out here."

At the top of the path, Doc Murdock came upon the Gatling gun abruptly, seeing it sitting back from the edge of the rocky ledge two hundred yards above Punta Del Sol. "I'll be damned," he said, out of breath, dropping both ammunition crates. "Talking about gambling . . . you sure took a big chance leaving that gun sitting out here in full view. Anybody coming along here could have spotted it."

"Luckily they didn't though," said Dahl matter-of-factly. He also dropped his two crates. Then he walked over to a rock half the size of a saddle, turned it over and picked up the Gatling gun's black metal firing mechanism. "Of course, the gun wouldn't have done anybody any good without this."

Murdock grinned, once again reminding himself how wise he had been not to kill this schoolteacher too soon. He would have been stuck with a machine rifle without a firing mechanism. But so much for waiting. Now was the time to get out of here. He glanced down at Dahl's dusty boots, sizing them up as he once again slipped his hand atop his pistol butt. "That was good thinking on your part, school-teacher," said Murdock. He looked all around for the horses, but saw none. Looking down at the ground, he saw only one set of fresh hoofprints in the dust.

"Looking for the horses?" Dahl asked in a quiet tone. As he spoke, his hand levered a round into his rifle chamber and kept the rifle pointed and cocked.

"Yeah, sort of," Murdock said warily. "I don't see but one set of prints here."

"That's because I lied to you. There's only one horse. Guess who's going to be riding out of here on it?" As if knowing what was about to happen, Junior moved out from between the two men and took a seat on the hot ground beside the Gatling gun. He looked back and forth, his tongue lolling from his gaping mouth.

"Whoa now!" Murdock tried to laugh off the seriousness of Dahl's words and actions, but it wasn't easy, seeing the deadly look in Dahl's flat, level stare. How the hell had he been caught off-guard like this? By a damned schoolteacher at that! "We made a deal! We both gave our word! What kind of man are you?"

"The kind who's going to leave you lying here dead. I've been listening to you tell me how nobody's life means anything but your own. You must be an idiot, telling me all that. Then you expect me to keep my word on anything I tell you?"

"Jesus, man!" Murdock sweated more freely. "I trusted you! I kept my end of the bargain. I could've shot you at any time, but I didn't!"

"Only because you fooled around, overestimating yourself, underestimating me. You figured, 'No hurry; what's this schoolteacher going to be able to do?'" said Dahl. "Well, now you know. You had a gun to my head; you should have used it. That was pitifully stupid, too stupid to stay alive out here."

"Wait!" Murdock shouted. "You're going to need me! How will you fire the machine rifle by yourself?" His hand made a fast, desperate grab for his pistol.

"I'll manage somehow," said Dahl, cool, calm, prepared for Murdock's move. He fired three times, spacing the shots a full second apart as he levered his rifle, taking a step forward each time Murdock rocked backward with another bullet hole in his chest.

Chapter 23

—————

Two soldiers had dragged a kicking and screaming Goose Peltry away and up the stairs. Sergeant Hervisu stood flanked by two armed guards in the narrow corridor among the prisoners. The guards held the prisoners at bay with their cocked rifles. Hervisu held a saber thrust out at arm's length, the tip of it almost touching Moses Peltry's chest. Still, Hervisu did not like the looks of this situation. "*Capitán*, let us move to the top of the stairs, *por favor*," he said to Oberiske. Any second, these outlaws could rush them. Oberiske had to be blind not to see it, Hervisu thought.

Yet Captain Oberiske stood with his hands folded behind his back, his chin tilted up at a haughty angle. Ignoring Hervisu, he said to Moses Peltry, "You have exactly ten minutes to decide, *Herr* Peltry. Either tell me where the Gatling gun is hidden, or your brother will be the next one to die."

Will Summers, Teasdale and Abner Webb held Moses back. "You dirty, low-down sonsabitch!" Moses bellowed in rage, struggling against Summers and Webb. "If you harm one hair on my brother's head, I'll rip your heart out and eat it!" His men stood seething, ready to make a lunge at the guards, waiting for only one word from Moses to start a bloodletting.

With no apparent fear, Captain Oberiske turned on his boot heels and walked to the bottom of the stairs. Hervisu and the two guards inched backward until they joined him. "Make no mistake; your brother *will* die!" He looked from one face to the next. "Every one of you will die if you refuse to turn over the gun—"

Oberiske's words stopped as three rifle shots resounded from the hillside above them. His eyes cut to Sergeant Hervisu and the two guards. "Sergeant, follow me. Let us see what the gunfire is about! You guards, stay here. If these men cause any trouble, shoot them. Shoot as many as you must to maintain order!"

"There it is," Will Summers whispered near Moses Peltry's ear as they continued holding him back. "That's our schoolmaster giving us a signal." Moses eased down a bit. They watched Oberiske and Hervisu bound up the stairs and close the thick wooden door behind them. They heard the large latch fall into place. "Get ready," Summers added. "The guard on the right has the key to these cuffs. As soon as we hear the Gatling gun, your men are going to have to rush him."

"We'll get the key, no problem," Moses Peltry whispered. "But how are we going to get through that door?"

"That's a good question," said Summers. No sooner had he said it than the sound of the Gatling gun rattled long and loud above them.

On the dirt street, Cherokee Rhodes and the two wagon guards had heard the three rifle shots as they'd returned to the supply wagon. Then, just as they'd found the other guard sitting propped up on the wagon gate with a trickle of blood running down the corner of his mouth, the Gatling gun began to spit lead down from the hillside two hundred yards above the streets of Punta Del Sol. "What the hell is going on?" Cherokee Rhodes shouted, staring into the dead eyes of the guard, who stared back at him as if in shock.

Bullets from the distant Gatling gun ran in a line along the roof of the old Spanish mission, kicking up chunks of orange clay tile. On its sweep coming back, bullets thumped into the water trough, split the hitch rail and toppled it and sent *Federales* diving for cover. In the dirt street, the bullets nailed the two guards who stood with their rifles aimed at Goose Peltry's chest. Goose grabbed a key from the belt of one of the fallen guards and quickly freed himself of the handcuffs and ankle chain. He snatched up a rifle and ran screaming and firing at the cowering *Federales* on his way back to the mission door.

"Someone kill him!" Captain Oberiske shouted, pointing his pistol and firing at Goose Peltry. He fired three shots. Two of them hit Goose—one in the upper arm, the other in the thigh—causing the outlaw to fall to the ground. Three *Federales* rose and fired with their rifles. One shot hit Goose low in the belly. Another sent a graze along the side of his head. Blood flew.

But Goose Peltry came up screaming, firing back, his shots sending Oberiske ducking for cover. "I'm coming, brother Moses!" He ran staggering toward the mission door.

"Somebody stop him!" Oberiske raged. He stood up and fired at Goose Peltry, but this time the sweep of the Gatling gun came back along the street and forced him down. Horses from the broken hitch rail ran in a frenzy, circling in confusion, their reins still tied to pieces of the broken rail. *Federales* ran back

and forth wildly in the dirt street, seeking cover from
the deadly assault of the machine rifle.

"We've got that bastard," Cherokee Rhodes
shouted, running over from the corral, the two
guards close behind him. Rhodes dropped onto one
knee and took careful aim at Goose Peltry with his
pistol as Goose stood up and grabbed the door handle. Rhodes' shot hit Goose in the center of his naked
back and slammed him against the mission door.
Goose slid down, then turned with his back against
the door, blood spilling from his lips. Through the
roar of gunfire, Cherokee Rhodes shouted, "I got that
crazy sonsa—!"

His words cut short as a shot from the rifle in
Goose's hands lifted him off his feet and slammed
him backward into the two guards, who were squat-
ting behind him. They threw Rhodes aside and fired
at Goose as he pulled himself up and managed to
fling open the mission door. Sergeant Hervisu saw
what Goose was attempting to do. He hurried, running in a low crouch through the heavy gunfire to
enter the mission behind Goose Peltry. He fired as
he hurried over toward the cellar door, where Goose
had pulled himself up and grabbed the latch with
both hands.

"No!" Hervisu shouted, seeing Goose struggle
with the heavy latch. He fired his last two pistol
shots. One hit Goose high in his shoulder. The other
thumped into the thick wooden door. But Goose continued to throw the latch open. Hervisu tossed his
empty pistol aside and hurled himself forward,
drawing his saber from its sheath.

Inside the cellar, atop the stair landing, Summers,
Webb, Teasdale and Moses Peltry stood poised, listening to the latch trying to come open on the other

side of the door. Behind them, the rest of the men pressed forward, eager to make their break. Tense seconds ticked by. At the bottom of the stairs, the two guards lay dead, their rifles gone, their pistols stripped from their holsters. "Come on, come on, hurry it up!" Will Summers pleaded with the slow-turning latch as if his voice could coax it open faster.

"Moses!" Goose cried out in agony as the big door swung open. He stood with one hand on the door, his free hand clasped firmly around Sergeant Hervisu's throat. Hervisu was past struggling. His bulging eyes stared glazed and lifeless. Half of his broken saber still hung in his hand. The other half protruded from the center of Goose Peltry's chest, the long point of it smeared with Goose's blood.

"No, Goose, no!" Moses lamented, grabbing his brother as Goose slumped down to the floor, releasing his grip on Sergeant Hervisu's throat. Webb, Teasdale, Summers and the rest of the prisoners poured out through the open doors. Moses lagged behind, holding Goose's bloody head in his lap. Holding one of the dead guards' pistols in his free hand, he wiped Goose's hair back from his forehead with the other. "Look at you, Goose," Moses said, weeping softly. "My poor, crazy brother. Why'd you do this fool thing? You shoulda took off and found some cover . . . not come back here."

"See?" Goose rasped, his breath beginning to fail him. "Bet you wouldn't . . . let nobody put me to sleep now."

"Damn it, Goose." Moses hugged his brother's head against his chest, careful of the sharp point of the broken saber blade. "You know I would have never let anybody harm you. You're my little brother."

*   *   *

In the street in front of the mission, the *Federales*, led by Captain Oberiske, moved back toward the corral and the livery barn, where there were more horses. Will Summers saw where they were headed and shouted to Abner Webb and Sergeant Teasdale, "Don't let them get mounted—they'll head up after the schoolmaster!" He stooped down and picked up Cherokee Rhodes' pistol from the dirt street and checked it quickly.

Three feet away, one hand pressed to his chest wound, Rhodes lay propped up on one elbow. "Summers, give me a hand. . . . I ain't done for. I was coming for you and the possemen. . . . I swear I was!"

"Lie still, Cherokee," Summers shouted above the pounding gunfire. "Try to die with some honor!"

"Honor hell," Rhodes moaned. As Summers moved away from him, firing the pistol, Rhodes reached a hand up toward one of the naked scalp hunters passing by. "Help me up! I'm one of you!"

Big Catt and Cap Whitlow came running up and slid down beside Rhodes in the dirt as the Gatling gun made a pass along the street, kicking up chunks of hard dirt. "You're Cherokee Rhodes, ain't you?" said Cap Whitlow.

"Yes, yes! That's me," said Rhodes, feeling hopeful. "Help me over there, out of the street. Hurry, before the machine rifle comes back!"

"Have you got a knife down here?" Cap Whitlow asked even as he jammed a hand down Rhodes' boot well and jerked out a long skinning knife.

"Yes, take it," said Rhodes. "Now let's go. Hurry!"

Big Catt grabbed Cherokee Rhodes' boot and began twisting it off his foot. "These are mine, Whitlow. You can have his britches."

Seeing what was going on, Cherokee Rhodes tried

kicking the two men away from him. "You damned, lousy vultures . . . get out of here!"

"We sure enough will," said Big Catt. "But I'm taking this along with me for luck!" He raised the front of Cherokee Rhodes' hair high and tight in his fist and deftly skinned him from forehead to rear crown.

"Lord have mercy, Big Catt. Look at you! You ain't even got drawers to hide yourself! You're taking hair?"

"I see no better time for it than now," said Big Catt, holding the scalp up as blood and fluid dripped from beneath it.

Rhodes writhed in the dirt, screaming. Big Catt slung the gore from the scalp and ran away in a crouch, veering off from the fleeing *Federales* and putting distance between himself and the sweeping Gatling gun. "I coulda told you he'd do that," Whitlow said to the screaming half-breed. Grabbing Rhodes' boot, he quickly twisted it from his foot. But before he could claim the other boot, a rifle shot from one of the fleeing *Federales* hammered into his forehead, causing his head to snap back and appear to explode from the impact.

Twenty yards away, Will Summers, Abner Webb and Lawrence Teasdale had taken a strong firing position behind an empty two-wheel oxcart. With rifles, pistols and ammunition belts they'd snatched up from the dirt and from the hands of dead soldiers, the three managed to keep Oberiske and the remainder of his men pinned inside the livery barn. Above them, the Gatling gun had fallen silent. Will Summers glanced upward through a thick sheet of dust in the air. "Either he's run out of bullets, or else he figures we're safely on our way out of here."

Lawrence Teasdale reloaded and checked the pistol

in his hand. "That's good—so long as he gets away before these boys ride through us and head up there. Oberiske wants that Gatling gun. Nothing else is going to satisfy him."

"Then let's fall back and let them ride out of here," said Webb. "So long as the schoolmaster is safe, what do we care about these *Federales*?"

"Yeah, you're probably right," said Summers as shots from the livery barn whizzed past them. A shot thumped into the oxcart near his head. He flinched and jerked his head back. He looked all around at the bodies lying strewn about in the dirt street. Then he said, "But you know something? I make it there's only seven or eight soldiers left, and that's counting the German captain."

"Yeah, so?" asked Abner Webb, not liking the look in Will Summers' eyes.

"So," said Summers, " I keep thinking how arrogant that pompous sonsabitch was . . . going to take us out one at a time and shoot us like we were brute animals or something. Does that sit right with you two?" He looked back and forth between them.

"Hold on, Will," said Abner Webb. "We've just about got what we came here for. Let these *Federales* ride out of here right now and go after the Gatling gun. Then all we've got to do is take down Moses Peltry and what's left of his men."

"That's the end of it all right," said Will Summers, realizing there was a lull in the firing from the livery barn, which meant that the soldiers were getting ready to make their move. "All we've got to do is let them ride out." He looked at Teasdale, then back at Abner Webb. "Is that what you two want to do? If it is, make up your minds and let's ease back away from here. They're coming any minute now."

Each of them considered their options as a ringing

silence fell over the dirt street. For a moment, the only sound was that of Cherokee Rhodes moaning in the dirt as his lifeblood continued to pour from his chest wound and the raw, exposed top of his head burned like fire. The three possemen stared at Rhodes for a second, then shifted their gazes back toward the livery barn. A few yards from the barn, Junior the hound had slipped back down the path into town. He stood beside the body of a *Federale,* his nose down against a wide circle of blood in the dirt.

"What's that dog doing?" asked Webb.

"What do you think he's doing?" Summers said, trading one question for another.

"He's lapping up blood is what it looks like to me," said Abner Webb.

"So he is," said Will Summers. "It looks like all the excitement finally got to him." Summers grinned. "Figures he's going to get his share of all this, I reckon."

"He's welcome to it," said Teasdale. "His share, and mine too." He looked at the two of them and let out a tense breath, letting the rifle slump in his hand. "As far as I'm concerned, let them pass."

"Yeah," said Abner Webb. "That goes for me too. If you think the schoolmaster is safe . . . let them pass."

"Consider it done," said Will Summers. He raised his voice toward the barn. "Captain Oberiske. We're backing away here. You heard the Gatling gun; you know where to look for it now. What do you say? Can we call it quits here? You go your way, we go ours?"

There was a silence, followed by Oberiske's stern voice. "If you are out there, we will have to kill you. If you are out of my sight, I will not waste time and supplies looking for the likes of you."

"Fair enough," Summers called out. The three posse-men backed away from the oxcart and watched from around the corner of a weathered shack as Oberiske cautiously led six mounted soldiers out of the livery barn. Summers spread a flat grin and said over his shoulder, "I hope the schoolmaster took out the firing mechanism before he left that gun sitting for whoever comes by."

"How do we know for sure he left it there?" said Webb. "He might be carrying it with him."

"No, he left it there," said Summers. "That's the way the schoolmaster would have it planned."

"You don't know that for sure," said Webb.

"You better hope I do," said Will Summers.

"I could use a drink right now," said Teasdale, leaning back and sliding down the side of the shack.

"So could I, but don't get too comfortable just yet," said Summers. "Soon as these men are out of sight, we've still got some bounty collecting to get started on." He gestured his rifle barrel toward the body of Cap Whitlow lying in the dirt with a bullet hole in his forehead. "There's one." He gestured farther along the street to the bodies of Thurman Anderson and Bert Smitson. "And there's two more."

"Who does that leave still alive?" Webb asked, looking all around the shot-up town.

"That leaves only two men: Roscoe Moore and Moses Peltry," said Will Summers. "I look for them to come crawling up out of the dirt any minute, now that they see the soldiers are leaving."

Teasdale stood up and checked the rifle in his hands. "All right then. Ready when you are. Let's get it done."

Chapter 24

Captain Oberiske and his six soldiers rode past without casting an eye in the direction of Summers, Webb and Teasdale. As the last soldier passed by, Will Summers let out a breath and shoved a pistol down into his waist. He started to speak to Webb and Teasdale, but before he could get his words out, Moses Peltry's enraged voice resounded along the dirt street, causing Oberiske to raise a hand and bring his men to a halt. "Oberiske! You've got to answer for my brother, you dirty, bloodsucking bastard you!"

"Uh-oh," said Will Summers. "Looks like a change of plans for the German captain." He took a step back out of sight around the corner of the shack, Webb and Teasdale right beside him.

As Moses Peltry stepped into the middle of the street, facing Oberiske and the six riders, he did so with his right hand holding one of his big Walker Colts that he'd managed to find. The big Colt was cocked and aimed at Captain Oberiske from less than twenty feet away. Along with his Walker Colt, Moses had also found his own trousers and galluses and put them on. He walked forward slowly, still barefoot, still shirtless, the straps of his galluses looping down his thighs and his long beard thrown back over one shoulder. "Stand down from that saddle, Oberiske! It's me and you!"

He cut a glance to the Mexican soldiers behind

Oberiske and spoke to them in Spanish, explaining that this was none of their concern. This was a matter of honor that had to be settled between him and the German. And when he asked the soldiers if they could ever respect and follow the orders of a man who refused a duel of honor, the young soldiers looked at one another, already knowing the answer.

"Damn," said Will Summers in a lowered voice, "it looks like Moses Peltry's got them stumped."

"That took some guts on Moses Peltry's part. You have to admire that," Teasdale whispered. The three watched intently.

"Shoot this filthy outlaw pig!" Captain Oberiske demanded, his hand clasping the pistol butt at his waist. But he dared not raise the pistol until the soldiers covered his move. "Shoot him now! That is an order!" He cut a harsh glare at the soldier nearest him. "Damn you, Corporal! What is the matter with you? Are you going to listen to him or to your superior?"

"To you, *Capitán*, of course," said the corporal. He shrugged and added, "But still, you have to admit . . . the man has challenged you. A challenge is a most sacred thing among fighting men such as us, eh?"

"Man to man?" said Oberiske, keeping a nervous eye on Moses Peltry as he spoke to the corporal. "You are out of your mind. This is the military, not some Mexican cantina brawl! Shoot this man!"

But the soldiers sat still as stone. One of them spoke in Spanish.

Oberiske cut a sharp glance toward the man who'd spoken.

The corporal said, "He told you that this is all about respect. Either a man deserves it or he doesn't."

"I know what he said, damn it!" Oberiske shouted.

"Step down, Oberiske," Moses said, the rage in his voice held in check. "It's a reckoning between us."

"Any man who refuses to obey my order is going to be shot when I report this to Mexico City!" Oberiske threatened.

A few of the men looked concerned and tightened their grip on their weapons.

From ten feet away on their blind side, Will Summers said in a low, even tone, "Anybody who interferes won't have to worry about getting shot in Mexico City. They'll be shot right here."

"Step down, Oberiske," Moses commanded.

Oberiske looked at Will Summers. Then he looked to Summers' right, where Abner Webb was holding a cocked rifle. Then to Summers' left, at Teasdale, holding a pistol in either hand. "You said the three of you would back away, call it quits here," Oberiske said to Summers.

"I know," Summers responded. "But it looks like I lied. We can't stand by and watch you kill a man who's offered an honest challenge, even if it is Moses Peltry. What kind of men would we be?"

"Step down, Oberiske," said Moses. As Oberiske's eyes turned to him, Moses uncocked the big Walker, shoved it down into his trousers and raised his hands away from it. "A fair fight is all I'm asking for," Moses said.

"*Sí*, and it *will* be fair," said the corporal, looking straight at Will Summers. "The least bit of trickery, and blood will spill. Make sure you remember that," he warned.

Will Summers lowered the gun in his hand. "That sounds right to us." Webb and Teasdale followed suit.

All eyes went to Captain Oberiske. He fidgeted in

his saddle for a moment, then took a deep breath. "Very well then!" Oberiske hastily unbuttoned his tunic, stripped it off and slung it down across his saddle horn. "I think it only fair to tell you that I was the crack shot in my village." He adjusted the pistol in his waist and swung his leg over his saddle to step down. "I will kill this fool quickly so we can get on with finding the Gatling—"

Before Oberiske's right boot fully touched the ground, three shots exploded in rapid succession from Moses' big Walker Colt. The impact staggered Oberiske backward a step with each shot. For a moment, he stood transfixed, blood pouring freely from his chest and his back. He shook his head like a wounded bull and tried to reach for his pistol. Moses shot him again, this time between the eyes.

Everyone in the street stared in disbelief. Then, as the realization began to sink in, Will Summers saw the corporal and the others reach for their weapons at the same time. "Damn you, Moses," Summers shouted, reaching for the pistol he'd just shoved down in his trousers, "you've really gone and done it now!"

On the far side of the corral, Sherman Dahl had led his horse down the steep footpath toward the streets of Punta Del Sol. From a distance, he'd seen what was about to happen between the three possemen and the *Federales*. He jumped up into his saddle just as the three shots from Moses Peltry's pistol exploded. Racing forward with his pistol drawn, Dahl watched the gunfight begin.

The Mexican corporal was the first to fall, a shot from Summers hitting him at the same time as Abner Webb put a rifle shot in his shoulder. Teasdale moved sidelong, firing as he went, taking out two of the soldiers but catching a bullet in his upper arm.

He jerked back with the impact of the shot and nearly went down. But then he caught himself and moved on, still firing as bullets sliced past his head.

From the direction of the cantina, Roscoe Moore came running with a double-barrelled shotgun in his hands, screaming aloud. One barrel exploded, lifting a *Federale* from his saddle and sending him sailing through the air. But as Roscoe came racing past an alley, Juan Richards came rolling out in his wheelchair, a shotgun of his own cradled in his lap. The two men collided in a tangle of wood, metal and flesh, punctuated by a blast of buckshot that sent both men and chair two feet into the air then dropped them sliding to a halt in a spray of dust.

Sherman Dahl veered his horse around the upside-down wheelchair and raced on, firing into the remaining Mexican soldiers, who'd begun to scatter along the street. Junior the hound raced alongside Dahl. At the last second, as Dahl circled his horse wide and fired into the melee, Junior leaped forward, downing a soldier who had dropped to the ground and was firing at Abner Webb. The soldier rolled back and forth, screaming as Junior, atop him, locked the man's face in his wide, powerful jaws.

Then, as quickly as it had begun, the fight ended. Horses raced back and forth with empty saddles, their reins dangling in the dust. The only sound above the pounding hooves was that of Junior's growls and the soldier screaming for someone to get the dog off him.

"Down, boy!" Will Summers shouted. But when the dog ignored him, Summers raised his gun and fired. The bullet struck the ground dangerously near the soldier's face, sending dirt up into Junior's muzzle. Junior let out a yelp and ducked away with his tail rolled back under his belly.

The soldier moaned and tried to sit up, one hand raised to his bloody face. His other hand rose toward Will Summers. Moses Peltry stepped in quickly and put a bullet in the man's head. The man flopped to the ground like a limp bundle of rags.

"Damn it, Moses! That's enough!" Summers shouted, swinging his pistol at him.

Moses Peltry only stared for a second. "Let me show you something, Summers," he growled. He reached out with his bare foot and kicked a small Uhlinger pistol from the dead man's hand.

"All right," said Summers, "but *that's* enough. It's over!" He scanned both directions and saw Juan Richards dragging himself along the street. Behind him lay Roscoe Moore with his face blown away. "Can somebody go help that poor bastard?" said Summers.

"Hang on, I'm coming," Lawrence Teasdale called out to Juan Richards. He walked away toward Richards as Summers turned back to Moses Peltry.

"Damn you anyway, Moses!" Will Summers continued. "You said that was going to be a straight-up, fair fight! That's the only reason we stepped out to back your play, you lying, double-crossing—"

"Whoa now, Summers." Moses cautioned him with a raised finger for emphasis. "That was vengeance for my brother! I didn't owe that German a damn thing. Besides, you heard him warn us all that he was some kind of crack shot back in his homeland. I'd have been a fool to let him get both feet planted on the ground, wouldn't I?"

Will Summers and Abner Webb looked at one another. Summers shrugged, accepting Moses Peltry's logic. "You could have let us know beforehand."

"Yeah? Now, just how the hell could I have done that?" Moses Peltry asked. "You've been around long enough to know how things go in a gunfight. Once I heard that crack shot story, I knew I had to make some quick changes if I was going to live through this." He stepped over to Oberiske's body and looked down. "Why would he tell me something like that anyway? That was plain stupid."

"Maybe he was lying, Moses," said Summers. "Maybe he figured he'd tell you that, and you wouldn't want to go through with it."

"If he was lying about it, that was even more stupid," said Moses.

Summers and Webb just looked at each other and nodded in agreement. "You realize what happens now, don't you, Moses?" Summers said, a grim tone coming to his voice.

"What? You're going to kill me? Going to take my head back to Rileyville or wherever and claim a reward for it? Go ahead then. Let's get it done." As he spoke, Moses didn't even look up at Summers and Webb. Instead, he stared down at Oberiske's snappy red and gray tunic lying in the dirt where it had fallen when Oberiske's horse bolted away.

Summers and Webb watched Moses pick up the tunic, shake it off and put it on. He adjusted the lapels and raised his arms up and down to see if it fit comfortably. "Not bad," he said. Then, looking up at Summers and Webb as Sherman Dahl came leading his horse up into their midst and Teasdale pushed Juan Richards along in his wheelchair, Moses said, "There's something about a military uniform I never could resist."

"You rotten, stinking pig!" Juan Richards shouted at Moses Peltry. "Somebody give me a gun. You won't have to worry about who kills him! I'll kill this snake myself!"

"Settle down, crip, before you hurt my feelings," said Moses Peltry. "What did I do to you that was so bad? I slept in your house, but I told you first. Look at it this way: I could have hung you up by your thumbs if I'd wanted to, and nobody could have stopped me."

"Are you going to kill him or not?" Juan Richards shouted.

"That's enough out of you, Moses," said Will Summers, stepping in between the two men. "Mister, if you're able to roll that chair, get on out of here. We'll take care of this man. But we're not killing him here. We're taking him back across the border with us to make sure he gets hanged proper for what he's done. Does that sound fair to you?"

"If that's the best I can get, it will have to do," said Richards.

"Good," said Will Summers. "When the next patrol comes through here, be sure and tell them what happened."

"Don't worry," said Juan Richards in a bitter tone. "They'll be passing through any day now. I'll be sure and tell them everything I saw. You can bet on it."

"I thought I could," said Summers, turning the wheelchair and giving it a push to get it started. "Now get out of here."

As soon as Juan Richards was out of hearing distance, Summers looked at the others and said, "We'll face a firing squad for sure if the Mexican government gets their hands on us before we reach the border. We'll never make it with that big, slow supply wagon and a bunch of outlaws' heads."

"What are you getting at, Will?" Abner Webb asked.

"I'm thinking we'd be better off if we holed up

somewhere for a while . . . let the dust of this thing settle some." He looked from Teasdale to Webb to Dahl. "What do you three think?"

"By now I'm a deserter," said Teasdale, "so a few more days or weeks or months won't make any difference. I'm all for staying out of sight if we can find a place."

"Moses has a place. Don't you, Moses?" said Will Summers.

"I might have," said Moses, "if you ask real polite." He grinned, then said, "But it'll be hard for me to show you the way if my head's chopped off and riding on the end of a rifle barrel."

"What about you, Webb?" Summers asked.

"Well, I started out a lawman, then a posseman. I don't know what I am now back in our country, but here I'm no more than an outlaw. We might have a price on our own heads once the word's out about killing all these *Federales*." He looked away for a second in the direction of the border. "Hell," he whispered. "I just as soon hide out down here for a while . . . just for a while though. I'm not staying forever."

"Neither are we," said Summers. "No longer than it takes." He turned to Sherman Dahl. "What about it, schoolmaster? You want to go or stay?"

"I'm heading to Rileyville just like we planned," said Dahl.

"What about the *Federales*?" Summers asked. "You're bound to run into them going back that direction."

"Maybe, maybe not," said Dahl. "There's nothing says I'm any more likely to run into them than you are. I think it's all over here, but you three just aren't ready to turn it loose. I went down that road once before, right after the war. Believe me, I don't want to do it again."

"What's that supposed to mean, schoolmaster?" Will Summers asked flatly.

"It means we've done what we came down here to do. It's time to make our way home. Whatever we run into, we'll have to deal with, same as we would no matter which direction we take."

"Well said, young man." Moses Peltry chuckled under his breath and turned toward the stray horses milling in the street. "If you army deserters, ex-lawmen and horse traders will excuse me, I'm getting a horse twixt my knees and hightailing it out of here. Anybody wants to ride with me, feel free. But hurry it up."

Moses stopped and turned, raising a pointed finger at Sherman Dahl. "And I'm warning you here and now: I better find my brother in one piece when I get to him!"

"Then you better get to him before I do," Dahl replied over his shoulder, walking away. "I don't owe you a thing, Moses Peltry. I'll cleave his head off the same way I would a poison snake!"

"Jesus, Dahl!" Will Summers whispered. "What kind of thing is that to say?"

Upon hearing Dahl's words, Moses Peltry stopped cold in his tracks and turned slowly. "What did you say to me?" Moses' voice rumbled like thunder from a dark, distant sky.

Sherman Dahl kept walking. "You heard me, Moses."

"Stop right there!" Moses demanded. "Turn and face me!"

"Why, Moses? So you can tell me what a crack shot *you* were back in your village somewhere?" Dahl kept walking.

"Why you—" Enraged, Moses Peltry snatched the Walker Colt from his waist, cocking it on the upswing.

But before he raised it level to Dahl's back, Will Summers shouted, "Dahl, look out!"

Sherman Dahl spun on his heel, his Colt appearing in his hand as if it had always been there. One shot split the silence on the dirt street, and Moses Peltry clasped his gun hand to his heart with his Walker still in it, then fell forward on his face, dead before he hit the ground.

"Well," said Abner Webb, "there went our hide-out idea."

"Yeah," said Will Summers in a lowered voice. "I think the schoolmaster did that on purpose just to make us go home."

The possemen left Punta Del Sol in the dark of night, Sherman Dahl atop the supply wagon, his horse reined to the rear of the wagon in case he needed it for a quick getaway. With Oberiske and his *Federales* out of the picture, Sherman Dahl and Lawrence Teasdale rode up above the town and brought back the Gatling gun and the last crate of ammunition Dahl had hidden between two rocks. They loaded the gun and ammunition in among the supplies, but in such a way that it could be gotten out easily should they have cause to use it.

While the others had prepared horses and gear for the trip back across the border, Will Summers, with the help of old Hector Roderio, set about the grisly task of collecting the outlaws' heads. Owing to his religious beliefs, Hector Roderio did none of the actual cutting. Instead, he watched Will Summers and, when the cutting was done, simply held out the bag. Summers offered to pay old Hector for his help, but

Hector would have none of it. "I do this for free, just to get you men out of Punta Del Sol and on your way."

"That's most kind of you, Hector." Will Summers smiled. When the four-man posse rode away in the moonlight, Hector Roderio and Juan Richards were the only two to see them off. In the dusty square riddled with bullet holes and stained with blood, Hector leaned on his cane and waved *adiós*. But Juan Richards spit at them from his wheelchair and cursed them under his breath.

For the next few days, the posse traveled unseen, following the river valley until at length they had to venture up onto the flatlands leading toward the border. The four men exchanged little conversation until they had crossed the border and were headed toward Diablo Espinazo. To their surprise, standing there outside the dusty little town to greet them was Trooper Frieze. "My God," said Abner Webb as he and Will Summers stopped beside the supply wagon and watched Sergeant Teasdale leap down from his horse and go running to his recovered trooper. "We left that boy on his deathbed at Little Sand River. He's made it all the way here—looking better than any one of us." Webb grinned with satisfaction. "And *you* said he was going to die."

"I never said he was going to die," Will Summers retorted. "It was his own sergeant there who said it." He nodded toward Sergeant Teasdale as Teasdale and Frieze shook hands and greeted one another.

Abner Webb said, "Maybe it wasn't his sergeant. Maybe it was Campbell Hayes who said it."

Will Summers replied, "It doesn't matter who said he was going to die. *He* kept saying he was going to live. And so he did . . . for the time being anyway."

He sighed. "Looks like that clears things up for Teasdale. He can return home a hero now. He's got a witness, and he's recovered the machine rifle."

"Good for him," said Webb. "I hope things work out that well for us in Rileyville."

"I don't know why things wouldn't," said Summers. "We brought back the outlaws. We even brought back most of the supplies they stole. Don't tell me you still dread facing the sheriff after all we've gone through?"

Webb chuckled. "After all we've been through, I doubt I'll ever dread facing anybody again for any reason." In Webb's saddlebags, wrapped in a bandanna, he carried the trigger fingers of both Moses and Goose Peltry for Wild Joe's son, Eddie.

"Does that include Renee Marie Daniels?" Summers asked.

"You had to mention her, didn't you?" said Webb, a look of dread coming to his face.

"Sorry," said Summers. He turned to Sherman Dahl, who sat in the driver's seat of the supply wagon. "What about you, schoolmaster? How do you feel now that this is all over? Think you'll have a hard time settling back into teaching kids how to read and write after this rip-roaring adventure we've been on?"

"I doubt it," said Sherman Dahl, reaching his free hand over and scratching the head of Junior the hound. Junior lay asleep like some ancient warrior sated from the kill, at peace now on a rough plank wagon seat, a fly circling close above his head. "If I do, I suppose I'll look you up, Will Summers. I've got a feeling you can always come up with something to do."

The three men laughed among themselves as townsfolk came forward from their abode and stood looking at them with curiosity. Some of the towns-men circled wide and walked to the rear of the wagon and nudged one another at the sight of Moses Peltry's head stuck atop a length of broken hitch rail. The dead face was stonelike and expressionless, peaceful with its closed eyes and its long gray beard asway on a passing breeze.

"Come say hello to these three possemen," said Sergeant Teasdale, "They've turned out to be good men all." He and Trooper Frieze walked over to the supply wagon, Frieze limping, but only slightly. On their way to join Summers, Webb, and Dahl at the supply wagon, Sergeant Lawrence Teasdale thought he saw something more than just curiosity in the townsfolk's eyes. He saw respect and admiration. In the eyes of the men, he was sure he saw envy.

JASON MANNING

Mountain Honor   0-451-20480-8

When trouble arises between the U.S. Army and the Cheyenne Nation, Gordon Hawkes agrees to play peacemaker-until he realizes that his Indian friends are being led to the slaughter...

Mountain Renegade   0-451-20583-9

As the aggression in hostile Cheyenne country escalates, Gordon Hawkes must choose his side once and for all-and fight for the one thing he has left...his family.

The Long Hunters   0-451-20723-8

1814: When Andrew Jackson and the U.S. army launch a brutal campaign against the Creek Indians, Lt. Timothy Barlow is forced to chose between his country and his conscience.

Available wherever books are sold, or
to Order Call: 1-800-788-6262